PACKING HEAT

Penny McCall

BERKLEY SENSATION, NEW YORK

THE BERKLEY PUBLISHING GROUP
Published by the Penguin Group
Penguin Group (USA) Inc.
375 Hudson Street, New York, New York 10014, USA

Penguin Group (Canada), 90 Eglinton Avenue East, Suite 700, Toronto, Ontario M4P 2Y3, Canada
(a division of Pearson Penguin Canada Inc.)
Penguin Books Ltd., 80 Strand, London WC2R 0RL, England
Penguin Group Ireland, 25 St. Stephen's Green, Dublin 2, Ireland (a division of Penguin Books Ltd.)
Penguin Group (Australia), 250 Camberwell Road, Camberwell, Victoria 3124, Australia
(a division of Pearson Australia Group Pty. Ltd.)
Penguin Books India Pvt. Ltd., 11 Community Centre, Panchsheel Park, New Delhi—110 017, India
Penguin Group (NZ), 67 Apollo Drive, Rosedale, North Shore 0632, New Zealand
(a division of Pearson New Zealand Ltd.)
Penguin Books (South Africa) (Pty.) Ltd., 24 Sturdee Avenue, Rosebank, Johannesburg 2196,
South Africa

Penguin Books Ltd., Registered Offices: 80 Strand, London WC2R 0RL, England

This is a work of fiction. Names, characters, places, and incidents either are the product of the author's imagination or are used fictitiously, and any resemblance to actual persons, living or dead, business establishments, events, or locales is entirely coincidental. The publisher does not have any control over and does not assume any responsibility for author or third-party websites or their content.

PACKING HEAT

A Berkley Sensation Book / published by arrangement with the author

PRINTING HISTORY
Berkley Sensation mass-market edition / April 2009

Copyright © 2009 by Penny McCusker.
Cover art by Corbis and Getty.
Cover design by Rita Frangie.
Interior text design by Laura K. Corless.

ISBN: 978-0-425-22805-0

BERKLEY® SENSATION
Berkley Sensation Books are published by The Berkley Publishing Group,
a division of Penguin Group (USA) Inc.,
375 Hudson Street, New York, New York 10014.
BERKLEY® SENSATION and the "B" design are trademarks of Penguin Group (USA) Inc.

PRINTED IN THE UNITED STATES OF AMERICA

10 9 8 7 6 5 4 3 2 1

Titles by Penny McCall

ALL JACKED UP
TAG, YOU'RE IT!
ACE IS WILD
PACKING HEAT

Anthologies

DOUBLE THE PLEASURE
(with Lori Foster, Deirdre Martin, and Jacquie D'Alessandro)

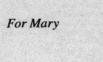

For Mary

chapter
1

HARMONY SWIFT ENTERED LEWISBURG USP—
United States Penitentiary—flanked by two prison guards. A
line of sweat trickled down her spine, and while it felt like
each door locking behind her would never open again, she
kept her pace steady and her expression calm, cool, and col-
lected. She knew because, well, she'd practiced in a mirror.

One of the guards unlocked a door, the other ushered her
into one of the rooms set aside for lawyers to talk to clients—
brick walls, industrial-grade table and chairs, one angry
handcuffed and shackled inmate. And another locked door.

She must be crazy. Or desperate. Truth be told she'd jumped
into this with both feet and it was too late to back out. But
hey, if she got caught, they wouldn't have to take her far . . .
which wasn't very funny when she thought about it.

She set the pile of clothes she'd been carrying on the table
and consulted the paperwork in her hands, hoping with every
optimistic bone in her body that it had held up, then muster-
ing every ounce of acting skill that had rubbed off on her in
the first eighteen years of her life. She hadn't grown up in
Hollywood, where waiters emoted over the appetizers and

cab drivers ran lines in bumper-to-bumper traffic, for nothing.

"Cole Montgomery Hackett?" she said with just the right amount of disdain and superiority.

He didn't respond. The guard confirmed it.

She nudged the pile of clothing across the table. "Put these on."

Still ignoring her.

The guard took a step forward, reaching for his nightstick.

Harmony held up a hand, he stopped, and she thought, *Cool*, resisting an urge to grin like an idiot. Sure, she was an FBI agent, but this was her first case . . . Okay, it wasn't exactly a case, not in the Bureau-approved, call-us-if-you-have-a-problem way, but it wasn't her fault she'd gone Rambo. It was theirs, and anyway, being in the field, where she could feel the power and respect of her rank for the first time, was a lot of fun, and, darn it, she was taking a second or two to enjoy it.

"Unlock the cuffs and shackles," she instructed the guard.

Cole Montgomery Hackett turned his cold, intense stare on her. He didn't lift his wrists, pull his ankles from under the table, or assist his own release in any way. Not exactly the reaction she'd expected.

Then again, nothing about him was what she'd expected. Harmony consulted the photo she'd brought along, the mug shot of a nerdy kid fresh out of college, soft around the middle, pocket protector, smiling and happy with a baby face and an innocent look in his eyes. The federal prisoner across the table bore little resemblance. Same black hair cut military short, same shape to the face except for the perpetual five-o'clock shadow and hollowed cheeks, all the baby fat gone to privation and resentment. The eyes were the same, too, so dark a brown they were almost black, but now they were intense, guarded, like his body language.

As soon as the guard had the cuffs and shackles off, Hackett crossed his arms over his chest. His left biceps sported a jailhouse tattoo of an owl with a bad attitude. Harmony stifled a smile that came as much from nerves as comprehension.

The tattoo would be some other inmate's commentary on Hackett's harmlessness, but harmless was a relative term when the company included rapists, murderers, kidnappers, and worse. And Hackett looked like he'd learned a thing or two in prison—and not about computers.

Hence the second-guessing. Running an op with a reluctant geek wasn't the same as riding shotgun on a dangerous ex-con while trying to track down someone crazy enough to take on the FBI. But she had a carrot Cole Montgomery Hackett couldn't resist chasing.

And sure, he looked bitter and angry, but it wasn't her fault he was in there. And it wasn't like he'd murdered anyone. He was a computer criminal. If he hadn't been prosecuted under the newly minted Patriot Act, he'd've been sent to one of the federal country clubs reserved for white-collar offenders. It would've been better for her if he hadn't gone to Miscreant U, but a good agent made the best of what she had to work with.

"You're being released into my custody," she said in her agent voice.

Hackett looked her over, head to toe, and it wasn't sexual—at least not entirely. The man had been locked up for eight years; his gaze lingered in the obvious places. But she recognized the moment when he made the decision, so it came as no surprise when he nodded. He knew he could take her. She knew it, too, but she wasn't counting on muscle to protect her.

He picked up the clothing and met her gaze, one brow lifted.

She crossed her arms, mocking his raised eyebrow with one of her own. "Shy?"

He still wasn't talking, but he began to strip, his eyes steady on hers. And he took his time.

Harmony didn't look away. This was where the real contest would be, her will against his. But she had weapons he'd never expect.

He had some weapons of his own. Incredible weapons. Before his shirt was off, her upper lip had begun to sweat. She managed to keep her gaze level on his, but she had really good peripheral vision, and he had muscles everywhere. Really nice muscles, good and firm without being over-pumped . . . He dropped his prison britches, and her breath stalled even though she couldn't see anything below the waist without breaking eye contact. Which she didn't do. As much as she wanted to find out if the merchandise matched the advertising, there was a lot more at stake than her prurient curiosity.

He dropped his eyes to tug on the jeans she'd brought, and she couldn't for the life of her think what. She knew he was dangerous, that she was putting her life on the line in every sense of the phrase, but she took a good long look at him and had to admire what she saw—from a strictly professional standpoint. Madison Avenue would love to get their hooks into him, she thought, because any American woman with a pulse—and more than a few men—would buy whatever he was selling. Especially if he did it in his underwear, on a billboard, in Times Square. And he'd caught her checking him out, judging by the smirk on his face when she lifted her eyes.

"Handcuffs." She tossed the set she'd brought in with her to the guard.

Hackett didn't like being put in restraints again, and there was a challenge in his eyes, when she met them. She wasn't falling for that. She thought better of the leg shackles, though. This guy had some pride; stepping on it wouldn't make him more cooperative.

As she'd previously arranged, the guards escorted Hackett out of the building and loaded him into the back of her government-issue SUV while she took the driver's seat.

She heard him checking the door handle and said, "Don't bother," adding, "the window's kick-proof, too," when she caught a glimpse in the rearview mirror of his feet coming up to do just that.

"Look," she said, twisting around so she could see him. "The FBI needs your help, and in return we're willing to spring you from jail. Permanently. If you can be patient for a little while longer . . . At least do me the courtesy of looking at me when I'm talking to you."

"Okay," he said in a startlingly deep voice, "but those guys are going to interrupt you anyway."

Harmony whipped around, and sure enough a couple of men in cheap black suits, expensive shades, and the distinctive expression she'd pasted on her own face for most of the day stood watching them. She started the Explorer.

Cole met her eyes in the rearview. "Those guys look like feds."

Who were running for a black Lincoln Town Car and giving chase.

"They are," she said, putting her vehicle in motion, but keeping to a non-panic speed, at least until they got out of the jail yard.

"I thought you were an FBI agent."

"I am."

"Then why are you running away from the other ones?" He ducked as something thunked into the back of the vehicle. "And why are they shooting at us?"

"They're not shooting at us, they're trying to take out the tires." Which would be a problem, but the real worry was why they wanted to stop Hackett's escape badly enough to draw their weapons.

"What the hell is going on?" he yelled at her.

Good question, she thought, putting her foot to the floor and pouring all her focus into driving because there wasn't much else she could do but drive and hope to hell inspiration struck.

Inspiration was going to need a damn good imagination.

Lewisburg Penitentiary was a maximum security facility a couple hundred miles north of Washington, D.C., and almost that far west of Philadelphia. The jail itself squatted in the middle of farms, the fields already harvested for fall. Flat landscape with nowhere to hide.

Lewisburg, Pennsylvania, sprawled along the west branch of the Susquehanna River just a few miles from the prison, a quaint, historic little town, population six thousand, give or take, all of them innocent bystanders going about their daily business. She'd rather not take this federal squabble, with its potential to produce serious nastiness, right down Market

Street. Robert F. Miller Drive had other ideas. Robert F. Miller Drive led right to Lewisburg with no consideration for the consequences.

Harmony took the first curve practically on two wheels, hearing a thump and a grunt behind her. She glanced in the rearview mirror and caught a glimpse of Hackett, hands still cuffed behind him, bouncing around the backseat like a pinball. Better that than the two suits in the government car catching up to them. They got caught, Hackett's twenty-five-year sentence would get amended to life. She'd rather not think about where she'd end up.

They'd hit a long, straight stretch of road. The government car whipped into the oncoming traffic lane and pulled up alongside the Explorer. The passenger side window slid down and a gun eased out.

Harmony slammed on the brakes, and the Lincoln shot ahead, the bullet going wide. Hackett crashed into the back of the passenger seat, but she didn't have time to worry about his likely tally of black eyes and bruises. She steered over behind the two agents in the Lincoln, straddling both lanes, swerving when they swerved, staying safely behind them and making it impossible for them to get off an effective shot.

The flat, empty fields had given way to woodland to their left, and between the tree trunks Harmony caught glimpses of the sun sparkling off the surface of a small river. It was really quite lovely, right up to the moment she crashed the SUV into the Lincoln's rear bumper, jammed the gas pedal to the floor, and forced the car off the edge of the road and hood first into the creek.

As they whipped past the Lincoln she said, "That was a rush, wasn't it?" trying to stop herself from grinning like a fool and not managing to. The stupid smile went hand in hand with the adrenaline popping through her bloodstream like firecrackers.

"Pollution is a federal crime," Hackett said from the backseat.

"Guess again, Clarence Darrow," she said, still grinning. "Dumping toxic waste is a federal crime."

"The toxic waste is inside the car," Cole said, adding "federal agents," like he had a mouthful of something disgusting. "And that won't hold them long. Toxic waste has a tendency to ooze."

Hackett had a point—about the hold-them-long part. But seeing that car settle at a forty-five degree angle, its back wheels spinning uselessly, was so satisfying she barely gave a second thought to the fact that as soon as they got out of there those two agents would have the place swarming with feds in record time. "We have to get far away from here."

"We?"

"We. I broke you out of jail because I need your help. We're going to be a team. Starting now."

He snorted. "I can't wait to hear how you're going to convince me of that."

Harmony grinned at him over her shoulder. "You won't be able to resist. Trust me."

"Trust a fed? When pigs fly."

AGENT SWIFT WAS A NUTCASE. SHE'D BARELY PULLED OFF a jailbreak with forged papers, then put two fellow FBI agents in a river, all with a big, white Hollywood smile on her face. They'd been shot at—okay, the car had been shot at, but they could have missed and hit her, or him—and she hadn't even broken a sweat.

And sure, she might be beautiful and blond, not to mention the first real live woman he'd seen in eight years, but she was heat. Even worse, she was federal heat, and in Cole's book that wiped out any good qualities she might have. It wasn't bad enough that the Bureau had played fast and loose with his life once; they were trying to con him again, like he was a fucking moron who'd lost his memory along with a good chunk of his life and the future he'd busted his ass to get.

If they'd left him alone, he'd have been a millionaire, with his own private island, for Christ's sake, in a part of the world where the temperature never dropped below seventy-five degrees. He'd be sitting on the beach right now, a bikini-clad woman in the chair next to him, tropical ocean as far as the eye could see, and a cloudless sky overhead. A wide-open sky.

And where had he been for the last eight years? Moldering in an eight-by-ten jail cell with a wall of Hugh Hefner's finest to keep him from going completely crazy. Not that he couldn't have found companionship if he'd wanted it, but he preferred his own devices to the alternatives available in a federal prison. He'd put on thirty pounds of muscle to ensure he had a choice.

The woman in the front seat was definitely three-dimensional and, sure, screwing her brains out was an ever-present urge lurking in the back of his mind . . . Okay, it wasn't his *brain* at a constant simmer. But he wasn't about to let her screw him back—in anything but the literal sense. He'd trusted the Bureau once. He wasn't making that mistake again, even when the Bureau came packaged in hair the color of ripe wheat; wide, innocent blue eyes; and a curvy little body covered in smooth, tanned skin . . .

"You have a name?" he asked, dragging his eyes off her body so he could put his brain back on the situation.

"Agent Swift."

"Is that an oxymoron?"

"It's a name," she said, the deadpan tone of her voice exactly matching the deadpan expression on her face.

She looked pretty ridiculous when she put on that blank, vaguely threatening FBI mask, like Betty Boop with a chip on her shoulder. Probably wouldn't help his cause to point that out.

She did a U-turn, taking them back the way they'd come, causing him a moment of panic when Robert F. Miller Drive made the swing back toward Lewisburg USP. Maybe she'd changed her mind, he thought, maybe putting two of her own in the drink had pushed her back to sanity and she was returning him to prison—stone, steel, and horny lifers—after a taste of freedom. His breath came short, and he broke out in a cold sweat. And he blamed Agent Swift.

She steered the Explorer off-road, but it took him a minute to fight down the image of his hands around her throat. He'd never been a violent man, but if it took violence to stay out of jail, he'd find a way to live with the regret. She kept heading steadily away from Lewisburg, though. And Cole kept his hands, cuffs and all, to himself. One of the first things he'd learned in jail was that anything could be turned into a weapon.

After a few minutes she left the relative smoothness of the harvested fields, turning into the same line of trees verging the same creek where she'd left the other two feds several miles downstream. The terrain worsened as they went. Cole put his shoulders against one door, his feet against the other. It cut down on the bruising, and kept him out of sight of the rearview mirror.

The leaves had just begun to turn with the onset of cooler weather, but they weren't falling yet. Agent Swift parked the Explorer under the thickest canopy she could find, and Cole shoved himself upright before she turned around.

"Worried about helicopters?" he asked her.

"There won't be any helicopters. Not right away at least. The FBI won't expect us to hang around a few miles from the prison, and they won't invite local law enforcement to go after one of their own, not as long as they think they can bring us in themselves. We've got some time."

WHATEVER CONCLUSIONS COLE HAD DRAWN FROM THE packaging, the mind inside that blond head wasn't too shabby. But then, she was FBI, and they only recruited the best. It would be a mistake to underestimate her. Or take anything she said at face value.

"Why me?" he asked, beginning where he always began to solve a problem—by gathering the facts.

"I need you to do some computer work."

"The geeks at the Bureau can't handle it?"

"They *won't* handle it," she said. "There's a difference."

Something the feds wouldn't dirty their hands with? No thanks. Except . . . She'd pushed his curiosity button. It was the one quirk of his personality even a stretch in the federal pen couldn't bastardize.

"Part of my sentence was zero access to computers," he

said. "I haven't touched so much as a calculator in ten years."

"Bull," she said, her back against the driver's side door so she could watch his face. "Prison doesn't prevent crime. As soon as the inmates with the power found out why you were incarcerated, the first thing they did was get you access to a computer. In there you were probably a god."

"There is no god in there."

She rolled her eyes. "Very dramatic. You have a brilliant career as a soap opera actor ahead of you."

"I'm probably not going to survive you."

"At least you'll die a free man."

"Yeah, well, I'm only staying free as long as the two agents chasing us don't catch up."

"They won't."

He snorted. "Between you and those other guys, my money is on them."

"Those guys?" She huffed out a breath, insulted. There were at least a dozen ways they could have stopped her from forcing their car into that river. The guy behind the wheel was probably an agent-in-training. Send a novice to catch a novice. After today, they wouldn't underestimate her that way again.

"Just sinking in, huh?"

"I got you out of there, didn't I? I had all the proper paperwork with the proper signatures. And they were real signatures, not forgeries."

"A cake with a file in it probably would have worked better."

She crossed her arms and glared at him. "You could at least say thank you."

Jesus, he was stranded with Emily Post. She'd broken him out of federal prison, perpetrated vehicular assault on two federal agents, and she was focusing on his lack of manners? She had no idea who they were really up against, and she worked for them. She was clueless or optimistic—and he'd take the former over the latter any day. Clueless could be educated. Optimism took years in jail to cure. Or death.

"What the hell is going on?"

She gave him a look. Probably didn't like the tone of his voice.

"Let's get a couple things straight," he said, using the same tone of voice. "You dragged me out of my life—"

"Your nice, comfy life in jail?"

"I was making the best of a bad situation," he said, clenching his jaw over the whiny note of defense in his voice. Damn federal agents, he thought, they did it to him every time.

"You have no idea what's at stake," she said.

"Don't I? I wound up in jail because of the FBI, but at least they asked nice last time."

"I know it looks bad, but you have to trust me."

He rattled the handcuffs.

She sighed, patience strained. "All right, I hijacked you, and you're cuffed in the back of my vehicle, but I had to make sure you would stick around long enough to hear me out."

"My ears are working fine. So's my bullshit meter."

She thunked her head back against the driver's side window but she didn't take her eyes off him. "Some new information has come to light regarding your case." It was a lie, hopefully the only one she'd have to tell. And she was only telling it because he'd backed her into a corner. Honesty was always the best policy; too many lies and you were stumbling over them and getting yourself into trouble. Besides, Cole Hackett was no stooge.

"What kind of information?"

"The kind that will get you a new trial."

Riiiight, and he was the King of England. "Let me guess, you're going to give me that information. After I help you."

"Well, you'd have no incentive otherwise," she said with a perky little smile.

Cole hated perky. He hated the way her blue eyes sparkled, and he hated the cheerful, glass-half-full way she was looking at him. What the hell was there to be optimistic about? He couldn't even enjoy his brief stint of freedom because he didn't believe it would last. Any moment the feds would show up and cart him back to Lewisburg, and hell, would that be so bad?

He'd come to terms with the fact that he was going to lose more than a third of his life. The best third. He'd even managed to make the best of a terrible existence. Now, along came the FBI again, making promises and expecting him to smile and nod and tell them what a fine idea it was. Like hell.

"I'm not that naïve kid the Bureau fucked over eight years ago," he said. "I'm not even a law-abiding citizen anymore, and I don't give a shit about national security."

And that, he realized, was a kind of freedom only someone staring down a twenty-five-year sentence could understand. There were options available to the man he was now that the kid he'd been never would have considered.

"There's no harm in hearing me out," she said.

Cole scrubbed a hand over his face and gave in to his curiosity. "So what's the story this time?"

"I can't tell you until you agree to help me. It's classified."

"It's not sanctioned, either. Let's start there."

"There are all kinds of sanctioning."

"What kind is this?"

"Fine," she huffed out, "it's not sanctioned. I'll do everything I said I would, just as soon as you agree to some ground rules."

"How about you give me the key to the handcuffs, I get out of this vehicle, and while you're trying to figure out your next move, I'll get so lost you'll never find me again. All I need is a computer and an Internet connection."

She turned forward and reached for the ignition. "I'll take you back before I let you es—"

Cole flipped his hands over her seat, laying the short handcuff chain across her windpipe. "It'll be hard to stop me when you're dead."

chapter
2

"YOUR HANDS WERE CUFFED BEHIND YOU."

"Now they're not," Cole said.

"You're a pretty flexible guy."

"The key."

She took a careful breath, no doubt considering her options. Cole put a little pressure on the chain.

"It's in the glove compartment," she wheezed out immediately. The look in her eyes wasn't so cooperative.

He eased off, enough for her to reach over . . . and pull out a gun, probably a .38. He had to guess at the caliber since she'd pointed it at him over her shoulder and all he could see was that little black hole in the end of the barrel. A .38 was what most women used . . . and that really wasn't the point here, he reminded himself, dragging his gaze off the gun.

Her eyes met his in the rearview, not so wide and innocent anymore, and when she wasn't trying to look like an agent, she actually did. Cool, determined, dangerous— Okay, the gun was dangerous, as long as he didn't take the package into consideration, because when he put Goldilocks and the gun in the same picture, he had a hard time taking the whole thing seriously. Then again, her hand wasn't shaking.

"Not much chance I can miss you at this range," she said, "even struggling to breathe."

"Go ahead, shoot me. If you think you can lift a couple hundred pounds of deadweight off your neck."

"Where's the good in both of us being dead?"

"One less fed on the planet."

"That's a stupid trade-off, and you don't strike me as a stupid man."

"Not anymore," he said.

But the pressure eased off. It didn't disappear, but Harmony could see she was on the right track. *Rule Number One in hostage negotiation: Keep the subject talking.* Probably would have been easier if she weren't the hostage, but you didn't get to pick your crises, that was what made being an agent such a rush.

"I'm offering you a chance to get your life back," she said.

"Spook bullshit. Last time it cost me eight years. This time around I'll probably end up dead."

Harmony bit back her impatience. She hadn't counted on this much resistance.

"Give me the gun," he said, "and I'll let you go."

Rule Number Two: Let the subject think he's in charge. The hell with that, she wasn't giving him the gun. She cocked it instead.

He tightened the chain.

She kept her eyes level on his, ignoring the gray at the edges as she popped the clip, turned the gun butt first, and handed it to him.

"Unlock the doors."

"You're not going anywhere."

"What? Didn't hear the magic word? *Please* unlock the doors or I'll strangle you," he said, voice dripping with sarcasm. "*Please* don't argue with me or I'll strangle you. *Please* let me go. *Or I'll strangle you.*"

Harmony rolled her eyes, but she got the point. He had her by the throat, literally. She hit the door locks, the chain disappeared, and he was gone, fast and quiet.

Rule Number Three: If you have a shot, take it. She very calmly pulled up her skirt to get her clutch piece from the thigh holster, stepped out of the car, sighted down the barrel straight at his back, adjusted her aim slightly, and squeezed off a round.

He stopped dead in his tracks and turned around.

"I won't miss next time."

"If you kill me—"

"I'll shoot you. I never said I would kill you."

"Just as long as I'm able to type?"

She popped up an eyebrow.

"You're in over your head, little girl," he said. "Go back to D.C."

"And tell them what? I broke a criminal out of prison and then chickened out?"

"Is your pride worth your life?"

"This isn't about pride. And it's not about my life."

"How about my life then?"

"They weren't shooting at us," she said, then clamped her jaw shut over the shrill edge to her voice. The adrenaline was wearing off, and she was having second thoughts, and third, and fourth. It didn't help that Cole Hackett was being an all-around pain in the neck. "Your life won't be in danger," she said to him, "so what are you afraid of? Carpal tunnel?"

"It's not fear; it's history. Considering my track record with the FBI, your assurances aren't exactly reassuring."

"Then I guess it's a good thing I've got the gun."

Cole's shoulders slumped. He stomped back to the Explorer, for the first time resembling that kid in his mug shot. But he wasn't a kid, and along with the baby fat he'd lost every ounce of naïveté and hope. Because of the FBI, which, being a federal agent, put her in a rather awkward position. The only way she'd get him to cooperate was to give him the choice.

She lowered the gun and turned away from him, reaching into the top of her dress to retrieve the handcuff key. When she turned back he was so close she all but ran into him. She took a step or two back, not because she was afraid he'd overpower her. It was the look in his eyes.

"If I'd known where it was, I'd have gone after it myself," he said. "My hands were right there."

She lifted the key into his field of vision—right about breast level—then closed her hand around it before he could take it from her. "You were close enough to 'go for it,'" she pointed out, "because you were threatening to kill me."

"And I could have." His hand closed around hers. "But I didn't."

She jerked her hand free, but she wasn't foolish enough to ignore the punch her system took from skin-to-skin contact with him. And so what if there was a bit of a buzz when she touched him? It was circumstance—circumstance and adrenaline. She'd wanted a field assignment forever. The excitement and danger of the day's events, and the high of making their escape was still bouncing around inside her, looking for an outlet. Next time she'd be ready for it.

Judging by the look in Cole's eyes he thought she was "ready for it" now. She chose to ignore the smirk.

"I'll make you a deal," she said to him. "You hear me out, and if you decide to take off, I won't stop you."

"Where's the catch?"

"No catch, except you'll be on the run."

"I'm on the run now. So are you."

"I can deal with the choices I've made. It'll be easier with your help, and the Bureau will be grateful—"

"Like the last time? They were so grateful they sent me on vacation. For twenty-five to life."

"You had a fair trial—"

"Fair!" Cole threw his hands up, cuffs and all, stomping a few feet away before whirling around to scowl at her, looking irritated, harassed, dangerously handsome . . . *Minus the handsome part,* she amended. *Not noticing the muscles, either.*

"The FBI fucked me over," he said, helping her out by looking just dangerous. "There's no point trying to convince you when you're part of the system."

He held out his hands, one of them palm up, and Harmony saw success flying away.

She didn't give him the key. "You're a federal fugitive. How long do you think you'll stay free?"

"I don't know, let's ask the guys on the Wanted posters in the post office."

"So you're going to turn into the Unabomber? Build a shack in the mountains? How's that going to get you back your life?"

"If I wanted my life back, I'd turn myself in and come clean."

"I saw your face when we walked out of jail. We both know you're not going to do that."

"I'll get a new life."

Great, now she'd pissed him off even more, enough that she had no trouble remembering he'd spent eight years in criminal boot camp. If he didn't get a new life when all this was over—a life that didn't include jail time—he'd blame her. Who was she kidding? She was FBI; he already blamed her.

"Take the front," she said.

"Because you trust me, or because you want to keep an eye on me?"

"I don't trust you any more than you trust me." But she handed him the key.

He unlocked the cuffs, rubbing his wrists. "It doesn't matter if you trust me. You need me."

"We need each other," Harmony said, retrieving the handcuffs from where he'd dropped then in the weeds.

He angled himself into the front seat. His body language was unreceptive at best.

"You can get a new life," Harmony said, climbing into the driver's side, "but you want more than that."

"Stop telling me what I want."

"Freedom," she said anyway. "And being a fugitive isn't freedom, not for you."

"You don't know me as well as you think."

"Why would you try to convince me you're innocent if you don't want to clear your name? You go on the run, the FBI will be the reason for every move and every decision you make. You'll still be their prisoner just like you were in Lewisburg. You won't settle for that."

"Spend almost a decade in jail and you'll figure out what's

really important," he said, trying to look all Zen and tranquil.

She'd struck a nerve, though. His jaw clenched, just once, but it was enough to tell her she'd gotten to him—and probably it would be best to back off before she pushed him too far.

They sat there for a minute, Harmony feeling like Cole and his big hands—which would fit so well around her neck—were way too close. She closed her eyes, took a couple deep breaths—

"Centering yourself?"

She frowned, cracking one eye open. Yep, he was sneering at her.

"You're from California, right?"

Her other eye flew open, and she narrowed both of them. "What of it?"

His gaze went to her hair.

"Here we go," she griped. "I have blond hair, which means I'm scatter-brained, and I'm from California, so I must be a kook."

"You broke me out of a United States penitentiary," Cole reminded her. "Kook doesn't seem to cover it. And when the time comes for explanations, you resort to deep breathing and stress relief exercises. Doesn't exactly inspire confidence. If there's more danger, I don't want to be hooked up with somebody who has to chant mantras to find some calm."

"I put two fellow agents into a river a half hour ago. I don't recall having to stop and 'chant mantras' along the way. And what I'm asking you to do isn't dangerous."

"There's all kinds of danger. Flying bullets, pretty dangerous."

"They were shooting at the tires, trying to get me to stop."

"I have a feeling it would take more than a flat tire."

Harmony took that for a compliment, turning to face him. "If there was a way to do this through regular channels—"

"To do what," he said, sounding exasperated—and antsy, like he was on the verge of taking off again. And she really didn't want to shoot him. She'd have to start over then.

"An FBI agent has been kidnapped and is being held for ransom," she said, jumping on the trust bandwagon and hoping he followed.

"You're the FBI," Cole pointed out. "You people are supposed to be the best at this kind of thing."

"The Bureau won't negotiate with kidnappers when the victim is one of our own. Sets a bad precedent."

"Kidnap a fed and get away with murder?"

"Something like that."

"And you think they should ignore their own rule in this case. Why?"

"The agent has some information we need. He was grabbed at the end of an assignment. He needs to be debriefed." And she was babbling, which he saw right through.

"So this guy means something to you personally."

Something? He was the closest thing to family she had left in the world, and the thought of him tied up and hurt, or worse—*Nope, not going there,* she thought before the tears burning in her throat leaked from her eyes instead. Richard was alive and she was his only hope. But she couldn't let it show. "What does that matter to you?"

"I need to know what I'm getting into. You're not exactly the typical FBI agent."

"Don't let my appearance fool you. I'm trained for this sort of thing." But she was too emotionally driven to be a field agent. At least that was the reason they'd given her the last time they'd passed her over. It didn't stop her from staying on at the Bureau, and it wouldn't keep her from trying to convince them they were wrong about her. If she still had a job when all this was over.

She took a deep breath and made the real commitment. The fact that she was steering the conversation away from uncomfortable territory only made it easier. "The ransom isn't money, not cash in a duffel bag, anyway. The kidnappers want the FBI to clean out the accounts that are frozen due to active criminal investigations."

Cole whistled softly through his teeth. "And since the FBI won't do it willingly, you want me to hack into their files and raid those accounts. Problem is, everything done on a computer is traceable, if you find someone who knows how to follow the trail. I'll be on the hook for the money."

"I'll make sure the hook passes you by. You have my word."

"Been there, done that, got screwed over for it." He reached for the door latch, but he didn't open it. "Although I have to say it's pretty ingenious. And nearly irresistible. You were right about that much."

She tore her eyes away from his grin—the white teeth, the wicked glint in his eyes—and gave her nerve endings a stern talking to. *Not getting personally involved with the convicted felon*, she told them. *He's here to do a job, not me.*

No reason he can't do both, her nerve endings retorted. Actually they gave a traitorous little throb, but it was the same thing. She was looking for a rebuttal when Cole gave her the perfect one.

What he actually said was "They want the funds transferred to a numbered, offshore account?" which reminded her what was at stake, and as long as she remembered that—and kept her eyes and her imagination to herself—she'd be fine.

"That's what they said."

He mulled that for a minute. "So give me the details."

Harmony rolled her shoulders. "I don't know all the details—"

He reached for the door handle again.

"I could have lied to you," she said. "I could have spun what I know into a coherent story."

"And sooner or later it would have fallen apart."

"By then you would have been committed. I told you the truth, not to mention busting you out of jail."

He snorted, more a soft rush of air that sounded almost companionable in the gathering darkness. There was definitely an edge of humor to it. "Still not sure you did me a favor there."

"If you decide not to help me, I'll take you back to Lewisburg, and I'll contact my handler. He's a good guy. He'll get you back in your nice, safe jail cell without any repercussion to you."

Cole's eyes cut to hers, then shifted, just slightly, toward the sun setting through the trees. "You think I'm worried about my safety? You think I want to spend the next seventeen years in there?"

The way he was looking at the forest, the sky . . . it was how she'd expect a blind person to react the moment their eyesight was restored. For the first time she began to understand what he'd been through and the risk she was asking him to take. If they failed and he was caught, his sentence would be doubled at the very least.

She wouldn't fare well, either, and losing her job was the least of what she'd face, although at the moment that was the worst thing she could imagine. Except Richard's death. But if you wanted a big payoff, you had to take a big risk, and saving the life of a man who'd been like a father to her—what bigger payoff could there be?

Richard Swendahl had stepped into her life at a time when she'd lost everything. When she was eight years old, her parents had both been murdered, victims of a botched kidnapping. They'd been wealthy, so she'd escaped the foster system, but the absence of any living relatives left her to the dubious care of a nanny and a guardian.

Richard had worked the case for the FBI, but unlike the other agents, he was haunted by their failure. He'd stayed in her life, the one adult who was there by choice, and eventually their relationship grew into affection. Years later, when she'd stated her intention to work for the FBI, he'd been the only person who didn't tell her she couldn't let the past dictate her career choices, or try to convince her she wasn't suited for it. Instead he'd calmly directed her educational path, and when the time came, he'd provided a recommendation—*the* recommendation, she believed—that had secured her a position with the Bureau. Richard had been the one pillar for most of her existence, and now his life was in her hands. She couldn't afford to worry about what would happen to her. Or Cole Hackett.

She took a deep breath and a huge chance. "We can't sit here all day, Hackett. Either you're with me, or you're not."

Cole went silent and still, absorbing the ultimatum and

weighing his options, all of which involved the FBI. Agent Swift might look harmless but she was just like all the rest of them. She asked him for a simple favor, nothing really, making big promises to bring him on board. It all sounded perfectly safe and reasonable, but he could be heading for a sharp left turn around a blind curve up ahead. Before he knew it he'd be driving off a cliff, and the FBI wouldn't just leave him to hope like hell he could learn to fly; they'd be waiting at the bottom just in case gravity didn't finish him off.

So why was he actually considering her deal?

Because she wasn't just offering him a chance to get out of jail, she was holding out the possibility of clearing his name. She had to know it was irresistible, but she had no idea who she was dealing with. No way would he put his trust in an FBI agent. And yet . . . If she was telling the truth, if there was the smallest possibility he could get a new trial, he had to take the shot. A new trial meant the chance of getting his reputation restored, which would allow him to put his life back on track—with a hell of a detour, sure, but exoneration was the closest he could get to wiping out the past eight years.

Besides, it wasn't like taking the deal meant he had to play the game by her rules. Any new information she had would also be in the FBI's files. She was asking him to hack into those files. If there was something new on his case in there, he'd find it himself, and then he'd ditch her and hire a shark of a lawyer to not only get his conviction overturned but take the government for everything he could get. If she was lying, he'd ditch her and look for his own evidence, and hell, the government could fund that, too, with the money she wanted him to clean out of those frozen accounts.

No matter what, he wasn't going back to jail, and he wouldn't be with her any longer than she was useful in dealing with their government pursuers.

"You have new evidence," he said.

"Yes."

"That might actually mean something if you were still in good standing with those jackasses in Washington."

"You do what I ask and you're a free man. Whether or not we get this agent back alive, I'll make sure of it."

He let that sink in for a minute, then said, "You have a first name, Agent Swift?"

"Harmony."

"Shit," he said. "Even your name is optimistic."

He reached over and turned the key, rolling the front window down and taking a deep breath of the crisp fall air. "It's getting stuffy in here, Harm. Go back to the beginning. How did you find out about the kidnapping, how much do you know, and what exactly do you want from me?"

"Is that a yes?" she asked him.

"It's not a no. Yet."

"I've given you all the assurances I can. What'll it take for you to say yes?"

"I don't know," he lied, because he'd pretty much decided he had nothing to lose by helping her, "but buying me dinner would be a good start."

chapter
3

"YOU HAVE A DESTINATION IN MIND?" COLE ASKED Harmony a half hour and three left turns later. "Over the rainbow maybe?"

"I'm from California," Harmony said, "not Kansas."

"It's not about geography; it's about make-believe. Optimistic bullshit. If you don't like the real facts of a story, pretty them up."

"They make horror movies in Hollywood, too."

"Yeah, I'm in one," Cole said, his face all hard planes and sharp angles in the faint glow of the dashboard lights. "It's just a matter of time before I open the wrong door and find your coworkers behind it ready to haul me back to hell. All that's missing is the ominous soundtrack."

"It's not going to end that way."

"This is reality. You don't get to write your own ending."

"Why not?" Harmony demanded, exhausted suddenly, and completely disgusted with his continual negativity. "If you want something bad enough—"

"Someone will come along and take it away just as you're about to get it."

She looked over at him.

He stared back, one eyebrow raised.

"I'm starting to regret not shooting you."

"You still have time," he said dryly.

"True. And hey, at least you got out of jail before you died."

He chuckled, a soft rumble of sound that seemed to fill the inside of the Explorer with companionship and comfort. "And at least I didn't spend my last hours with someone boring."

"Wow, was that a compliment?"

"Just drive, Calamity Jane. Preferably away from the other agents as fast as you can."

"Whatever you say, Captain Smith."

"*The Titanic?*" he said. "Seems about right. Not even Hollywood could make that story have a happy ending."

"Didn't you see the movie? Jack and Rose ended up together."

"But they were dead."

Harmony smiled, feeling more optimistic than ever, despite Cole's lack of confidence. He didn't believe she could do it. What mattered was that she believed. She'd rescue Richard from his kidnappers, and if she had any skill at all, she'd not only make sure the kidnappers didn't get a dime for their trouble, she'd put them in Cole's jail cell before it was all over.

They came to another intersection, a couple of two-lane roads with nothing but nature as far as the eye could see. "Eeny-meeny-miny-mo," she said, and because her lack of a plan seemed to annoy Cole she took a right at random.

"This road'll take us back to that little town," he said, "I don't remember the name, but we went around it about an hour ago."

"And now we're going back."

"Nope."

"Not even for food?"

"Food?" Cole repeated, slightly embarrassed but hardly surprised that the word came out on a breath of air and laced with longing. His stomach had been growling for hours, but he'd learned to ignore it in Lewisburg since the remedy for his growling stomach was prison food, which, as far as Cole was concerned, qualified as cruel and unusual punishment. The possibility of eating real food in a real restaurant made him dizzy—but not so dizzy that he couldn't see the looming spectre of a return to Lewisburg. "Do you think eating dinner in a restaurant is a good idea?"

"Not even the FBI would expect us to show our faces in Podunkville, Pennsylvania."

"I'll bet they have televisions with cable in Podunkville, not to mention network programming."

"Relax, we aren't on the evening news yet. It's too soon for the FBI to go public. The embarrassment-to-recapture quotient is still too high. It's only been a few hours, and you're not a dangerous criminal, so they can justify saving face by keeping this secret until they find you. Which they're certain they will."

"I'm not so sure that's misplaced confidence."

"A while ago you asked me some questions," Harmony said, sidetracking him from the whole fear-of-discovery thing that would keep him from the food. The only thing he wanted more than food was information.

"How much do I know about the kidnapping, and what, exactly do I need you to do," she continued. "You want answers, or should we keep discussing our travel plans?"

Cole figured the two were linked, but he was willing to take it at her pace. "I'm listening."

"My handler, Mike Kovaleski, told me about the kidnapping."

"And it pissed you off," Cole said. She looked pissed off now just thinking about it, which was like seeing a rabid bunny. It was all cute and soft until you noticed the demented look in its eyes, but by then it was too late because it had sunk its teeth into you. The idea of Harmony sinking her teeth into him wasn't exactly unwelcome . . . Oh, hell, she could bite him anywhere, anytime, she wanted. In fact, he had some suggestions, and now would be a really good time.

But then he wouldn't get the explanation, so he made a valiant effort to tame his raging lust. She'd still have teeth, and he'd still have all those places later, he reminded himself before he had to resort to chanting mantras. And hopefully they'd both be alive.

"So you decided to take matters into your own hands," he prompted.

"We've been over this already," Harmony said, still channeling Jessica Rabbit with blond hair. And PMS.

"Right, he's a friend, a fellow agent. What I'm wondering now is what's the hidden agenda."

She glanced over at him. "Like what?"

"Like you were tired of riding a desk."

She hesitated long enough to tell him he was on the right track, before she confirmed it. "There was some of that, but it wasn't my main incentive. It isn't right to leave a federal agent, who's served his country for thirty years, out in the cold."

At least there wasn't anything personal between them, Cole thought, unless she was into much older men. Not that he cared about her romantic entanglements, he assured himself. He just wanted to understand her motivations. "That kind of black-and-white attitude will get you into trouble."

"You mean like jeopardizing my career and putting my life on the line?"

"Not to mention mine."

"Regretting your choice?" she said, keeping her voice light, amused, and not fooling Cole in the least.

"I haven't made a choice yet," he reminded her. "I won't until you give me all the facts."

"Oh. Right." She did her California act, taking a couple of deep breaths, and when she answered, she sounded more relaxed. A little. "I lifted the file when Mike wasn't looking and read it."

"So we're relying on your memory?

"I had to get it back before he noticed it was missing."

"Why not copy it?"

"You can't just leave the FBI building with a stack of classified documents, even copies. I took down the contact information."

"And they let you out with it?"

"I wrote it on my underwear," she said, which stopped him in his tracks—verbally.

Physically he'd gone into overdrive, his eyes dropping to her halter dress, and she knew he was betting she didn't have a bra on under it. He was right, too. She'd never gotten the hang of the FBI dress code. Probably one of the reasons she hadn't been promoted to field agent, but she just couldn't bring herself to wear those ugly, boxy suits, and the shoes . . . Ick.

When she'd aimed her career at the FBI, she'd pictured herself more like a Bond girl—a smart Bond girl—than Eliot Ness. She wanted to wear gorgeous, designer clothes and never chip a nail or smear her lipstick while she was saving the world. The truth was, they'd stuck her at a desk and given her a computer, and she figured if they weren't going to let her do what she wanted, they could take their dress code and—

"Earth to Mata Hari," Cole said, less snark than heat.

She glared at him anyway.

"If you're done centering yourself."

She added pursed lips to the narrowed eyes.

"We were at the point where you went commando so you could pilfer government secrets on your thong," he said, most of the way back to sarcasm, which was what she wanted.

And then she said, "I don't wear a thong," which was the wrong thing to say because he went back to picturing her in her underwear, which might not take the form of floss in his imagination, but probably involved black lace, considering the faraway look on his face and the heat pumping off him.

"Earth to Dirk Diggler," she mocked, and when he only smirked a little, she added, "White cotton."

He huffed out a breath. "You ruined the fantasy."

"I'd've thought my being an FBI agent took care of that already."

"In my fantasy you have a different job."

"Used to leaving money on the nightstand?"

"I never had to pay for it."

She snorted softly. "I saw your mug shot."

"Ouch," he said, deadpan. "Ever heard of the Bill Gates effect?"

"No, but I can tell you're dying to enlighten me."

"Not all women are interested in looks."

"No," she said, getting his inference, "apparently some women are future planners. Who knows when you might stumble across a computer nerd who's about to get insanely rich off some revolutionary new piece of software."

"Yeah, I kept a supply of blindfolds in the nightstand, right next to the condoms."

Harmony rolled her eyes, not missing the undertone of insult beneath the sarcasm. "Suppose we agree that sex—past, present, and future—is out of bounds."

"I don't have any blindfolds with me anyway."

They wouldn't be necessary anymore—not that they ever were, but Cole Hackett the nerd would have appealed to a certain type of woman. Cole Hackett the ex-con had a wider appeal, as in any woman with a pulse who wasn't a candidate for same-sex marriage would find him appealing. Except her, of course.

"We were talking about the kidnapping," she said. "It appears Richard was snatched by members of the Russian mafia. The voice on the single phone call had a Russian-type accent. The call was traced to Los Angeles."

"A lot of the computer crime that goes on now originates in Eastern Europe."

"And those guys know how to cover their electronic tracks."

"You sure it wasn't bounced all over the planet?" he asked.

"The experts at the Bureau were sure."

"So we're heading to Los Angeles."

She glanced over at him, then back at the road.

"I may not look like that pasty kid in the mug shot," he said, "but my IQ didn't decrease with my body fat percentage. You know as well as I do that giving them what they want is a death sentence for your friend. You're planning to rescue him."

"Yes," she said without hesitation. "You're just the backup plan. If this goes the way I want it to, they're not getting their hands on one red cent."

"YOU HAVEN'T ANSWERED MY SECOND QUESTION," COLE said.

"I didn't think it was necessary, you having that big IQ." Not to mention big eyes, and hopefully a big stomach.

They were in a small town somewhere in western Pennsylvania, at an old farmhouse converted into a restaurant. It was a little mom-and-pop place, dingy but welcoming, with creaking wooden floors, mismatched furniture, and the kind of menu that was loaded with salt, saturated fat, and enough calories to put half the state into a food coma.

"Okay," Cole said, "so I know what you want from me. Do you have any idea what the risks are? I'm good, but your friends in computer security at the FBI keep a close eye on their firewall. Anybody tries to get through, they make it their mission in life to track him down. And they love to make examples of people like me."

"We've already had this discussion. I knew what the risks were when I took this assignment."

"But you're one of *them*, and I'm an escaped convict. I'm the likely scapegoat if things go wrong."

Harmony sighed heavily.

It was turning out to be a lot harder to convince Cole to help than she'd expected. Because of his history with the FBI. Understandable, since the FBI had put him in jail—for good reason. There hadn't been a lot of time to plan and prepare, but before she'd embarked on this course, she'd read his file. Not much there; from all outward appearances he'd been nothing more than a stupid kid who'd hacked into the Bureau's system for kicks, and had the colossal bad judgment to do it at a time when every intelligence agency in the world was on high alert.

Except Cole certainly wasn't stupid. Or judgmentally challenged. And he kept talking about doing the FBI a favor and being screwed over, and she couldn't ask him what he meant. Not after she'd lied about having new evidence. Sure it had been a tiny little spur-of-the-moment white lie meant to nudge him closer to helping her. But that lie put her in an awkward position, because it implied she knew more about his predicament than she actually did.

So she'd just have to figure it out as they went along. It wasn't like she hadn't expected Cole to be uncooperative. And suspicious. She'd just have to keep an eye on him, and guard her words. Cole would learn he'd been played eventually, but timing was everything. If he found out now, he'd bolt, and she'd lose her only hope of buying enough time to find out where Richard was being held. If . . . *when* they freed Richard, the Bureau would have no choice but to commute Cole's sentence. He'd still be angry, no doubt about it, but she imagined freedom—permanent freedom—would have a pacifying effect on his temper.

"Look," she said, "I know you don't trust me—"

"I just want to make sure I'm not being set up again."

"Do you want me to make promises you won't believe anyway? I've given you all the assurances I can."

"And none when it comes to actually accomplishing your end of the job, except you have the kidnappers' contact information written on your panties."

A woman at the next table sucked in her breath and scowled at him.

"Can we try not to draw attention to ourselves?" Harmony said, keeping her voice down.

"In case you haven't noticed, people have been staring at us since we walked in."

Harmony glanced around the room. "It's mostly women, and they're staring at you."

"Probably all that million-dollar software I'm going to write."

Probably they were thinking she was the luckiest woman alive. "I doubt they're interested in getting their hands on your software."

He reached across the table and closed his fingers around her wrist, loosely. "What are you thinking about?"

She tried to pull away, but he moved his hand down to

hers, twining their fingers. "They'll stop staring if they think we're a couple."

Another quick look around proved he was right, for the most part. Other than a sidelong glance now and again, most of the female diners had gone back to minding their own business. But she had a feeling Cole Hackett had left an impression.

Their dinner arrived, netting them more attention, out of curiosity this time, since the waitress brought enough food to feed half the town, including dessert, which Cole had told her to bring right along with the main courses. The good news? He took his hand back so he could eat. The skin-to-skin havoc was over, but it didn't end the assault on her libido.

This time the attack came by way of her ears, which suddenly seemed to be connected directly to her nerve endings. He cut into a rare steak, put the first bite into his mouth and moaned, eyes closed, head falling back, a low, sexy sound that made her nerves vibrate like plucked cello strings.

Every woman within hearing distance broke out in a sweat. Harmony experienced an internal earthquake that nearly jolted her off her chair.

"You're not eating," he said. "Don't tell me you're one of those women who only eats salads and pretends not to be hungry all the time."

"No." She indicated the spread in front of him with her fork. Roast turkey with stuffing, pork chops, and the steak, with all the sides: buttered noodles, mashed potatoes, the vegetable of the day, and a small tossed salad with ranch dressing so thick it could masquerade as mayonnaise. And then there was the lemon meringue pie, Harmony's favorite. Not that she was letting him know it. "You're going to get fat eating like that."

His voice dropped another notch, becoming impossibly deep, impossibly slow. Incredibly suggestive. "You could help me work it off."

"Having sex burns less than a hundred calories. You've got about ten thousand there."

"Who was talking about sex?"

She gave him a look. "You were."

"Don't ruffle easy, huh?"

Harmony wasn't sure what she was feeling, but ruffled was definitely too mild a word for it. "Why are you trying to ruffle me?"

"Just having fun. It's been a while." He took her hand again. "Not that it's such a bad idea—sex, I mean. We could keep pretending to be a couple. It would be a good disguise."

"We don't need a disguise. You're here to strip bank accounts."

"Okay, but it would give me more incentive to toe the line."

"You actually want me to hold sex over your head."

"Every woman gets around to it eventually."

"I'm insulted for all womankind, not to mention personally. And you don't need me to have sex."

"Uhhh . . . I'm out of prison now."

"I meant, if you want sex, you can get it from any woman here."

"With you watching?" he asked, effectively shutting her up. The problem with that was that it left him alone with his thoughts, and his thoughts weren't exactly comforting because he was thinking that he didn't want sex from any other woman there. He wanted it from Harmony Swift.

That was troubling until he realized he'd only fallen back into his old pattern, afraid to approach women. He didn't even like Harmony, and he sure as hell didn't trust her. But he knew her now, he could talk to her, and that had always been half the battle for him.

He wasn't that nerdy kid anymore, though. After eight years in jail he didn't think he'd have any trouble breaking the ice with women, no gunfire necessary. Not that it was going to be an issue, anyway, seeing as he was stuck with Harm—with Agent Swift—for the next little while . . . And if she ever looked at him the way she was looking at the lemon meringue pie, they were both in real trouble.

Her tongue crept out to wet her lips. He focused on his meal. And changed the subject. "I do what you want, I get the new evidence, right?"

"Yes, but there are some ground rules."

"Such as?"

She put her fork down, met his eyes. Making sure he heard her. "I'm in charge," she said.

"Nope."

"But—"

He stood, his chair legs screeching over the wooden floor when he shoved it out of the way and walked off.

"I have to pay . . ." Harmony half rose, then sank back into her seat, smiling at the other diners. "Sorry," she mumbled, grabbing the lemon meringue pie before she went up front to pay the bill.

When she got outside, Cole was pacing in the cool evening air, keeping to the gloom at the side of the building. At least her speech about keeping a low profile had sunk in.

"What's that?" he asked, pointing to the takeout box in her hand.

"Dessert."

"You're going to get fat."

"It's a new diet," she told him, "the irritation diet. I figure as long as I'm around you, I'll burn enough calories to eat a pound of sugar every day."

"You're an FBI agent," he said in his own defense.

"And you don't trust me, I get it. But you have no idea what's at stake."

"Because you're holding back. And you don't trust me, either."

"No, I don't, so I'll be running this show until you prove I can trust you."

"But you don't have to prove anything to me?"

"You can still go back to jail and serve out your sentence," she said. But she wasn't looking at him.

Cole turned and saw what she saw, two police officers heading into the restaurant.

"What's it going to be," Harmony said, "me or them?"

chapter
4

"STATE TROOPERS," COLE SAID. "HOW DO YOU KNOW
they're looking for us?"

Harmony sidled over to the window, peering through a
couple decades' worth of grime and the dim lighting inside
until she spotted the police officers, standing at the front of
the place in a huddle of staffers. "They're showing around a
photo." Probably hers since Cole bore no resemblance to his
mug shot. Then one of the cops lifted his hand to about Cole's
height. Even from there Harmony could see one of the waitress's eyes light up. "Uh-oh."

Cole crowded close to look over her shoulder. "I thought
you said they wouldn't notify the local authorities that one of
their agents defected."

"This isn't Russia; I didn't defect," she said, her voice
rasping out on a soft wheeze because she'd just realized he
was all but wrapped around her, a warm, solid, comforting
hulk of a man who smelled like a man and felt . . . safe.

"Why else would they be here?"

"The warden. According to his file he has a pretty good

relationship with the Pennsylvania State Police. He must have alerted them before the Bureau gagged him."

"Great, a federal employee with initiative."

"Hey, I'm a federal employee."

"Not a recommendation in my book."

"Maybe you'd prefer those two guys, and whoever they just called in as backup." Harmony eased away from the window—and from Cole—turning back when she realized he wasn't behind her. "Look," she said, "this means the FBI isn't the only agency after us. We'll have to avoid the local police. I expected it, but not this soon."

"Kind of complicates things."

"Not really. Your choice is still pretty simple."

"Is it?"

Harmony shrugged, but after the day he'd had she knew what he was thinking. Seventeen more years in jail couldn't compete with wide-open spaces and restaurant meals. By the time he said, "We can't go back to the car," she'd already managed to suppress a self-satisfied grin. But she didn't even pretend to agree with him, heading toward the Explorer.

"Their cruiser is blocking the drive," Cole said, trying to muscle her off into the darkness.

"And the parking lot is completely surrounded by trees, I get it," she said, ducking out of reach, "but if I don't get my laptop we might as well give ourselves up." She opened the rear passenger door just as the two cops came out of the restaurant and shouted at them to stop, crossing the parking lot at a dead run.

Their hands were on their holsters, but they hadn't drawn their weapons, and Cole wasn't giving them the chance. He headed for the bigger of the two, walking calmly, hands spread to show he wasn't armed. When the cop got close enough, Cole sucker punched him. The officer went down, not out cold, but definitely groggy. Which left officer number two. He was smaller than his partner, but he had a good sixty pounds and six inches on Harmony. What he didn't have was a takeout container of lemon meringue pie.

Harmony opened the little takeout box, scooped out the pie, and hit the cop square in the face, all in one slick Three

Stooges move that left him blind. And enraged. He swiped at the lemon in his eyes with one hand, swinging wildly with the other.

Cole slipped up behind the officer, wrapped a hand around the back of his neck, and had him folding in a boneless heap to the pavement.

"Pie?" he said to Harmony, his eyes on her mouth.

"I didn't want to shoot him," Harmony said, choosing to respond—at least verbally—to the professional criticism rather than the way Cole had watched her lick lemon meringue off her fingers. Her physical response was completely involuntary and absolutely inappropriate given the fact there was an unconscious police officer at their feet and a groggy one just a few yards away. Not to mention the whole convicted felon thing.

And on that note, Harmony hit the locks on the Explorer's key fob and pulled out a duffel and a laptop case, slinging the latter over her head so the strap lay between her breasts.

"Not taking a chance on losing the computer," Cole said. "A woman after my own heart. What's in the duffel?"

"My clothes, and I don't want to lose those, either."

He took the duffel from her and said, "We can work on that. Do you have any idea where we are?"

"A small town in western Pennsylvania."

"Not a lot of options." He cocked his head and smiled. "But there are possibilities."

He wrapped his hand around her wrist and took off for the street, putting as much distance between them and the state cops as he could.

It would have been a good plan, if not for porch lights and barking dogs marking their path through the pitch black. The residents of this little town might be in for the night, but they weren't sleeping. And they were probably armed.

"We have to get out of town," Cole said, echoing her thought process. "Every one of these people has a gun in the house, a hunting rifle if nothing else. We keep this up and it's only a matter of time before somebody takes a shot at us."

"Not if the police get to us first," she said, red and blue lights flashing against the white siding of the nearest house.

The police cruiser pulled into the driveway and two state troopers jumped out, one of them sporting a lemon meringue hairstyle, the other a nice lump on the jaw. Both of them displayed a singularity of purpose born of humiliation.

Lemon Meringue Guy stayed in front of the house, but the other cop came around the back, right toward the spot where Cole and Harmony crouched behind a rotting old shed Harmony suspected had once been an outhouse. This time his gun was in his hand.

"Keep to the shadows," Cole said, which was great in theory, not so much in reality.

Harmony took off after him, but suddenly there was light everywhere, not to mention puddles, ditches, fences, a variety of gardening equipment, and the odd gnome. Cole blasted through every obstacle, Harmony struggling to keep up in his wake and quickly losing him in the darkness. The good news was that she'd lost the cop, too. She didn't delude herself he'd stay lost forever.

"Man," she wheezed when Cole appeared out of nowhere, dragging her behind a handy thicket of lilac bushes.

"Fake a twisted ankle," Cole said, trying to shove her back out into the open. "I'll circle around and take out the cop."

Harmony grabbed two handfuls of shrubbery and refused to be thrown under the bus. "You'll take off."

"You're the one who keeps saying we have to trust one another," Cole reminded her, his voice low but fraught with frustration.

"Fine, you fake a twisted ankle," she said. "I'll circle around and take out the cop."

"How are you going to manage that?"

"These hands are lethal weapons," she said, holding them up, French manicure and all.

She could all but see Cole rolling his eyes. "Twisted ankles are chick territory, and the cop is less likely to shoot a woman."

"Wow. You managed to be a chauvinist twice in one sentence."

"I've always been an overachiever," Cole said.

"Then you might be able to handle chick territory," Harmony said. "With a little help." She kicked him in the shin, and when he jackknifed to clutch at the assaulted body part she planted her foot on his butt and sent him stumbling out from behind the bushes.

"Hey," the cop yelled, "I mean, freeze."

Harmony heard the pounding of feet as she cut the opposite way around the bushes, coming up behind the cop and kicking him in the knee. She used her gun butt on the back of his head at the same time, and he crumpled into a satisfying heap at her feet. And then he jumped back up and lumbered toward her, murder in his eyes and his gun completely forgotten for the more primal urge to strangle her.

Harmony danced out of his way, heart pounding, no idea how she was going to live up to her big claims to Cole, let alone avoid arrest, when the cop dropped again. This time he didn't get back up. Any self-congratulatory urges or notions of delayed reaction died when she saw Cole behind the cop. The look on his face was . . . bloodthirsty.

"You didn't, uh . . ."

"He's not dead," Cole said, "but it won't be long before his partner finds him or he wakes up." He took her by the wrist again. "And then we're going to discuss your definition of teamwork."

"I can walk by myself." Harmony gave her arm one good, twisting yank that broke his grip, then she set off, getting about two steps before the heel of her shoe caught on some obstacle unseen in the utter darkness and she fell on her backside, hitting Cole below the knees and nearly taking him down with her.

"You can walk," he said, his face a white blur above her. "It's staying upright that seems to be a problem."

"Stop manhandling me," she hissed as she climbed to her feet.

"You're lucky I didn't fall on top of you."

"It's these shoes," she whispered back. "They're not exactly outdoor gear."

But they made her look like she had a mile of leg. "We have to go cross-country," Cole said, putting her incredible mile-long legs—and how they'd feel wrapped around him—out of his mind before he lost the blood flow to his brain. "We don't have a choice."

"Then we go cross-country."

They didn't go fast enough for Cole's preference. He kept the pace down for Harmony's sake, not to mention his own. He couldn't afford for her to fall again and maybe turn an ankle. But it worked against them.

They hit the edge of town and headed into the woodland beyond, Cole pulling her to a stop behind a handy tree while he got his bearings. Noise had a tendency to travel in the country, and there wasn't anything to mask it, no crickets chirping, no frogs croaking, no sounds of the sidewalks being rolled up since that had apparently happened while they were in the restaurant.

The troopers were crashing through the underbrush, swearing and making enough noise to wake the dead as they split up and went in different directions. He and Harmony were both wearing dark clothing, but there was enough moonlight coming through the trees to reflect off their skin like neon. If the cops looked in the right direction . . .

Harmony curled her hand around his arm, and all Cole could think was that he ought to be paying attention to the guys with the guns. But her face was close to his and her breath was short, heat and excitement pumping off her. He was right there with her, adrenaline sparking along his nerve endings, but it wasn't fight or flight he was thinking about.

She turned to him, started to speak, and he took her mouth. She sank in, just for a moment, her lips softening under his, her breath easing out on a small moan, her tongue tangling with his. And then she punched him in the gut.

There wasn't a lot of oomph behind the shot—they were too close for that—but it was enough to startle a grunt out of him, and that, coupled with her snarling, "What are you doing?" was all it took to get the other cop's attention. He sent up a shout for his partner and came after them at a run.

"Keep up," Cole said, pointing himself into the darkness and setting a ground-eating pace, not full speed, but fast enough to put some distance between himself and Pennsylvania's Finest without slamming into a tree trunk or stumbling into a hole. His heart was chugging like a freight train, from a combination of exertion, fear of arrest, and the conflicting urge to either kiss Harmony Swift or throttle her. She wasn't exactly helping the situation.

"Every man for himself?" Harmony said, breathing hard, her voice dripping sarcasm.

"You're not facing another twenty years in jail," he shot back, "not to mention what they'll tack on for this little field trip," but the important thing was she was right behind him. She was the key to exoneration, he told himself. He almost believed it—he might have believed it if that kiss wasn't still sizzling across his skin like heat lightning, if he didn't taste her again with every breath he took.

Think, he told himself, or there won't be any more kisses, or wide skies, or choices. There wouldn't be any more freedom, which was enough to send his hormones packing and re-engage his brain.

The troopers weren't stupid enough to keep blundering around in the dark with no idea where they were going. Sooner or later they'd stop and do what he'd done, listen for sounds of movement. He pulled Harmony into a copse of saplings big enough to hide them both, and they froze except for their breath steaming on the chill autumn air. Sure enough the night was silent, the cops playing the waiting game, too.

Harmony was on the same page, head cocked, listening hard. All her attention was on the threat, Cole figured, or she never would have shifted closer to him, one hand on his stomach, the other creeping around his waist. Cole moved away, far enough to keep himself from being muddled by her again.

After a minute or two there was some crashing and swearing behind them, but it seemed to be headed in the opposite direction, back toward the town. Cole didn't believe for a moment it meant they were off the hook. But they had some breathing room.

"What now?" Harmony asked, her voice no more than a breath of sound—with an unmistakably arctic overtone. Pissed off, Cole realized with a mental eye roll. One minute she was cranky because he'd gotten close, now she was angry that he wanted distance. Typical woman.

"Hear that?" he said close to her ear. He couldn't resist brushing his lips, just a whisper of a touch, over her skin.

She shivered, but she moved away. He had to admire her self-control. It was a hell of a lot stronger than his, especially since taunting her had only backfired on him and it took her saying, "Seventeen more years of jail," to shock him back to the fugitive-on-the-run stuff.

"Listen," he said.

"Is that what I think it is?" Harmony asked, just as the faint throb of an engine was joined by the mournful wail of a train whistle. "Are you talking about the train? Or the dogs?"

Cole listened some more and off in the distance, in the direction of the town, he could hear the baying of hounds. "Crap."

Harmony put a hand on his arm before he could walk away. "Maybe we should circle back around to the Explorer instead."

"They'll have a trooper watching it by now, and even if they don't, the dogs will catch up to us before we get there."

"That train isn't going to wait for us."

"There'll be another."

"When?"

"Don't know." And he was done arguing. "I'm for the train. Come or don't come, it's up to you."

"You're not leaving me a choice," she muttered.

"I know how you feel," he said, because he really didn't have a choice either. He'd made it while they were sitting in the woods that morning. He'd go along with Harmony's plan, and he'd do what she wanted, for exactly as long as it took him to complete his own agenda: find the new evidence by himself or, if she was playing him and there was no new evidence, hack into those frozen bank accounts and siphon some of the money off for himself, enough that he could go anywhere and be anyone he wanted without trouble or hardship. It wasn't stealing, the way he saw it. It was payback for nearly a decade spent in hell—not to mention his life's work stolen from him.

Harmony took his arm, this time dragging him off at a tangent from the direction he'd been going.

"What?" she said when he hauled her to a stop. "The train is this way."

"No, it's not."

"Yes, it is. The sound came from up ahead."

"The sound came from over there," Cole said, correcting back to their original course.

"Fine," Harmony said, "you go that way and when I get to the train I'll—Hackett! Damn it, put me down."

Cole straightened, hiking her a little higher, then bending his knees until he was low enough to snag her duffel from the ground where he'd dropped it—not easy with a hundred twenty pounds of pissed-off, struggling FBI agent draped across his shoulder.

"Hold still."

"Put me down."

"I wonder what's in here," he said, unzipping her duffel and digging into it until he heard the jingle of chain.

She went immediately still.

"Not so much fun when the cuffs are on the other wrists," he said, his brain making the leap from her restrained in the backseat of the Explorer, to him back there with her— Okay, that was a mental picture he really didn't need at the moment. It was going to be difficult enough to lug her around without any other . . . impediments.

"We'll do it your way," she said, the tone of her voice and her body language pretty strong arguments against the pretense that she'd given in, even when she added, "I promise."

Cole wasn't sure putting her down was the right decision, but there was the trust issue. He set her on her feet, stepping back out of striking distance, for which he received a look that smoldered, and not in a good way. She was keeping track, that look said, and there'd be a reckoning.

"Lead on, Moses."

"Cute," Cole said, and struck out for the train, hoping like hell he was right and they didn't have to wander around for forty minutes, let alone forty years. Aside from the whole going back to jail program, he really didn't want to look like an idiot.

And then he heard the dogs again, and getting to the train was more about the possibility of ending his life as a chew toy than appearing directionally challenged. He took Harmony by the wrist, and when she couldn't keep up with him in her impractical heels, he wrapped an arm around her waist, boosted her off the ground and ran, flat out. The train whistle sounded closer, but so did the dogs, and he barely registered Harmony prying at his arm because his world narrowed down to the train whistle and the dogs, the dogs and the train whistle, all of them on a collision course.

They broke out of the woods, Cole's lungs burning, his thigh muscles shaky, and there was the train—on the other side of a ditch, up a hill, moving slowly away from them—already halfway gone. The dogs, sad to say, were right behind them. Cole looked over his shoulder and saw them straining at their leashes in the wildly oscillating flashlight beams of their handlers. Way too close for comfort. Or rational thought.

He dropped Harmony on her feet and towed her through the ditch, ankle-deep in water, and up the hill on the other side without stopping, boosting her through the open door of an empty freight car as it chugged by. He tossed her duffel in after her, and then his strength started to flag. Lifting weights was something you could do in the pen, running not so much. He didn't have the stamina or the lung capacity to keep up with the train, and it started to pull off without him. Harmony hanging out the door yelling, "Get your butt moving, Hackett," did nothing to motivate him. And then she shrieked, "The dogs," pointing over his shoulder with a touch of real panic on her face, and he dug deep, put on a burst of speed, and threw his upper body onto the edge of Harmony's freight car just as a hound latched onto his pant leg.

Harmony hit the floor on her belly, grabbing him by the armpits, and pulling for all she was worth, but he had a full-grown hound hanging off his leg, deadweight, and he could feel himself slipping.

And then Harmony let go.

chapter
5

A COUPLE HUNDRED POUNDS OF CONVICTED FELON plus eighty pounds of homicidal hound equaled disaster for Harmony's one hundred twenty pounds. And getting dragged head first off a moving freight train wasn't going to make her day, even without the yapping, snarling pack of dogs. So she let go of Cole. And grabbed the first thing that came to hand—an ear of feed corn, which was hard as a rock. She winged it at the dog. The corn bounced off its skull without any discernible consequence.

Cole was having more of an effect, kicking the leg with the dog attached to it, trying to scrape it off with his other foot. And he was yelling at her the entire time, swearing, making threats, promising retribution, as he slid farther and farther to the edge of the car. The dog finally let out a yelp and disappeared into the darkness below the speeding train, just as Harmony braced herself with her back against the very edge of the open door and reached for Cole. He grabbed onto her, dragging himself into the car an inch at a time. He wasn't very careful about where he put his hands.

"Jesus," he said, flopping on his back, breathing hard, "my life flashed before my eyes."

"Let me guess," she said, rubbing the places his fingers had dug in, including her right breast, "puberty, college, jail. All woman-free zones in your case."

"Too bad I can't say that now."

"It's a big freight car," Harmony said, climbing to her feet. She lurched to the far end, taking her duffel and her laptop case with her.

"I think we should get off," Cole said, his voice just barely loud enough to carry over the sound of the train clattering down the tracks, "while we're in the middle of nowhere."

"I'm not jumping off this train while I'm wearing a dress."

"Your choice, but I'm not hanging around until this thing gets to the next station."

Cole was still lying in a heap by the door, so despite his big talk she wasn't all that worried about him taking off on her. Especially when she stripped off her jacket and lifted her skirt.

Out of the corner of her eye she saw him sit up.

"Dogs and cops," he said. "Waiting. For us."

He seemed to be really worried about the possibility of arrest, but he still wasn't moving. And she could feel him watching her.

Not that he could see that much, but she turned her back anyway, unbuckled her clutch holster from around her thigh and tightened it up to fit around her ankle.

"I've never been into James Bond," Cole said, "but I'm beginning to see the attractions of being a spy."

"I'm not a spy." She slipped her clutch piece into its holster and straightened. "And James Bond isn't exactly a realistic version of what I do."

"Hell, Cupcake, you're not a realistic version of what you do. You're more like FBI Barbie."

"Cupcake?" She tore a pair of jeans out of her duffel and dragged them on, then whipped her dress over her head. "FBI Barbie," she fumed, shimmying into her bra and whipping around to face Cole.

It was pitch-black away from the door, but it felt like she was standing in a spotlight, bright and hot and exposing. She fumbled her T-shirt on and slipped into her shoulder holster, feeling a lot better when she tucked her Smith & Wesson into it. Nothing like a loaded firearm to inspire confidence.

"Don't call me Barbie again," she said.

"You kicked me in the shin," he shot back. "If that's not a Barbie move I don't know what is."

"It worked, didn't it?"

"Yeah, right up to the moment the cop jumped back up and came after you."

"And if you hadn't horned in I'd have dealt with him."

"How? Scratched his eyes out? Or maybe you could have strangled him with your designer jeans."

That stopped her. "How do you know these are designer?"

"Even in jail there's television. Any show with supermodels was real popular."

"There's a mental picture I could live without. And just for the record, I was taught there's no wrong way to handle a situation as long as you come out of it alive and with your goal accomplished."

"Next time ask for help."

"Next time I'll just pretend it's you."

She slung her jacket back on and pushed her feet into a pair of running shoes, stuffing her dress into her duffel before she shouldered it, along with her laptop. "So, how do we do this?" she asked, stepping into the open doorway, the wind whipping cold across her skin.

"They don't teach you how to jump off trains in FBI school?"

"They don't teach any of this in FBI school."

Cole came to stand beside her, looking, as she was, down at the ground rushing by. "Just jump," he said. "Gravity will take care of the rest."

"Just jump," Harmony repeated. Or get shoved, which was what Cole did when she balked at the idea of flinging herself into the darkness and taking the landing on faith.

She slammed into the ground feet first, tried to go into a tuck and roll but wound up flopping uncontrollably, arms and legs windmilling, until she came to a graceless stop. In a marsh. Facedown. If not for the cold water seeping through her clothes she would have stayed where she was, taking stock and getting her breath back, but she jumped up immediately, only to have Cole blunder into her and knock her down again—and then fall on top of her.

"Oh, there you are," he said, not making any effort to get off her. In fact, he was resisting her efforts to shove him off, laying the whole hard length of his body on hers. The parts of her that had managed to stay dry were losing that battle. And Cole was getting aroused. Big surprise. The man had been in jail for eight years, a picket fence with a convenient knothole would probably turn him on.

"We're in the middle of a swamp," she said. "It's cold and wet."

"Not from where I am." His hand crept up from her hip, spreading heat and making her forget about the cold air and the frigid water and the possibility there were state troopers combing the railroad tracks for them. Until she realized his fingers were inches from her gun.

She slipped her left leg out from under him, braced her hand on his left shoulder, at the same time hitting his right arm at the elbow and when it collapsed she flipped him off her. He landed on his back next to her with a satisfying little splash. "How about now?"

"Let me guess—they taught that in FBI school?"

"You're lucky I used my FBI training," she said, climbing to her feet. "My self-defense instructor taught me to use my knee. Or my hand."

Cole levered himself upright. "I get the knee. I'm guessing I wouldn't like what you'd do with your hand, either."

"I'd grab your testicles and squeeze as hard as I could for as long as I could. It's for getting away from a rapist."

He sucked some air in through his teeth. "Makes me glad I'm just a terrorist."

"You're not a terrorist; you were just a dumb kid."

"Yeah," he said on a rush of breath, "and now I don't even have the excuse of youth. What are you doing?"

"Looking for my laptop," Harmony said, walking a couple more steps back along the path she'd have taken when she came off the train. "It has to be around here somewhere."

"Shit. Why the hell didn't you hang onto it?"

"Hmmmm, let me see. Because somebody shoved me out of a moving train and I was busy trying not to break my neck?"

Wisely, Cole decided not to respond to that, pacing along about five feet away from her, back toward the train tracks. Luckily, it wasn't far away, and it was dry. Her duffel hadn't fared so well. Harmony slung the laptop case over her shoulder again, but when she took the duffel from Cole it weighed at least five pounds more than it had, and she could hear it dripping. So much for dry clothes, not to mention ones that didn't chafe.

But she was still alive, still free, and as far as she knew, Richard was all right, too. As long as there was hope for success, a little chafing was a small price to pay.

"So what's the plan?" Cole wanted to know.

"Start walking." And that's what she did, scanning the darkness ahead and praying for inspiration. What she got was Cole, sounding like the voice of her own insecurity.

"Where?"

"We head west."

"Do you know where west is?"

"I will as soon as the sun rises."

"Sunrise isn't for hours. I'd like to get dry and warm some time in the near future."

Harmony stopped, looking back to where he was still standing by the railroad tracks. "You should be used to privation."

"Even in jail I got a bed and a hot meal."

"You've had the hot meal. That will have to do for a bed."

Cole came over to her and peered in the direction of her pointing finger. "What is it?"

"A big, red barn."

"How do you know it's big? And how do you know it's red?"

Harmony took another look. The ground rose up gradually away from the tracks, and at the top of a distant hill sat a farmhouse, outbuildings, and something that was definitely a barn, its distinctive roof shape a darker patch against a sky studded with a million stars. "It's a lot bigger than the rest of the buildings," she said. "Does the color really matter? It's close and it will be warm."

"What about the farmer? I'm assuming there's a farmer in your mental picture, probably wearing overalls and holding a pitchfork."

She huffed out a slight laugh. "Who's the one with the imagination?"

"I had a lot of time to develop it in jail," Cole said.

"Don't get out of practice. You're going to need it."

"Wouldn't dream of it." Cole smacked her on the backside as she walked by. "But it always helps to have inspiration."

THEY WALKED FOR LESS THAN AN HOUR, BY COLE'S ESTI-mation. It felt like forever. He was tired and damp and cold, and hungry since he hadn't eaten enough of his dinner to dent his appetite. And then there was Harmony, walking in front of him with her trim little ass swaying. She'd had her back turned on that freight car, and it had been pretty dark, but even if her pale skin hadn't reflected what little light there'd been, he wasn't kidding when he said he had a hell of an imagination. He had no trouble filling in the blank spots. Hell, he was probably making her look better than she actually did. For one thing, in his fantasy the FBI badge was nowhere to be found.

Too bad it was reality he had to live with.

When they got to the farm they gave the house and the other buildings a wide berth, approaching the barn from the rear.

"Hayloft," Cole said, indicating a door sitting about twenty-five feet off the ground, at the top of a conveyor.

He took her hand and pulled her up the ramp, wincing

when he opened the door and the shriek of unoiled hinges cut through the still night air. A dog barked from the farmyard, but Cole relaxed when he heard the faint rattle of chain that told him the animal wasn't roaming around free.

Cole wouldn't have risked it, but Harmony went past him, continuing across the loft to look out the window on the other side.

"The house is still dark," she said softly, "and the dog has stopped barking."

"What about tomorrow morning?"

"We'll be gone before anyone knows we were here," she said, and then for the second time that night she decided to torture him, digging through her duffel. "Yes!" she said, pulling out another pair of jeans. "They're still dry. Mostly."

She toed off her shoes and peeled out of her wet jeans one agonizing inch at a time. Cole turned his back. He could still hear the rustle of cloth, imagine too well what she was taking off and regret what she was putting on, but at least he had the self-control not to watch this time.

"It feels good to be dry again," she finally said, dropping down onto the hay.

"I wouldn't know," Cole said. "I don't have anything to change into. But we can share body heat."

"You want to share body heat?" she asked, her voice dropping from chipper to sultry. "I think that's a wonderful idea."

"Really?" His voice shot up about three octaves and broke at the end.

"Sure. There's a cow right down there."

Cole stomped to the other side—okay, it was more like wading, since it was impossible to stomp in knee-deep hay. "It's your fault I'm cold," he griped. "You didn't bring me a coat."

"Sue me," Harmony said groggily, the hay rustling as she settled down, her duffel under her head.

Cole waded back and lay down behind her, but she scrambled away before he could get too cozy.

"Time to get some things straight."

Cole blew out a breath and rolled onto his back, crossing his arms behind his head. "You do like your rules, don't you?"

"Not rules," she said, "these are more like guidelines."

"Guidelines."

"Suggestions," she amended. "Obviously you've decided to help me, and I think it would be a good idea to agree—"

"Agree?" Cole sat up, exasperated. "Sweetheart, if you want to be in control, just take charge. Don't ask or suggest or supply guidelines. Tell."

"Fine, I'm the FBI agent—"

"Having a job title doesn't make you the boss, either."

"Back off, Mr. Chips."

"That's better," Cole said. "Nice snap to the voice, good touch with the sarcasm."

Harmony didn't say anything.

"Earth to Blondie."

"I'm reminiscing about our first meeting, when you refused to talk to me."

Cole smiled before he could stop himself. It was surprising. And troubling—even more because he was feeling . . . friendly. Lust he could understand; anything else was sheer stupidity. Sure, she was attractive, and yeah, he enjoyed the fact that she could keep up with him. Hell, she gave as good as she got, mentally and physically. But she was FBI, and if she hadn't lied to him outright, she definitely hadn't told him everything. She'd managed to answer all his questions, and she'd looked sincere while she did it, but the FBI operated on a need-to-know basis, and he wasn't in the loop.

"You have something to say, say it," he said, feeling as grim as he sounded.

Harmony must have heard it too because she got right down to setting boundaries, no edge, no banter. "Like I said, I'm the FBI agent, so I'll deal with any threats and I'll handle strategy."

"Nope. I'm laying my life on the line, too. I get a say in what we do."

"I have contacts at the Bureau," Harmony countered. "I'll have the intelligence—"

"And you'll share it with me."

"Your job is to hack into the accounts and move the

money," she reminded him, "but only where and when I tell you."

"Because?"

She huffed out a breath, but she didn't answer his question.

"You're right," Cole said. "I agreed to help you. That makes us partners in my book, and partners watch each other's backs. I can't do that if you're not straight with me."

"We're partners?" she said in a voice that sounded like an *awww* should go along with it. But she dropped that tone and became all business again. "You were right. I'm going after Richard. I need you to move enough money to fool the kidnappers into thinking we're cooperating. I'm scheduled to call them tomorrow night. We only have to show them enough progress so they believe we're doing what they ask. So they won't hurt Richard." Or kill him. "And we need to get as many miles behind us as we can."

"To give you time to find out where he is and come up with a way to rescue him."

"Yes, but you won't be in danger."

He snorted. "You come with your own warning label. And then there are the people trying to capture me and take me back to jail."

"That problem will be going away," Harmony said. "Once we get out of Pennsylvania, we won't have the state police to worry about anymore, and as soon as they're out of the picture, the FBI won't have any way of knowing where we are."

"Famous last words," Cole said. "Those are your last words, right? We're going to be partners in this. Full partners. No secrets." Except the ones he was keeping.

"Yes," she said, no hesitation, which didn't mean she was telling the truth, just that she'd decided her course, same as him.

"Except . . ." she added just when he'd begun to relax, "you can't have a gun."

"I don't want a gun."

"Why not?"

"People have a tendency to shoot back at you for one

thing. And when I get caught with a gun, it'll only go harder for me."

"*If* you're caught," she said. "You really should try to have a little faith in me."

"No problem," Cole said. "I have just as much faith in you as you have in me."

chapter
6

HARMONY WOKE UP WITH COLE WRAPPED AROUND her like a big, warm blanket. Straw poked her everywhere, and she had a face full of dog parts. It was still dark, but she could see two black-and-white speckled dog legs and a blaze of white dog chest about two inches in front of her face. The dog was licking Cole's face, and since Cole was behind her, there were a couple of soft dog ears brushing across her cheek. Not to mention the drool.

Cole didn't seem to be enjoying the adoration. "A little help here?" he said, his breath warm on her neck.

Harmony shifted, the dog backed off far enough to snarl at her, upper lip curled back over really big teeth. She froze. "You're on your own."

"If he doesn't like you, he's not going to like me," Cole said.

The dog sat down and let out a low whine, which told Harmony two things. "It's a she," Harmony said. And apparently Cole was a babe magnet regardless of species. "I think she has a crush on you."

The dog snarled at Harmony again.

"He's all yours, Fido."

The mutt's ears perked up.

"Awwww—" Harmony began.

Cole's arm tightened around her ribs. At the same time Harmony heard the barn door roll open, followed by the sound of footsteps and the clank of something metal. She raised her head—careful not to piss off Cole's canine fan club in case the bite was worse than the bark—and peeked over the edge of the loft. A farmer, complete with overalls and a straw hat, hung a lantern from a hook on the other side of the barn and pulled out a small stool. He hunkered on the stool and proceeded to get intimate with a cow. The cow looked less than invested in the process, chewing her cud and staring placidly at the wall. The cats were a different story. About a dozen barnyard tabbies sat to the farmer's left side, which made perfect sense when he aimed a teat in their general direction and squirted one of them in the face.

"There's a farmer down there," Harmony whispered to Cole.

"What happened to 'We'll be gone before anyone knows we're here?' " Cole asked, managing to put an amazing amount of snottiness into a whisper.

"Who knew farmers milked cows in the middle of the night?"

"Everyone who didn't grow up in Hollywood, where apparently milk appears magically on store shelves."

"Why didn't you wake up before milking time? Apparently you're the expert on dairy production."

"It's your show, remember?"

"Maybe you could can the sarcasm and help me come up with a plan," she hissed, shifting to aim her narrowed eyes at him.

The dog growled. Harmony's glare hadn't worked on Cole, so she decided to try it on the dog, who went into full-blown Cujo mode, lip snarled back, growling low in her throat, half-crouched and ready to spring.

"Dot," the farmer thundered, his voice echoing off the rafters about a mile overhead, *"kommen sie hier."*

"I think this guy is Amish," Cole said, putting the lack of

overhead lighting and the German-studded commentary together.

"And how does that help us?"

"They don't believe in guns. That's got to be a plus."

"Unfortunately, they believe in dogs."

Dot took offense to Harmony's observation, loudly.

"Dot," the farmer bellowed, sounding at the end of his patience, "come down from there and leaf the mice for the cats."

"Mice!" Harmony squeaked, Cole pulling her back down on the hay before she could bolt to her feet and give them away. Just for good measure he laid his long body over hers, clamping his hand over her mouth.

Dot sank her teeth into Cole's pant leg and tried to pull him off Harmony, growling and snarling.

"Dot!" the farmer yelled again. "You haf a skunk treed up there?"

Harmony's eyes cut from the dog to Cole, and they all froze, listening to the creak of the ladder leading up to the loft. The crown of a straw hat appeared, followed by the farmer's head. He lifted the lantern, his eyes taking in the scene, Cole on top of Harmony, his hand over her mouth, her eyes wide with fear.

"*Schwein!*" he yelled, charging the rest of the way up the ladder. Amish people might not believe in guns, but they had no moral objection to pitchforks. The farmer grabbed one from the corner and brandished it, one-handed, at Cole.

Cole scrambled off Harmony, both hands up to ward off the tines that were pointing his way. "It's not what it looks like," he said, backing away slowly.

The farmer took a couple steps forward, stopping when he was beside Harmony. "You all right, Miss?"

"I'm better than all right," she said grinning at Cole.

"A little help here?" he said through clenched teeth.

"He won't hurt you. The Amish don't believe in violence."

"The pitchfork says otherwise."

Not to mention the guy was built like the Hulk with ZZ Top facial hair. And he was pissed.

Harmony got to her feet, grabbed her duffel and laptop,

and went to stand beside Cole. "Really, everything is fine," she said to the farmer. "We're together. No problem here. Everything was consensual."

It wasn't quite the tension defuser she'd hoped it would be. In fact, it had the opposite effect, the farmer looking at the flat spot in the hay, then at them, his face getting redder as he leapt to conclusions.

"Noooo," Harmony said, "we weren't . . . you know. We just needed a place to spend the night."

"You English," the farmer said, followed by something unintelligible in German. But when he stepped forward he got his point across loud and clear. It was a whole different dynamic, Harmony decided, when that pitchfork was aimed at her.

She put her hands up in the universal I-mean-no-harm gesture, making her jacket gap open—which made the farmer's eyes bug out and his face go even redder.

"You bring a weapon here?" he thundered.

"Time to go," she said, slipping her hand into Cole's and backpedaling to the door they'd come through the night before. They hightailed it down the conveyor, Cole taking a precious moment to look it over in the predawn light.

"It's horse-powered," he said. "Pretty ingenious."

Harmony rolled her eyes. "Nerd."

"The Amish are really good at engineering," Cole said defensively, following her into the cornfield, the dry stalks rattling around them like bamboo wind chimes.

"I'm just happy they don't believe in guns. Or phones."

"They believe in the police, and that one believes we snuck into his barn to have sex."

"You speak German?" Harmony asked, surprised enough to look over her shoulder at him.

He waggled his brows back at her. "Didn't need to understand German to get that."

Neither did she, but she'd decided the subject of sex was off limits so she let it go. "Do you really think he'll go to the police?"

"He was pretty mad. We probably aren't the first couple to sneak onto his property for a booty call."

"We're not a couple, and that wasn't a booty call. And why would anyone do that?"

"Don't know," Cole said with a shrug in his voice. "It's probably like the Mile High Club."

Harmony had never really understood that one, either. Why have sex in a tiny airplane bathroom or a scratchy hayloft when you could—

"You're thinking about sex, aren't you?"

"Yep," she said, mostly because he wouldn't expect it, "in a bed, with satin sheets and champagne, and all night so you don't have to race through it, because if you're with someone who counts, you don't need some kind of stupid thrill to get in the mood."

There was silence behind her. She glanced back. Cole had stopped walking—and breathing. He was about twenty yards behind her, his eyes on her backside. She turned the rest of the way around and his gaze rose about eighteen inches, so she crossed her arms over her breasts and waited until he made eye contact.

"You're playing with fire," he said.

"You're the one who keeps bringing up sex."

"And you're supposed to keep shooting me down."

"I'll try to remember that," she said, which wasn't just a smart-aleck comeback. Testosterone might be making him forgetful, but there were moments . . . Take the way he was looking at her right now. Hot, burning her up, making her remember the heat and solidness of him against her last night and the way he'd kissed her, strong and hard. If she hadn't been shocked enough to shove him away, she wouldn't have cared if there'd been a bed. Hell, she wouldn't have cared if there'd been a horizontal surface. The tree would have done just fine as long as she got him inside her, just as fast and hard—

"Stop looking at me like that," he said, his voice even deeper than usual, impossibly deep, stroking over her nerve endings and throbbing in places she shouldn't be thinking about in Cole Hackett's vicinity.

"I will if you will."

He let his chin drop to his chest, and she could see him taking slow, even breaths.

"Chanting mantras?"

"Reminding myself you're a pain in the ass," he said, "with an FBI badge."

"Whatever works for you." Harmony started off into the corn again, but in a couple of steps Cole overtook her.

"I think you should walk behind me for a while."

Harmony couldn't help but smile over that, even if it was sadly unprofessional of her. Sure, she was a federal agent, but she was also a woman, and what woman wouldn't be flattered to know she was so distracting to a man? Even one who'd been in jail for nearly a decade, working out every day and getting a butt she wanted to sink her teeth into—

"Do you think the farmer is going to report us to the police?" she asked, seizing on the first thing that didn't have anything to do with Cole's butt, flexing with each step in a nice steady rhythm . . . "I know they don't have telephones, but he could drive his buggy into town."

"The Amish take a lot of crap from tourists. Not to mention your gun might make him think twice about overlooking our visit."

"He'll finish his chores first, though. I mean, you can't not milk a cow, right? That'll give us time to get to a town and find some transportation."

"You mean steal a car."

She shrugged. "It's better than walking."

"It'll get us arrested," Cole said. "By now every cop in the state is on the lookout for us. We steal a car in a city smaller than Pittsburgh, and we won't make it to the city limits. Why can't you just . . ." He swirled his hand in circles, a forthcoming gesture that didn't mean a thing to her.

"What?"

"You know, get a car the same way you got me out of jail? Use your FBI wiles."

"Wiles?"

"Do what you do. Get us some transportation the cops won't be looking for."

"But the Bureau will. They'll be watching the buses, airlines, trains, and car rental agencies in the area. I could use my FBI *wiles*, maybe arrange for a car using another agent's name. But there'll be no way of knowing we didn't get away with it until we see the agents or cops in our rearview mirror, and I'd rather not be surprised that way."

"So we steal a car."

"Eventually."

"Not liking the sound of that," Cole said.

"Even if we could find a car, stealing one in farm country, where the crime rate is probably zero, would get everyone's attention. And the state police have you on their radar. Much as I'd like to stop right here and put you to work on those bank accounts, the smartest thing we can do is get out of Pennsylvania before we do anything the cops might connect with your escape."

"Then I guess we walk," Cole said.

She knew it was the right decision, but that didn't make the prospect of an all-day hike any more palatable. Not to mention the time they were wasting. Harmony took a deep breath and let it out, stiffening her spine before she set off after Cole. The kidnappers were expecting a call from her in less than twelve hours. When they found out she hadn't gotten the money yet, they weren't going to be happy, and Richard would be the only one they could take it out on. Walking a few miles was nothing to complain about.

By mid-afternoon wide-open spaces had lost of lot of their appeal for Cole. The morning had started off breath-steaming cold. They'd begun their trek at cow-milking time, also known as four A.M. By the time the sun came up they were in heavy woodland that kept them shaded. And cold.

As they wound their way farther west, headed for Ohio, the terrain had gradually changed from hills and valleys to flatter country. There wasn't a tree in sight or a cloud in the sky, just the sun, big and bright and hot, beating down on Cole, turning every inch of exposed skin into cracklings. His feet hurt, he had a couple pounds of dirt in his eyes, and car exhaust caught at the back of his throat. Every step took him farther from Lewisburg, USP. Otherwise the day would have been a total waste.

"We have to get off this road," Cole said.

Harmony nodded, too busy concentrating on putting one foot in front of the other to form actual words.

Aside from a brief stop at a roadside fruit stand, they'd been walking for most of the day. The cornfields and dirt lanes had given way to paved roads a while ago, and the paved roads were getting wider, more lanes, more traffic. More cops.

"At least two police cruisers have gone by in the last hour," he said. "It's just a matter of time before one of them wonders why we're walking down the side of the highway and takes a closer look."

Almost before the words were out a white Lincoln Town Car pulled off the road a little way ahead of them, tires crunching on the gravel. The car was a late-seventies model, big as a parade float, and tricked out with tinted windows, lots of striping, and enough shiny chrome to be visible from outer space. Moby Dick with wheels. One of the windows slid down and an insanely beautiful woman stuck her head out, jet-black hair, porcelain skin, cheekbones like razorblades.

"She looks like Snow White's evil stepmother," Harmony said under her breath.

"Y'all need a ride?" the woman called out.

"No—"

"Yes," Cole overrode Harmony. He wrapped an arm around her waist and propelled her to the car, stuffing her into the backseat before she could object again. He'd intended to take the front passenger seat until he realized it was already occupied. He slid in beside Harmony instead.

Harmony poked him. Cole ignored her, busy making eye contact with the woman behind the wheel.

"Where y'all headed?" she asked, her voice deep and slow, her gaze mesmerizing. A visual invitation.

"Cleveland," Cole said without giving it any real thought.

Harmony elbowed him in the ribs. He hissed in a breath and fielded the look she shot him. Definitely not happy about something, he deduced, but at least she was keeping the disagreement to herself. He was in for it when she got him alone, though.

"Y'all have names?" the woman in the front seat asked in a slow, husky, Deep South drawl.

"Janet and Dick," Harmony said before Cole could make that decision, too. Cole suspected she'd given him that name for a reason. "How about you?"

"You can call me Irene. This is my brother, Leo."

Cole took his first good look at the guy in the front seat, and thought, *Brother, my ass*. Irene was supermodel material. Leo belonged in a circus sideshow: no neck, shoulders up around his ears. His body consisted of roll on top of roll, starting with his three chins and ending with the spare tire in his lap. Leo looked like a seven-footer accordioned down to troll size. On top of which he had hands the size of dinner plates, a hairline so low it blended in with his unibrow, and several personalities, at least one of which he was conversing with in a constant under-the-breath mutter that began to rise in volume.

"Leo!" Irene snapped out before he got to an audible level.

Leo had what appeared to be a minor seizure, and subsided into his seat, silent but staring daggers at Irene. Not someone he'd like to meet in a dark hallway, Cole thought. Leo was scary. Cole didn't want to know how Irene was keeping him in line, but he had to give her credit.

"He has these outbursts," Irene said. "He's really not a bad person." And she put Moby in gear and they floated out into traffic, her eyes meeting Cole's again in the rearview mirror. "Y'all been together long?" she asked him.

"It feels like forever," Cole said.

"Oh, honey." Harmony slipped her arm through his and snuggled up to him, laying her head on his shoulder.

Cole understood it was just an act—mentally. Physically he went into full-on, heart-thumping, white-hot hormonal overload. Some soft part of her was pressing against his arm, there was a bunch of really nice-smelling blond hair tickling his chin, and he could feel her hands shaking. Either she was royally pissed off, or she wasn't as unaffected by him as she pretended to be.

"Lovers' quarrel?" Irene asked.

Harmony lifted her gaze, narrowed, to his. Cole grinned down at her.

"Everything's fine," she said with a bright, sunny, completely believable smile. Whatever Dick's investment in their fictional "relationship," Janet was clearly living in a shiny, pink heart-shaped bubble of love-conquers-all.

"So, Cleveland, huh?"

"I know, right?" Harmony said. "Who lives in Cleveland? I mean, Ohio, what's up with that? We broke down and we couldn't even get a cell phone signal."

"We're still in Pennsylvania," Cole pointed out.

"Huh, Pennsylvania. Don't even get me started. Did you know there are people here who don't believe in electricity?"

"Cleveland?" Irene prompted.

"His parents live there," Harmony said, making it sound vaguely accusatory. "You can drop us at the nearest bus stop and we'll take it from there."

Irene waved off that notion. "Gotta go right by there," she said. "Y'all just set back and enjoy the ride."

Cole was prepared to do just that. He hadn't slept much the night before, for the same reason he couldn't relax now. He pried Harmony off, told his hormones to heel, and slouched down in his seat, eyes closed, arms crossed over his chest.

Unfortunately, Irene kept asking questions. And Harmony kept answering them.

"How did you meet?" Irene wanted to know. "No offense, but y'all don't exactly seem . . . He's . . . And you're . . ."

"Oh, I know, but Dick didn't used to look all"—Harmony fluttered a hand in the air—"muscular. He used to be, like, sensitive. We met in college. I was pledging this sorority because, well, they needed me. I mean, those girls were totally clueless when it came to makeup and clothes. It was like they thought sororities were all about academics or something.

"Anyway," she continued, ignoring the part where Irene wanted to get a word in edgewise. Leo kept up a constant low-key mutter. Everyone ignored him.

"I went to this frat party with Tommy Morrison," Harmony was saying. "He turned out to be a complete loser. Why do men think they're Tom Cruise in a white naval uniform when they get drunk? Like I'm going to be all hot for some guy who will either throw up or pass out halfway through, you know?"

"I kn—"

"So there I was, like, stuck at the frat house with a bunch of drunk Casanovas, and there Dick was. He was a grad student at the time, and he didn't look like this, either. He looked smart." She leaned forward and lowered her voice. "Just between you and me, he was kind of a geek, you know, crazy smart but a little flabby and pasty. He was like this big, clumsy puppy you can't help but love. He gave me a ride home and that was it for me. I think we'll be together for a really long time."

"What do you think, Dick?"

"He's asleep," Harmony said. "He does that all the time. I just remember where I left off and pick up the conversation when he wakes up. We're going to visit his parents, and I'm kind of hoping it's a sign. I'm not getting any younger, you know."

"You're what, twenty-five?"

"I don't want to be one of those forty-year-old moms. I want to have kids and still look good. I want to be a MILF."

"MILF," Leo shouted.

Irene reached over and gave him a shot to the arm, which Cole saw because he'd given up trying to sleep, and not just because of the constant chatter. Harmony was up to something, and he felt a need to keep his eye on her.

Leo was back to muttering, Harmony was back to talking, and Irene's foot seemed to be getting heavier on the gas pedal. Irene wanted to get to Cleveland bad.

Cole couldn't blame her. Harmony managed to talk the entire four hours without stopping.

"You can drop us off here," Cole said to Irene as soon as he saw the WELCOME TO CLEVELAND sign.

Irene took the first exit ramp, barely slowing down long enough for them to jump out at the first intersection. As soon as Cole's feet hit pavement, she peeled off, back door still hanging open, leaving an inch of rubber on the pavement.

"I think Irene is happy to hear the last of you," Cole said.

"Irene could have let us off any time she wanted."

"She didn't have much use for you, but she liked me."

"Everything female within view likes you. And hey, at least that one was human. I think."

Cole gave her a look, but he wasn't all that insulted.

"We should get moving before Boris and Natasha come back."

"Boris and Natasha? Irene had a Southern accent."

"Southern accent, my aunt Fanny. They were Russian."

"You're being paranoid."

"If you'd been paying attention instead of thinking with your hormones, you'd know I was right."

"Jealous?"

"Puh-lease. If I wanted you, I could have you."

That was true. And annoying. He took off, keeping his strides purposefully long so Harmony had to trot to keep up. But walking away in a snit wasn't going to keep him out of jail. Neither was the FBI. The only protection he had was knowledge. "How do you know they were Russian?" he asked grudgingly.

"A Russian accent is hard to lose completely unless you mask it with another accent. Southern is the strongest."

Cole thought about that a minute, tried to replay some of Irene's conversation in his head, which wasn't easy since all he could remember was Harmony talking incessantly. "Why didn't you say something?"

"And let them know I was on to them? We were stuck in the backseat of their car going ninety on the highway."

"Jumping off a moving train was enough fun for one day, huh?"

"I didn't jump," she reminded him. "And it wasn't fun."

"I wasn't thinking about the exit. I was thinking about the landing."

"I prefer the part after the landing."

Cole knew she was talking about flipping him into the muck, but he was thinking about being on top of her. Okay, he wasn't really thinking, and if he didn't get a grip he wouldn't be walking either, at least not without limping. He could just imagine how smug Harmony would be then.

"I think you're jumping to conclusions," he said. "Just because they're Russian doesn't mean they're working with the kidnappers. And even if they were, they must've known who you were when they picked us up, so what's the point of channeling Paris Hilton on speed?"

"They didn't know that we knew, and she wasn't being honest with us, so she deserved it."

"They're criminals. And you didn't tell her the truth, either."

"I didn't tell her anything."

"Despite four hours of constant chatter, which is quite an accomplishment."

"I'll take that as a compliment." Harmony jogged up next to him, puffing a little.

Cole took pity, shortening his stride and hefting her duffel.

"She was trying to get information from us. Where we were going and why. How long we'd been together." Harmony snorted. "She *really* wanted to know who you were and how much you knew."

"She didn't want to tip her hand, and she didn't want a confrontation," Cole finished, seeing it plain as day now that Harmony had pointed him in the right direction. "Why?"

"I don't know." And she looked worried—for all of ten seconds before the optimist surfaced again. "Once I realized they weren't going to strong-arm us, I needed a way to control the conversation. Everyone looks at me and sees a dumb blonde, so I went with it." She shrugged, not the least embarrassed. "And it was fun."

"You said 'like' nine hundred and sixty-three times. I counted."

"You were asleep."

"Who could sleep?"

She grinned up at him. "If it makes you feel any better, I gave myself a headache."

chapter
7

"HOW DID THEY KNOW WHERE TO FIND US?" COLE asked as they walked deeper into the city of Cleveland. "Why did they let us go? Do you think we're still under surveillance?"

"Boris and Natasha—Irene and Leo—*whoever* they are, they must have been following me. It's the only thing that makes sense. They know I got you out of prison, and they're wondering why."

"Which is the reason Irene asked all those questions about who I was and how long we'd been together. Why didn't you just tell her the truth? That I'm here to move the money."

"They're the enemy. The less they know about our plans, the better."

Cole took his customary pause to digest what he'd learned. She was really beginning to hate that pause. He always came out of it with a question she didn't want him asking.

"Why didn't they just kidnap you and force you to get the money for them?"

"I'm already doing what they want. They don't gain anything by grabbing me. And they could blow their whole game.

If the FBI lost another agent, they might decide there was more than greed going on and get involved. They were just keeping tabs on me."

"On *us*, you mean."

Exactly, and that was the part that worried her.

"What about—"

"Can we save the rest of the postmortem? At least until I get some painkillers, a shower, a meal, and a bed, in that order." She wasn't kidding about the headache. Her jaw ached, too. She had a new respect for those vapid, posturing celebutantes. Doing nothing was exhausting.

A couple miles off the highway they came across one of those travel motels where each room had an outside entrance. Harmony went into the office and got a room in the back. Cheap, clean, two beds, one of which she collapsed onto as soon as they got inside.

Cole wasn't on the same page. Cole was getting his second wind, and it was blowing in from skeptic land. "Cops, feds, now Russians," he said. "This thing isn't going to happen if you don't get the pressure off long enough for me to work."

Harmony cracked one eye open. "How do you expect me to do that?"

Cole shrugged. "You're the one with the contacts."

In other words, he was calling her bluff, and she had no choice but to make good on her big talk. She shoved herself upright and reached for her duffel, stifling a groan when her head pounded in protest. She had her FBI-issue cell phone, and a second disposable one she'd bought because it was untraceable. She pulled out the second phone, taking a deep breath as she punched in her handler's number. She'd been dreading this moment, but it had to be done.

Mike Kovaleski answered the phone by growling "Yeah," which was polite for him.

"Hey, Mike," she said, "it's Harmony," and then she waited for him to ask her what the hell she was doing.

Instead he said, "Kind of late for work, aren't you? Like thirty-six hours late," sounding like he had absolutely no clue she'd gone rogue.

Mike was damn good at playing a role, but he had no reason to pretend he was in the dark on her extracurricular activities. Just the opposite, in fact. He was her handler; her actions reflected directly on him. If he'd been questioned about her activities, he'd have sent more than a pair of agents that included a novice.

"Don't tell me you're worried about me," she said, keeping her voice light, teasing, and giving up any attempt to puzzle out the mystery. Keeping Mike ignorant was more important at the moment than figuring out why no one had asked him about her in the first place.

"Who said I was worried? You haven't missed a day of work in five years. I knew you'd call in eventually."

She covered the phone and said to Cole, "FBI ears only," and took the conversation to the other side of the room, lowering her voice. "Nice to know I'm so predictable," she said into the phone.

"You're upset about Swendahl," Mike said, sounding like a shrug went along with the observation.

Harmony took a second to absorb that—not that she should've expected him to react any other way. He'd always told her she was too sensitive to be a field agent. Disappearing because she was all broken up about Richard was exactly what Mike would expect her to do. Still, it stung to be written off to emotional paralysis when she was doing what no one else at the Bureau had the guts to do.

"I don't agree with the Bureau's policy, but I understand it," she said, swallowing her pride. "I just need a few days to get my head around it."

"Your number came up as not available on caller ID."

"I'm at my aunt's house in the Poconos. No cell towers."

Mike didn't say anything, but his silence felt skeptical.

"I haven't taken a vacation, ever," she reminded him. "It's not like the copyright pirates are going to blow up the world if I'm not around to enforce the FBI warning for a little while."

"I didn't say no."

"You didn't say anything."

"I was thinking."

"That's what worries me," she said, only half in jest. "Anything . . . interesting going on?"

"Besides Swendahl? Nope. Why, what did you hear?"

"I caught the tail end of the news when I was driving through Pennsylvania. Sounded like something happened there."

"Pennsylvania's a big black hole as far as I know."

"Okay. Has . . . is anything being done?"

"Nope. It's been quiet all around. I'm finally writing that novel." There was silence for a couple beats, then, "I'll see you in a week."

"Or two."

"Two?"

"I came up here to relax and see the trees change. You never know when peak color will hit."

"Swift—"

"Bye, Mike."

"Well?" Cole said the second she disconnected. "Did you ask him about me?"

"I didn't have to. He'd have mentioned you if you were on the radar."

"I'm a federal prisoner. Shouldn't the FBI be looking for me?"

She bumped up a shoulder, as flummoxed as Cole was. First Mike didn't know about her freelance activities, now he had no idea there was an escaped felon in Pennsylvania? "Either they're keeping your escape really quiet, or they're not talking about it at all."

And as puzzling as it was from an FBI standpoint, it answered a couple of questions about Irene and Leo. They must have followed her from D.C. to Lewisburg, with no intention of interfering as long as she did what they wanted. And then she hooked up with Cole, but since the FBI wasn't releasing the news of his escape, the Russians had no way of knowing who he was and why she'd gone out of her way to pick him up. As long as he remained a mystery man he was safe. Losing Irene would only be added insurance, but she'd make that a priority anyway.

"They sent feds after us. And cops."

"The Pennsylvania cops aren't a problem anymore, now that we're in Ohio."

"What about your coworkers?"

"They're not a problem anymore, either," she said, knowing Cole would take it to mean they'd been called off.

In truth, she found it troubling that Mike hadn't heard anything about the jailbreak at Lewisburg. The handlers were only supposed to know about their own cases, but Mike had a way of nosing out trouble, whether or not it involved his unit. He always said the Bureau's practice of compartmentalizing was incompatible with his ability to do his job properly. If Mike didn't know about Cole then Cole was really off the grid, and if that was the case, then why?

She glanced over at the convict in question and wondered. There were only a couple reasons to keep a prison escape quiet. For instance, if the guy was so dangerous they didn't want to alarm the public unnecessarily. Cole wasn't a mass murderer or a serial killer. He hadn't done anything violent. He'd hacked into the government's computer system—not an easy feat, but hardly threatening to the average American going about his daily business. Terrorist organizations, now, they might be interested in Cole, which was a hell of a reason to keep his freedom a secret. Access to the FBI's files would be priceless to anyone who hated America.

Of course, the FBI's computer system had been overhauled since Cole's incarceration. New security had been installed, supposedly hack-proof security, but nothing was perfect. In her two years at the agency going after computer criminals, Harmony had learned a lot about tracking and hacking, but she wasn't good enough to break into the FBI's banking system, and money was her only leverage with the kidnappers.

"What's going on in there?" Cole said, tapping a finger on her temple.

She'd been so caught up in her own thoughts she hadn't heard him come up behind her. Not good. She needed to stay sharp and focused, even around Cole. The authorities outside of Pennsylvania didn't know he'd escaped. As long as it stayed that way she probably had nothing to worry about. But there was no point taking chances.

"All we have to do is keep our heads down and do what needs to be done," she said, "and this will all be over."

Cole smiled grimly. "That's what worries me."

HOT WATER SHOULD BE ONE OF THE SEVEN WONDERS *of the world*, Harmony thought, *even in a mediocre shower*. She stood under the hot spray and imagined the dirt and exhaustion of the last thirty-six hours washing down the drain. The stress stayed with her. What she'd gone through already was nothing compared to what she'd face in the days to come. She couldn't put that out of her mind, and if she didn't put it out of her mind, she wouldn't sleep, and if she didn't sleep there'd come a moment when she needed to make a split-second life-or-death decision, and she wouldn't be up to the challenge.

She needed a stress reliever. She needed to go out and run. Physical exertion was always good at calming her nerves. Running would be her first choice, but she didn't trust Cole enough to leave him by himself. Which meant she needed to do something else, maybe yoga or just dance around like a maniac until she was exhausted. Or sex. Yoga or dancing in front of Cole would make her feel stupid, but sex would involve him, and he'd made it clear he was willing, so it would be the perfect solution. Except she couldn't have sex with Cole. They had a working relationship, nothing more, and since she was the one who'd drawn that line she couldn't cross it now. All her credibility would be gone—not to mention he'd rub it in every chance he got. So, definitely not having sex.

There was just one problem. Sex was all she could think about now. She soaped up a washcloth and started scrubbing a little too hard. Her skin tingled, but her thoughts were still racing, back to Cole on top of her, behind her, his large body hard and hot against hers. He was contrary and pushy and ungrateful, she tried to remind herself, but then she remembered him at the jail, his shirt off, and his pants off, and somewhere along the line the remembering turned into fantasizing, and the scrubbing turned softer as she imagined him easing into the shower, his hands wet and soapy, sliding over her skin under the hot spray, over her aching breasts and down, across her belly, easing between her legs—

And then the hotel room door closed, the sound muffled by the running water, but the change in air pressure and the slight tremor she felt in her feet were unmistakable.

"Cole?" she yelled, but she was already ducking her head under the spray, taking precious seconds to rinse because she'd be no good to herself with shampoo running in her eyes.

She grabbed a towel and raced out of the bathroom, already knowing Cole was gone—along with the small roll of cash she'd had in her backpack.

"Damn," she yelled. "Damn, damn, damn." Grabbing the first T-shirt she found and fighting it over her wet head and damp skin, no bra, she stepped into panties and reached for her jeans, berating herself the whole time. "Idiot," she said, "stupid, trusting moron who had to take a shower because she can't handle a little discomfort," and then she heard the doorknob rattle.

She froze just for a split-second, jeans halfway up one leg, still covering her foot, before she let go of the waistband and grabbed her gun, running across the room as silently as she could with a denim shackle. There was no time to look through the window or the peephole. She barely made it behind the door when it began to open, and she was blind, the door between her and whoever was coming through it, so she eased out and put her gun to the person's back.

"I know I didn't ask you what you wanted before I left, and the restaurant here is only one of those school cafeteria-style places so there wasn't a lot of variety, but I'll give you first choice," Cole said, his voice unmistakable, both for its depth and the way it made her insides shiver.

"Cole," Harmony said, exhaling in relief as she lowered the gun.

"Who were you expecting? Jimmy Hoffa?"

"Boris and Natasha. They found us once."

"And you figured I was long gone." He turned to face her, his eyes dropping immediately to her breasts, then lower. "Nice outfit. Is that the way you always greet Russian kidnappers?"

Harmony glanced down, then did a double take. Even from her vantage point it looked like she was participating in a wet T-shirt contest. "I was in the shower," she reminded him, adding, "and don't forget about the gun," because she almost had, and if Cole kept staring at her like she was a buffet, the gun wasn't all she'd forget.

"I thought you were going to start on the bank accounts."

He shook his head. "Can't concentrate on an empty stomach."

She pulled her jeans on the rest of the way and escaped to the bathroom before Cole saw her anxiety, her fear, before she put her gun to his head and made him hack into those accounts so Richard didn't have to suffer one more second.

If ever there was an occasion for chanting mantras, Harmony thought as she toweled her hair, this was it. Too bad she didn't know any. She settled for some deep breathing and concentrated on putting one foot in front of the other.

She changed her top—and added a bra. Once she'd managed enough control to make a reappearance, she found Cole already seated at the little round table, eating with a focus that amazed her.

"I thought you were giving me first choice," she said, taking the seat across from him and surveying the sad array of edibles still remaining: a tuna sandwich, a small salad, two varieties of pie, and something that might have been a chili dog before twelve other kinds of food had been piled on top of it and turned it into a pile of orange glop.

"That was when you had a gun pointed at my spine. And before you spent a half hour in the bathroom. Not that I'm complaining," he added, leering at her over the top of the taco he was eating.

His teeth bit in, strong and white, but he never took his eyes off her, his intent gaze setting off the kind of heat that made her remember what she'd been thinking in the shower before she heard him leave the room. Suddenly her clothes felt too tight, every movement rubbing cloth across sensitive places, and food was the furthest thing from her mind. Luckily for her, she hadn't forgotten about Richard.

Cole finished off his taco, dusted his hands together, and got to his feet all in one motion. "I'm going to take a shower."

And she was going to take a walk so she didn't have to hear the water running and think about him all wet and naked and muscular.

BY THE TIME SHE RETURNED, BETTER FOR A HALF HOUR of fresh air and solitude, Cole was standing by the table with her duffel bag open in front of him, a pair of her panties in one hand, her notebook computer in the other. And so much for her fantasies, because it wasn't her panties that had him all hot and bothered. If there'd been anything personal between them, she'd have been jealous.

"Like what you see?" she asked, going over and pulling her bag across the table.

He didn't even look at her, still staring at the computer, face flushed, pulse pounding in his neck. "Do you know what this is?" he said, then proceeded to tell her, his voice low and reverent. Seductive. "It's a Pentalon A1A. State-of-the-art, custom built, largest memory of any notebook computer on the market, and it can handle nearly unlimited simultaneous tasks. And is that one of those mobile broadband modems?"

"Yep, you can access the Internet anywhere, just like a cell phone."

Cole popped the laptop open with a little catch in his breath, hesitated, then put his finger on the start button, closed his eyes, and pushed it. When it whirred to life, Harmony swore he got a little orgasmic jolt out of it.

He ran his fingertips lightly over the keyboard, crooning low and fast to it under his breath, like he was talking to a lover. If he stroked her the way he was stroking those keys, she'd melt into a puddle at his feet.

"You and the computer want to be alone?"

He opened his eyes and grinned at her, not the least embarrassed. In fact, he looked annoyed at being interrupted.

"I can give you some privacy. Just don't get . . . anything on the keyboard."

"Jealous?"

"Relieved." She reached across the table and plucked her panties out of his hand. Then she tore the plastic wrap off the tuna sandwich and scraped the tuna off the bread onto the salad.

"Hey, I was going to eat that."

"Not anymore," she said, carrying the salad to the bed closest to the door. "I didn't get any dinner last night since you decided to leave."

"Neither did I, and you threw my dessert at a cop."

"Would you rather I'd shot him? They wouldn't have given up so easily then."

"They sicced dogs on us."

"They would have chased us to hell and back if we'd wounded a police officer." She took another bite of salad, chewing it for all she was worth. "And stop watching me eat. It makes me self-conscious."

"That's not what it makes me."

"Men get turned on by the stupidest things."

"There's pie, but darn, no clean forks. You'll have to eat it with your fingers."

Harmony rolled her eyes and ignored the box he held out. "Eat it yourself. You have work to do."

Cole shrugged and sat at the table, opening the box in his hand. He tore a chunk off the wedge of pie with his fingers and dropped it into his mouth, head back, groaning softly as he licked the filling from his fingertips.

Harmony couldn't take her eyes off him.

And he noticed. "Men get turned on by the stupidest things, huh?"

She walked over to the table and opened the other pie box. Chocolate cream. She broke off a piece of pie and put it into her mouth, closing her lips around her finger and pulling it out of her mouth one agonizing centimeter at a time, never taking her eyes off him.

"You're playing with fire," Cole said.

"You started it."

"And I'm willing to finish it."

And if she didn't know exactly what he meant, her body sure did. If he kept looking at her like that she'd have an orgasm on the spot. But as much as she liked the idea of that, the fallout would be a nightmare.

"I don't think I'll be able to concentrate on your problem as long as I have this"—he dropped his eyes—"huge need," he finished with just the hint of a smile that was directed at himself, she suspected, as much as her.

Harmony put the pie down and left the table before she could give in to the urge to smile back. They had a long night ahead of them, and it would be a mistake to give him even that much encouragement. She came back with the phone book, dropping it in his lap.

"This is Ohio, not Nevada," he said. "I don't think I'll find what I want in there."

"Try 1-800-lunatic. Any woman who takes you on after eight years of deprivation has to be crazy."

"You took me on."

"This is a professional relationship."

"I could leave a twenty on the nightstand when we're done."

"You don't have any money."

He shrugged. "I'll steal some."

She rolled her eyes and pointed to the phone.

"What am I supposed to do with that?"

"Don't tell me you've never heard of phone sex—1-900 numbers?"

"After nearly a decade in jail that would just be more of the same."

She came around the table and got right in his face, her mouth a whisper away from his, her hand resting lightly on his chest. "Use your left hand."

She pushed away, but before she could escape he came to his feet and caught her by the upper arms, his grip just a bit too tight for comfort. "If you ever do that again . . ." He didn't finish the threat. He didn't need to, holding her there, against his body. She could feel his hunger, and not just because of his erection. Heat was radiating off him, along with a depth of anger and frustration she could only guess at.

Her heart thumped hard against her ribs, her eyes searching the angles of his face, seeing the darkness in his eyes, remembering what he'd been through and at whose hands. He was a dangerous stew of emotions, and she'd been stupid to stir him up like that.

"You're right," she said. "I'm sorry."

He let her go and stepped back, pushing both hands through his hair, the anger disappearing as fast as it had come over him. "How sorry?" he quipped with a slight smile. But there were shadows in his eyes, and Harmony was ashamed of herself for helping to put them there.

This time she answered his smile with one of her own. "Not that sorry." *Yet.*

chapter
8

THE CITY OF CLEVELAND, OHIO, SPREAD ITSELF ALONG
the south shore of Lake Erie. If Harmony and Cole had
been there for pleasure they could have visited the Rock and
Roll Hall of Fame, the Great Lakes Science Center, or they
could hit a Cleveland Indians game. Hell, if they'd been interested in pleasure, Cole's vote would have been to stay in
the hotel.

He indulged himself for a moment, stopping before the
fantasizing took him to a point where he'd have a hard time
walking, since that was the only physical activity on the
agenda. They needed to disappear, and disappearing meant
they had to go out in public. Crazy but true.

"Tell me again what you accomplished last night," Harmony said, and by *again*, she meant for the fourth time.

Cole blew out a breath and humored her. "I wrote a password generator and started running it, but it hasn't come up
with anything yet, which is no surprise. This is the FBI we're
talking about, and their system has a hell of a security com-
ponent." He ought to know. "It's not going to run while the

laptop is shut down, but we can stick around here for a while, see if anything interesting happens."

"No, we need to get moving. Ohio law enforcement doesn't seem to have us on their radar, and it appears we've lost the feds. The Russians are another story. There's not much chance they dropped us off yesterday and kept driving."

"I don't know; you were pretty obnoxious."

"Trust me, it'll take more than verbal diarrhea to shake Irene loose, and I don't want her to know what we're up to."

Since he felt the same way about Harmony and his plans, Cole let that comment pass. Besides, he'd done exactly what he'd said. He just hadn't told her what he was going to do with the password when he got it.

"Smell that air," Harmony said, taking a deep breath when they stepped outside, eyes closed, savoring the cool morning breeze.

"Smells like car exhaust," Cole said. He'd been up late putting together the password generator, then he'd tried to sleep. He hadn't had much luck.

Mentally he was exhausted. Physically he was a mass of straining senses and unsatisfied lust, all because of a wet T-shirt and a piece of pie. Hell, who was he kidding? Just being in the same room with Harmony all night, listening to her breathe, hearing the rustle of the bedclothes as she shifted position, had kept him on edge.

"Look at that sunrise," she said, all bright and bubbly.

Cole hated bright and bubbly. Why wasn't she cranky like he was? And he wasn't just talking about sex- and sleep-deprivation. "Why are you so cheerful? This thing has fiasco written all over it."

"I prefer to believe we'll be successful."

"Right," Cole muttered, "you're an optimist." Another thing he hated. "How can you prepare for the worst if you refuse to acknowledge it's a possibility?"

"What, did you minor in philosophy or something?"

"I majored in life."

"Wow. Sounds ominous, but it's still better than the alternative."

"Stick around, Pollyanna. Life will beat all the hope out of you—probably in the near future." Which meant he'd most likely be around to see it. That went a long way toward cheering him up, along with knowing they didn't have another day of aimless wandering ahead of them. Somewhere in the depths of the sleepless night, he'd remembered he had a possible safe haven in Cleveland, which was probably why he'd thought of it to begin with. Under normal circumstances, he wouldn't want to risk bringing trouble down on a friend, but Juan Esposito was more than able to handle a couple of Russian thugs.

"So tell me about this friend of yours," Harmony said. "Is he a geek?"

"He's an ex-con."

"Oh boy. Should I ask what he did?"

"Once you meet him, you won't have to."

"Does he at least have a name like Crusher or Mad Dog? I feel kind of cheated being stuck with a convict named Cole."

"Your choice, remember?"

"Circumstances dictate."

"Yeah, well, circumstances dictate that you be my girlfriend while we're there."

"Pretend to be your girlfriend, you mean."

"That could work, too."

She gave him a look, trying to appear annoyed, but still way too chipper to pull it off.

"If they find out you're a federal agent it won't be pretty. For either of us."

"I'll keep my mouth shut if you will."

"Don't make promises you can't keep."

Harmony didn't have a witty comeback for that. Harmony was letting her silence speak for her. Making a point. Cole didn't expect it to last.

They caught a cab from the motel to the nearest bus station, bought tickets to Detroit, then lost themselves in the early-morning crowd.

They headed into an industrial section of the city, following the directions Cole had gotten off the Internet. The route led him into the parking lot of a huge warehouse, big bay doors open to the brisk air and early-morning sunshine. The place was a beehive of activity, hi-los trundling around with pallets of shrink-wrapped merchandise, truckers backing semis into loading bays, employees bustling about with serious intent. An adjacent lot held vehicles of all shapes and sizes, in all stages of cannibalization.

"This can't be right," Cole said to Harmony. He approached a man standing by a chest-high desk cluttered with papers held down by random auto parts. "I'm looking for Juan Esposito."

"Over there," the guy said, pointing into the gloomy depths of the warehouse.

Cole shrugged and, taking Harmony by the hand, walked inside. They hadn't gone two steps before a voiced boomed out, "Doc!" and a bull of a man with gang tattoos on his neck, face, and arms caught Cole in a spine-cracking bear hug.

When he stepped back, Cole pointed to a pair of teardrops, the sign for gang killings, tattooed under Juan's left eye. "I thought you were going to get rid of those."

"And lose all my cred?" Juan shook his head and shifted his gaze to Harmony, giving her an appreciative up and down. "Who's the *chica*?"

"Harmony Swift, Juan Esposito," Cole said.

Harmony offered her hand. Juan hooked thumbs with her and pulled her in, kissing her on both cheeks. "Your taste in friends is improving," he said to Cole.

"It has a lot to do with my accommodations." Cole pulled Harmony back to his side, slipping his arm around her waist. Keeping up the pretense. "You're married, remember?"

"Married and respectable." Juan did a *Price Is Right* pose, both arms raised with a little half-spin to showcase the warehouse and its industrious staff. "What do you think?"

"This is all yours?"

Juan nodded, smiling from ear to ear.

"Not exactly low profile."

"I'm legit now, bro."

Cole took a long look around, shelves filled with auto parts, from small boxes all the way up to hoods, fenders, and entire car chassis.

"Yeah, wild, eh? When I got out, I went back to my roots, you know? Boosting and stripping cars, but I sold the parts on the Internet, just like you said. Nobody local to finger me for the cops.

"Before I knew it the business got so big it didn't make sense to keep stealing and risk losing everything, so I started buying parts in bulk. Businesses going under, wholesale, direct from the manufacturers, anywhere I can get 'em cheap, you know? I even have a salvage yard for older models where the parts are hard to get. That's real lucrative, man. I sell online, and I can't keep up with the demand.

"So what's your story? I thought you had at least another dime and a half to go."

Cole shrugged. "Overcrowding."

Juan laughed. "Yeah, you never were too much of a threat."

"I got out not too long ago, spent some time in Philly and hooked up with Harmony. We're on our way to Seattle, and I remembered you live here, so I thought I'd stop in and see how you're doing."

"It rains a lot in Seattle, man."

"It's also a major computer hub, and I need to get a job."

"I could put you to work here. My webmaster is useless." Juan turned to Harmony. "This guy has magic fingers."

"I know," she said, sending Cole a sizzling look that left Juan open-mouthed and speechless.

Cole inadvertently tightened his arm around her waist, and she shot him another look with a different kind of smolder. Chances were good the second look was more in line with her true feelings.

"You were telling me about Cole," she said, all smiles for Juan's sake. "Start with the nickname."

"Doctor Who," Juan said, punching Cole lightly on the arm and grinning. "Most of us just call him Doc. His protector gave it to him."

"Protector?"

"Louie F."

"Louis Frambelli, of the New York mob family?"

Cole tightened his arm again, this time in warning.

"I grew up just outside New York City," Harmony lied without blinking an eye. "I went to school with Louie F.'s grandkids. He was a pretty big crime boss, right?"

"Outside," Juan said. "Inside he was still a pretty big boss, but he wasn't a bad guy where it counts, you know? And he knew what was going down in Lewisburg before the warden did. Day Hackett arrived, Louie was right there. Said Cole looked like an owl, all wide eyes, blinking at everything like he had a million questions and didn't know which one to ask first."

"The wide eyes didn't last long," Cole said.

"But the nickname stuck, right Doc?"

"And thanks to Louie F.," Cole said, "I'm still in one piece. Louie said he took one look at me and knew I wouldn't last twenty-five days let alone twenty-five years, and there were only two ways for me to leave the place, dead or broken."

"You're neither," Harmony said.

"Because he knew I'd be useful."

"First thing Louie did was have me pick a fight with your boy, here," Juan said. "Gave the guards a reason to toss him into solitary."

"It doesn't sound like help," Cole put in, "but there was a bed, a toilet, and a weight set, compliments of Louie F. I spent sixty days alone putting on muscle and making a mental adjustment. I was looking at twenty-five years in that place, and it was up to me how I served my time. When I came out of solitary, I agreed to work for Louie, and he agreed to watch my back. But he couldn't guarantee around-the-clock protection."

Cole met Harmony's eyes for the first time since they'd begun rehashing the nightmare. "Louie told me the first fight would send a message. If I didn't fight hard and fight dirty, I'd be a target no matter what he did."

"First guy cornered Doc here never walked right again," Juan said.

Cole bumped up a shoulder. "I kept up the workouts, had a couple more altercations, but after a while I stopped being a target. There were always newcomers." He looked out the door, trying not to remember the screams, the times he'd heard sobbing from some new inmate's jail cell, the haunted looks in the eyes of some poor bastard who would have been him if he hadn't possessed skills Louie F. could use. He'd tried to help when he could, but Louie was right, you couldn't be everywhere. After a while you had to turn a blind eye, put on blinkers, keep the anger from spilling over onto the guards who did nothing to protect the weak. All that would get him was trouble.

He traded a look with Juan and knew he was thinking the same thing.

"The tat," Juan said, bringing a reluctant grin from Cole and the predictably inquisitive look from Harmony. "Wasn't long before Hackett's attitude went from *What the hell am I doing here* to *Who can I punch out?*"

"Which is why the owl has a bad attitude," Harmony concluded. "So where does the 'doctor' part come from?"

"Jailhouse award," Cole said. "I was working on my thesis when I was arrested. The FBI took that away from me, too."

Harmony kept her eyes on his, and there was sympathy there. Cole didn't want to see it. He moved his arm and was already walking away from her when he said to Juan, "Give me the tour."

"Not much to see besides auto parts," Juan said, "but wait till you get a load of the hacienda."

The hacienda was more like the Kennedy compound at Hyannis Port, except it was a few blocks from the shores of Lake Erie and there were no overbites in sight. Lots of light brown skin, warm brown eyes, and dark curly hair, since the hacienda was busting at the seams with Juan's Hispanic family members.

The place consisted of a huge, rambling old house that had probably been built for some famous Ohio personage a century or so ago. There were a couple smaller houses off to one side of the property, newer construction, and a building that looked like it had once been a barn or carriage house, but had been converted to a guesthouse. Juan had insisted they stay with him, and Cole, without consulting her, had agreed. Since they were supposed to be a couple, she had no choice but to go along.

Besides, she had something she needed to do, something she'd put off as long as she could.

She took out her government cell phone and speed-dialed a number she'd programmed in. The phone was traceable, but since she wasn't undercover, it would also come up on caller ID. That was a requirement.

"Agent Swift," the person who answered the phone said with a Russian accent. "I expected your call yesterday."

"I couldn't because—" Anything else she might have said was cut off by a bloodcurdling scream that trailed off into muffled sobbing.

In the back of her mind there'd always been the possibility of turning back. She scrapped that notion right there and then.

"This happens when you do not meet our demands."

"I need to talk to Richard."

"Nyet."

"I get proof of life or I'm out."

"You hear the screaming."

"That could have been you for all I know."

There were a few seconds of silence, then Richard came on the line, his voice shaking and weak. "Harmony? Is it really you?"

"Yes, Richard."

"Oh, thank god," he said, the words ending on a small sob. "I didn't think anyone gave a damn about me—" He ended with another scream, then the kidnapper came back on the line.

Harmony was struggling to pay attention, but all she could hear was Richard's pain.

"Agent Swift," the kidnapper yelled, his Russian accent becoming thicker as he grew agitated.

She swallowed, but she wasn't in an emotional place where words were possible. The most she could force out was a sound that meant she was still there and still listening.

"The money. You transfer it, yes?"

"It's not that easy," she said, her voice getting stronger as she managed to tune out Richard's soft moaning. "It's not like I can just pull up the accounts and push a button. I have to hack in. It takes time."

"Your friend, he is running out of, how do you say it, exposable body parts."

"Expendable," she said, stifling the urge to throw up.

"I would hate for him to no longer be a man when he comes back to you. If he comes back."

"You'd better hope—"

"Two days, same time, you call." And he hung up.

"I take it you weren't ordering pizza."

Harmony swung around and there was Cole. She didn't ask how long he'd been standing in the doorway. He'd clearly heard enough, and even if he hadn't, it wouldn't be hard to guess who she'd been talking to. Her hands were shaking, and when she scrubbed one over her face it came away wet.

"You okay?"

"Fine," she said, which was clearly a lie. She couldn't chance the possibility Cole would try to comfort her. If he lent any sympathy, she'd fall apart.

"Good," he said, "nothing worse than a hysterical female."

She turned away, went to sit on the seat in the front bay window, pulling her legs up and hugging them to her chest.

Cole came over and stopped in front of her, looking uncomfortable and fidgety. "Juan is expecting us to stay the night. They're having a barbecue. The whole family is coming."

"Paying homage to the man who inspired the Esposito auto parts empire?"

"Entertaining a friend."

"Then we eat barbecue. But tomorrow we head west, put some distance between us and Ohio. For the sake of your friend."

"You think we're in danger here?"

"No, it's just a precaution." Except for the fact that she'd had to use her government issue phone, which was traceable. She wouldn't have worried about it, but those two FBI agents showing up at Lewisburg still troubled her.

Cole didn't say anything, taking his customary moment to deliberate.

"Richard was working in Los Angeles," Harmony said into the silence, not in the mood for any of his uncomfortable questions. "We have a long way to go, and I'd think you'd want this over with as quickly as I do."

"How do you know he is still alive?"

Harmony looked out the window. "He's alive. Trust me." She'd never get the sound of those screams out of her head.

chapter
9

COLE SET THE LAPTOP TO CONTINUE RUNNING THE
password generator, then took a stab at making himself pre-
sentable, which consisted of running water over his head
since he didn't have any clean clothes.

He wasn't really in a party mood. Sleep he could use, and
maybe some time to process everything that had happened in
the fifty-five hours since Harmony Swift had blasted into his
life. They walked out of the guesthouse, Cole got a whiff of
barbecue, and suddenly crowds of strangers and music that
made his skull vibrate weren't too much to endure if he could
get his hands on a rack of spareribs.

Three huge grills anchored one end of a large patio behind
Juan's house, manned by three Hispanic guys bickering good-
naturedly in two languages over who was the best griller. Every kind of barbecued meat imaginable came off the grills
and was moved to a series of tables already loaded with bowls
of fresh fruit, tortillas, and dozens of homemade Mexican
dishes that defied identification but tasted like heaven.

There was enough food to feed an army, and over the next
few hours, one showed up. It started with Juan's extended

family—his wife and seven children, and a couple of *abuelas*, dressed in black and giving Cole the eye out of wrinkled faces. There were cousins, aunts, uncles, nieces, and nephews of all shapes and sizes, most of whom seemed to live in the other two houses on the property.

After that people started wandering in from the street in ones and twos, packing into the backyard and attacking the food tables like locusts. Couples danced to the music piped out from the house; kids ran around screaming and playing.

The main connection seemed to be Hispanic, with a few other ethnic groups peppered in for diversity. As long as he stayed seated, Cole thought he blended okay. Harmony stood out like a sore thumb. She was whiter than anyone else there, blonder than anyone else there, and she was trying to outdo everyone as far as liquor intake went. Quite the undertaking considering the crowd involved and their fondness for tequila.

She'd made a half-hearted visit to the food table when they'd arrived, and then she hit the bar. Repeatedly.

Cole made an attempt to rein her in at first, but he couldn't forget how shaky she'd been after that phone call. She said the kidnappers had let her know Swendahl was alive—alive and hurting. Cole bet they'd made it clear he was paying a price every time she kept them waiting. Maybe it was just hearing someone in pain that had turned her into a wreck, but Cole would have bet she had a personal involvement with the guy. And if she'd lied about that, what else had she lied about?

He might have asked her, if he'd had the time to accomplish any of his own goals. But until he got the money or the proof he needed, he had to stay on the roller coaster with her. He just had to hope she wasn't going to get him killed in the meanwhile.

At least they were in a safe place. Harmony needed to escape reality for a little while, but as long as one of them was sober what was the harm? And sure, the ugliness would still be there when she sobered up, compounded by a wicked hangover, but he couldn't deny her a moment of oblivion. He kept an eye on her, nursing a beer and keeping a clear head.

He had things to forget, too, but he'd come to terms with his demons a long time ago.

At the other end of the stone patio from the grills, a live band played in front of a wooden dance floor. People came and went; Harmony was apparently there to stay. She had a beer bottle in one hand, and she was moving to the music. Every now and then a man—or a woman—would dance with her for a bit, but mostly she was dancing by herself. She wasn't the only one going solo. The floor was packed with people, some of whom had no partners, some who were dancing in a group. Harmony wasn't all that unusual. But she stood out.

Cole would have chalked it up to the blonde thing again, but it was more than that. Harmony was sexy, even on a normal day. Hell, even when she was involved in a car chase that ended with two FBI agents in a river, there was an energy about her that spoke directly to a man's most basic urges. And when she was drunk and completely without inhibitions, well, if she'd been wearing a G-string and straddling a stripper pole, she couldn't have stirred up a bunch of men more than she did wearing jeans and holding a bottle of beer.

Cole decided it was time to get her out of there, before she started a riot. And then the police showed up. They weren't in uniform, but they had cop written all over them, both of them walking in from the street like they were still sporting cop tool belts and shoulder radios. They wandered through the throng, hands loose at their sides, eyes missing nothing. One of them stopped and took a long look at Harmony, nudging his partner so they were both staring at her.

"Shit," Cole said under his breath. His first instinct was to drag her out of there. He stifled it. If the cops were looking for a couple with their description his best bet was to stay away from her. All he could do was sit there while the younger of the two police officers headed straight for Harmony. And began to dance with her.

"You look like you saw a ghost, man," Juan said.

More like his life flashing before his eyes. "Sneaking up on me?"

"You were busy watching the cops. Want to tell me again how you were paroled?"

Cole didn't say anything, still watching Harmony shake her booty with one of Cleveland's finest, clearly oblivious to the whole low-profile program.

"They didn't come here on business," Juan said. "They're friends of mine. Some of my neighbors think I'm a detriment to the community."

"They're probably right."

Juan grinned like he was reliving his glory days. "When there's a complaint, these guys show up and make middle-class America feel like their tax dollars are well spent."

"You have cops for friends? You really have gone legit."

"Don't mean I can't tell when somebody ain't being straight with me, and you're not being straight with me, Doc." Juan took a seat at a nearby table. Cole joined him.

"You were convicted under the Patriot Act," Juan continued. "The feds didn't let you out seventeen years early."

"Not entirely true," Cole said. "Harmony is a fed, and she got me out early because she needs me to help her with a case."

"Shit, man, didn't you learn anything the first time around?" Juan shook his head, not believing one man could be that stupid twice in one lifetime. Juan knew Cole's history.

"It's a chance to get out of jail for good."

"If you do what they want."

"You got it on the first try."

"I got some experience in these matters," Juan said dryly.

"On the positive side," Cole said, gesturing to Harmony's dance partner, "the Ohio cops don't appear to be looking for us yet, and the feds don't know where we are." Just a couple of Russian enforcers Cole chose not to mention since they didn't seem to be a threat to anyone. For the moment.

"Fuck," Juan said.

"We'll take off."

"Nah, like you said, the cops aren't looking for you and the feds don't have a clue. Spend the night." He looked off in the general direction of the dance floor. "But I think the party's over."

Juan got to his feet and made his way through the crowd to the dance floor. Cole watched him shake the hand of the spectator cop. By the time that cop got the attention of his partner, Cole had circled around the dance floor. The moment Harmony was alone he swooped in and towed her away, ignoring the protests of the male gallery. A glance over his shoulder told him the cops had missed the getaway, and Harmony was stumbling along behind him, laughing and looking happy. She tripped over a rough patch of grass and fell on her ass. Her hand pulled free of Cole's and she stayed there, giggling uncontrollably. Cole caught her under the armpits and hauled her to her feet, slinging his arm around her waist and half carrying her toward the guesthouse.

"You're pretty," she said, smiling blearily up into his face and draping herself over him so that when Cole pushed the door to the guesthouse open he had to put his hands on her waist and walk her backward into the darkness.

It wasn't bad enough that he could feel her body against his from breasts to knees, she had to nuzzle his neck, too. Then her hands got in the act, running over his back and down to his butt, and she added a moan, her warm breath washing over his skin.

Cole put her at arm's length, ignoring her pout. It would be the easiest thing in the world to take what she was offering. Hell, she probably wouldn't even remember it in the morning. Except he had philosophical objections to taking advantage of her that way. And if they were going to have sex, she was damned well going to remember it.

"Time for bed," he said, giving her a light shove toward the end of the room that was set up as a sleeping area.

She went, still pouting. Cole turned his back, hoping to hell she didn't come after him again, but knowing if he watched her undress he'd go after her, and their relationship would get way too complicated. He couldn't help himself, though. He looked across the room and saw Harmony, facedown on the bed, snoring softly, and something inside him shifted. Something that scared the hell out of him.

He was on his feet and heading for the door before he thought about it, and when he did think, his feet kept right on moving. He could find a computer somewhere, he said to himself; he could do exactly what he wanted without having to worry about Harmony's mission. And then he'd have the FBI after him for real, not to mention Juan would get jacked up because no one would believe he hadn't helped.

Cole stopped with his hand on the doorknob, looking back at Harmony and rethinking his options. All she wanted him to do was hack into the FBI and commit a little larceny, right? And serving Harmony's ends meant serving his own. And if he was being strictly honest with himself, he had to admit that that look on Harmony's face when she'd called the kidnappers had something to do with his decision. He knew how it felt to be an innocent victim, and to be helpless to do anything about it.

A faint beep from the table where he'd left the laptop cemented his decision, especially when he crossed the room and discovered that the password generator had finally gotten past the FBI's first line of security.

He was working his way past the second line of defense when he was kicked out. He went back in, and was kicked out almost immediately. A system that plugged its own holes. Revolutionary. And familiar. Because he'd created it. Every programmer left himself a back door, so he typed in a series of commands and hit enter. Nothing happened.

Cole took to his feet, but it was no use. Anger blasted through him, wave after wave until he was shaking with it, red crowding the edges of his vision.

They'd stolen his system. He'd known that before he started, but coming up against his own handiwork and being repelled by it . . . He paced across the room and back, hands fisted so hard they ached, struggling against the urge to smash something. He'd never really believed they could get his software up and running. But they had. And they were using it against him.

It felt like being fucked over again, like finding out his best friend had scored him a face-to-face with his old man, a guy named Victor Treacher, who just happened to work in computer security at the FBI. Cole had been so high just to get the opportunity to pitch his new security software he'd have handed over a kidney, no questions asked, if Treacher had requested it. Hacking into the FBI's system to prove they needed to upgrade their security had seemed an entirely reasonable request. Until he was arrested under the new Patriot Act.

When he'd tried to defend his actions, he'd discovered that every scrap of hard copy and every file on his computer had disappeared, leaving him with an interesting story but no proof that he'd ever created revolutionary new security software. And that wasn't the worst of it. His best friend had set him up, stolen his future in every way possible. And there hadn't been anything Cole could do about it. Until now.

SURPRISINGLY, COLE MANAGED TO SLEEP AFTER ALL that. Apparently anger was exhausting. He'd shut down the laptop and passed out sometime after midnight. He woke up to the sound of bedclothes rustling, and unfolded himself from the too-short couch, rubbing at the crick in his neck.

Harmony stirred in the bed again, but he kept his eyes to himself. No point adding a snapshot of her, all warm and drowsy and sexy, to the picture album in his head. Unfortunately he got a sound bite instead.

"Cole?" she whispered, her voice husky, the question ending on a little moan as she stretched. "Are you up?"

"Yeah, I'm up." In every way possible.

"What time is it?"

"Time to get moving."

She sat up and stretched; she must have pulled her jeans off sometime during the night, and the sight of her in just a T-shirt and panties brought on the familiar rush of heat and need. He welcomed it this time because it blunted the frustration. "Great party last night," she said, already wide awake and sounding chipper.

"I'm surprised you remember any of it. You had a lot to drink."

"Did I?" She shrugged and went into the bathroom, oblivious to her lack of meaningful coverage and humming something that would have been played by a mariachi band.

"Why aren't you hung over?" Cole wanted to know.

"I never get hung over," she said, coming to the bathroom

door and talking around her toothbrush. "I think it has something to do with burning off the alcohol. I tend to do a lot of dancing when I drink."

"I remember," Cole said. "You danced with a cop."

That took some of the pep out of her attitude. She stopped brushing, went into the bathroom to spit, and came out, looking a little sick to her stomach.

"I'm sorry," she said, which surprised the hell out of him. "I should have kept my head, no matter what."

"You had to face something horrible," Cole said, "but you're going to have to toughen up if you want to get through this thing alive and bring your friend out with you."

She looked like he'd slapped her, but he wouldn't be doing either of them a favor by babying her. "You handed out the job assignments," he reminded her. "I move the money; you handle the secret agent part of the program."

Harmony crossed the room and got in his face. "I'll handle my end of it."

"You might want to put some pants on first."

"It's not pants I need." And she went over to the table and pulled her shoulder and ankle holsters out of her duffel.

Before she could slip into the former, there was a knock on the door, then Juan shouted, "Hey, you lovebirds awake in there?"

Cole exchanged a look with Harmony, and she sped across the room. She was zipping her jeans when Cole opened the door. Juan came in and dropped a couple of bundles on the table, stopping when he got a load of the guns.

"I can explain—" Harmony began.

"I already did," Cole said, adding, "I told him you're a fed and you need my help with a case," because she had a tendency to concoct stories if left to her own devices.

"I guess I owe you an apology, too," Harmony said to Juan. "We should have been straight with you right from the start."

"No sweat. Cole told me you were trying to keep me in the clear. I appreciate that."

"Cole tells me there were cops here last night. Cleveland PD?"

"Just a couple buds of mine," Juan said. "Not as big a deal as having a real live fed at my place."

"I'm sorry I wasn't honest with you, but it's need-to-know."

"No skin off my nose. You're going to keep Cole out of jail, right?"

Harmony met Juan's gaze. "Do I hear a threat?"

Juan shrugged. "Just want you to know I got Cole's back."

"Cole's not going to be in danger." Harmony put her foot on one of the chairs and strapped on her ankle holster.

Juan nudged Cole with an elbow. "She gives the word *heat* a whole new meaning, huh?"

"You have no idea."

"You two know I can hear you, right?"

They ignored her, Cole poking at one of the bundles on the table. "Going away presents?"

Juan grinned. "Just want you to be prepared, man. For anything. Including her coworkers, who are trampling civil rights on the next block."

Also known as a house-to-house search, Cole interpreted. "And you thought it might have something to do with us."

"I'm not the only one."

Harmony was already packing. It didn't take long, since her belongings consisted of two changes of clothing and a laptop. "You're sure they're FBI?" she asked Juan.

"I sent my oldest boy over there on his bike. He says there are roadblocks manned by the Cleveland PD, but the guys in charge are wearing cheap black suits and driving a black car, unmarked."

Cole looked at Harmony. He didn't have to ask the question.

"Somebody at the FBI didn't get the word to lay off us," she said.

"Call that Mike guy."

"It's too late for that. If they catch us, I'll be detained, and you'll go back to jail while they're sorting it all out, and once they get you back in Lewisburg, it's game over."

Juan put into words what they were all thinking. "You guys have to vamoose, and you're going on foot."

"That's the best way to avoid them anyway," Harmony agreed, joining them at the table. "We're going to stick out with all this luggage, though. Any ideas?"

"Head for the lake."

Cole was already stuffing the parcels into Harmony's duffel and shouldering it. "I'm sorry," he said to Juan.

"No problem, man. Most of these assholes around here are bigger crooks than I ever was. Guy next door defrauds old dudes out of their life savings, you know? He calls it the stock market." Juan held out a wad of cash.

"I can't take that," Cole said.

"Consider it royalties. Paid in full."

Translation: Don't come back.

Harmony reached over and took the cash. "Thanks," she said to Juan, giving him a hug. "We really appreciate your hospitality, and I'm sorry if we caused you any trouble."

Juan squeezed her ass. "I'm glad my wife didn't see that," he said. "Take care of her, Doc."

Cole snorted. "There's a pretty good chance she'll get me killed."

Juan thumped his fist on his chest, then lifted it in Cole's direction, first two fingers extended in a sort of loose peace sign. "Stay cool," he said.

They all trooped outside and headed for the back of the yard. Juan opened a gate. Cole looked through it and saw a small wooded area, mixed oaks and pines. No feds.

He and Harmony threaded their way between the tree trunks, making no effort to stay quiet. It would have been impossible anyway, walking through dead leaves ankle deep. The trees began to thin out, and Cole stopped while they were still hidden, Harmony coming to stand beside him.

"Practically no cover," he said, taking a good long look at what lay ahead of them.

They were back in a residential area, the houses set pretty far apart, as they'd been built a hundred years ago in an affluent area. The lots were landscaped, bushes and trees older than the houses, big enough for both him and Harmony to hide behind, but too far apart to be all that useful.

Off in the distance, a few streets ahead and between the houses, they could see the sun sparkling off water.

"I don't see any activity," Harmony said, clearly more focused on who was in the area rather than what. "If they're going to search this block, it doesn't look like they've made it here yet."

"I say we stay hidden for a while, lay low, see what happens."

"I think we should head for the lake, like Juan said. The longer we stay here the more likely we'll get trapped."

"I don't like it," Cole said. "It feels off."

"Off."

"I spent the last eight years breaking the law under the noses of federal prison guards."

"Some of them were paid to look the other way."

"And some of them weren't," Cole countered. "Ask any ex-con. You develop a feel for trouble. It's too quiet for a weekday morning. Where are the people going to work? Why aren't there any kids waiting for the school bus?"

"What do you suggest we do?"

"I'd suggest we wait for dark," Cole said, "but it's too far off. When they don't find us, they're bound to widen the search area."

"We don't have a choice," Harmony said, and before he could stop her, she eased out of the trees and ran, almost silently, across the lawn to the back of the house directly ahead of them. When she got there she looked back, crooking a finger when she saw him still standing in the shadows of the pine trees.

Cole had no choice but to follow, heart thumping as he crossed the wide-open expanse of lawn. Even when he made it, his pulse was still kicking. But so was the adrenaline. He took Harmony by the hand and crept toward the street. When they got to the front of the house, Cole hesitated briefly before stepping into the open again. No skulking this time. He walked to the curb, hand in hand with Harmony, as if they were out for a morning stroll.

"See—"

"Stay where you are," a bullhorn-enhanced voice said into the eerie stillness, "and keep your hands where we can see them."

Harmony's hand tightened in his, and when he looked into her eyes, he knew exactly what she was thinking, even before she shouted, *"Run."*

chapter
10

HARMONY LET COLE PICK THE ROUTE BECAUSE HE
was taller, that and he let go of her hand and took off, and it
was all she could do to keep up with him. He headed straight
for the water, no concern for what lay in their path. It was a
flat-out, top-speed footrace over a suburban obstacle course.
Harmony ran full tilt across lawns, through koi ponds, around
backyard swings, and under rose arbors, vaulting fences and
ignoring various mutts who, thankfully, seemed to think they
were there as playmates and not chew toys.

The team of feds had split up, taking positions at either end
of the street behind Juan's house, safely out of bullet range but
badly situated for a chase on foot. It was one of two things she
and Cole had going for them, Harmony thought, the other
plus being they were only a couple of streets from a good-
sized marina.

Cole clearly didn't plan to spend a lot of time playing tag
with guys who could make sure he never saw the outside of
prison walls again. They hit the docks, and he took a sharp
right, heading for a sleek little speedboat that looked like it
could skate on a molecule-thin layer of water.

"Not that one," Harmony yelled. She slowed, searching the place until she found what she wanted, then taking off again at full speed.

Footsteps pounded the dock right behind her, so either Cole had abandoned the speedboat or the feds had caught up.

"What the hell are you doing?"

Okay, so it was Cole, but Harmony didn't waste any time acknowledging his presence. She didn't even look over her shoulder; it would only slow her down, and she couldn't afford that since she was already running out of steam. She dug deep, found one last burst of energy and poured it on, vaulting over the side of a big old cabin cruiser that was immaculately maintained but made entirely of wood.

Her toe caught on the brass railing and she sprawled onto the deck, the laptop slapping painfully against her back. Cole came on board right behind her. He hauled her to her feet and dragged her under the tarp covering the bridge. To the right was a control panel with a bunch of gauges and a captain's wheel with a chair on a pedestal in front of it. To the left was another chair, and in between there was a door leading down to the galley and, presumably, sleeping quarters. The entire boat was made of varnished wood and brass fittings, battened down under clean white canvas.

"I don't think they saw us," he said, "but it's just a matter of time before they go from boat to boat."

Harmony was already on her knees by the control panel. The wind had been knocked out of her, and she had to take a few seconds to get her breath back.

Cole took it as uncertainty on her part. He had no faith in her abilities. "I hope you know how to hot-wire this thing," he said. "I was a law-abiding citizen before I got arrested, and hot-wiring isn't one of the skills I learned in the joint. If you want to know the best way to shank a guy, I can help with that."

"It can't be that different from a car. Just get this panel— *Jeez*," Harmony shrieked, covering her head and barely diving out of the way when Cole slammed his foot through the thin wooden panel that covered the boat's controls and gauges.

"Sorry," he said, not sounding particularly apologetic.

"You'll be sorry if those guys catch up to us."

"Good point. Anything I can do to help?"

"Untie the boat."

"You mean cast off?"

Harmony rolled her eyes. "Whatever you want to call it, Ahab." She pulled a bundle of wiring out of the space where the panel had been. She quickly isolated the ignition wire, made a cut, stripped the ends, and sparked them together. The motor caught to life with a throaty roar. Unfortunately it also caught the attention of the federal agents.

Harmony heard a shout, Cole came racing back to the wheel, and put the boat in motion. She tried to stand up, but he wasn't worried about the surrounding watercraft or the dock, scraping and banging his way out of the slip and keeping her from finding her equilibrium. She wrapped her arms around him, it was that or eat the deck again.

He caught her and set her back on her feet. "You have a problem with balance."

"You drive like an old lady with cataracts," Harmony shot back, letting go of Cole to take hold of the back of the captain's chair with one hand and the brass railing with the other.

They lumbered out of the marina, motor chugging and smoking, adhering to the NO WAKE signs. As if they had a choice.

"Shit," Cole said, clearly on the same wavelength, "this thing couldn't make a wake in a hurricane, and it has a draft like a hippo. I had a nice little cigarette boat all picked out. Why the hell didn't you follow me?"

"This boat isn't as fast, but it's what we need," Harmony said. "Trust me."

Cole shot her a look, not amused. He pushed the throttle up, the engines got louder, the back of the boat bit into the water, and the front nosed up in the air.

"This is more like it," Cole shouted. He pointed the boat out into Lake Erie and pushed it to maximum speed.

He looked like he was having a lot of fun, considering the circumstances. Harmony really hated to bring him down, but he got so cranky when she kept things from him. So she tapped him on the shoulder and pointed behind them, where a sleek powerboat was clearing the marina and coming up to full speed. There wasn't much to the speedboat, just seats and horsepower—and two guys in black suits and dark glasses. Not your typical boaters out for a pleasure cruise on the lake. Of course, they got their jollies by arresting escaped felons and rogue FBI agents, so pleasure was a relative term in their case.

"Let me drive," she yelled, nudging Cole aside.

He didn't move, his eyes on the speedboat. "I'm still waiting to hear why you picked this old wooden monstrosity."

"Get out of my way, and I'll show you."

If he'd wanted to push the issue, Cole could have kept control of the boat. But after his customary moment of deliberation, he moved aside.

Harmony got behind the wheel, immediately taking it into a big, wide left turn. As she came around at a right angle to the speedboat she whipped the wheel around, putting the cabin cruiser into a tight hairpin turn the boat hadn't been designed to make. It wallowed, heeling hard onto its side and slowing drastically, almost capsizing before it righted itself, all forward momentum lost. Cole went down, sliding on his ass on the spray-slick deck until he came up hard against the opposite side of the boat.

"Having trouble with your balance?" Harmony asked sweetly.

"You drive like a maniac," he shouted, climbing to his feet. "You almost foundered the boat."

"I wanted them to think I did," she said, waiting while the feds slowed and assessed the situation, waiting while they punched their boat back up to full speed and came straight for them.

"The Coast Guard has a post in Cleveland," she continued, one hand on the wheel, the other on the throttle. "These agents won't want to bring them in unless there's no other choice. We need to take these guys out before they can radio back for help."

"Jesus," Cole said, his hands on the top of his head like he was afraid his skull might explode.

"I'm not going to kill them." She pushed the throttle up as

far as it would go, shouting over the roar of the engine. "I'm just making sure they have a nice, long swim."

"What if they can't swim?"

"I'd expect you to be happy at the prospect of two less federal agents in the world." She steered straight for the smaller boat.

The agents kept on coming, until they realized she'd turned the tables on them. They tried to steer off, but it was too late. They dove for cover over opposite sides of the speedboat, making it to safety seconds before she crashed the big wooden boat into their play toy. Fiberglass shattered, engine parts smoked and gurgled their way underwater, the two feds yelled and shook their fists. Harmony kept going, taking the boat out of firing range.

She steered around them in a big circle until she and Cole were heading west again, keeping the boat to an unremarkable speed.

Cole was staring at the two federal heads bobbing off in the distance. "You—" he said. "They—" He threw his hands up in the air and stomped to the opposite railing, turning around to shake a finger at her.

"Speechless," she said with a grin. "The icing on the cake."

Cole scowled at her, arms crossed. "I'm waiting to hear how you justify this one."

"First of all, I can't believe there are four FBI agents that inept, so those guys have to be the same two agents who came after us at Lewisburg." No experienced agents would have fallen for the foundering boat trick, or stuck around long enough to be run over. "They haven't learned any new skills since the last time, either."

"And?"

"And we have at least two hours before they make it to shore," she said, "and probably another hour while they deliberate over whether or not to bring in the Coast Guard. By the time they make up their minds, they won't know where we are. That's another reason I chose this boat. The new models have built-in GPS and locator beacons, but they won't be able to track this one. The bad news is we don't have that much fuel. The owner was probably getting ready to winterize, and he let it run low."

"Oh, good," Cole said, "I was really worried we might actually get away with this."

THEY MOTORED ALONG WITHOUT TALKING. ONCE THE adrenaline wore off, neither of them had the energy to shout over the din of the engine. Harmony kept out of sight of the shoreline until the gas gauge got so low she feared they'd run out. When the engine started to sputter she aimed the boat for shore and let it ground.

Cole knew before the motor went quiet, before Harmony turned around, that it was time for a reckoning. "You're wondering how your friends at the FBI knew where to find us."

"Aren't you?"

Nope. Cole knew exactly how the feds had found them. He'd underestimated Victor Treacher. Again. Treacher was slime, but he was slime with a brain. Treacher must've kept tabs on him, even in jail, which meant he knew when Cole had broken out. The two federal agents at Lewisburg must have come from Treacher as well, and not because Harmony's paperwork had been sloppy. They'd managed to give Treacher's goons the slip—until Cole went online last night.

He could picture Treacher sitting in his big corner office, just waiting for Cole to open that back door he'd written into his software. And he'd walked right into the trap, eyes wide open. He'd given Treacher a starting point to narrow their location down to a neighborhood, and then he'd slept like a baby, allowing Treacher's agents the time to set a trap. And almost catch him.

Such a close call should leave him doubting his course of action. It only reaffirmed it. It was about revenge now. He'd be damned if he'd let Victor Treacher fuck him over twice. This time it was war. And it was his war, not Harmony's. He probably ought to tell her the truth, but she wouldn't take on one of the top dogs at the FBI, and he was afraid if she knew he planned to do it, she'd turn him in.

"You were online last night," Harmony said, reminding Cole that she might look like she had fluff for brains, but in her case looks were definitely deceiving.

"Yeah," he said, "I was online last night."

"That must be how they tracked us."

"I didn't even get in. Every serious hacker in the world has tried to breach the FBI's computer system. If they tracked down everyone who slammed up against their firewall, they'd never do anything else. Any chance they could have traced your phone yesterday?"

"Maybe," Harmony said, even though she didn't believe it for a second. Officially, she was on vacation. There was no reason for the FBI to be watching her phone. She'd been tracking computer criminals for most of her time with the Bureau. She knew the feds had shown up because Cole had tried to breach the system. He knew it, too. She could see it on his face; he just wouldn't admit it. The question was why? What was he hiding from her? And how did the FBI figure into that secret, because if she knew one thing, it was that something was going on at the Bureau, and whatever it was it involved Cole Hackett And there was only one way to find out what it was.

She took out her second cell phone and held it up. "Yesterday I had to use my FBI phone so it would come up on caller ID. This one is prepaid. Untraceable."

"Calling your handler again?"

"Got a better idea?"

Cole heaved a sigh and went to the far end of the boat.

Harmony punched in Mike's number. "Remember when I told you I was on vacation?" she asked when he came on the line.

"You're not staying with your aunt in the Poconos."

"How did you know?"

"You work for me, remember? At least you used to."

Harmony's stomach rolled in sick waves. But she held her moral ground. "Somebody had to go after him, Mike."

"Maybe," he grumbled sourly. "Somebody with experience."

"I don't have experience because you wouldn't put me in the field."

"You're not ready. Not until you can keep your feelings out of your work."

"There's nothing wrong with emotion."

"There is when it can get you killed."

"Is that why you sent agents after me?"

Mike was silent for a beat, then he said, "Spill it."

Harmony told him everything. Mike couldn't help her if he didn't have all the facts. "Look, Mike, you have to call off the chase. I know those guys must be pretty ticked off, since I put them in a river, and a lake—"

"Good for you," Mike said, but absently, like his mind was working a mile a minute, which it probably was. Mike Kovaleski was one of the best handlers the FBI had, always one step ahead of his agents. This time he sounded several steps behind. "You had release papers for Hackett, right?"

Harmony smiled a little. "You signed them."

"Yeah, we'll talk about that another time. So everything looked kosher?"

"Yes. I can't figure out how the warden knew they were fake so fast."

"There's something going on we don't know about," Mike said. "Someone we haven't factored in."

Harmony's eyes cut to Cole. "Definitely."

"It doesn't matter. If you come in, I'll salvage what I can of your career—and mine, since I'm in charge of you, and my ass is on the line, too. Stay out in the cold, and I can't guarantee anything."

Her stomach rolled again, and her career flashed before her eyes. Along with Richard's dead body. "You know I can't do that, Mike."

"Then I guess I'll sit here and wait for a call from some morgue."

"It won't come to that," Harmony insisted. "I have a plan—"

"Let me guess, you're going to have the geek hack into the frozen accounts and transfer the money, but just enough to make the kidnappers think you're cooperating while you get a bead on where they're holding Swendahl."

It wasn't a question, it was a pretty accurate statement of her intentions, and Harmony felt no need to reply.

Mike clearly wasn't expecting her to. "Problem one," he continued, "you can't control Hackett."

Harmony's eyes cut to the man in question. "I have so far. He agreed to help."

Mike snorted. "I looked him up. He wasn't dangerous before he went into jail, and I'm willing to bet he's still not or he'd have knocked you over the head and taken off by now. But he's no dummy, either. He's working an angle. The minute he gets whatever it is he wants, he's gone and you're screwed."

Harmony sat down hard, feeling stupid. If her plan was that transparent, would the kidnappers figure it out, too? And would she even get the chance to find out?

"Look," Mike said, sounding like he was at the end of his patience, "just sit tight, let me wrap my head around this, and I'll get back to you."

"Don't worry about me, Mike. I have all the training."

"There's more than training to being in the field. Intuition, experience, and a little cynicism wouldn't hurt. You can't afford to think the best of everyone. Think the worst, and if you're proven wrong, it'll be a pleasant surprise."

"Just get those agents off our backs," Harmony said. "Oh, and if you hear about charges against a guy named Juan Esposito in Cleveland, can you get them dropped? All he did was give us a place to crash for the night."

Mike sighed. "I'll handle it. Let me talk to Hackett."

That surprised her. She looked at the phone, then at Cole.

"What?" Cole said. "He wants to talk to me?"

She shrugged and handed him the phone. Cole took it back to the other end of the boat. He and Mike had a short conversation, which consisted of nothing more than a couple of "uh-huhs" from Cole's side of the conversation, then Cole said something Harmony couldn't hear—but she could guess at, from the tone of his voice and the way he snapped the phone shut before he tossed it to her.

"What did Mike want?"

Cole didn't answer, just walked away, gathered her duffel and laptop, and jumped over the side of the boat. He didn't seem to care that he landed in a couple inches of water. Harmony was surprised it didn't steam.

She didn't have a clue what Mike had said to Cole, but whatever it was, it had put her back to square one with him.

chapter
11

HARMONY HAD GROUNDED THE BOAT IN A MARSHY
area, waves lapping gently at the stems of weeds and shallow-
water plants growing higher than Cole was tall, anchored by
two inches of muck.

He stomped through water and mud, not caring that he
looked like a three-year-old having a temper tantrum at the
beach. He was entitled to sulk for a little while, he told himself, slapping cattails aside, fuming and wondering how he
kept getting the shaft. Fucking FBI, that was how.

Last time he'd been a naïve kid who wanted to help his
country and make his mark in the world of computer security. His reward had been a jail cell. He should have learned
something from that, but along came a beautiful blonde with
a get-out-of-jail-free card and he'd followed along like a dog
on a leash. He could have lived with that, as long as further-
ing Harmony's cause meant his own agenda got served. Instead, here he was with his nuts in the wringer again.

Victor Treacher was headed for a comeuppance; Harmony
he could handle. The guy on the phone just now had been scary.
If anything happened to Harmony, Mike Whatsis had said,

there wouldn't be anywhere to hide. He'd make it his mission in life to hunt Cole down and toss him in the deepest, darkest hole he could find. It was a promise, not a threat, one that would be kept if things didn't turn out well for Harmony Swift.

Shit.

He could already see the writing on the wall. Somehow she'd come out of this smelling like a rose, and he'd end up in an even worse place than Lewisburg. Like a grave.

Cole sent her a sidelong glare, wading through the marsh a short distance away.

She huffed out a breath. "All right, what did Mike say to you?"

He hunched his shoulders, not wanting to replay it again. Of course she couldn't let it go.

"Let me guess, something about you watching out for me, along with a dire threat about what he'll do if I get hurt."

"Dire?" he ground out with a puff of disgusted laughter. Dire didn't even begin to cover it.

"We made a deal," Harmony said, "which is all that matters."

"And what if you're dead?"

She shrugged, but she looked pretty grim, staring through the weeds at the little road they'd come to. "If I'm dead, you'll still be free, and you can get lost in the world just like you said you could."

Except he'd have every local, state, and federal law enforcement agency on his ass, not to mention Harmony's personal guard dog, who had all the weight of the FBI behind him.

"Nothing has changed," she said. "We have a deal and I'm holding you to it."

And he was all in, Cole thought, Mike's threat notwithstanding. He stood more of a chance of getting what he wanted as long as he had someone on the inside running interference.

"So, where we going, Captain Bligh?" he said.

"Don't call me that," she said, looking like a woman who carried two guns and was thinking about using one of them on him.

"We have an agreement, remember? Shooting me wasn't part of it."

She nodded, and let it go at that. "We can hole up for the night or we can find something to drive. A good-sized city works best either way. Toledo is the closest."

"Do you think we lost the Russians?"

"Even if they tailed us to Juan's, I don't see how they could have stayed with us this morning."

"We won't be that hard to track if they ask the right questions. I think we should put some more distance between us and Cleveland."

"Then we need transportation."

"How?"

"Boats aren't the only things I can hot-wire."

Cole heaved a sigh. If—when—*if* the feds caught up to him this time, at least they wouldn't need a frame.

IT HADN'T TAKEN HARMONY LONG TO FIGURE OUT they were in a state park, signs for boating, swimming, and hiking cropping up fairly regularly as they walked. The roads were narrow, trees and underbrush crowding right up to the paved edge, which kept them out of the blistering Indian summer sun but left them in biting and stinging insect territory. She didn't appreciate the trade-off. And being out of the sun hadn't helped her temperature a whole lot, not with Cole staring at her backside. At least it felt like he was staring at her backside. She'd glanced behind her a couple of times, and he'd been looking off into the trees, or down the road over her head, but when she faced forward again, it felt like his eyes were glued to her butt.

She slapped at a mosquito, amazed it hadn't burst into flame just by landing on her arm. Her clothes felt constricting, her throat was dry, and there was a constant hum running through her, like a low-grade electrical current that settled in the obvious places and left her . . .

A car whooshed by, sporting a *Honk If You're Horny* bumper sticker complete with a picture of an antlered deer. She burst out laughing.

"What's so funny?" Cole wanted to know, sounding as

cranky as she'd been a moment ago, which set her to thinking things she shouldn't have been thinking. Like how he'd been in jail for eight years, and he'd made it clear that sex topped his list of "making up for lost time."

Dangerous thought to have. She'd been simmering for two days—not that she was on the verge of ripping her clothes off and shouting, "Take me," or anything—but the . . . awareness of Cole had been there since the moment she'd first seen him. In that little room at Lewisburg. Taking his clothes off. And remembering him stripping down wasn't helping her predicament. Even toting up all the ramifications of getting physically involved with Cole didn't help, especially since most of them weren't true any more because something had changed.

Yesterday he'd been going through the motions, on board, but poised to jump ship the minute things went south. Being in ex-con safe territory hadn't helped. Juan would have helped Cole ditch her in a heartbeat, and no way could she have taken on half the Hispanic population of Cleveland, headed by a guy who had committed two murders, if she believed his body art.

She'd slept like a rock after the party, exhaustion—and booze—finally catching up with her. Cole should have been gone this morning, but when she woke up there he'd been. Heck, he'd led the escape from their FBI welcome-to-Cleveland party, which didn't mean anything on the surface since the feds would put him back in jail if they caught him. And even though he could have easily ditched her at the marina, he'd gone along with her willingly when she'd insisted on taking the big wooden boat.

Yep, something had changed, and while her brain worked to fit it into the bigger picture, her body was taking his cooperation as a green light. Good thing they were in the middle of a forest, probably carpeted with poison ivy and inhabited with fire ants. What deterrents she'd find when they landed somewhere with a bed she didn't know. Maybe the urge would go away by then. *And maybe pigs would fly.*

Cars slowed as they passed, a couple of drivers seeming

like they'd be willing to offer assistance. Harmony waved them on. Cole didn't object. Neither of them wanted to chance a repeat of their encounter with Irene and Leo. It wasn't a good idea to take a ride from strangers, either. Drivers passing them on the shoulder would only remember seeing a man and woman. If they spent time in the backseat of somebody's vehicle, their identity could be confirmed. Another low probability, sure, but one she wasn't willing to risk.

"I thought you were going to hot-wire something," Cole said, still irritable.

Harmony rolled her eyes and shook her head. "And you call yourself a criminal."

"The FBI gave me that distinction."

"Didn't you learn anything in jail?"

"Not a lot of opportunity to steal cars in jail. My hosts preferred to limit travel opportunities."

And he'd been a geek before that. A law-abiding geek. For the most part. "A car gets reported stolen around here, the cops will find the boat."

"Doesn't mean the feds or the Russians will find out." Cole held up a hand. "I know, we can't take that chance. I'm just antsy."

"I get it," Harmony said. "I didn't expect to be on the run so much, either."

"Lot easier to be on the run in a car."

"Jeez, will you give it up about the car already?"

"You could always threaten to shoot me if I don't shut up."

Harmony kept covering ground, one foot in front of the other, not thinking about Cole's eyes and where they might be looking. "Shooting you would definitely solve some problems."

"For both of us," Cole retorted, "but you'd also sign your friend's death warrant."

"I could get the money without you," Harmony said.

"Then why did you break me out of jail?"

Harmony whipped around, went toe-to-toe with him. "I'm wondering that myself," she said, drilling a finger into his chest. "I'm trying to remember why I went to all this trouble, just so I could be saddled with a whiny," poke, "obnoxious," poke, "cranky ex-con hacker who hasn't got the sense not to mess with the f—"

Before she could finish the acronym, or poke him in the chest again, Cole caught her by the wrist, gave her a quick, hard tug, and jerked her against him.

"The FBI asked me to mess with them," he ground out, "and you broke me out of jail."

And he kissed her, a rough kiss at first, angry and full of frustration. Then his mouth gentled on hers, his tongue swept inside, and Harmony lost herself to the heat and taste and scent of him, to all that rock-hard muscle pressed against all the places her body ached to feel him. Okay, not all the places. She moved into him, sank into the kiss, let the simmer turn into a full-out boil—

Brakes screech, they jumped apart, Cole trying to sweep her behind him.

"I'm the one with the gun," Harmony said, refusing to be swept.

Besides which it was just an old RV, eighties' brown-and-tan paint job, rusted around the wheel wells, piloted by retirees if the white-haired guy behind the wheel was any indication. He slid the driver's window open, trying to get a better look, judging by the sparkle in his eye and the "Carry on" he tossed out the window.

"Ron!" a voice shouted from the depths of the RV. "What are we stopping for this time? Oh." A woman with short salt-and-pepper curls came up beside Ron, leaning over to peer out the window at them. "You youngsters need a ride?"

"He was about to get one, Veda," Ron said, leering at Harmony.

Veda gave Ron a good swat with the back of her hand across his chest. "I bet you're on your honeymoon, right?"

Harmony held up her naked left hand.

Veda shook her head, abjectly disappointed. "Don't understand you young kids."

"Makes me wish I'd been born forty years later," Ron said.

"That'd only make you a young pervert," Veda said, "which'd

land your cute bee-hind in jail since young perverts can't get away with near's much as old ones."

"You got a point, you old bat," Ron said with a hoot of laughter.

"You two out for a hike?" Veda asked.

"Nah, they don't have any backpacks," Ron said. "Not dressed for it, neither."

Harmony looked down at her jeans, T-shirt, and walking shoes, still squishing from her unplanned interaction with Lake Erie. Cole was dressed similarly. She wasn't sure what constituted hiking gear in Ron's mind, but considering the general direction of his thoughts, she wasn't about to ask him what she should be wearing.

"We ran out of gas," Cole said, which wasn't exactly a lie. For a criminal he was disturbingly honest, didn't have a devious bone in his body. And now they were stuck with his story.

"Well," Veda said briskly, "c'mon then, hop in and we'll take you as far as the nearest gas station."

Cole gave her a look, realizing his mistake, Harmony figured, and coming to the conclusion there was no getting around it.

"Let's go, Pinocchio," she said.

They circled the RV. Veda met them at the door. Harmony stepped up first, hesitating at the entrance. It looked pretty normal inside, typical RV setup: small galley in the center, driver's and passenger's seats up front, tiny bathroom and sleeping quarters at the other end. Lots of fake wood paneling, neutral colors, no immediate threat.

It was almost worth the risk, Harmony decided as cool air washed over her. And anyway, what was the chance Veda and Ron would run into FBI agents asking questions?

"Where are you headed?" she asked Veda, moving out of the way so Cole could come in, too.

"Me and Ron are headed to Branson to see Tony Orlando."

"And Dawn," Ron put in from the front.

"Dawn isn't going to be there," Veda said for what must have been the hundredth time, judging by her tone.

"Then what the hell are we going for? I don't want to see

some old fruitcake singing about ribbons. You promised me backup singers."

"They're my age, you old pervert. And it's not like they're going to give you a lap dance or anything."

Now that she wasn't right on top of him, Ron appeared not to hear her.

"Took his hearing aids out," Veda said, sliding onto the bench seat at the U-shaped table and gesturing them to join her. "Truth is, I tune him out half the time, too. Dr. Phil'd tell you communication is the secret to a long, happy marriage, but he's a quack. Lack of communication, that's the real ticket. Knowing when to overlook your partner's crap, just like he overlooks yours. 'Course, once in a while you miss something important, but hey, there's always a downside, right?"

Yep, Harmony thought, there was always a downside, and the downside of riding with Veda and Ron was that Veda never stopped talking. And she had an opinion on everything. By the time they pulled into a gas station Harmony was wishing she had hearing aids to take out. The upside was getting to civilization a lot faster than they would have on foot.

Toledo Express Airport was about thirty-five miles from where Ron and Veda dropped them. Harmony had no intention of walking thirty-five miles. That meant public transportation, and the safest mode of public transportation for them was bus. By and large people who rode the bus were used to minding their own business. Even if they were remembered, Harmony knew odds were low that the information would get to the authorities.

It was after noon by the time the bus dropped them at the airport, but Harmony bypassed the terminal completely.

Cole slowed as they passed the entrance. "There's probably food in there," he called after her.

"There's also security," Harmony said, despite her own growling stomach.

She headed for the parking lot, and Cole fell into step with her, looking cranky again.

"This is America," Harmony said, taking her time, looking for just the right car to boost. "There's a restaurant on every street corner and highway off-ramp these days."

"I was in jail, not a coma. We had restaurants back in the Dark Ages, eight years ago."

She saw a man taking a suitcase out of the trunk of a black Ford Taurus, and not one of those little wheeled carry-ons, either. This suitcase had some heft to it.

"That one," she said to Cole. "Wherever he's going, he'll be there awhile. He won't miss the car for a few days."

The man headed for the terminal; Harmony headed for the Taurus. She had it unlocked and running in under a minute.

"You want to take the first shift driving?" she asked Cole. "Or should I?"

Cole pulled her out from behind the wheel and shooed her to the passenger side. "My stomach is taking the wheel," he said.

"Okay by me, but you might want to tell your stomach to stay away from donut places. Just in case."

chapter 12

FAST-FOOD RESTAURANTS TENDED TO HUDDLE TO-
gether in high-traffic areas and around freeway interchanges.
Cole drove as far as the closest conglomeration, loading up
on fat and cholesterol, before he pulled into a parking space
at the last one and switched places with Harmony.

Surprisingly, he pulled her laptop out of the backseat first,
booted it up, and mapped out a route that took them south
and west. Then he dug in.

Harmony sipped on a Diet Coke and snacked on fries
dipped in chili. Cole reached over and draped a napkin across
her front, tucking it into the neck of her T-shirt. His fingers
brushed across the upper swells of her breasts, her heart shot
up into her throat, and she almost put the car into the ditch.

Cole, when she met his eyes, had a grin on his face. "The
shoulder's far enough," he said.

She scowled at him, but she didn't say anything, not when
she couldn't keep what she felt out of her voice. No point letting him know that pulling over to the shoulder was the least
of what she wanted to do.

She got the car back under control and steered it up the Highway 24 westbound ramp. Cole kept his hands to himself, and as long as she didn't look his way, everything was fine. It helped when he fell asleep, not waking up until they hit the outskirts of Fort Wayne, Indiana.

He took the wheel then, steering them around Fort Wayne on I-469, and almost directly south on I-69 toward Indianapolis. Harmony would have stopped there, but Cole insisted on pushing it another two hundred and fifty miles or so to St. Louis. Harmony didn't object; it was two hundred and fifty miles closer to Richard, and St. Louis was a large city with a lot of suburban sprawl around it. They could get lost there long enough to rest and recharge, and make a real start at putting this thing to bed.

"You don't have any ex-con friends here, do you?" Harmony asked when they hit the outskirts of the city.

"Not the kind you'd want to run into," Cole said. "They're not what you'd call 'rehabilitated.'"

"Neither are you."

"True, but I'm harmless."

Not in the ways that really counted, she thought. When she'd cooked up this crazy scheme, she'd factored in things like how difficult it would be to control a man who'd been in prison for eight years, a man who had to hate the FBI for putting him there. When she'd first laid eyes on the nerd-turned-muscleman, she'd almost put the kibosh on the whole thing. Only the fact that she'd gone too far to turn back had kept her moving forward.

Now she was wondering how she would've ever gotten this far without Cole. It was more than his cooperation, more than the comfort of having someone at her side, and it was more than the fact that she desired him. *More*, however, was a term she couldn't begin to define at the moment. And it was a term that might never need definition.

Harmony was almost a hundred percent positive Cole was working some angle of his own, some way to keep himself out of prison in case she couldn't. It stung that he didn't trust her, but she could live with that as long as he did what she needed him to do.

"This place looks like it'll do," Cole said. "What do you think?"

Harmony read the sign in front of the little travel motel Cole had pulled into. "Hurry Inn?"

"They have weekly rates."

"We're not staying for a week," she said, but absently because she was busy looking the place over and deciding Cole was right.

The Hurry Inn looked like one of the once-charming little travel motels that had popped up along the route west in the fifties, when Mom, Dad, and the kiddies took vacations in faux-wood-sided station wagons. It ran at a forty-five degree angle from the road, with a little business office in front. All the rooms had outside entrances, and there was just enough parking for the residents.

The building was showing its age, some of the brick needed repointing, and the wood trim could've used a coat of paint. But the parking lot was clean and it didn't seem to be a by-the-hour place. It wasn't filled with families, either, but with weekly rates it probably appealed to single men on the low end of the pay scale.

Harmony handed Cole a hundred-dollar bill. "Go in and get us a room. In the back would be best."

He looked at the money then at her.

"What's wrong?"

"Nothing." He got out of the car, went into the little office at the front, and came back a couple minutes later. He drove to the far end of the motel, parking in front of the last room on the end.

Harmony took a deep breath and levered herself out of the car, following Cole into the room. It didn't surprise her to see a double bed instead of two singles. That's the way her day had gone. "The accommodations are going to be a problem."

"Anything else would have been suspicious," he said, "and requesting two beds would have defeated the purpose. You sent me into the office alone for a reason."

"So I did." She pulled her wallet out of the duffel and went back outside. "I'm going to find some food that doesn't come in a paper wrapper," she said. "I'll be back in a little while."

But she didn't get into the car.

Cole went to the door and looked out at her. "Don't worry. I'll be here when you get back."

"If I didn't know that, I wouldn't have given you money, and I wouldn't be leaving you alone here."

"Then what's the problem?"

"Nothing," she said. They both knew it wasn't the truth, but there was no way she was telling Cole that she wanted him to trust her in return.

Things got worse from there. Measurably worse. Cole dug into the steak, baked potato, and asparagus she brought back like a man who'd been starved. For sex. He moaned, he groaned, he closed his eyes and let his head fall back. Harmony checked below the table while she had the opportunity. No obvious bulges. Okay, so he wasn't that excited about the meal, but he made a good show of it.

Harmony did a lot of restless shifting in her chair and concentrated almost desperately on her chicken, rice, and broccoli. It tasted like cardboard.

"What's for dessert?"

His deep voice struck a sympathetic chord on her already overworked nerves, all but jolting her out of her chair. She slid a smaller take-out box over to him, already regretting its contents even before he opened it and said, "Lemon meringue pie. I'm touched."

"I owed you," she said, getting to her feet before he could open the take-out container. "Don't read anything into it." She snagged her duffel and headed for the bathroom, pulling out the last clean item of clothing she had with her, a pair of running shorts. She slipped them on, and bolted out of the bathroom, straight through the room, and out the door to the parking lot.

The idea was to exercise herself into a stupor. She didn't have much hope either cardio or yoga would work. As tense as she was it would take the Dalai Lama himself to meditate her into a state where she had any hope of sleep. Since she doubted he'd come down from his mountain to help her work off a case of hormonal overload, a couple hours of exhausting exercise might do the trick. Or it might not. Maybe the only thing that could help her work off this much tension was the man who'd caused it.

Cole Hackett, however, was the one remedy she didn't dare try.

HARMONY JOLTED AWAKE, GROGGY, HEART POUNDING, a scream echoing in her ears.

Richard.

She stared bleary-eyed around the room, dimly lit by the fluorescent parking-lot lights leaking through the thin drapes, and tried to shove the nightmare out of her mind. Except it wasn't a nightmare. Richard was being held captive somewhere, hurting and afraid for his life. She couldn't do anything about it, at least not by herself, and there was a price to Cole's assistance that she hadn't expected.

Take tonight, for instance. After her run she'd taken a shower and popped into bed, without sparing Cole a word or a look. Back off, she was saying, keep your distance. She couldn't have sent a clearer message if she'd written it on his boxers with a Sharpie.

But did he back off? Did he take the chair or the floor and leave her in peace? No. He'd climbed into bed with her some time after she drifted off to sleep, and now there he was, the jerk, right beside her, looking all warm and sexy. And here she was, wide awake and afraid to breathe for fear the sight and the smell of him would lure her into doing something she'd regret later. And she wasn't just talking about sex.

Though she was only inches away from Cole, she felt alone, lonely, and uncertain and anxious. It would be so easy to roll over and steal a little comfort. It would have been a lot more tempting if she hadn't known he'd take it as an invitation—and as much as she'd like to offer one, she couldn't. She needed to keep her distance, and not just for her own self-respect. Mike Kovaleski, heck, everyone at the Bureau thought she had trouble separating her emotions from her work. But she could. It just took a little self-control . . .

Cole rolled over and draped his arm over her waist, sliding his hand around her butt and snugging her against him. *Okay,* she amended, *a lot of self-control. And willpower.*

She tried to shove him off, but he only slung one of his legs over hers and wrapped himself around her so she was well and truly trapped, her face against his neck, drawing him in with every breath she took so she couldn't even escape into herself and find peace. She made a last-ditch effort to push him off, but he was deadweight, sleeping the sleep of a man with a full stomach and a clear conscience. Well, maybe just a full stomach. He didn't deserve a clear conscience.

For the first time in days she felt good. Comfortable, safe, protected. The tension drained out of her muscles, and her mind went fuzzy, sliding down into exhaustion. She fought it. There was no way she intended to wake up wrapped in Cole's arms.

She attempted to muster up some outrage over his criminal past, but the most she could manage was mild irritation. He had an abrasive personality, she reminded herself. He was high-handed and sarcastic, and borderline chauvinistic. None of that worked either. Even the normal sexual buzz wasn't enough, and the next thing she knew it was morning, and she was surfacing from the best sleep she'd had since Richard had been snatched.

She resisted full consciousness because she was having the best dream of her life. She stretched, sighed, her breasts aching and the kind of tightness deep inside that made her move restlessly, needing . . .

"Keep that up and we won't be getting out of bed for a while."

Harmony went still. She kept her eyes shut, reaching out with one hand and encountering firm, resilient flesh. Cole's flesh. Worse, she was draped half over him, one of her legs nestled between his, his thigh riding high against her center. And that wasn't all. His mouth was on her neck, his hands were on her bottom, and there was something hard poking her in the side. And she liked it. All of it. She wanted more. In fact, she wanted that mouth to keep moving over her skin, and she wanted that hardness deep inside her, and clearly she was getting that message across loud and clear because he skimmed his hand up, along her ribs, heading for territory she couldn't allow him to explore, at least not while she was awake. If he touched her breast, she was going to climb the rest of the way on top of him—after she took off what little she was wearing.

She scrambled off him and kept going until she was completely out of bed. Cole had turned the air-conditioning unit up to arctic last night, so it was cold, especially on all the places her body was damp. That wasn't why her nipples were still peaked, though. It was the way he was looking at her. And the fact that she still wanted him to do more than look.

She crossed her arms over her breasts, expecting him to make some smart comment. But he wasn't laughing, and the look in his eyes . . .

"I thought you'd take the chair," she said, feeling a need to defend herself.

"If I knew you were going to climb on top of me then back off, I would have."

"I was sleeping."

"So was I."

"Not when I woke up. If you were a . . ."

"What? A gentleman? If I was a gentleman, I'd have taken the chair." And Cole got out of bed, still hard and even more magnificent.

He knew she was looking, too, and she must have done a pretty poor job of hiding her feelings.

"Your choice," he said.

"It would be a mistake."

"Women," he muttered, as he walked by her. "Always screwing up sex with emotion."

He dug through Juan's parting gifts and came up with a clean pair of jeans and a T-shirt, disappearing with them into the bathroom and leaving Harmony stung. But only because he'd hit a sore spot. It had nothing to do with the fact that he could have sex with her and feel nothing beyond physical gratification. Wanting him to feel something meant she was feeling something.

That would be the biggest mistake of all.

chapter
13

WHEN COLE FINALLY VENTURED OUT OF THE BATH-room, feeling like he had some self-control, thanks to cold water and distance, Harmony was working on the laptop. Every guy had his trigger; for Cole, seeing a woman he had the hots for with her hands on his keyboard only made the hots hotter.

She glanced over her shoulder, did a double take. "You were in there so long I was expecting George Clooney to walk out."

"If you want Clooney, just close your eyes and pretend."

"Even I don't have that much imagination."

"Your loss," he said, taking the chair across the table from her. "What're you doing?"

"I thought I'd take a stab—"

The next thing Cole knew he was across the room and bending over her shoulder. He didn't hear the rest of what she said, his eyes scanning the screen, his hands flying on the keyboard as he shut it down.

"Tell me you didn't use a recognizable ID."

"No," she said. "And I, uh, b-bounced the signal through Eastern Europe."

Cole backed off, the breathiness of her voice, the quaver in it spearing straight through his panic. He went from terror to desire so fast it left him light-headed, and then he went back to terror—a different kind of terror that had to do with who and what she was, how drastically he wanted her, and what it would cost him to have her. By the time he found his emotional feet again, he could see that Harmony was every bit as rattled as he was.

So he pretended like the last five minutes had never taken place, knowing she would do the same. "No harm done," he said. "You weren't even close to the FBI firewall."

Harmony let out a soft sigh.

"So what's the plan?"

"I think we've put enough distance between us and our pursuers to stay here a day or two. Get some rest, and see what kind of progress you can make on moving the money."

Two days with her in that tiny room with one bed? There'd be no rest for him, Cole knew. Hell, she'd probably shoot him before they checked out. It was the only form of rejection she hadn't tried yet, and if she gave him even half the encouragement she had last night, it would take a gunshot wound to stop him. "I thought you were in a hurry to get to LA."

"I am, but I have to call the kidnappers again tonight."

Or maybe just her, sounding forlorn and looking a little scared and sick to her stomach. The urge to get her into bed wasn't gone completely. It never really was, but it was a hell of a lot easier to ignore when she looked like that.

"They'll be expecting progress," she continued more briskly, putting on her FBI agent face. "If they don't hear it . . ."

"I haven't broken into the bank accounts yet." He hadn't broken the system yet, for that matter.

"You're not sure you can get in without being tracked," she said.

Cole shrugged, conceding the point. "I have to make sure I'm not being tracked, and there's no way I can get in safely and accomplish what you want in the next few hours."

She mulled over that for a minute. "Can you open an off-shore account and give them access to view the balance without making withdrawals?"

"Child's play." At least it was after a decade in jail, but he decided it was better not to let her know just how many laws he'd actually broken while he was being rehabilitated from his honest former life.

"Good," she said, "let's start there."

Cole shut down her browser and pulled up another, using one of several fake IDs he'd set up while incarcerated. Even if Treacher knew he'd been hacking in prison and put geeks on it around the clock, there was no way for them to tie Joe Smith to Cole Hackett. There were literally millions of Joe Smiths in the western hemisphere. That was why he'd chosen it. As long as he stayed away from the FBI's system, they should be perfectly safe.

"So," he said while he worked, "are you really going to steal the money?"

"Yes and no." Harmony got to her feet, came around the table, and leaned over his shoulder. "I'm not going to hand over the money unless there's no other option, but we have to transfer enough to make the kidnappers think we're doing what they want us to do, and that means millions."

Cole glanced over his shoulder at her, which only made matters worse since her breasts were right in his face. "Why don't you just climb into my lap?"

"I'm sorry, is this bothering you?"

Cole lifted his eyes to hers.

"I just wanted to see what you were doing."

He still didn't respond verbally. He let his expression speak for him.

She stopped smiling and eased off a couple of steps.

It wasn't nearly far enough, but he faced forward again and took some deep, calming breaths.

"Chanting mantras?" she asked sweetly. From a safe distance.

"That's the second time today you were all over me. Do it again and there won't be enough mantras in the world."

"I wasn't 'all over you.' I didn't even touch you. I only wanted to watch. Call it a learning opportunity."

He could have given her a learning opportunity. But she had a point that couldn't be ignored. "In case I get killed?"

"Or run off."

"I'm not going anywhere," he said.

"I noticed." Harmony gave him a wide berth, circling the table to take the chair across from him again.

If he kept his eyes on the screen and slouched a little, he couldn't see more of her than the top of her head. And if he concentrated hard enough, it kept the mental pictures at bay. Now, if he could just get her to shut up.

"I never really had to hold you at gunpoint, Cole, but I always had the feeling you were holding back, waiting to see if I could pull any of this off. After Juan's that changed. Why?"

He shrugged. "I decided to make the commitment to your cause." An obvious lie, and even after saying it he agonized over telling her what was really going on. But he still couldn't quite trust her, and short of torture she wasn't going to drag Victor Treacher's name out of him. "It's getting you what you want, so just go with it. I really need to work, and I can't with you breathing down my neck."

She got to her feet and wandered over to the window, then to the bed. She was wearing the halter dress again, the one she'd had on that first day at Lewisburg. The one that left nothing to the imagination, especially as the jacket was nowhere in sight.

"Or pacing around the room," he said, adding, "or watching television," when she retrieved the TV remote and sat on the end of the bed.

"I guess I could wash some things out."

Right, like the idea of her rinsing out her panties was any less distracting than her lounging on the rumpled bedclothes with her long legs bare and just a couple of thin halter straps between him and paradise.

"I could use something to eat."

There was a split second of silence while Cole tried to

convince himself they weren't both replaying that sentence and considering the possibilities.

Then Harmony shot off the bed, and raced across the room. "You want food," she said, slipping on her shoes and taking a tiny little purse out of the duffel. "I'll get you food. What do you want? No, never mind, I'll surprise you." She all but ran out the door.

It took Cole a few minutes, and he had to open a window, get the scent of her out of the room, but after a little while he managed to lift his hands to the keyboard. The familiarity of it helped put Harmony out of his mind, enough that he was able to set up the bank account she'd asked for. And another for himself.

ONCE SHE WAS OUT OF THE ROOM, HARMONY FIGURED it would be a bad idea to go back any time soon. Cole would probably gripe about his stomach, but at least he wouldn't be looking at her like he wanted to take a bite.

Great, now she had to start all over again, forgetting the way he looked at her, and the way he felt wrapped around her, his arms and his chest and—

Fantasies were off-limits, too, especially when they were backed up with enough firsthand knowledge to make them sizzle but not enough to stop the ache. It didn't help that she was buying him underwear. Boxer briefs. Which meant she had to guess at his size, except there wasn't a whole lot of guessing involved because she'd seen him in his boxer briefs, in just about every state possible for a man, from couldn't-care-less to oh-my-god.

She tried to concentrate on his face, which was too rugged for her taste, not to mention his expression was almost always some form of barely disguised tolerance. Except when his eyes went all bedroom, smoldering from under half-closed lids. And there was his mouth, and no matter how she tried to focus on the snarky comments that usually came out of it, he'd kissed her with that mouth, and it had been a hell of a kiss because he put his whole body into it. Which led to her wondering what else he could do with that mouth and that body, and that led to her trying to find a loophole in her ground rules.

It would ease the contention between them if they slept together, she told herself. He'd stop being so touchy, and she'd be able to concentrate on Richard. Sex was the elephant in the room. Once they'd slept together, it would be out in the open and out of their systems, the elephant banished. And she'd be an idiot if she believed that. For her, having sex with Cole would send the elephant on its way. Maybe. But the elephant would still be there for Cole, and it would have a big blue *V* tattooed on its side. Her capitulation would be like putting him on a mammoth dose of Viagra. As things stood now, he was at half simmer most of the time. If she jumped in the sack with him, he wouldn't let her out for a week.

Not that she thought for one minute she was the great love of his life, or even to his taste, as women went. In fact, he'd made it more than clear that under normal circumstances she wouldn't be the kind of woman he preferred. But the man had been in jail for eight years, and she was the only game in town.

Except it wasn't a game. She had a phone date later that evening with Richard's kidnappers to remind her of that.

She put all but the immediate necessities out of her mind while she visited a moderately priced chain store and an Italian restaurant before heading back to the Hurry Inn. She expected Cole to gripe about his empty stomach, but he didn't mention the hours of absence, just thanked her for the clean clothes and dug into his dinner. He didn't lift his head until his food was gone, and even then he focused his attention on her take-out box.

"You going to finish that?" he said.

Harmony met Cole's eyes, but he was keeping his feelings to himself, like usual. She slid her chicken Caesar salad across the table. "Be my guest," she said, taking to her feet.

No point in putting off the inevitable, and she wasn't calling the kidnappers while she was sitting across the table from Cole. He didn't have a lot of respect for her or her abilities; letting him see how much these calls tore her up would hardly help his opinion.

She dialed the number on her regular cell, and the call was picked up on the first ring.

The same man answered, with the same Russian-accented arrogance. "Who is the man with you?"

"There's no man with me," she said. "Let me speak to Richard."

"I tell you before, you don't make demands."

"And I told you before, I talk to Richard or the deal is off."

There was nothing from the other end of the call, and for one sick second she thought they'd called her bluff. Then Richard came on the line. "Harmony?" he asked, sounding weaker, but not like he was in pain.

"Hello," she said, turning to the window and blinking furiously, swallowing to keep the tears out of her voice. "How are you holding up?"

"Not very well," he said, his voice going hoarse before he cleared his throat. "You're doing what they want, right?"

"Richard—"

"Just do what they tell you to, Harmony."

"But—"

"I know you won't respect me for begging, but you can't imagine . . ." His voice dropped. "What they've done to me so far is nothing. They have all these knives and torches . . . Don't be a hero, Harmony, just get them the money, and they'll let me go."

"Do you really believe that, Richard?"

"That is a dangerous question, Agent Swift," the Russian said. In the background there was a hoarse scream. "Your friend suffers because you do not follow instructions."

"Stop hurting him or I swear it's all over." She put as much steel into her voice as she could with Richard sobbing at the other end of the line. She pulled it off because she had nothing to lose. No matter what Richard believed out of desperation, the Russians wouldn't let him go if they got the money. But he wasn't going to stay alive long enough for her to rescue him if they kept up the torture.

"I will not be threatened by a woman," the kidnapper snapped.

"It's not a threat."

"So far you have accomplished nothing. Perhaps I should simply kill him."

"No, I have made progress." She flew across the room, waving a hand at Cole. That and the panic that must have been in her eyes had him tapping the keys.

"I opened an offshore account," she said to the kidnapper, giving him the account number that popped up on the screen. "There's no money in it yet, but I'm getting closer to breaking the FBI's banking system."

"This is a disappointment. You have twenty-four hours to demonstrate your ability to meet our demands. If you cannot, we send body part."

"What did you do, read the *Kidnapper's Handbook?* Chapter Four: Chop Off a Finger."

"What is this *Kidnapper's Handbook?*"

"I mean you have no imagination."

"We need none, Agent Swift. Just very sharp knives and earplugs. And it will not be a finger."

chapter
14

"I TAKE IT THEY DIDN'T APPRECIATE YOUR HUMOR."

"Russians," Harmony said. Probably she'd intended for there to be some level of derision. Hard to pull off with her voice wavering.

Her hands were shaking, too, and she paced the room with a restlessness that told him she was trying to outrun her own thoughts, not make sense of them.

"We have to get some money in that account," she said. "If we don't they said they'd start chopping off body parts."

"You're right, they don't have any imagination."

"I know you haven't had much luck breaking the FBI's system. If you're worried about getting traced, maybe we could steal the money from somewhere else."

Cole stepped into her path and caught her by the shoulders. He shook her, hard enough to have her head snapping back. Her eyes focused on him, and she seemed a little confused.

"Listen to yourself, Harm. You're talking about stealing money from innocent people. Would Richard want you to do that?"

She dropped her eyes, still trembling but coming back to herself. "He was begging."

"I'm sorry, but you aren't going to drain random bank accounts."

"There are some people out there who wouldn't miss a few million dollars. Movie stars, oil companies, the Russian mafia. That would be poetic justice."

Yeah, poetic justice, Cole thought. And he needed another big-time enemy like he needed another hole in the head. "So the kidnappers win, right?"

"What?"

"You're talking about paying them. One phone call—"

"Two. And you didn't hear him—"

"You're right, and I'm sure he was suffering, but that means he was alive. We both know the minute you pay the ransom he's dead."

Harmony took a deep breath, nodded once.

"Then we stick with the original plan. The whole point of raiding the frozen accounts is that the theft won't be noticed right away. It buys you enough time to find Richard and get him out. We just have to be careful. We can't help him if we're caught."

She met his eyes again, and then she stepped forward, lifting her face to his, her eyes fluttering closed. Cole took a step back. Clearly it surprised her as much as it did him.

"I thought—"

"If you were thinking, you wouldn't have—"

"You're right." She went to the window, looking between the edges of the drapes without opening them. Night was falling, and the window looked out over the parking lot, so there wasn't a lot to see.

"Do you have a boyfriend?" Cole asked her out of the blue.

"No. Do you?" She turned to face him, but she stayed on the other side of the room.

"I had a few offers."

Harmony gave a slight laugh. "So did I, and they were probably the same kind you got." She leaned back against the wall between the window and door. "Dating in Washington,

D.C., is like a social prize fight. Only the most ambitious men go to work there, and they approach finding a wife like it's a political campaign. It's all about the win, and marriage is less about romance than it is about finding a lifelong campaign contributor—and I don't mean money, that's easy to come by. Who you know is who you are.

"I'm not connected, so unless I call myself Iowa and assign myself some electoral votes, I'll never be more than one-night stand material."

"Politicians are stupid."

She waved that off. "It's not like I want to get married. But it would be nice to have a relationship that lasts longer than the salad, which is generally when my date discovers I don't do casual sex and reads the latest of the text messages he incessantly gets. The next thing I know there's some emergency on Capitol Hill, and democracy as we know it will be in great danger unless my date races to the rescue. And I get stuck with the check."

"Great leftovers," Cole said.

"It's still dinner for one. And that was more information than you wanted."

"I was trying to get your mind off the phone call."

She pushed away from the wall and crossed the room, stopping in front of him. "There are better distractions."

This time she didn't kiss him. And just in case he didn't get her meaning, she lifted his hand and sucked his thumb into her mouth, lapping her tongue across his skin and giving it a little nip before she slid her mouth away. She kept her eyes on his the entire time.

"Tell me to stop," she said.

"You're joking, right?"

"We both know this is a mistake. If we do this, it's going to complicate everything."

"Yep." And he could see the war raging in her. She was right about sex complicating everything, but wild horses, driven expertly by Roman charioteers, couldn't have dragged him away from her again. He framed her face, threading his fingers back into the wealth of her blond hair, and kissed her.

He felt her surrender, knew the second when she abandoned the high moral ground, ceding what was smart for what she wanted. And what she wanted, thank god, was him.

Her body went soft against his, burning him up in all the places they were touching, moving restlessly as he dropped his mouth to her neck, down the vee of her top to tease along the inner curves of her breasts. Her head dropped back. She moaned softly, and the breathless, pleading sound slammed through him, shooting heat and need to his groin until he was so painfully hard it was all he could do not to throw her down and take.

It helped that she gave, or rather demanded, saying, "Now," as she stepped back and flipped the button at the back of her halter. She did a little shimmy with her shoulders, and as the dress whispered down her body, she slid her fingers beneath the top of her bikini panties and slid them off with a wriggle of her hips.

Cole had his shirt off before her clothing hit the floor. He shucked his pants, too, then retrieved them, grabbing something out of his back pocket before he dropped them again.

Harmony looked at the condom in his hand, one eyebrow inching up.

"I believe in always being prepared," he said.

"I don't think the Boy Scouts have a badge for this."

"There's one too many badges around here already."

For a minute he thought he'd said the wrong thing, and then she was in his arms and they were on the bed, her mouth on his, her hands rushing over his skin.

She tried to push him onto his back. He wouldn't go. She got to be in charge everywhere else, he'd be damned if he let her tell him what to do in bed.

He rose over her, his mouth on her breast, working a hard nipple between tongue and teeth. She arched up, every tug drawing a shudder or moan from her, and when he slipped his hand between her thighs, slipped two fingers inside her, she came, hands fisted in the bedclothes, her body convulsing around his fingers, once twice, as she sighed his name. He fumbled on the condom, lifted her knees, slid his hands under her backside, and entered her before the last echo of her orgasm, feeling the fading ripple of it as she sheathed him in heat.

Her eyes opened and met his, still dazed with pleasure, her mouth curving up as she ran her palms up her belly, over her breasts, keeping her eyes on his as she began to move, meeting him stroke for stroke. There was only her, the hunger and frustration of the last eight years and the previous three days building and building, all but blinding him so he could only feel, the heat and friction of her body around his, her hands skimming along his skin, the way her body was tightening around his.

Her breath rushed out on the little moan that seemed to be a trigger for him. He lifted her higher, drove into her one last time, locking himself there as her body pulsed and shuddered, and his skin felt so tight he was afraid he'd explode. And then he did, the dam inside him burst, all the pressure and heat and pleasure from a million nerve endings rushing down from his head and up from his toes, focusing into the climax, making it so intense he felt incandescent with it, years of darkness turned to light. He held onto it as long as he could, held onto her, until all his strength was drained away and he collapsed next to her and just concentrated on breathing for a few minutes.

The bed shook, and he cracked open an eye to find Harmony leaning up on one elbow next to him, still a little out of breath, her skin sheened with sweat and her mouth curved up in pleasure.

In a lifetime of fantasies he could never have imagined this moment. Or her.

"That did the job," she said, and he knew the moment was over. Her mind was back on the case, and the phone call.

"I feel so used," he said with sarcasm he didn't come close to feeling because that was the problem he'd had before, he realized. It wasn't about her making the first move; it was her motivation that bothered him. He didn't make an effort to figure out why. *Why* was dangerous territory for a man whose future was so uncertain.

"I think we used each other," she said. "It was inevitable

that we'd get horizontal together at some point, given our mutual attraction. And I wasn't the one with the condom," she pointed out.

"Juan asked me if I needed anything," Cole said with a shrug.

"And that was your first thought?"

"I was in jail for eight years. My first thought is always about sex."

"Now who's feeling used?" She started to get up.

Cole put his hand on her stomach and she stopped, meeting his eyes. "It doesn't have to get in the way," he said.

"It won't."

WAKING UP IN COLE'S ARMS THE NEXT MORNING WAS an entirely different experience than it had been the first time. He was wrapped around her, just like yesterday, and she wanted him with every throbbing nerve ending, just like yesterday, but this time she didn't shove him away. There was too much mental activity for her physical urges to overpower.

She didn't bother listing all the reasons why having sex with Cole was wrong. That ship had sailed. How it would affect the case, that was the real question. And the answer was it wouldn't. To Cole she was only a way to make up for the years of forced celibacy. To her he was a way to free Richard without giving away the farm. And if sleeping with him felt like it might be about more than sex, she'd keep that to herself.

Besides, he was hiding something from her.

She slipped out of his arms, out of the bed, pulling on her T-shirt and panties. She had to have the distance even if it left her feeling cold and alone again. She'd needed his comfort last night, but she couldn't allow it to become a habit to turn to him when her own strength wasn't enough.

"Setting boundaries?" Cole said from the bed, his voice rough with sleep and even more tempting. "For my benefit or yours?"

Now she looked over her shoulder at him, smiling slightly. "I thought my job description was the only boundary you needed."

He shrugged. "As long as you don't start thinking about fairy tales, we'll both be fine."

"I'm FBI and you're . . . you. Not exactly Cinderella, Prince Charming, and happy endings."

"You don't think I'm Prince Charming?" Cole slapped a hand over his heart. "I'm wounded."

"Just as long as you can type."

"I think I can manage it." He headed for the bathroom, turning back halfway there. "I, uh, could use somebody to wash my back."

"I thought you liked showering alone."

"I like showering alone when my choice is showering with a hundred other guys."

"Well, just consider me one of the guys."

He gave her a leisurely once-over, his smile coming slow and wide as he did. "Too late for that."

Too late was right. Almost. If he kept looking at her with that combination of heat and appreciation, she'd shuck her determination and her clothes, and join him in the shower. He didn't press her, though, and once he disappeared into the bathroom, it was a lot easier to stick to her guns. Sure, hearing the water run, thinking of all that naked, muscular flesh under the hot spray, remembering what he felt like against her, in her, was almost more than she could resist.

Once he walked away, though, it was a lot harder for her to make the first move. True, she'd done just that last night, but she didn't have an excuse this time. If she went into that bathroom she wouldn't be looking for simple human comfort or a distraction from the horror of Richard's torture. She'd be going in there because she wanted Cole, and Prince Charming notwithstanding, there'd be more to it than just satisfying a physical need. And he'd know it. That was what really held her back.

He came out, shirtless, his jeans unzipped and unbuttoned. She barely spared him a glance, ducking into the bathroom and showering in record time, leaving her hair wet and sleek. It wasn't much as disguises went, but if someone was looking for a blonde with shoulder-length curls she wouldn't immediately come to mind.

She put on clean underwear, a pair of jeans, and a soft cotton sweater she'd bought for herself the day before, and slipped out of the bathroom. Cole was already at the computer, lost in his own little world, and since it was almost noon, Harmony left him there and walked to the nearest fast-food restaurant. She brought back two salads and two iced teas, unsweetened.

"You consider that a meal?" Cole said when she handed him his half of lunch. "I'm working hard here. Not to mention last night. I need to keep up my energy."

"I did just as much of the work as you did last night."

Cole grinned, acknowledging the truth of it with a slight waggle of his head.

"You're sitting on your butt in front of a computer," Harmony pointed out. "If you keep eating like you have been, you're going to start looking like your mug shot again—which is probably appropriate since you're breaking the law."

He dug into his salad, made a face. "I never broke the law before I went to jail."

"Except for that one time."

His head lifted, his eyes going hot on hers. "I didn't know I was breaking it."

"Right, you were pudgy and naïve."

Cole went silent, not all that unusual for him, except this time there was a dimension to the silence that made her replay her comment and regret making it. Cole wasn't the kind of person who did what he'd done, at least not for money. He didn't have a devious bone in his body. What he did have was a moral streak a mile long. "I'm sorry," she said. "What really happened?"

"It doesn't matter."

Which, along with the fact that he'd shoved the salad away and gone back to work, was code for *leave me alone*. She did, but she knew it was important to him. And she knew it was connected to the FBI. He was usually a pretty even-keeled man, but every time he tried to break into the Bureau's system he became angry and frustrated.

It didn't take him long to prove her point. Less than ten

minutes later he lurched to his feet, shoved both hands back through his hair, and paced across the room, stewing.

Harmony looked at the screen but it was all a bunch of *Matrix*-type gobbledygook, and Keanu Reeves wasn't handy to interpret for her. "What's the problem?" she asked Cole.

He held up a hand and kept pacing. She could almost see him thinking, his brain working at warp speed before the proverbial lightbulb popped on over his head. He raced back to the table and plopped down, almost missing the chair but not bothering to adjust his seat as his fingers flew over the keyboard. His eyes were glued to the screen, intense, the re-flected glow making him look fanatical—and a little scary when his mouth curved into a Grinch-comtemplating-Whoville grin.

"What are you doing?" she asked, putting her hand on his shoulder when her voice wasn't enough to get his attention.

He punched the ENTER key and sat back. "I'm going after your money," he said.

"Should I pack?"

"Nope. Your IT friends at the Bureau won't be expecting me to hit the banking system. And, anyway, I made sure they'll be too busy to notice I slipped in and diverted four million dollars."

Her heart jumped, partly because she'd just taken an irre-vocable step, partly because it was a step closer to saving Richard. And then reality crashed her party. One minute he was seething, the next he was so elated she could feel the ex-citement coming off him in waves. Either he was manic or . . . "Wait a minute, what did you do?"

"I infected them with a little virus," he said in a singsong, *take that* tone of voice.

Harmony ripped his hands off the keyboard, knowing it was already too late. "Jesus, Cole," she breathed, "how . . . what . . ."

"Relax, all I did was scramble some of their files for a lit-tle while." He shook her off and picked up his tea, taking a long pull from the straw. He was trying to look like he didn't care, but the Grinch was gone, and in its place was a sulky little boy who'd played a trick and wasn't getting the appreciation he'd expected. "I put some dancing cartoon characters on their screens."

"Cartoon characters," Harmony echoed faintly, sitting down hard on the other chair and trying to wrap her brain around it. Dancing cartoons or not, she was responsible for putting the FBI out of commission for god knew how long. Thanks to the lunatic she'd unleashed on them.

"Cinderella and Prince Charming," the lunatic said, still not getting it. "I thought you'd appreciate my choice." When she didn't respond, Cole snapped his finger in front of her face. "Hello. It's supposed to be funny."

"Funny? You think the FBI is going to find this funny just because it's cartoon characters and not something obviously destructive? You're insane. Or you have a death wish."

"Did you miss the part about the four million dollars?"

"No." She took a deep breath, and thought, okay, so it hadn't exactly happened the way she wanted. There was four million dollars in the kidnappers' account. Now all they had to do was deal with the fallout of Cole's virus.

She got to her feet and started throwing her things in the duffel.

"What are you doing?"

"We have to get out of here."

He shook his head, looking smug. "It'll take them a few hours to get the system back up, and even then they won't be able to track the source."

She put both hands flat on the tabletop and just concentrated on breathing for a minute. "You're sure?"

"Like I said, they won't be expecting a hit on the frozen bank accounts, and even if they do, it'll look like the money is still there because they'll have to reload their last system dump, which was probably midnight."

"It's not like they don't monitor those accounts. They'll figure it out before long."

"Doesn't matter. Even when they realize the money is gone, they won't be able to track me. I bounced the signal all over the known universe. It'll take them days to find this motel, and we'll be long gone by then."

Harmony resumed her packing. "I still think we should go."

Cole looked like she'd just kicked his favorite dog.

"It's not that I don't trust your abilities. I broke you out of jail for exactly this reason, remember? It's just that we've been here for two days, and I guess I'm feeling like we need to move on. Just to be safe."

"Okay," he said, looking somewhat mollified. "I'm with you. As long as we stop somewhere for real food."

chapter 15

SINCE IT WAS GETTING ON TOWARD MIDNIGHT AND
they were in farmland, where towns rolled up their sidewalks
at nightfall, real food turned out to be a bar off I-44, a good
fifty miles out of St. Louis, headed southwest toward Springfield, Missouri. It was a typical small-town watering hole.
Lots of dark paneling, a bar that ran the length of the place,
fronted by stools, and a scattering of small tables along the
opposite wall. The bartender was clearly the owner. He knew
everyone in there, and Harmony and Cole stuck out like
Twinkies at a fat farm. But after a curious once-over by the
locals, they were left alone.

Harmony had called the head Russian and reported four
million dollars' worth of progress. The head Russian had
checked the account and been quietly pleased. He hadn't said
as much, but there'd been no screaming or sobbing or threats
of lopping off body parts, and he'd given her two days to show
more progress.

She'd show him progress, all right. If sheer determination
was any guarantee, Richard would be free in two days—
hopefully before she went broke from feeding Cole.

"I'll have a beer, whatever's on tap," he said when the waitress appeared at their table, "and two cheeseburgers. How about you?" he asked Harmony before the waitress could jump to conclusions and walk away.

"Not the heart attack special." She plucked the small, plastic-coated menu out from behind the salt and pepper shakers. Her choices were severely limited, and they all included beef and buns. Cheese was optional, and why not, she figured? "Cheeseburger and a Diet Coke."

The waitress took herself off having written nothing down and spoken not a word. But she'd taken a really good look at Cole. She appeared immediately with their drinks, and less than five minutes later with their food in paper-lined plastic baskets. Cole attacked his meal with the same kind of focus he approached the computer. Harmony didn't attempt to sidetrack him with conversation.

They were at the bar paying their tab when a Special Alert came on the television over the bar. Since it preempted football, the place erupted in catcalls and boos.

And then Cole's eight-year-old mug shot flashed across the screen and the ruckus cut off like somebody had clapped duct tape over everyone's mouth simultaneously. All eyes were glued to the TV, some of them narrowed in a puzzled attempt to place that face, as the voice-over talked about Cole. *Terrorist* was the first thing they called him. After that it was hard to hear much. She caught the terms *armed and dangerous* and *escaped felon* over the din of voices, but she was probably the only one who heard the part about Cole hacking into the FBI's computer system—*allegedly*—and setting loose a virus.

Then she saw her own face, taken straight from her FBI identification badge. Nobody had trouble recognizing her. The word *reward* was just the catalyst that got them moving.

Several people pulled out cell phones. Cole raced for the door, and Harmony was right on his heels, getting a flash of Veda and Ron, backdropped by their RV, telling a roving reporter how they'd been in fear for their lives.

They hit the car, Cole taking the passenger seat. "Did you see—"

"Yeah," Harmony said over the sound of the engine roaring to life when she sparked the ignition wires together. She straightened and put the car in gear, backing out of the parking space. "The guys in the bar are already calling the cops."

"I don't think you have to worry about the guys *in* the bar."

She swung around and looked past him, out the passenger side window. A half-dozen locals were piling out of the bar and heading for their vehicles, all of which said 4WD on them somewhere. "Damn!" She stomped on the gas and the Taurus sent up a plume of gravel before the tires caught and it shot forward, the back end fishtailing until they hit the paved road.

"We'll never outrun them in this," Cole said.

"I didn't pick it for speed." She'd picked it for anonymity, which was no help now that they'd been outed on national television.

"We don't know the roads around here, either."

"We don't have to." She hit the ramp to the interstate, narrowed down because of repaving. She flew across the two open lanes without using her signal, then put as much distance between them and the bar as she possibly could. Since it was after eleven at night, there wasn't much traffic and what there was had eighteen wheels.

"With any luck we can get lost in all these trucks," she said, tucking the Taurus between a car hauler and frozen food truck pacing each other in the right lane.

"You mean the ones with the CB radios?"

"Don't you ever have good news?"

"You're optimistic enough for any five normal people," Cole said. "Somebody has to represent reality."

"Choosing to think positively isn't ignoring reality. Sometimes you get good news."

"The good news is I won't survive to see the inside of a jail cell again."

"The hell you won't. There's no way I'm letting you die before you tell me what's really going on."

"I thought you were going to keep me out of jail."

Harmony glanced over at him. "You're changing the subject. There's no way the FBI would go on television and admit you hacked into their system if they didn't want you bad."

That shut him up. The pickup truck that roared up next to them kept her from gloating. She hit the gas, cutting the wheel sharply to the left in a feint that made the pickup driver slam on his brakes automatically, and gave her time to cut over into the left lane in front of him. The Taurus's engine sounded game, and the speedometer inched up, but not nearly fast enough to keep the rear window from filling up with an F-150 grille.

"Shit," Cole muttered, bracing himself between the door and the console.

The F-150 nudged their back bumper, its engine roaring as it accelerated, pushing them toward the rear of the semi in front of them. There was another truck in the right lane. To their left were orange construction barrels, and beyond them the remaining lanes of the highway were nothing more than an open pit corrugated with reinforcement steel, waiting for concrete to be poured in. Harmony let the car drift toward the barrels. Cole grabbed the steering wheel, trying pull it back to the center of the lane. Harmony brought her fist down on his wrist as hard as she could.

"Ouch. Jesus, Harm!"

"I can't fight you and him at the same time," she shouted back.

"But—"

"If you touch the steering wheel again, I'll shoot you." The threat might have had real teeth if her gun hadn't been in her duffel, which was in the backseat. But Cole appeared to have gotten the message.

The pickup hit them again. Still hugging the barrels, Harmony let it drive them toward the semi, waiting, waiting, her eyes glued to the truck ahead, and when the Taurus's hood nosed beneath it, she swerved right, almost into the semi beside them. The pickup driver shot ahead, and being an amateur, he jerked his steering wheel just slightly to the left to avoid hitting the truck. He tried to correct but it was too late, his left front tire slipped over the edge of the pavement and towed the vehicle into the pit. Rebar came flying up and then they were past.

"I hope he's okay," Cole said.

"If he's not, it's his own fault," Harmony shot back, her eyes on the rearview mirror. "His friend certainly hasn't learned anything."

Cole twisted around to look over his shoulder. "Jesus," he said, "what is this guy thinking?"

"He's thinking that I'm female and blond and I probably can't drive a vacuum cleaner in a straight line. People constantly underestimate me."

"I've noticed," Cole muttered.

"Noticed? You've done it yourself."

"I won't again."

"Let's hope you get the opportunity to prove you mean that."

The semi in the right lane had dropped back, probably wanting to get out of the danger zone. Harmony pushed the Taurus up to top speed again and went around the truck in front of her, cutting in and out of traffic as fast as she could. The second pickup stayed right on her bumper.

"Shit," Cole said again. "He's on the radio."

Harmony looked over at him, both of them coming to the same sick conclusion just as two big rigs lined up on the road ahead. A pig hauler with an open top and slatted sides took the left lane, a tanker pacing it on the right.

"At least the tanker isn't carrying anything explosive," Harmony said. Just cooking oil, judging by the name-brand logo on the back.

"It'll still hurt when we smash into it."

Sure enough, the two big trucks seemed to be answering the pickup driver's call to aid. They lined up together, as the pickup inched up close behind the Taurus just like the first truck had.

"Apparently he did learn something," she said, because the pickup driver stayed on their rear bumper, keeping his truck at a speed she couldn't outrun. A big SUV roared up beside the pickup, the two of them herding her across the white line and forcing her between the two semis. Then all four trucks began to slow, leaving them trapped, nowhere to go.

"They're trying to hold us until the police can get here."

"The hell they are," Harmony said. She floored it, sending the Taurus shooting ahead.

The semi drivers fought back, nosing the cabs of their trucks together. They'd expect her to stop. Harmony poured on more speed. The Taurus shuddered, smoke beginning to seep out from under the hood. But it gave her a couple more miles per hour. Out of the corner of her eye she saw Cole leaning back in his seat, his right leg straight, like he was pushing an imaginary brake pedal. She kept the speedometer pegged and her hands steady on the wheel, and if there was a prayer running through her mind, who could blame her as they rocketed toward a vee of steel and rubber with an increasingly small opening.

She hit that seemingly tiny gap, steel shrieking as both sides of the Taurus scraped against the semis' cabs. They had enough speed for the car to make it past the front doors, before she felt it jerk, the rear quarter panels hanging up. For a minute she didn't think they were going to make it through. Then the Taurus shuddered, there was the sound of steel screaming as it tore, and they were free.

The man driving the pig hauler reacted with lightning speed, Harmony saw in the rearview mirror, hand-over-handing the wheel to steer the truck straight again. The tanker driver didn't have the same skill, or reflexes. The sudden absence of the Taurus caught him off guard, causing him to jackknife the truck.

Air brakes shrieked. The pig hauler tried to turn but there wasn't enough time. It hit the tanker, sending it over onto its side. The last thing she saw was pigs being catapulted from the hauler and landing on the highway, still moving, thankfully, slipping and sliding in the fountain of cooking oil spilling out of the top of the tanker. If there were any other guys chasing them from the bar, they were behind the brand-new roadblock.

"I hope that thing doesn't catch on fire," she said, bringing the car down to the speed limit. "The whole state will smell like a pig roast."

Cole didn't say anything, and when she glanced over at him, he looked kind of green. "Do you remember when you asked me to trust you," he said, "the day you broke me out of jail?"

"You told me 'when pigs fly.' "

"They didn't have wings," Cole said, "but I'm pretty sure a couple of them were airborne, at least briefly, and if they weren't, I'm still willing to take that as a sign."

Harmony didn't even try to hide her grin. "I wonder if hell froze over, too."

HARMONY STAYED ON THE INTERSTATE UNTIL THEY HIT an exit that wasn't circled by gas stations, party stores, and chain restaurants. By then the cloud of smoke billowing out from under the Taurus's hood was nearly too thick to see through. She pulled the car as far off the road as she could, trusting the darkness to hide them.

"Spill," she said, turning to Cole, her face lit faintly by the dashboard lights. "Any more surprises like the last one, and we're not going to make it."

"Give me a minute to enjoy the fact that we survived this one, and the air bags didn't even go off."

"We're not out of the woods yet. The police are going to be looking for us. We can't stay here very long."

Just long enough for her to get an explanation. Cole knew she was right. He had to take a risk and come clean, but he gave it a minute anyway.

"Let's start with what you were thinking when you sent that virus," she prompted.

"I wasn't," he admitted. "At least not clearly."

"No kidding." Harmony settled back in her seat, facing the darkness through the windshield. "Every time you try to get into the FBI's system, you get angry. If you'd been thinking instead of striking back—"

"I know."

"We're supposed to be a team," Harmony said. "I realize

it didn't exactly start out that way, but you just got done telling me you trust me. So trust me."

Saying it and doing it, Cole thought, were two different things. But she was right. The time had come for honesty. Her life was on the line, too, the more so because of one bad decision on his part.

"My freshman year in college I roomed with a kid by the name of Scott Treacher, and we became friends."

Harmony said something that sounded like "fuck" under her breath. He'd been expecting that kind of reaction, but hearing her say it felt like Tinkerbell had flown up his pants and done something obscene. It also gave him an idea how she was going to react to the rest of the story. Not that he blamed her.

"Scotty and I got an apartment off campus, and we lived together the whole six years I was getting my undergrad and master's degrees," he said. "Kid was a total screwup. It took him all that time just to get his bachelor's degree, but I helped him get through it, and he got me a face-to-face with his father."

"Victor Treacher, head of Systems Security for the FBI." Harmony sounded like she wasn't sure she wanted to hear the rest of the story.

Cole told her anyway. "Not back then," he said. "Treacher's career had stalled. Computer technology changes at light speed, and guys like me, coming right out of school, have the edge over anyone who's been in the industry awhile. I spent every second of my spare time working on a new kind of software security system. By the time I was starting on my doctorate, I had it pretty much perfected. Victor was tired of watching younger men get promoted over him. He saw my system as an opportunity to move to the top of the ladder."

"So he stole it from you."

"Right after he got me to hack into the FBI's computer system in order to prove to them they needed an upgrade.

"Scotty got into trouble right about that time," Cole continued, "big trouble. Drugs. His old man wouldn't help him out of the jam unless he stole all my paper documents. Then he copied my hard drive and wiped it so I had no proof I'd created the system." Cole gave a slight, humorless laugh. "It never occurred to me to hide anything from a guy who'd been my friend for so long."

"That's because you don't have a devious mind. Or a cynical one. Not back then, at least."

"Yeah," he said, feeling demoralized, victimized, and pissed off all over again. "Victor won himself a lot of kudos by 'catching' me. I went to jail, and once I was safely out of the way, he sold my system to the Bureau, with Scotty as the author."

"Ouch."

An understatement if he'd ever heard one. Victor couldn't claim to have written the system because anything he'd created as a federal employee would automatically be the property of his employers. So Scott Treacher had gotten a big payday, Victor had gotten a big promotion, and Cole had gotten the shaft.

"I'd be willing to bet Treacher's been getting regular updates on you," Harmony said. "He probably knew every time you had a visitor—heck, he probably knew what you had for dinner every night. And he knew it the minute you checked out of Lewisburg."

"I'll bet he sent those agents day one."

"Yeah, and they were the same two guys on that boat in Cleveland. My guess is they're a couple of secret agent wannabes who work for Victor. That explains why they're so inept. It also allows Victor to keep their activities off the books, which is why Mike doesn't know anything about it. So what happened tonight?"

Another subject Cole didn't want to revisit. He took a couple of deep breaths, vowing never again to give Harmony grief for doing it, and plowed on. "You're right about Treacher. I underestimated his paranoia. The first time I tested the FBI's firewall—*my* firewall—he probably knew it was me. When I got into the system at Juan's, he kicked me out right away. Today I got in, no problem, and I didn't get kicked out. I figured it was a trap."

"You were right. And it ticked you off so you wrote that virus, and while they were dealing with fairy tales you hijacked four million dollars. Not a bad strategy, except for the part where Treacher plastered our faces on every television and website in the country."

Cole scrubbed a hand over his buzzed scalp. "I didn't expect him to do that. Putting me on the nation's radar as a federal fugitive might help get me caught, but it also gives me a pretty big soapbox."

"Not if you're dead."

"Shit. I didn't think of that."

"That's what I'm around for," Harmony snapped.

"You? Mary Sunshine?"

"There's a difference between recognizing trouble and borrowing it. Just because I'm an optimist, it doesn't mean I can't understand the workings of a criminal mind."

She had a point there.

"If you'd told me you were taking on someone like Victor Treacher, I might have been able to anticipate this kind of situation and avoid it. What else haven't you told me?"

"That's everything."

She shook her head, and there was nothing cute about her expression. She didn't look like Barbie or Jessica Rabbit or any of the other harmless sexpot characters he'd likened her to. She was furious, and for once he was glad she chanted mantras to calm herself down. Otherwise she'd probably be shooting him.

"At least we know what we're up against now," Cole said into the silence. He'd been hopping to defuse her anger, but the look she shot him said he'd missed the mark. "You can call your guy now, right? Get them pulled."

"They're not the problem anymore."

No, he'd been an ass and let loose that virus, pushing Treacher into going public. By now everybody and their brother was looking for them, probably with guns drawn, and there was a pretty damn good chance they wouldn't be talking to anyone ever again. "So I signed our death warrant with that virus."

Harmony didn't say anything, the tension in the car growing thicker as the seconds ticked by, until Cole couldn't take it any more.

"Harm—"

"We have to split up."

Cole closed his eyes and just let that sink in. He'd known from day one how she would feel going up against a high-ranking FBI official. "I guess I should be glad you're not taking me back to jail."

"What?" She turned to him, puzzlement overlaying the anger still on her face. And then it sank in. "Our deal still holds. But it's nice to know how little faith you have in me."

"Taking on Treacher is a career ender for you."

"Yeah, well"—she looked away—"I think it's too late to worry about that. They're looking for a man and a woman together, and I'm a lot more recognizable than you are. That's why we have to separate. Just for a little while. We have to get as far away from the last confirmed sighting as we can, and the best way to do that is separately."

Cole digested the implications of her decision, and what it said about their partnership. "How do you know I won't take off and leave you hanging?"

"Because Treacher won't stop until you're dead, Cole. I'm the only hope you have."

"What makes you think he won't kill you?"

She shrugged. "Arrogance. He's confident the Bureau will sweep this under the rug."

"He's probably right, but as far as he knows, you're not working for the FBI on this one."

"He has no way of knowing if that's true. Mike could have made it appear I was out in the cold for a reason. Treacher can't risk taking me out without there being a lot of uncomfortable questions asked."

"So how does that help me?"

"Mike will back me up," she said with absolute conviction. "And I believe you, which means he won't just write you off as a crackpot with an axe to grind."

"Great, I can see how far I get with a murderous FBI computer geek on my ass, or I can trust an FBI agent and her FBI handler to take my side when the shit hits the fan."

"There's really no choice, is there?"

Cole heaved a sigh. "I'll meet you in Tulsa."

"Another ex-con friend?"

Cole didn't say anything.

"Don't you think Treacher will have agents on anyone you knew in Lewisburg?"

"Fine, no friends."

She handed him some cash and the prepaid untraceable cell phone. "My number's programmed in, and I-44 will take you straight to Tulsa. Call me when you get there. And be careful. The instructions will be shoot to kill."

Unnecessary advice, Cole might have said. If there'd been any point. He opened the door, then thought better of it, leaning across and taking her mouth. He let the heat and sweetness take him, just as she did, sinking in for a few rushing heartbeats.

She didn't push him away, but as soon as he pulled back, she said, "What was that for?"

"I don't want you to forget me."

She exited the driver's side and looked at him over the roof. "I'm pretty sure that would be impossible, even without the kiss." She started to walk away, then turned back. "But it was a nice touch."

chapter
16

COLE FOUND HIMSELF ON THE OFF-RAMP OF I-44 alone in the dark. Tulsa was a bit under four hundred miles from St. Louis, as the crow flies, and a crow could probably make it in a few hours. It would take a man on foot a lot longer.

He had a phone, a wad of money, and absolutely no game plan except to take the quickest route. Stay on I-44, Harm had said, probably because she knew he didn't have the kind of skills it took to be on the run for long. It didn't bother him. She was right. He didn't carry a gun, he couldn't hot-wire a car, and he didn't have the first clue about how to blend in and fly under the radar. If he hadn't learned to think like a criminal after eight years under the tutelage of some of the best in the world, it was probably a lost cause.

The only thing he had going for him was unrecognizability. His mug shot was eight years old; he'd changed so much since it had been taken he was basically a different person now. But he was still a person on foot. He took out the untraceable cell and called information. The nearest bus station turned out to be in St. Louis, and heading back the way he'd just come, where people had already connected him to the guy on TV and the cops were probably all on alert, didn't seem a very bright idea. The next bus station was in Springfield, over two hundred miles away.

Hopefully he'd find some sort of transportation before then, but at the moment he was surrounded by a whole lot of nothing. Walking along the highway, where he'd be at the mercy of every dozing driver and backlighted by every car that went by, including state police cruisers, was out of the question. Cole opted for the service drive, keeping just off the shoulder. He could still see the road, but the dark hid him pretty well, and if anyone did see him and got nosy, he could disappear into the wilderness.

Two hours later, he was willing to try his hand at car theft. Or bicycle theft. Or horse theft. Any mode of transportation besides his own two feet would be a welcome relief. He could just imagine Harmony in some nice, warm car, gliding comfortably through the night, while he was cold and tired and pissed off, and wondering if it could get any worse. And then it began to rain. Torrentially. A gully-washing, cats-and-dogs, Noah's Ark downpour that had him scrambling for high ground. That part of Missouri had clearly had a lot of rain over the last couple of weeks; there was standing water everywhere, and the dirt and gravel shoulder was striped with runoff channels. Even as he made that observation, the ground beneath his feet washed away, dumping him into the overflowing ditch, along with a ton of mud.

Cole came up, sputtering for air and clawing the phone, his only lifeline to Harmony, out of his pocket. He almost fumbled it because his hands were slick and clumsy with the cold, but he managed to hang onto it and flip it open. Water ran out. The display blinked half-heartedly a couple times, then went dark.

"Shit." He dragged himself back up the embankment and stood there in the pouring rain, not daring to think things like *It can't get any worse*, or *At least it would be warm and dry in the back of a police cruiser*. But when a car pulled over just ahead of him, he didn't think twice, or factor in how bad his luck had turned since Harmony had deserted him. If Victor Treacher had been driving that car, with his goon squad in the back, Cole wouldn't have hesitated.

What he found instead of FBI agents was cats. A car full of cats, piloted by a woman who looked like she belonged in a car full of cats. She was old and wrinkled and feisty-looking. Not to mention ornery.

"You just going to stand there," she yelled at him through the open passenger-side window. "The upholstery is getting all wet."

The upholstery looked like worse things had happened to it. "It's going to get a lot wetter if I sit on it. I'm kind of dirty, too. I fell in the ditch."

"That's why I pulled over. I don't normally pick up strange men, but I felt kind of sorry for you. I'm a sucker for strays."

"I can see that," Cole said, but he still wasn't sure. It didn't seem like an old woman should give him pause, but an old woman with a car full of cats struck him as crazy, and he'd had enough crazy in his life lately.

"No offense," she yelled, "but it ain't like a fella in your sort of predicament can be picky."

She had a point. He pulled open the door and angled himself into the passenger seat, the window motoring up as he did, so that when he pulled the door shut he felt trapped.

"I'm Maizie," the old woman said.

Cole took her hand and shook it, saying, "Pleased to meet you, Maizie."

"What, you don't have a name?"

He smiled faintly. "You can call me Dick."

"Hmmmm." Maizie sounded unconvinced, but she didn't comment. "What are you doing wandering around in the middle of nowhere in the dead of the night in a thunderstorm, Dick?"

"My car broke down on the highway," Cole said, shaking his head a little over how easily the lie came. He'd spent eight years with criminals and nothing had rubbed off on him. Less than a week with Harmony Swift and he was lying like a pro. "I figured it would be a bad idea to walk along the highway, but that was before the shoulder of the service drive gave way and dumped me into the ditch."

"Sounds like you had a disagreement with god," Maizie observed.

"It's been that kind of night." Hell, it had been that kind of decade. "I'm sorry about getting your seat all wet."

"Can't hurt this car none."

She had a point. The rest of the interior of the ancient Chrysler wasn't any cleaner than the passenger seat. It smelled, too. In all fairness he probably didn't remind anyone of a flower garden, but he'd had a rough night. And as long as he didn't resemble a scratching pole or a litter box, he was happy. There had to be twenty cats in the backseat, and when he ventured a look over his shoulder, he saw that they were all staring at him, not moving or making noise or even blinking, just their yellow eyes shining in the darkness.

"Not a cat person, huh?"

"Nope," Cole said, keeping his eyes on the cats and trying not to be freaked out. Not that he really had anything against cats, but as best friends went they left something to be desired, especially if you were a kid. They didn't fetch or catch a Frisbee or greet you at the door after school like you were the best thing that had ever happened to them. Cats were independent. And sort of sneaky.

"You strike me as the kind of person who favors dogs," Maizie said.

"I was until recently."

"Nasty, slobbery things."

It was more their teeth Cole didn't like. Hounds especially. "So, where you headed?" he asked Maizie.

"Home, but I won't take you there."

"I'm surprised you picked me up at all."

"My babies won't let anything happen to me."

Cole turned his head and got a face full of cat because one of her "babies" had hopped onto the back of his seat. He sneezed. Twice. It hissed at him both times.

"Sounds like you're mildly allergic," Maizie said, "and I'm going a bit beyond Springfield. You sure you want to tag along?"

Cole considered his chances of finding another ride. Springfield was a bit over halfway to Tulsa, so about two hundred miles. Even at old lady speed it shouldn't take more than five hours. He could catch a bus from Springfield and be in Tulsa by noon. Maizie was right about his allergies being mild, too. As long as the cats stayed in the backseat, he seemed to be all right. And it would be worth a few hours of sneezing to see the shock on Harm's face when he beat her to the rendezvous.

"So, you in?"

"Yep, let's go."

Maizie put the car in gear and guided it back onto the road. "It's your funeral."

It wasn't long before Cole wondered if she'd been trying for humor or making a prediction. Maizie hadn't figured out that cars went faster than forty miles per hour in the twenty-first century, and she wouldn't let Cole drive because he "didn't look like a rapist or serial killer, but that there Ted Bundy fella didn't either." Apparently she was afraid he'd take her to a remote location, kill her in some gruesome manner, and bury her in a shallow grave.

Cole couldn't think of anyplace more remote, and he had no sexual designs on the old lady, violent or otherwise. Murder was a different story. He could have worked himself up to a nice strangulation, if not for twenty pairs of cats' eyes watching his every move. One of them hissed at him whenever he sneezed; he could just imagine what they'd do if he went for the old lady—which became more of a temptation as the hours dragged by.

Not only was she slower than Christmas Eve for a five-year-old, but she stopped once an hour to let the cats out, and then it took forever to round them all up again. And she always stopped on some deserted stretch of road, which made her the best of a bad situation every time. What should have been a five-hour trip at most took them well over eight, but Cole managed to get some sleep, mostly because he'd been bored into a stupor.

Maizie nudged him out of a light doze about mid-morning, and Cole straightened in his seat, puffy-eyed, congested, and itchy from the dried mud in his clothes. And he smelled like wet cat.

"Where are we?" he asked, yawning and stretching.

"Shawville, just like I told you."

"I wanted to get out in Springfield."

"Then you shoulda said something."

Cole sighed dejectedly, not bothering to muster up the energy to point out he'd been asleep. "What's in Shawville?"

"Farmers," Maizie said, "but they got a mall here now."

"That works for me."

Mall wás the last thing he'd have called the blocky, industrial-looking brick building she took him to.

"Used to be a manure factory," she explained when he just sat in the car and stared for a minute.

"That explains it." He shooed the cat off his lap and reached for the door handle. "Thanks, Maizie," he said, getting out of the car and taking a deep breath of the fresh air—through his mouth since his head was filled with goo from the cat allergy.

Maizie peeled off on her bald tires, and he headed for Sears, the mall's big anchor store, outfitting himself from head to toe in less than ten minutes. The sales clerk took the twenties he handed her, eyeing the wrinkled, damp bills, then studying him suspiciously before she deposited the cash in the register and gave him change.

He hit the bathroom next, stripping down and washing up as best he could, including his hair, then dumping everything he'd been wearing into the trash. Getting rid of all evidence of cat. It helped, but putting wet paper towels on his eyes was even better. Sure, he felt a little girly, but it worked. Some of the swelling went down, and the congestion seemed to clear up a bit, enough that he could feel his stomach talking to him.

There were maybe ten stores in the Shawville mall, but it boasted a small food court. Since it was mid-morning, his only choice was one of those huge cinnamon buns and coffee. Not that he was complaining. He was clean, he had food, and a table all to himself at the edge of the seating area. Things were looking up. For all of about five minutes.

Cole's coffee had barely cooled enough for him to drink it

comfortably when a kid with acne and ADD wandered by. He was wearing droopy, three-sizes-too-big Levi's, hanging so low Cole could see a pair of Simpson's boxers between the waistband of the jeans and the hem of his khaki security guard shirt. There was a name tag on the shirt pocket that read TED JASPER, and since he wasn't wearing a holster, Cole's level of alarm dropped sharply.

His mouth should have been classified as noise pollution, though. He decided to stop at Cole's table and chat, and by chat, Cole meant talk nonstop. Every sentence ended in a question mark, and he didn't seem to notice that he was crossing the line from annoying to nosy.

The third time Ted asked where he was from, Cole said, "I'm just passing through," deciding it probably wasn't a good idea to ignore the kid. It certainly didn't discourage him.

"I could swear I've seen you somewhere before," Ted said. "You ever get to Kentucky? I got kin over that way."

"Never been to Kentucky."

"Huh, you sure look familiar. Like I knew you a couple years ago or something."

Cole got to his feet. "Time for a refill," he said, holding up his coffee cup. "Nice talking to you."

Instead of taking the hint, Ted followed after him like a puppy, still asking questions but not waiting for answers. "What do you do for a living?" he wanted to know. "Are you between jobs? I mean, it's the middle of the morning on a weekday and you're not at work. And you're not dressed like you have a job, unless you work at a real casual place. One that allows tattoos . . . Shit."

Cole turned around. Ted was backing away slowly, his eyes riveted to the tattoo Cole's new T-shirt sleeve wasn't long enough to hide completely. The tattoo that must have been used on TV as an identifying mark of the dangerous federal fugitive who'd just unleashed a virus in the FBI's computer system.

Sure enough, the kid pulled a square of paper out of his pocket, unfolded it, and held it up, looking from the paper to Cole, paper, Cole, his eyes shifting back and forth so fast it was a wonder he didn't make himself dizzy.

Cole's streak of luck—all bad—was holding strong. Ted reached into his other pocket, pulled out a pistol, and pointed it at him.

It wasn't like that was a first for Cole, but with Harmony he'd thought she wouldn't shoot. He was afraid this kid's gun would go off and kill him accidentally. Ted's hand was shaking, his eyes darted back and forth, and if he didn't hit Cole, he'd likely take out one of the innocent bystanders. There weren't a lot of people in the food court, and most of them were employees, but they all decided to leave their cash registers and grills to come out and gawk. And get in the line of fire.

"Linda," Ted said to a cute brunette in a striped apron, "scoot off and call the sheriff."

Linda dimpled at Ted and scooted right off.

Before he could even begin to think of a way out, Cole found himself handcuffed and bundled into the back of a white SUV with a county sheriff's shield on the door. He was taken to the sheriff's office, the FBI was contacted, and the sheriff was only too happy to inform him that there were a couple of agents in the area.

Cole just sat there in a daze of disbelief, no question in his mind who the agents were and who they answered to. Victor Treacher was about to get his hands on Cole again, and Harmony was nowhere in the vicinity. Even if she hadn't made it to Tulsa, she was too far away to help him.

So much for her promise to keep him out of jail. Then again, he was probably headed for much smaller accommodations than a jail cell. Like a coffin.

EVEN MILES AWAY FROM COLE AND THE TAURUS, HARMONY was still chugging along, fueled by anger and righteous indignation, seeing all her hard work spiral down the drain. Along with Richard's life. Walking like a maniac wasn't helping much, so she finally screamed, "*Fuck*," at the top of her lungs because, although she rarely saw the use in profanity, that had been her first reaction to Cole's story, and it still seemed to sum up the situation pretty completely. *Shit* was a good word, too, as in, she'd stepped in it. Big-time.

The Russians she could handle. Somehow. And anyway, they were criminals. They deserved whatever they got. She'd already cleared herself with Mike; he wasn't happy about it, but he was watching her back. Victor Treacher was a roadblock she couldn't see a way around, and he was a roadblock with a hell of a motivation. His whole world was riding on silencing Cole—and by extension her—and criminal or not, Treacher was a powerful man. If she'd known what she was getting into . . .

What? She'd have found another geek to handle the computer work? There hadn't been time. No law-abiding computer expert on the planet would have broken into the FBI voluntarily, and dealing with the hacker community was risky. Unless she had leverage. Cole had been her only option, so she'd put on blinders and bulldozed ahead, and now here she was, at the edge of a cliff, hanging by her fingertips, weighed down by the sheer magnitude of her own shortsighted overconfidence.

Cole had told her more than once that the FBI had framed him, but she'd written it off as the typical jailbird's protestation of innocence. Even after she knew Cole was basically an honest, moral guy who was keeping his word despite his distrust, she'd stayed focused on Richard and ignored the warning signs. It was all her fault. All of it. And it wasn't bad enough that her neck was on the line, she was going to pull Cole and Richard down with her. True, Richard had been in trouble to begin with, but if he died she'd still blame herself.

She kicked at a clump of roadside weeds. It didn't help. Neither would shouting more obscenities, because the truth was, she admitted with a heavy sigh, she wouldn't change any of it, even if she could. There was no way she'd leave Richard to die. *No. Way.*

She'd find a method of neutralizng Treacher; she really couldn't imagine any other possibility. She wasn't without skills, and she wasn't without resources. Mike had said he wouldn't put his career on the line, but she knew him better than that. He talked a good line, but he was the human equivalent of a Tootsie Pop. It just took a little patience to work your way through the hard shell to find the soft center. Mike would be there if she needed him.

She kept on a circuitous route through the urban sprawl around St. Louis, on foot for a while longer, then briefly in a car she boosted, as much to create a diversion for Cole as anything else. Hopefully the cops would focus on the stolen vehicle and come after her, leaving Cole free and clear. He was a smart guy, but he was a computer geek, and his thought process was linear; it didn't allow for the kind of quick adjustment necessary when the authorities were on your tail and a split-second decision was all that stood between you and iron bars.

She abandoned the car not far from a truck stop and hitched a ride with a long-distance trucker. Risky under normal circumstances. Having a couple of guns made it less dangerous. For her.

The truck driver looked a lot scarier than he turned out to be. He was a bear of a man with a lot of gray, bushy hair everywhere: face, arms, ears, and sticking out of the collar of his T-shirt. He didn't watch the news, he preferred books on tape to the radio, and he had a soft spot for his daughter. Since Harmony reportedly resembled the aforementioned daughter, that worked for her. He'd told her to call him Bull, a nickname he said came from his tendency to spin a good yarn. And his hard head.

They pulled into Tulsa around daybreak, Harmony taking in the sunrise with bleary eyes. She hadn't slept, worried about Cole and second-guessing her decision to split up. How much of it, she wondered now, had been anger?

"How 'bout I treat you to breakfast," Bull said once he'd manhandled the big rig into a parking space behind the diner at the truck stop.

"I really need to be on my way." She was hungry, Cole-level hungry, but she didn't want to parade her face in front of a group of twenty-four-hour diner workers who probably spent the slow night hours watching television where no doubt she was starring on the morning news. "Thank you for the ride," she said, smiling and waving as she slung the laptop case over her shoulder, hefted the duffel, and headed for the main road.

As soon as she got out of sight of the diner windows, she ducked between two parked big rigs and slipped into the motel parking lot next to the truck stop. She went to the farthest corner of the parking lot, hunkering down against a block retaining wall, with a minivan parked about five feet in front of her. Not the best scenery, and it was chilly in the shadows there, but it kept her out of sight.

She took out her official cell and called Mike, thanking providence when he picked up the phone.

"That explains a thing or two," he said after she'd given him the high points of Cole's run-in with Victor Treacher. "You know—"

"I know."

"He'll—"

"Want Cole dead. I'm on it."

Mike whooshed out a breath, and she could almost see him scrubbing his hand back through his grizzled, marine-cut hair. "Gotta hand it to you, kid. You're an emotional crackpot, but there's nothing wrong with your brain. Just one thing, though. Hackett was arrested last night."

"Oh, *man!*" Harmony shot to her feet, fighting the urge to do something. *Anything.* She wound up turning in a circle, caught between wanting to rescue Cole and knowing she'd never get the chance if she got arrested herself. She got a grip, mainly because she refused to give in to the picture that tried to form in her mind: Cole, behind bars again, miserable and blaming her. Like she was. "He's not very good at this sort of thing. I never should have sent him off on his own."

"Don't apologize," Mike snapped at her. "Splitting up was the right decision. Man can't watch his own back—"

"He's basically a computer geek, Mike. He was in prison for eight years, but there's a big difference between watching your back inside and watching it out in the world."

"You're defending him."

Mike was right. Shocking but true. "Not the point" was what she said out loud. "I need him to save Richard. Where is he?"

"I'm not sure I should tell you."

"You wouldn't have dropped the bomb if you didn't want it to go off."

"Treacher's guys were in the area," he said, not beating around the bush, giving her the bad news straight. "Hackett was his problem eight years ago, so he was allowed to handle the retrieval."

"And?"

Mike heaved another windy sigh. "I can't let Treacher have your geek killed."

She might have protested the "your" part of that comment, if she wasn't so busy being relieved to have Mike's help.

"Treacher's guys are going to get there first," she said.

"I'll call the sheriff's office and make sure they don't let Hackett go."

"Long enough for me to show up and get him out."

Mike was silent.

"Right?" she prompted.

He gave her a Springfield address, not sounding very happy about the situation. "There'll be a car waiting for you there, with GPS. Hackett's current location will be programmed in."

"Any idea how I can spring him without getting arrested myself?"

"I figure history will repeat itself," Mike said with a shrug in his voice.

"History included forged paperwork."

"You're not getting paperwork, forged or otherwise. It won't do either of us any good if I get jammed up, too."

"It's not like I can get him out of jail without doing something you won't like."

"If you finish your operation, and it works out, I can explain it away. Just don't shoot any good guys."

"I'll try to remember that."

Mike chuckled. Mike probably knew she was rolling her eyes. "You're in over your head, kid, and there's probably not a chance in hell you'll be working at the Bureau when this is over, but I'm too old to start a new career."

"Nice to know your priorities."

"I shouldn't even be talking to you, Swift."

Yeah, she knew that, too, but she didn't thank him. He wouldn't expect it and he wouldn't want it.

"Harmony?" he said. "I'd tell you not to do anything stupid, but it's a little late for that. Just don't do anything really stupid."

chapter
17

COLE WAS LIVING HIS WORST NIGHTMARE, HAND-
cuffed to a bench in the Shawville sheriff's office, waiting for
FBI agents to arrive and drag him back to Lewisburg. And
that was the optimistic scenario. If Harmony was right—and
she had a disturbingly accurate track record—he'd never
make it back to prison alive.

He should have stuck with her. He should have argued
when she suggested splitting up. His gut feeling had been
"bad idea," and then she'd hit him with logic, and he'd caved
in, which was the really odd thing since logic was more his
thing than hers. She'd been right, though, everyone would be
on the lookout for a man and a woman traveling together, and
even he had to admit they made an eye-catching couple.
Problem was, his luck had run out eight years ago. And even
if the last few days had seemed like a light at the end of a
long, dark tunnel, he'd have been better off if Harmony had
left him where he was. He could have survived another seventeen years in prison. He didn't figure he'd make it to the
Shawville city limits alive.

The sheriff's office was a converted storefront, sitting at

the end of Shawville's main drag. The town itself was surrounded by corn and wheat farms with barns full of cows,
pigs, and chickens, and houses inhabited by farmers and their
extended families, none of them between the ages of eighteen and thirty because the minute they came of age, kids
went to college or joined the army. Cole couldn't blame them.
Even inside the building it smelled faintly of manure. He'd
gotten used to that. It was the other occupants he found annoying, namely the current bane of his existence.

"I'm gonna get, like, a cert-certick—that whatchamacallit
they give you for doing something good, right?" Ted Jasper
said, hiking up his pants for the umpteenth time. No one was
paying attention to him, but he never stopped talking, and he
never stopped moving, pacing the floor, swinging his arms,
checking out the Most Wanted board where Cole's poster
still hung with a big black X through his face. "I wanna be a
real cop—I mean police officer—even if Granddaddy Jasper
don't approve. We got us a family trade, you know," he said
to Cole, "like the Bushes are politicians, the Jaspers do flea
markets. My daddy says we both deal in garbage." He laughed
uproariously. "But I wanna be a cop. They won't let me go to
the academy without a college degree, and I'm not so good
with, you know, learning stuff. I shouldn't need to now, right?
I should get a special, uh, something-or-other because I caught
a fugitive."

The deputy behind the front counter and the sheriff sitting
at his desk on the other side of the room shared a look, eyes
rolling, heads shaking.

"I mean he's *dangerous*," Ted said, doing a little shadow
boxing in Cole's general direction, bouncing on the balls of
his feet then hitching his pants up over his Simpsons boxers a
little too forcefully so he had to do a wedgie removal.

"What genius gave him a gun?" Cole wondered out loud
when it fell out of the kid's pocket and spun around in a circle
on the floor.

"That's a really good question," the sheriff said. He came
out from behind his desk and held out a hand.

Ted bobbled the gun, finally getting it turned around so he
could show it to the sheriff. "It's not even loaded, see?"

"Christ," the sheriff said, "it's just a BB gun."

Cole let his head fall back to thump against the wall behind him. He'd been caught by a moron with a popgun. If any of his former cellmates found out, they'd make him hand in his tattoo.

"Feeling like an idiot?" the sheriff asked Cole.

"You have no idea."

Stick to I-44, Harmony had said. That was the quickest route. She hadn't factored in his bad luck, or a wet-behind-the-ears security guard with delusions of grandeur.

The phone rang, the deputy picked it up, and went through his greeting, then said, "Yes, ma'am, the sheriff's here. Yes, we caught that escaped felon."

"I caught him," Ted said, outraged to be left out of the headlines. "Tell her I caught him."

The deputy ignored him. "You gonna be around awhile?" he called to the sheriff over Ted's continuing protests.

"'Cept for lunch," the sheriff called back.

The deputy repeated that information into the phone, then said, "Hold on," when the street door opened.

Two men walked in, looking like the guys in the Matrix, dark suits, perfect hair, and vaguely familiar faces. Cole had seen them before. Bobbing in Lake Erie. One of the agents glanced over at him, and Cole saw retribution in his eyes.

"Can I help you?" the deputy asked them.

They ignored him, walking around the counter to the desk where the sheriff sat. They flipped out wallets and flashed their badges, and even though they didn't say a word the sheriff was already bristling before they gave their names, Special Agents Jones and Carter. Cole wondered if those were really their names.

The sheriff didn't seem to care. He hardly glanced at their badges. "You have a warrant?" he asked them.

Agents Jones and Carter exchanged a look, appearing to communicate telepathically. Creepy. "We don't need a warrant," one of them said.

"Now that's a real oddity, since I got a call from a Mike somebody or other a little while ago. Told me he was with the FBI and there'd be two agents coming to collect this yahoo."

The sheriff aimed a thumb in Cole's general direction. "And we better turn him over or else. Said he didn't know how a podunk outfit like ours had managed to catch him, but we better not think about hanging onto him so we could get ourselves some good press."

The sheriff came out from around his desk and stopped a couple feet in front of the feds, resting his hand on his tool belt and putting an extra measure of "hick" into his voice. "Now, the idea of a press conference never occurred to me, but hanging onto him, why, poor fella ain't even had lunch yet."

Agent Jones, or maybe it was Agent Carter, started to say something. His partner stopped him with a hand. "We'll be back," he said.

Ted followed them to the door and watched them go through it. "You don't think they're going to drive a truck through the front of this building, do you? You know, like the Terminator? The police wouldn't let him have Sarah Connor, so the Terminator said 'I'll be back' and then he drove a truck into the police station and went in and killed all the cops. Can I have a real gun?" he asked the sheriff, "and some bullets, because, you know, if those guys are going to come in here blasting I want to shoot back."

The sheriff and the deputy shared another eye roll. Cole was right there with them.

"You still got the phone in your hand," the sheriff said to the deputy.

"Shit, you still there?" he said into the receiver, then shrugged. "Must've hung up. Probably just a reporter."

"C'mon, Ted," the sheriff said. "I can't give you a commendation, but I'll spring for lunch. We'll bring you back a burger," he said to the deputy on the way to the front door.

"Wife has me on a diet," the deputy said back.

"What she doesn't know won't hurt her." The sheriff stopped at the front door and looked out. "The government stiffs are nowhere in sight, Ted, so it looks like we're safe." And they left.

Nobody thought to ask the dying man what he wanted for his last meal.

They couldn't have been gone ten minutes when the door opened again. Cole's bench was against the wall, opposite the front counter, and his hands were cuffed to the arm of the bench farthest from the front door. He twisted around, expecting to see Agents Jones and Carter coming back to try their luck now that the sheriff wasn't around to give them a hard time.

Harmony came in instead. Cole almost swallowed his tongue, he was so surprised. It took a minute for his brain to kick in, and when it did, his thoughts were hardly comforting because what he was thinking was, *Great, now we're both going to die.*

THE GPS LED HARMONY TO A SMALL, LOCAL COUNTY sheriff's office in a town that must have been centrally located, since it had little else to recommend it as a hub for county law enforcement. There was a main street with a few businesses, surrounded by side streets with homes that looked to have been built in the late nineteenth century: wide front porches, dormer windows, white picket fences. There were absolutely no living souls in sight, as if no one wanted to be seen populating the place. Even the sign outside of town, welcoming visitors, had been so badly rusted the name was illegible.

She parked in front of the sheriff's office and got out of the car immediately. No time to rethink or overplan—not a problem since the sum total of her preparation consisted of "go in when the fewest people are around, and do whatever it takes to get Cole out alive."

She'd done all the reconnoitering she could from a distance, but she took a moment to familiarize herself with the building itself and its immediate environs.

The sheriff's office had once been a storefront. Through the wide, street-facing windows she saw a long counter with a guy around her age in uniform behind it. She gave it a moment or two, but she saw no other signs of life. The deputy didn't talk to anyone else, and since he'd answered the phone, she figured it was a safe bet there wasn't a receptionist on duty at the moment.

She stepped through the door and paused just inside, surprised when she spied Cole on a bench in the corner, handcuffed. He jerked upright when he saw her, which got the deputy's attention and gave her a few precious seconds to hide her own reaction, which consisted mostly of elation that she didn't have to spring him from a jail cell. Heck, she thought, managing not to pump a fist in the air, she might actually pull this off.

"Can I help you?"

Harmony stepped up to the counter, flashing her FBI badge in the deputy's face. She looked the part, too, wearing her blue dress and jacket. And her guns. "Agent Smith," she said, using a false name that was close to her own in case he'd gotten a better look at her ID than she'd intended. "I'm here to collect a prisoner. Paperwork is on its way."

"Um, the sheriff is out to lunch right now. He told me not to . . ."

Harmony took off her dark glasses and leaned in close. His eyes dropped to her cleavage, and his sentence trailed off. Cole's cuffs rattled, but she didn't spare him a glance.

"I know Mike Kovaleski called you," she said, making it a confidence. "Just between you and me, he's a real pain in the neck when it comes to interagency cooperation. Always worried the FBI isn't getting the credit it should. There's really no paperwork necessary in this case since there aren't any local warrants. He's only wanted by the FBI, so you can just turn him over to me, one law enforcement officer to another."

"I, uh . . ."

She leaned both elbows on the counter and took a deep breath, making the most of what she had. "I'll just take him into custody and walk him out quietly. It's best that way."

Cole did some more rattling, which broke the deputy's fascination with her god-given endowments. He looked over and so did she, chagrined to find Cole scowling at the deputy, hands straining at the cuffs.

"What about those other two agents?" the deputy said.

Harmony glared at Cole for another second, giving her head the slightest shake. He was still pissed off for some reason she couldn't fathom, but he subsided to a low simmer.

"The other two agents called me," she said. She leaned in again, sharing more secrets.

His gaze didn't budge off her face this time, though, and his eyes were narrowed. Not good. "Your voice sounds kind of familiar," he said. "And now that I think about it, you look familiar, too. Have we met before?"

"It's possible. I've been stationed in this area for some time, and I make it a point to attend the policemen's charity ball every year."

"Nope, that's not it."

He looked around the office, puzzled, searching for something to jog his memory. By the time he'd finished turning in a slow circle, his gaze ended up on the phone. And recognition dawned. When he lifted his gaze to Harmony again, she had her gun pointed at him.

His eyes crossed on the tiny black hole at the end of the barrel.

"Hands," she said.

He lifted them about shoulder high, his left hand dangerously close to temptation.

"Away from the radio," she ordered, meaning the small personal communication device he wore on his shoulder.

The deputy moved his hands out to the sides, but they were still in Wyatt Earp quick-draw range.

"Don't," she said, seeing in his eyes that he was considering it.

"You won't shoot me."

"You really don't want to—"

She moved the gun a couple inches to the right and squeezed off a shot.

"—dare her not to shoot you," Cole finished.

"Yeah," the deputy said, "I'm getting that."

"Men," Harmony muttered. "You'd think after millions of years of evolution you'd stop thinking of the half of the species that can push out a seven-pound human being through a ten-centimeter opening as the 'softer sex.'"

She went around the counter and secured the deputy to one of the metal supports holding up the counter, using a spare set of cuffs she found on a shelf. Then she retrieved the key from his pocket and unlocked Cole.

"Nice jailbreak, Mata Hari," he said.

"Can we talk about my methods later? The sheriff is going to be back any moment."

That was all the urging Cole needed. He snagged the envelope holding his personal effects off the counter and followed her outside, halting abruptly when he got a load of the Ford GT, a black wedge that was barely waist high on him, sitting at the curb just out of sight of the windows.

"I talked to Mike," she said, "told him the whole story. I won't say he's behind us a hundred percent, but he arranged for a car."

"That isn't a car, it's a wet dream."

"Thanks for the visual. Get in."

"I'm driving."

"I left you alone for ten minutes; you got arrested."

Cole simply lifted her up by the armpits and moved her aside, angling into the driver's seat. He was already revving the engine before she made it around the car, and he had it in gear and moving before she'd completely folded herself into the passenger seat. A glance at the speedometer told her they were going close to sixty by the time she got her door closed and her seat belt buckled.

"This is a small town," she pointed out.

"Tell them," Cole said, eyes on the rearview.

She looked over her shoulder and saw a black sedan right on their rear bumper, a gun just appearing out the passenger-side window. "Treacher's agents."

"Yeah," Cole said. "I don't think having a traffic accident is our biggest worry at the moment."

He gave the GT a bit more gas and it leapt ahead, the leather-covered wheel thrumming lightly under his hands, vibrating with the leashed power of 550 horses. Harmony's handler couldn't have picked a better car if he'd talked to Cole first. If he'd never run afoul of Victor Treacher, and if he'd sold his system and gotten rich, as he'd planned, he'd have one of these in his garage.

"They were probably watching the sheriff's office," Harmony said, "waiting to see if I got you out of there."

"Yeah, and now we're going to die."

"You should've let me drive."

"No way."

"In need of a little redemption because you let yourself get caught?"

"Oh, yeah," Cole said, choosing not to tell her exactly who'd caught him. He checked the mirror; Treacher's guys hadn't caught up yet, and he wasn't going to give them a chance. "There's no way they can outrun this car. It tops out at over two hundred miles per hour."

"They'll only find us again," Harmony said.

"What happened to the eternal optimist?"

"You want optimism? I'm positive they'll find us again."

Cole shrugged. "Maybe we should take them out permanently this time."

That stopped her, but not for long. "We can't kill two FBI agents, even if they aren't exactly working in the best interest of the Bureau . . ." She put her hand on his arm. "I have an idea." She turned on the GPS and brought up a map of their immediate surroundings. "Take the next left," she said. "Don't lose those guys."

A shot rang out. "And keep out of gunshot range," Cole said before she could. Irrationally, it was concern for the car that made him say it. "What's the plan?"

"There's a fair-sized town about fifty miles straight along this road."

"Won't it have a fair-sized police force?"

"That would be my guess. But they won't be able to outrun this car, either."

Cole grinned. He couldn't help himself. He wasn't passing up a chance to tweak his nose at any law enforcement agency. "Neither will Treacher's pet agents."

"I've driven some of the cars the FBI calls company

vehicles," Harmony said. "That one's a step above, but that's really not saying much."

"So what next?"

"Next we call the local authorities and let them know there are two very irresponsible drivers on their way into town." And that's exactly what she did, calling Mike directly after and letting him know what she was up to. "All you have to do is keep us out of custody," she said to Cole, "and hope they're not that lucky."

"They're FBI agents. Even if they get arrested nothing will happen to them."

"Except they'll be making a one-way trip back to Washington, D.C. They're not exactly on a sanctioned mission. Hell, they're not even agents. Treacher will have a lot of explaining to do. Mike will make sure of it."

The inner workings of the FBI had never made much sense to Cole, so he didn't ask any more questions, just punched the GT up to about eighty miles an hour. The government-issue sedan kept pace, even when Cole blew by two black-and-whites sitting on either shoulder of the road about two miles outside of town.

The police cruisers swung out behind the agents' sedan, lights flashing and sirens blaring. One of them stayed behind, and the other blasted around it to take up a position on the GT's back bumper. Cole just smiled and hit the gas. The GT shot forward. The cruiser didn't even attempt to stay with them. It slowed, making a wide turn that left it sitting across both lanes of the road.

The last thing Cole saw was the government sedan bracketed by the two police cars. He slowed down to about sixty, bypassing the town and keeping to little-used roads, following Harmony's instructions and trying to keep a low profile in the GT.

"That was fun," Harmony said.

Cole glanced over at her. She'd been half-turned during the short car chase, watching the feds out the back window. Now she'd relaxed into her seat, head back, her face alight with laughter.

"I told you I wouldn't let you go back to jail," she said.

That pissed Cole off, although he knew it was irrational he didn't stop to ask himself why he was burning. "You put me in that position to begin with."

"How do you figure? I was three hundred miles away when you got arrested."

"Exactly."

"And as soon as I found out, I put my own ass on the line to get you out."

"It wasn't just your ass."

"What's that supposed to mean?"

Cole pulled the GT into a narrow dirt road, more a path than anything else, that led into an unharvested wheat field edged by trees. "You let that deputy drool all over you," he said, jamming the car into park when he was sure it couldn't be seen from the main road.

Harmony turned sideways to face him, arms crossed, her mood notching down to his level. "I didn't want him to focus on my face," she shot back. "I was on TV, too, you know."

"It worked. He wasn't looking at your face."

"Until you turned into Mr. Hyde and broke his concentration."

"Concentration? Nice euphemism. Good thing he didn't know about the thigh holster. He'd have concentrated you right there on the counter."

"You mean this?"

She hiked up her skirt to show the leather holster, and the heat in Cole turned from anger to lust in the space of a heartbeat. Or maybe it had been lust all along, mixed with jealousy, he admitted before he dove at her. She met him halfway, the kiss wild, almost a continuation of their argument with both of them trying to come out the winner.

She pulled back and met his eyes, and then they were both out of the car and heading around it, meeting at the hood on the passenger side because Cole's legs were longer. He thought his need was more extreme, too, but Harmony stripped off her jacket and shoulder holster, slipped out of her panties, and leaned back against the hood of the car wearing nothing but a wisp of blue dress and that band of leather around her thigh.

"This is only adrenaline," she said, apparently mistaking

his hesitation for something it wasn't. "Danger gets you wired, and once the danger is over, you need a place to work it off."

"I'm just taking a moment to enjoy the scenery," Cole said. He wasn't talking about the countryside.

She must look like an ad in one of those car magazines, Harmony realized. And judging by Cole's ability to spout the GT's specs at a moment's notice, he had to have seen his share of half-naked women draped over prime automotive machinery. She wasn't quite sure how she felt about that.

Cole took a step forward and put his hands on her thighs, his touch like fire on her sensitized skin, and she knew exactly how she felt about it. Like the foreplay was over. She popped the snap on his jeans, and he pushed them down along with his boxers.

His hands moved up, curling around her bare bottom and pulling her toward him as he drove forward and surged inside her, hot and hard and deep, touching some part of her that sent pleasure rippling outward in waves so strong she thought she saw the air shimmer around them. She felt a fumbling at her neck and then her breasts were free, and his mouth was there, taking in one throbbing crest and working it as his body moved within hers.

All she could do was brace herself, overloaded with sensation, barely able to breathe as her body wound tighter and tighter. The pleasure became so impossibly intense she heard herself begging and didn't know what for until his hand slipped between them and rasped over her flesh, and she exploded even as he drove himself deep one last time, the clenching of her body easing enough to feel the echo of his climax from deep inside her.

He slipped away and collapsed onto the ground, and Harmony slid off the car, her muscles lax and her body limp, to lie beside him. Her breasts were still bare, the warm sun and soft breeze playing over her skin, but she didn't care.

"You really know how to concentrate," she said to Cole.

He laughed, still a little out of breath. "Those car magazines are going to have a whole different meaning for me from now on."

"What meaning did they have before?"

"Touché," he said with a little chuckle, his breath coming more easily. "Let's just say the attraction is gone, because the fantasy could never live up to the reality."

chapter 18

"SO HOW DID YOU GET CAUGHT?"

They were back in the car again, heading for the interstate. Cole was still driving, and for a second Harmony thought he wasn't going to answer her.

"An old lady with cats, and a mall security guard with a nose for trouble," he finally said.

"Mall?"

"Food court. And that's all I'm going to say about it."

Harmony grinned, but she decided to leave it at that. Maybe it had something to do with what had just happened in a stranger's wheat field, maybe it didn't. Whatever the reason, they were on pretty good terms at the moment, and she was enjoying the peace too much to ruin it. She already knew it wasn't going to last.

If anyone had asked her a week ago if she really thought they'd make it this far, she'd have said no. Richard was the only family she had; she wouldn't have been able to live with herself if she hadn't gone after him. But she really hadn't thought she could pull this off. Then. Seven days down the road she was beginning to believe she might succeed. Because of Cole.

And it wasn't just the mission that was better. She'd been lonely a long time. True, she was always surrounded by people—coworkers, friends—but she'd never connected with any of them the way she had with Cole. Really connected, in all the ways that counted. They could practically read each other's minds. Of course it wasn't that hard to do when your life was on the line.

And that was all Cole was thinking about, she reminded herself. His life, his future, his freedom—complete freedom, including from her. Sure, he was enjoying her company now, but he was sex-starved, not lovelorn. His heart wasn't involved, and she'd better put hers on ice before it got any foolish ideas about long-term commitments with a man whose trust she was about to destroy. If he couldn't trust her, he couldn't love her. Not the way she wanted to be loved. Unconditionally.

"How did you know where to find me?"

"Mike Kovaleski," she said, putting her head back in the present, which was all she and Cole would ever share. "He was keeping an eye out for activity involving either one of us. When I called to fill him in on your history with Treacher, he told me you'd been arrested. Mike did a little digging and found out where Victor had sent his stooges. We both knew they'd get there before me, but—"

"He called and pissed off the sheriff so he wouldn't hand me over," Cole finished from firsthand knowledge. "I only have one question, did you have a plan when you walked into the sheriff's office?"

"Yep, get you out and don't get caught."

"That was it?"

"I called just before I got there."

"So that was you on the phone."

"Posing as a reporter," she confirmed. "I needed to know whether or not you were still there, and I was lucky enough to hear Treacher's agents come in and get turned away. When I got to town, I did a quick reconnoiter, so I knew the sheriff and at least one deputy were there, and I knew Treacher's guys were somewhere in the vicinity. When I saw the sheriff leave with that kid wearing a security guard's shirt . . . Hey—"

"I was hungry. Get over it," Cole said. No point in revisiting his humiliation.

She grinned again. "I always said your stomach was going to get you into trouble."

He glanced over at her, unamused. "You were filling me in, remember?"

"Right. After they left I knew there was still at least one guy in there aside from you, but it was the best odds I was going to get."

"That deputy was outnumbered," Cole said. "One poor guy against you and the girls."

"It's not my fault he was so easy to distract."

Cole didn't say anything, just stared out the windshield. She had a feeling that steering onto the highway wasn't what he was so focused on. "What?"

He bumped up a shoulder. "I was wondering what Mike said when you told him about Treacher."

"He didn't say anything, really. He didn't seem all that surprised, either, and I know he's checking into it."

"There won't be anything for him to find."

"No crime is foolproof," Harmony said. "There must be some truth to what you're saying—"

"Some truth," Cole repeated, shaking his head.

"Look at it from our viewpoint, Cole. All we have to go on is Victor Treacher's suspicious behavior. He wouldn't be so hot to get his hands on you if he wasn't afraid of who you'd talk to and what you'd say."

He did his silent routine, but she knew his brain was worrying over the facts of the matter, so it was no surprise when he said, "You're right, but he doesn't want to get his hands on me. He wants me dead."

"At the moment he has no way of accomplishing that. By now his agents are on their way back to Washington, and Treacher is being asked what they were doing and why it wasn't on the grid. He won't be able to send anyone after us until this blows over, and he's not going anywhere."

"Okay," Cole said, "so we go get Richard. Tomorrow. Tonight we get a room and a meal, not particularly in that order."

"Your stomach talking again?"

"I missed lunch, but I was thinking of you. It's going to be a long, rough night."

Her mind went in the obvious direction, her body helping by going halfway down that path just at the memory of that wheat field. But she hadn't forgotten about the phone call she had to make later.

Or the confession.

COLE DIDN'T FEEL COMFORTABLE ENOUGH TO GO INTO a restaurant to eat, but he had Harmony order dinner from one of the medium-priced chain restaurants that brought the food out to your vehicle. That way he could keep his head down and go unnoticed. He hadn't factored in the car.

"Cool ride," the girl who brought them the take-out bag said. "How fast does it go?"

"Give me the food and I'll be glad to show you."

"Oh, sure." She handed him the bag and took the money he gave her in return, backing into the restaurant, her eyes on him and the GT the entire way.

"This car isn't exactly low profile," Harmony said, watching the waitress watch him. "Maybe we should get different transportation."

"I wouldn't worry about that waitress too much," Cole said, handing her the food. "She forgot she was holding a bag full of take-out boxes she picked up five minutes ago."

"Right after she got a good look at you in this car. And how about the rest of the people who work here? Not to mention the diners."

Cole took in the faces peering out at them, some from the hostess's station at the front door, others whose tables overlooked the parking lot. "You might have a point."

"And it wasn't inflating your ego."

"I figured that out a long time ago."

"We've only been together for seven days."

"Really? It seems longer."

"Yeah."

They both went silent, mulling that for a few seconds.

"It hasn't all been bad," Cole said, backing out of the parking space and heading out to the I-44 service drive. "I'm not in jail. And I'm still alive. At the moment."

Harmony smiled over that. "Feels pretty good, doesn't it?"

"Peachy," Cole said, his eyes cutting in her direction with a look that matched the sarcastic drawl. "So how about the car? Do we have to ditch it?"

"A black GT with white racing stripes? There are what, five of these things on the road? And I'd be willing to bet none of them are in farm country, Oklahoma."

"Okay, it's not exactly a stealth vehicle, but it's a definite asset if we run into any more cops. And I don't think we have to worry about the Russians. They might want to keep tabs on us, but they won't interfere as long as we're doing what they want us to do."

Harmony didn't agree, but she really couldn't refute his logic, either. They'd finally made it to Tulsa, stopping a little past midway through the city where the neighborhood was working class verging on working poor, and the inhabitants would be used to minding their own business. Cole found a small travel motel not far off the interstate, took a room in the back, and parked the GT where it wouldn't be easily seen.

They ate in silence, letting the upheaval of the day slough off in quiet and decent food and, at least in Harmony's case, there appeared to be some dread involved. She was jumpy, barely picking at her meal before she gave up and took to her feet, prowling the room—and watching him, although whenever he glanced her way she was looking elsewhere. Strange—and troubling, considering the change in their personal relationship. She wasn't exactly a poster child for emotional detachment, and sure, she was the one who'd felt a need to set boundaries, but that was days ago. He had no clue what was going through her mind now, and he didn't want to find out.

"I think it would be a good idea to put more money in the kidnappers' account," he said, because if Richard wasn't the one on her mind, he should be. "It won't take me long, and between the virus and the trouble his guys are in, Treacher is probably too busy to bother with me tonight. Why don't you take a shower and try to relax before you have to call them."

She kept pacing, and just when he decided she hadn't heard him, she whipped around and said, "I lied, Cole." She collapsed into a chair, looking exhausted and miserable as she met his eyes for the first time since they'd walked into the room. "There's no new evidence. I figured once we rescued Richard the Bureau would be so grateful they'd commute your sentence, but the way this is going— Now that we're up against Victor Treacher . . ." She shook her head. "He has a lot to loose. And Mike's not too happy with me. I'm probably out of a job."

So much for his ego, thinking she was all torn up about him. He ought to be feeling something, anything, but he was just . . . numb. And then it all started to crowd in.

"Say something."

"*Say something?* What the hell do you want me to say?"

"I don't know, yell at me. Call me names, whatever works for you."

"Why? It's not like I actually believed you." But somewhere along the line he'd come to trust her.

Cole was usually a thinker, but he couldn't contain this with a moment of silence and the application of logic. He surged to his feet, paced across the room and back again, struggling to contain the swirl of anger and betrayal. And failing. He wanted to shove the confession back down her throat so they could keep going as they had been, working together. Sleeping together. So he didn't have to walk out that door and leave her on her own.

It was what he should do, what he'd learned to do in Lewisburg. Protect your own ass at all costs. It was a decision he'd already made, to walk if this thing went south. And now it was a course he couldn't take. Because she wasn't the only one to blame.

He'd lied to himself, too. Not in the beginning. When he'd made his every-man-for-himself game plan, he'd been ready, willing, and able to carry it out. Now he couldn't, and sacrificing himself to a hopeless cause was the worst kind of self-betrayal.

She came to stand in front of him, her blue eyes, wide and brimming, focused unwaveringly on his face. He banded his hands around her upper arms, lifted her onto her toes.

She bit into her bottom lip, but she kept her eyes on his. "God, Cole, I'm so sorry."

He let her go so fast she stumbled. He wasn't ready for mea culpas or explanations, so he turned his back. It wasn't enough, neither was pacing, but it was all he could do to work off the anger and sort out a million clamoring thoughts.

"Why now?" he finally asked her.

"If we're not honest with each other, we won't get through this alive."

Wrong answer, was his immediate reaction, but he didn't know why. Hell, he didn't know if there was a right answer.

"After you told me about Treacher," she said, "I was pretty mad."

"I never lied to you."

"I know. It didn't take me long to realize it was all my own fault."

Just like it was his fault for trusting her. Not only was she FBI, but he'd watched her lie to just about everyone they'd run across. When had he convinced himself she wouldn't do the same to him?

"I had no time to plan or prepare," she was saying. "I read your file, and as far as I could tell, you were just another hacker. You suited my purposes and I didn't care what you'd done."

"And now?"

"If I'd known what I was getting into, and what I was getting you into—"

He whipped around. "You'd have done it anyway."

"Yes," she blazed up, striding over to face him. "I can't leave Richard to die," she said, the rest of her breath sobbing out.

"So you put your own neck on the line. And mine."

"And that's another reason you should know the truth. You're innocent—"

She kept talking, but he lost the rest of what she said. It felt like a cleansing wind blew through him, not strong enough to completely clear the storm, but the clouds thinned enough for him to savor that one word he'd been waiting to hear for eight years. That Harmony was the one who believed in him, though she had little more than his word to go on, gave it even more meaning.

Everybody in the joint claimed to be innocent. Cole actually was, but nobody had believed him, including the lawyer who'd sucked him dry before leaving him to the mercy of the system. The young public defender who'd caught his case knew there was no point in filing an appeal when the accuser was one of the top suits at the FBI and the accused was a kid with no connections and no resources, just parents who, if Cole had let them would have mortgaged everything they owned to try to help him.

Fucking feds, he thought for the millionth time. But he couldn't dredge up enough anger to really mean it. The sense of vindication, at least in that moment, was too sweet.

And then reality crashed back in.

"Cole? I'm serious. I think you should take off."

"You don't need me anymore, now that I've transferred enough money to satisfy the Russians."

She stared at him, her eyes filled with what he would have sworn was hurt before she shifted her gaze left and said, "You're right. You've done what I wanted, and I don't need you anymore. Leave me the account numbers and go. I wish . . ." She stopped, shook her head slightly. "I'll make sure Mike gets your case reopened. If you call him in a couple weeks, he'll let you know what it'll take to prove Treacher framed you."

"Being a martyr now?"

Her gaze shot to his, filled with heat before she banked it. "The Russians are my problem, not yours. I told you that from day one."

"You also told me you'd get my sentence commuted to time served."

"I just said Mike—"

"*You* promised, not Mike."

It took a few seconds, but she finally put the hope in her eyes into words. "Are you saying you want to help me finish this?"

"Do you really think the Russians are going to settle for four million dollars?"

"No."

"Then you still need me."

"Yes."

He walked back over to the table and righted his chair, pulling her laptop in front of him. He didn't boot it up; he was busy watching her.

She didn't seem to notice. She sat on the end of the bed, swallowing hard a couple of times, her fingers absently pleating her dress. Cole felt like a heel. She was grateful he hadn't walked out on her, but the real reason he'd stayed was the money. He'd transferred funds into the kidnappers' account, but in the fallout of his viral sabotage on the FBI's computer system, there'd been no chance to set himself up, let alone search for the evidence to clear himself, because Harmony had insisted on leaving.

Since the new evidence didn't exist, all he had left was diverting some money to fund his disappearance. He could get it on his own, but it was so much easier with her. And the second he'd done it he'd walk away, he told himself. Guilt-free.

"No more lies," Harmony said into the silence. "Okay?"

"Okay," Cole said. After all, it was the truth. He'd been keeping this secret all along.

chapter
19

"I THINK I WILL TAKE A SHOWER," HARMONY SAID
after another half hour of uncomfortable silence.

Cole waited until she'd disappeared into the bathroom
and he heard the water running. For once he had no trouble
keeping his mind off what was going on behind the shower
curtain. He booted up her slick little laptop and went straight
into the FBI's banking system, for the first time with no worry.
Before the water cut off, he'd added several million to the
kidnappers' bank account, and he'd done a little creative ac-
counting for his own benefit.

By the time Harmony came out of the bathroom, he was
able to fully appreciate the sweatpants and matching tank
she must have bought for herself when she'd supplemented
his wardrobe a couple days before. The pants were the kind
that skimmed across her hip bones and left a strip of bare
skin before the hem of the tank got in the way. The material
was all clingy, too . . .

And he'd just rediscovered his detachment. He couldn't
afford to lose it again if he was going to put himself first. "So
what did you really do at the FBI?"

She moved away from him, keeping her eyes, and her thoughts, to herself. "I tracked computer criminals."

That stopped him. "If you're good enough to catch hackers, what do you need me for?"

"I didn't exactly catch hackers."

"Offshore cyber-criminals?"

"Uh-uh."

"Lonely geeks who unleash worms and viruses from their mom's basements?"

"No."

"High school kids who trash their friends on Facebook?"

"I track down copyright violators, okay? You know the FBI warning at the beginning of a movie you rent or buy? That's me."

"You're the DVD police?"

"I'm the person who takes down bootleg movies on the Internet and prosecutes the perpetrators."

Cole was feeling a lot better suddenly, trying-not-to-laugh-his-ass-off better. "How long have you been with the FBI?"

Harmony's eyes narrowed on his mouth, probably because it was twitching. "Almost five years."

"And you've been the DVD police all that time?"

"I'm not the DVD police," she snapped. "And no. I've only been in Cyber Crime the last twenty months or so."

"There must be a reason you weren't put in the field."

She clamped her jaw shut for a minute, then said on a little burst of temper, "They think I have trouble compartmentalizing."

Cole didn't bother trying to keep a straight face. "In other words, you get emotionally involved."

"No, those are pretty much the exact words they used. And you should be grateful, since that's the reason I decided to break you out of jail."

"You broke me out of jail because you have something to prove."

Her gaze flew to his, and she looked a little startled, probably because he'd pegged her. She didn't like it, her expression going sulky. But she told the truth. He had to give her credit for that.

"I'm here to get Richard free," she admitted. "That's first and foremost. If I prove something to somebody along the line, that's great, but I'm going to carry out my mission."

"Sure, because you have all those skills from tracking down the high school audio/visual nerd and confiscating his bootleg copy of *Girls Gone Wild*."

"I haven't let you down yet, have I? And when Richard is free I'm going to make sure you don't go back to jail."

She took a deep breath, and he got the impression she was mentally squaring her shoulders. In actuality she came to hover behind him again, warm and fresh-smelling, and completely distracting.

"If you're done laughing at me, can we get back to business?"

"Sure," Cole said.

He'd gotten into the FBI system without being kicked out or feeling like he was being tracked. He'd moved the money for the kidnappers, and he'd taken steps toward securing his own future. He had a full stomach and a beautiful woman draped over him, like the icing on the cake. He pulled Harmony into his lap.

"I don't think this is a good idea," she said.

"Neither do I." But he kissed her anyway, the rush of heat and pleasure no less incredible for being familiar. The way his heartbeat thundered in his ears, the feel of her mouth on his, her body a living flame he threw himself into—

Until she tore herself out of his arms.

It took a second or two for reality to batter its way past the need. The look on her face was a big help, not to mention she was staring at the door. Cole wasn't sure he wanted to know why. But he turned slowly and there were Irene and Leo. The molding around the door was splintered, the door hanging on one hinge behind them, smashed in while he was lost in a sexual haze.

Leo stationed himself in front of the opening, a Russian fireplug with one goal, to keep them from leaving, which he accomplished pretty handily.

It was a typical motel room, with the door and a large window on one side, Leo and Irene effectively blocking both of them. A bed, a small round table, and a cheap dresser with a television on it completed the décor. There was a window in the bathroom, but Harmony couldn't fit through it, let alone him. That left the table or TV, which he could throw and they would duck, and then laugh at him.

"Irene and Leo," Harmony said, edging ever so slightly away from him. Toward her gun, which she'd left on the other side of the table.

Cole couldn't believe the Russians were unaware of her intentions, but they did nothing to stop her.

"Irina," the woman corrected on her own behalf. She felt no need to perform the same service for Leo. It was probably hard enough to get him to answer to one name, let alone confusing him with another.

"How did you find us?" Harmony wanted to know.

"We have been following from the first," Irina said. "At prison, monitoring police radios, in Pennsylvania, being talked to death," she added with a slight sneer.

"It was your choice to pick us up. Why didn't you just kidnap us then? We were stuck in the backseat of your car for hours."

Irina's lip curled. She didn't want to be reminded. "You lie to us about him." She stabbed a finger at Cole.

"Right, and what happened to your Southern drawl, which, by the way, wasn't very convincing."

"It's probably not a good idea to piss off the Russians," Cole said.

"If they wanted us dead, we wouldn't be having this conversation," Harmony told him, never taking her eyes off Irina. "But since we are, I have some questions. How did you find us again? We lost you back at Shawville."

Irina shrugged, looking smug since she'd remembered she had the upper hand again. "We split up. We know you are going to Los Angeles. We know you drive fancy car. Tulsa logical city to stop for night. Leo not so good at drive car, but he do it."

"Are you saying you just drove around until you found us?" Cole asked.

"*Da.*"

Damned car, Cole thought, trading a look with Harmony, and damn him for getting into an adolescent fever over it.

"It's not your fault," Harmony said to him. "They haven't pulled their weapons, so I'm guessing they have something to say."

Irina bumped up an eyebrow and nodded once, a sort of Russian touché. "We have come to make offer," she said.

Harmony was already shaking her head. "I'm not interested."

"Is not for you." Irina jerked her head in Cole's direction. "Is for him."

Harmony nearly gave herself whiplash, she looked at him so fast.

Cole was just as surprised. "Me? Why?"

"There is reason she break you out of jail." Irina's gaze shifted to the laptop on the table, then lifted to Cole's again. "When we see you on television, when we have name, we find out how you break into FBI computer. She cannot get money without you. Is only reason to take risk."

"Did you miss the part where I wasn't good enough to keep myself from getting caught and sent to jail in the first place?" Cole interjected. True, he'd been set up, but they didn't need to know that. He didn't like where the conversation was headed. And he really didn't like that Harmony was still edging toward the shoulder holster she'd left on the table. If bullets started to fly, he'd be the only one unarmed. That had seemed okay a few days ago when he'd considered the consequences of getting caught in possession. It didn't seem such a wise decision under these circumstances.

"She has kept you from being caught again," Irina was saying. "We will do same. And we will compensate you."

"What makes you think I'm not compensating him?" Harmony asked.

Up went Irina's eyebrow again, up went the corners of her mouth into that irritating little sneer. Her gaze shifted to the single chair in front of the table. "We will give him money."

Harmony gave a slight, shocked laugh. "I think I've just been insulted, Cole."

"I think you're right."

"I think you have no liking for FBI," Irina said to Cole, getting in the act and managing to follow her own agenda at the same time. "They put you in jail for stupid reason. She will send you back when she is through with you."

Cole was still fighting off the immediate, sphincter-clenching thought of going back to Lewisburg, when the rest of Irina's implication sank in. He glanced over at Harmony and knew she'd already gotten the gist of what Irina's deal meant for her.

"You're going to kill me," she said.

"They don't have weapons," Cole pointed out.

"They're not going to take a chance of shooting a gun in here. Not only would it bring the police, they might hit you."

"And they need me. But not you, and if they let you go, you'll interfere."

"They can't take the chance I'll let the FBI know what's going on and cut off the money."

"Very good," Irina said.

"What guarantee do I have that you won't kill me once I've done what you want?" Cole asked.

"Dead bodies are very messy," Irina said.

"And you'll be long gone by the time someone starts asking who made the mess."

"The FBI will not keep promise to you, Cole Hackett. You will be returned to jail."

Harmony kept her mouth shut, wisely, letting Cole make his own decision, even though, on the heels of her fit of honesty, she couldn't know what he'd do.

But even though he didn't trust the FBI, he'd made a deal with her. "I guess I have to turn you down," he said to Irina.

"That is unfortunate. And unacceptable."

Leo had gone dormant while they talked. Irina made a slight hand gesture, and he came to life, lumbering toward Cole as all hell broke loose.

Harmony dove for her gun, but Irina got to her first. Cole couldn't do anything to help her because Leo threw himself the last few feet. Leo wasn't built for speed, and his mental capacity was a big question mark, but he made up for it with sheer bulk, slamming into Cole like the Berlin Wall.

Cole hadn't spent eight years working out just to look good, though. In prison his body had been a deterrent, especially after the first year or so when the other inmates had stopped taking him on to see if he had the meanness to back up the muscles. It had been a while since he'd had to fight, but he hadn't forgotten the basic rules of jailhouse self-defense. Never back down, and fight dirty. And this time he had extra motivation.

He shoved the Russian off and jumped to his feet. He should have taken Leo out while he was still down, but he had to see how Harmony was doing against Irina. The answer was "not good." The other woman had six inches and at least twenty-five pounds—all muscle—on Harmony, not to mention focus and attitude. Her task was to take Harmony out, and she clearly didn't know the meaning of failure.

Harmony had enough training to give Irina a good fight, though; even as Cole watched she got in a beaut of a punch to Irina's face, putting her whole weight behind it. Irina was going to need dark glasses for the next few days. But it was just a matter of time before big and mean won the day, Irina coming back with a blow to Harmony's midsection that made Cole's breath whoosh out in sympathy.

He started for the women, but Leo was on him again, and Cole had to concentrate on staying out of the reach of his massive arms. Pretty simple, since Leo was all bulk and no speed or planning. He just kept coming on, arms wide, trying to crush Cole in a massive bear hug. And he had stamina, damn it, along with a jaw of granite. Cole hammered his midsection and his face and it didn't stop him until frustration and panic had Cole taking Leo out with a roundhouse kick to the head. Leo went down and Cole made sure he wasn't getting up anytime soon, grabbing a handful of hair and rapping his head against the floor a couple of times for good measure.

He lunged to his feet and spun around, fearing the worst and finding it. Irina flipped around behind Harmony and wrapped one arm around her neck, the other coming up to the other side of Harmony's jaw so that Irina's arms were crossed in front of her windpipe. One quick twist and Harmony's neck would be broken.

The table was between them. Cole knew he couldn't get there in time to save her. He met Harmony's gaze, saw the bare, stark knowledge of her situation before he shifted his attention to Irina. She looked back at him, eyes still hard and bright, a little anticipatory smile lifting one corner of her mouth. She didn't go for the kill, letting the pleasure of it spin out. It was her only mistake.

Cole blew out a breath, then said to Harmony, "Remember the day you came for me? In the SUV?"

Harmony nodded slightly. She might not be a warrior, but she had the quickest mind he'd ever known, and she had no trouble connecting her predicament with Cole's handcuff chain around her throat. She'd been threatening to shoot him then, and he'd asked her what she'd do with two hundred pounds of deadweight slumping against her windpipe. Harmony wasn't two hundred pounds, but she'd have surprise on her side.

Irina was no slouch in the mental department, though, her eyes narrowing on Cole's face as she realized they were going to pull something.

It all happened at once then. Irina's muscles bunched to make the kill, but Harmony sagged against her, dropping all her weight against Irina's arm and dragging her off balance. At the same time, Cole ran three steps, vaulting over the small table, snagging Harmony's holster with one hand and tearing her gun out of it with the other. He had it pointed at the side of Irina's head before she could muscle Harmony back into a coup de grâce position.

Irina contemplated her situation for a split-second, then let Harmony go, raising both hands in surrender. Harmony slumped to the floor, but Cole kept his eyes on Irina's, kept the gun pointed at her, watching as she backed away, toward Leo. She kicked him in the side, then again until he grunted and started to stir. She never looked away from Cole, and her eyes were dark and glittering with rage.

A voice in his head screamed at him to shoot her. In eight years of living with the worst of the worst, no one had ever looked at him like that. But he couldn't bring himself to pull the trigger. He held Irina's gaze as Leo dragged himself to all fours, shook himself like a big, clumsy bear, then climbed the rest of the way to his feet and shuffled out of the room, Irina backing out behind him. Cole crossed to the door and watched them get into a nondescript car and drive off.

He knew it wasn't over.

All he could hope was that he and Harmony had a lot of backup or some really big guns when they found Richard. Or that they didn't find him at all. Because if they actually had to take on Irina and Leo a second time, one on one, he didn't think they'd walk away.

chapter
20

HARMONY DRAGGED HERSELF TO HER FEET AND tried to get her things together while Cole went to the door and watched the Russians leave. He came back and shouldered her duffel and the laptop case. He would have carried her, too, but she waved him off. Everything hurt, even the roots of her hair, but she hid it as best she could, considering she couldn't stand fully upright without feeling like someone was stabbing her in the side.

She made it to the car, though, and she didn't argue when Cole insisted on driving. "Back roads" was what she said, regulating her breathing so he couldn't tell how much pain she was feeling. "One lane."

"I'll keep an eye on who's behind us," Cole said. "Except . . . do you think they put a tracking device on the GT? I watched them leave, but they could have put one on before they busted into the room."

"They didn't think it would be necessary," she said, her words punctuated by shallow, wheezing breaths. "They didn't intend to leave without you, and they thought I'd be dead. As long as the police don't stop us, we're good."

"You don't sound good."

"I'm in better shape than I should be under the circumstances."

"You can choose to dwell on what went wrong, or you can look at what just happened as critical training. You need to learn to fight dirty when your life is on the line. Next time—"

"There won't be a next time. Mike is right. Everybody is right. I have no business being an agent. They told me it was because I couldn't separate my emotions from the job."

"They had a point," Cole said.

She snorted out a breath. It hurt like hell, but she got her point across. "They were trying to spare my feelings. They should have told me all the self-defense and fighting classes in the world weren't going to keep me alive because I'm a pantywaist."

"A pantywaist?"

"A weakling, a puffball, all brains and no brawn."

"A puffball having a pity party. Where's the optimism?"

"You were right about that. There's no percentage in thinking positive. When reality hits you between the eyes"— and in the ribs, and the kidneys—"it's just that much worse."

Cole didn't have anything to say to that. After a while, he glanced over at her, his face looking concerned in the reflected glow from the dashboard lights. "Why don't you get some rest?" he suggested.

It was a wonderful idea, the thought of putting her seat back and letting it all go. She needed to make sense of what had happened so she could figure out what direction to take, but her thoughts kept running in circles. She tried to reach into the small space behind her seat, and only wound up gasping in pain because she'd let herself sink into the humiliation of getting soundly defeated, and she'd forgotten about her ribs.

Cole reached back and got the duffel for her, setting it carefully in her lap.

"Thanks," she said, trying for a minute to remember why she'd wanted it in the first place before it came to her. She pulled out her cell and dialed Mike.

When he answered, she wasn't quite sure what to say. Cole came to her rescue again, taking the phone and filling Mike in on what had just happened.

Once he'd finished there was silence for a few seconds, then he said, "They found us because they knew we were headed to LA." Another stretch of silence, then Cole said a couple of uh-huhs and disconnected.

"Get some sleep," he said to her. "When you wake up, we'll be somewhere the kidnappers can't find us."

She reached over, ignoring the stab of pain, to grab his wrist. "I was supposed to call them tonight."

"Fuck them," Cole slashed out.

"Richard—"

"They already know why you're not calling. And they won't hurt Richard. They screwed up by coming after us."

"They took a risk, a pretty good one actually." She let go of his wrist and relaxed back into her seat, squirming a little until she found the most comfortable position—not pain-free but the best she could hope for under the circumstances. "In their place I'd have done the same thing."

"And you'd have gotten the same answer."

"Why?"

Cole slowed to take a turn, then looked over at her.

"Why did you turn them down?" Harmony pressed. She should have let it go, but she needed an answer.

"Once they were done with me, I'd be deadweight. Literally."

He'd accused Irina of that much to her face, and it made perfect sense. Harmony still didn't believe he was telling her the whole truth. But maybe it was just wishful thinking.

"Get some sleep," Cole said, not a suggestion this time so much as a conversation ender. "And don't worry about the kidnappers. We have something they want, they have something we want. It's time we stopped letting them run the show."

Harmony wanted to argue, but her brain had given up what little clarity it had, and it was just too much effort to worry about anything or anyone. She didn't complain when

Cole reached over and buckled her seat belt. She let the darkness steal over her and put her out of her misery.

COLE PUNCHED THE DESTINATION MIKE KOVALESKI HAD given him into the GPS and pushed the GT as fast as he dared without risking police involvement. He didn't believe Harmony was in any medical danger, but he was worried about her. Once she finally drifted off to sleep, he'd checked her pulse and her temperature. Sure, he hadn't used the most scientific method, but her heart rate seemed steady, her breathing was even, and she wasn't warm to the touch. She'd have lots of bruises, including the one blooming along the ridge of her jaw and cheek, and she was obviously in pain, but he didn't believe a hospital was necessary. What concerned him more was the mental toll of losing the fight with Irina.

Her phone chirped and he grabbed it before it could wake her. The voice on the other end had a Russian accent. Not as thick as Irina's; this guy had been off the boat for a while, but he was Russian all the same.

"You missed your appointment," he said.

"We were kind of busy. I imagine you've already heard about it."

"Yes," the head kidnapper said. "You have made a very foolish choice, Mr. Hackett."

"Did you really expect me to take you up on your offer?"

"Yes."

"I know you're Russian," Cole said, "I never thought you were stupid."

"That will earn your friend more punishment."

"He's not my friend," Cole said.

"He is a friend of Agent Swift's, yes? I think you are reluctant to upset her."

"Why?" Cole shot back. "Because I turned you down? I'm pretty sure she's not planning to kill me when this is all over. Can you say the same?"

"Now who is stupid? The FBI cannot be trusted."

"I've been through all this with the two Cossacks you sent after me. I'm not changing my mind." But he wondered just how much of his history they knew. "Let's get down to brass tacks. Unless you're low on your quota of small talk for the day."

"Yes, let us get down to facts, shall we? One would think you are coming after Swendahl."

"One would be right," Cole said. He didn't have a devious bent, as Harmony had pointed out more than once, so he was going to handle this his way. "We're on our way to California."

"We are not in California."

"Cut the bullshit, Ivan. You're somewhere in Los Angeles."

"My name is not Ivan." There was a beat of silence, then, "What makes you think we are in Los Angeles?"

"Because I'm not stupid, and neither is Agent Swift."

"You will never find us."

"We'll see about that," Cole said. "We're taking a few days to rest and recuperate, and if your comrades show up, you can call the whole thing off."

"And Agent Swendahl will be dead."

"I don't care if he takes another breath. Agent Swift does, but she won't blame me if you guys murder him. You either play this my way, or I'll tell her he's already dead and you can go to hell for all I care. But wherever you go, you won't be taking any extra rubles with you unless I make it happen."

There was another brief silence. "There is only seven million dollars in the account. We will not release the agent for this amount."

"There'll be enough," Cole assured him, as Harmony would have done. "And you won't get the password to transfer the funds unless we make the trade face-to-face. And Swendahl had better be up to walking or the deal is off."

"If what you say is true, he will be improved."

"Good. And if I see either one of your flunkies again, it's over. I'll be gone and so will the money." Cole hung up and, as an afterthought, said, "Harm?" concerned that she'd heard his threats, including his disinterest in Richard Swendahl's welfare.

She didn't stir. Cole reached over and shook her gently. No response. There was a moment of blind terror where he couldn't decide what to do, including steer the car, apparently. The GT wandered onto the potholed shoulder, jumping and bouncing. Harmony shifted and groaned, and by the time Cole brought the car back onto the road, she was back asleep again, and he was wondering where the panic had come from.

When he didn't have an answer twenty miles later, he decided to go with "knee-jerk reaction," with a little bit of selfishness thrown in. Harmony was high-handed, bossy, and worst of all, perky, but somewhere along the road she'd grown on him, Cole admitted. He'd hate to see her suffer some major injury or worse, not to mention she was the only person standing between him and jail—if they succeeded in getting Swendahl free. And he'd begun to believe they could pull it off. Of course, that could be because he was flying high on the fact that he'd not only kicked Leo's ass, he'd also pulled off a Hollywood stunt that ended up with him holding a gun to Irina's head and rescuing the damsel in distress. He intended to rub Harmony's face in it the first chance he got— once she stopped feeling sorry for herself. And it would be kind of hard to lord it over her if she was really hurt. So thank god she wasn't.

THE GPS LED THEM TO AN RV PARK OUTSIDE OF COLO-rado Springs. Not what Cole was expecting. RV parks made him think of retirees, not crime. He sat at the entrance for a minute, looking through the windshield, wondering what kind of an active case would be important enough to prompt Mike Kovaleski and the FBI to send an agent to this place. A Metamucil theft ring? Or, if he was being serious, maybe someone was scamming the old folks because the few that were out and about seemed to be wearing clothes from the Salvation Army thrift store like long, old-fashioned dresses and sandals, although he could see their breath fogging the air. A giant of a man stepped out of an RV not far along the main thoroughfare, dressed in what appeared to be long johns and a robe that was way too short . . .

And then Cole looked closer, peering through the early-morning gloom, and realized the people he saw weren't all that old. And the man in the robe—check that, tights and tunic?—was heading straight for the GT.

He halted at the driver's-side window, stooping down to peer inside, his eyes skimming past Cole and resting for a long minute on Harmony, huddled in the passenger seat. His gaze shifted back to Cole, but he didn't say anything, just pointed at the RV he'd exited a moment before, held up an index finger, and then walked away.

Cole waited until he'd made it back to the RV and then pulled down the road, easing the car in between two of the big vehicles where it would be hidden from the road. Before he could decide whether he'd reached safety or the Twilight Zone, the man in the tights opened Harmony's door, gathered her in his arms with a gentleness belied by his size, and carried her around the RV. By the time Cole got out of the GT, they'd disappeared inside.

He didn't remember getting to the door, but when he found it locked, he tried to go straight through it. Who would've guessed RV doors were so sturdy. All he could do was pound on it like a maniac until it opened up. And then it was filled with the big guy in the tights.

"She's fine," he said, coming out and shutting the door behind him without ever giving Cole an opportunity to slip by.

The tights left little doubt about his level of muscular fitness. Cole figured at best it would be an even fight—if the other guy hadn't been a good six inches taller and looked like his idea of working out was bench-pressing wenches. Or small automobiles.

"Connor Larkin," he said.

Cole took the hand he offered, but his eyes were on the RV's door.

"Mike sent you, so I think we both have to agree there's no danger here."

"Except whatever you're investigating," Cole pointed out.

"Not sure what you're talking about," Larkin said. There

was a smile on his face and a warning glint in his eyes. "A friend of mine is looking Harmony over. Annie's not a doctor, but she does a lot of the minor health care for this bunch."

"Bunch?"

"Renaissance reenactors. We travel from fair to fair, mostly selling handmade goods. We're resting up here for a month or so now that the summer and fall fairs in the northern states are over, and before the winter ones start in the South."

Cole nodded, not missing the "we" and wondering what kind of trouble a bunch of harmless kooks could get into that required an FBI investigation. But he respected the other man's undercover status and kept the questions to himself. "Let me guess, you're the blacksmith."

"Armorer."

The RV door opened and Larkin turned around, Cole joining him by the steps. A woman Cole assumed was Annie stepped out and closed the door softly behind her. She was older, with a quiet confidence that said she gladly owned every single wrinkle on her face, and a calmness of manner that put Cole instantly at ease.

"She's pretty banged up," Annie said to Larkin. "I'd guess she has a mild concussion and at least one injured rib. Bruised would be my assessment, but it might be cracked. Her pulse, breathing, everything is steady, so I don't think there are any internal injuries. It looks like someone beat the stuffing out of her," she finished, her gaze shifting to Cole for the first time, anger icing the blue of her eyes and catching Cole off guard.

Not as much as having Larkin slam him up against the side of the RV and hold him there with one hand, his feet a good twelve inches off the ground.

Cole tried to defend himself, but having the breath knocked out of him, along with a shot of pain he hadn't expected, left him speechless. Unlike Larkin.

"Where were you when she was getting the shit kicked out of her? Or were you doing the kicking?"

Annie put a hand on Larkin's arm and said his name, and the rage leached out of him, enough so he put Cole down.

"The boy is hurt, too," she said quietly. "May I?" She lifted his T-shirt, sucking in a breath at the bruises blooming along his left side, from below the waistband of his jeans up to his armpit.

"I guess Leo got in a couple of good shots," Cole said, pulling his shirt down.

"You guess?"

"Honestly, I was just . . ."

"You were trying to get to her," Annie said softly.

Cole pulled his eyes off the RV again.

Annie patted his arm. "I'll go inside and check on her."

Larkin waited until she was gone. "I told them I was running from my past," he said once the RV door shut behind Annie again. "She probably thinks you're part of that past. They respect privacy," he added with a measure of regret that puzzled Cole.

But he had bigger problems than an FBI agent who seemed to be having mixed feelings about his current assignment. "They wanted her dead," he said to Larkin.

"They?"

Cole gave him the high points of the last few days, ending with the offer Irina had made in that Tulsa motel room, and the fight that had followed. "They tried to kill her," he finished. "I couldn't get to her right away, and she couldn't get to her gun."

"Jesus." Larkin paced off a little distance, running a hand through dark, shoulder-length hair. If he'd had armor and a sword he would've looked like the Black Knight, which was probably why he wore his hair like that. "What was she thinking, going out on her own like this?"

"That she had to rescue this Richard guy."

Larkin huffed out a breath, still working on temper control.

"What's he to her?" Cole asked, not really sure he wanted a straight answer. Harmony claimed there was nothing going on between her and Richard Swendahl, but she had to have strong feelings for the guy to put her life on the line for him.

Larkin studied him for a minute, then said, "How much do you know about Harmony?"

"Nothing," Cole said, surprised and a little embarrassed. He'd never thought to ask about her background, just labeled

her FBI and spent the rest of the time thinking the world re-
volved around him and his troubles.

"Harmony was born and raised in California," Larkin
began.

"I know that much."

"What you don't know is that she's a trust-fund baby. A
trust-fund orphan more like. Her parents were kidnapped
and killed when she was eight years old. She never really
knew them."

"Shit," Cole said, his turn to take a few steps away while
he tried to wrap his mind around it. "But . . . she's so optimistic and happy."

"Yeah, something, isn't it? Maybe it helped that she was
so young when they died. I know she misses them, or the
idea of them, especially having a mother. But maybe they're
like a fantasy to her, you know? The best kind of parents, in
a way, because you can make them into whatever you want
them to be."

Larkin sounded like someone who'd lived the other side of
that coin. "Richard Swendahl isn't just a friend," he continued.
"Harmony was raised by a guardian, and there was a succes-
sion of nannies when she was younger, but none of them were
close to her. Richard and her father roomed together in college;
Richard worked her parents' kidnapping, and when she decided to apply for a spot at the FBI, Richard helped her get in.
Away from the Bureau, she refers to him as her uncle, and I
know she considers him the only family she has."

Cole couldn't imagine anyone not being charmed by her.
But then, for a woman who had such difficulty separating her
feelings from her duties, she also set boundaries that kept
others at an emotional arm's length. Maybe because she'd
grown up in an environment where she kept putting herself
out there, and no one had cared back. Or almost no one.

No wonder she was desperate enough to risk everything,
including her own life. "She couldn't do anything about her
parents, but she can do something about Richard."

"Exactly."

"You don't like him," Cole observed. "Why not?"

"It's not jealousy, if that's what you're thinking. I can't say

I didn't take one look at her and have the obvious reaction, but once I got to know her, well, she's like my little sister. And I'm not the only one who feels like that. She's like a mascot at the Bureau, like a soft little clumsy puppy. Everyone who knows her loves her, and they'd all put their lives on the line to help her."

That hadn't been Cole's experience. Sure there'd been lust, but it hadn't been until he'd gotten to know her, until he could see beyond the FBI badge, that he started feeling . . . He took a deep breath and admitted something impossible, something he'd never expected to have to deal with. He was falling in love, with someone he'd nicknamed Harm. He'd gone into this knowing there was a good possibility he'd lose his life, but never his heart.

He should walk away, he told himself. If he stayed with Harmony until her mission played out, he was going to end up in some kind of confined space, and between a coffin and a jail cell, he'd prefer the latter. There was money in his account, and Harmony was safe. There wouldn't be a better time to cut himself loose. And yet he couldn't.

In light of his emotional concerns, he thought it best not to ask himself why.

Annie poked her head out. "She's asking for Cole," she said.

Larkin stopped him on the way by. "Go in and put her mind to rest, then we're going to talk."

"About?"

"How to handle this case. I can't go with you, but I can give you some pointers."

"Thanks, but I already called the kidnappers. Told them we're taking time to recover and then we're coming to them. We'll make a face-to-face exchange, Swendahl for the password to the bank account."

"They'll kill you both."

Cole met Connor Larkin's eyes. "They can try."

chapter
21

HARMONY OPENED HER EYES THE NEXT MORNING—
at least she thought they were open, and she assumed it was
morning. Hard to tell with it being pitch-black. She was lying
on something soft, and there was a pillow beneath her head,
covered in silk. She didn't hear anything, but there was a
cloying flowery scent hanging on the stale air, and when she
reached out, her hand contacted something hard and smooth
not more than six inches from her right side, and her head,
and her big toe when she arched her foot. *Coffin,* her exhausted mind shrieked. Not a sound came out of her mouth,
though, it was impossible to say anything with all her breath
exploding out of her.

There were tiny flashes of light sparking in her vision, her
ears were straining to hear any sound, and her lungs labored
to draw in air. She flailed out with her arms, heading for full-
blown panic when a voice said, "Harm," and then she felt
like a fool because it wasn't the voice of god, it was Cole, and
when she calmed enough to start breathing again, her vision
cleared and she could see him sitting on the edge of the bed,
a blacker silhouette against the rest of the darkness.

She rolled to her side, hissing in a breath through her teeth because it hurt like hell.

"How are you feeling?"

"Stiff, groggy, sore." She shifted a little and winced. "Humiliated," she added, feeling an echo of the desperation she'd felt when she understood she'd lost the fight, that Irina's arms were around her neck and she was about to die. "That was some stunt you pulled."

He turned on a light somewhere behind her, and she blinked, as much from confusion as anything else. "Where are we?"

"You don't remember anything after the stunt?"

"Bits and pieces. I remember being in the car, and I remember you talking to someone."

"Your friend Mike, at the FBI."

She leaned back a little, surprised. "You called the FBI?"

"You called him, but you weren't in any shape to talk."

"So you did."

"I didn't have a lot of options," Cole said. "We needed a safe place to go. We're just outside Colorado Springs right now, at an RV park full of Renaissance fair people."

"You're joking," she said with a slight laugh that still wasn't shallow enough, but then everything hurt. Even the blood running through her veins caused a faint throb of pain. "Why would Mike dump us with Renaissance kooks?"

"Some guy name of Connor Larkin."

"Conn's here?" Harmony forgot reality and tried to jump out of bed. She made it up to one elbow before she collapsed again.

"You can see him later."

"You read my mind," she said. "Where exactly are we?"

"We're in Sal and Larry's RV. They've gone to Vancouver to visit their new granddaughter."

Harmony took in the faux-wood paneling surrounding what passed for a double bed, dressed in silk ruffles. She lifted her head far enough to see past Cole down the length of the RV, a straight shot to a set of curtains that must close off the living space from the cab at the other end. "Sal has a heavy hand with the perfume," she said, "but I'm grateful." It might not be the Four Seasons, but she was alive and safe.

Because of Cole.

After all her big talk, she'd nearly been killed the first time she'd really been tested. If not for Cole . . . She closed her eyes, too tired to hide from the truth any longer. She had feelings for Cole, feelings that went beyond trust and respect, wandering right into love. She wanted to believe Cole had chosen her over the Russians because he had feelings for her, too. But that would be foolish.

Cole was looking out for his own interests, and who could blame him? He'd spent a week with her, and while he couldn't possibly trust her, he must be reasonably confident she wouldn't shoot him in the head the moment she didn't need him anymore. He couldn't say the same about Irina. He could have taken off once he'd put Leo out of commission, but Cole wasn't that kind of man. He wasn't in love with her, but he wouldn't leave her to die, either. "Did I thank you?"

"Not necessary," Cole said.

She shifted onto her back, staring at the ceiling over her head. "I don't think I can do this."

"So you're just going to leave Richard to the kidnappers? Look, you ran into a woman who's been doing this a while. You're new at it. And it's not like you to sit around feeling sorry for yourself."

"I'm not. How can I rescue Richard when I can't even defend myself?"

"That's a question you have to answer for yourself."

He stood up. "How about some breakfast?"

It was so typically Cole to be thinking of his stomach that she couldn't help but smile. She wasn't sure how to salvage the mission, but she began to feel a little glimmer of hope again.

AFTER COLE LEFT, HARMONY DRAGGED HERSELF INTO the tiny shower in the tiny bathroom that turned out to be where the light had come from. The hot water loosened up her stiffening muscles enough that she felt better. Not well enough to bother with a bra; her ribs were still too sore for that, and wrangling herself into that particular undergarment just seemed like too much trouble. She borrowed a shirt from Sal's closet, loose and oversized, hanging almost to her knees. She was just stepping into her own jeans when there was a knock on the door, the person on the other side not waiting for her to answer but stepping inside, a covered tray in her hands.

Harmony was more interested in the woman behind the tray. She appeared to be in her fifties, and the wrinkles on her face were clearly from smiling, since that's what she was doing.

"Annie Bliss," she said, setting the tray on a small table and turning back to Harmony, her eyes sparkling.

"From last night," Harmony said, recognition kicking in.

"That's right. I'm glad you remember. It means you weren't as out of it as you appeared to be."

Harmony waited, expecting the obvious questions. Who wouldn't wonder about a woman who'd shown up in the middle of the night looking like a punching bag?

"I brought you some breakfast," Annie said, still smiling that serene smile, apparently not the least bit curious.

"I'm not really hungry," Harmony said, and then Annie uncovered the tray to reveal a bowl and a glass. The bowl contained some kind of hot cereal. The aroma of brown sugar and melted butter wafted to her, making her mouth water and her stomach growl.

Annie handed her a spoon and nudged her into a chair. Harmony took a bite, the slightly nutty flavor of the cereal mixing with the sweet sugar and the salty creaminess of the butter, all of it warm and comforting from the moment it passed her lips all the way down to her stomach.

"That is really amazing," she said, spooning up another mouthful. "It's not oatmeal. What is it?"

"It's a special blend made by a friend of mine. It's actually after noon, but I wasn't sure how your stomach would be, so I thought this would be best."

"You were right. Thank your friend for me."

"You'll meet her later. You can thank her yourself."

"I, uh, don't know how long I'm going to be here, Mrs. Bliss."

"Annie."

"Annie," Harmony repeated dutifully.

"Your young man said the two of you would be here a couple days at least."

"Oh." Harmony ate two more bites without tasting them because she was concentrating on sounding casual when she said, "He's not actually my young man."

"No? He was quite frantic last night," Annie said calmly, as if she hadn't just implied a life-altering possibility.

And as soon as that thought surfaced, Harmony rejected it. Cole was worried about staying out of jail. He needed her for that.

"Well," Annie said as if she'd read Harmony's mind and wanted to reassure her, "sometimes it's best not to overthink these things. Just accept today for what it is, try to make the most of it, and above all enjoy it. Tomorrow can take care of itself."

Harmony nodded, thinking that was a really nice fantasy for someone like Annie, but Harmony had a hard time accepting today for what it was when it meant Richard was still a hostage and she couldn't do anything about it. She forced herself to sit there a few more minutes, but her stomach wasn't going to let her put anything else into it.

Annie seemed to understand. She took the tray and left with nothing more than a parting smile. Harmony eased out of the chair and folded the hem of the shirt up until it was around her waist, tying the ends into a knot. She slipped her feet into her athletic shoes, not bothering to tie them, took a deep breath, and opened the RV door, blinking in the bright sunlight.

She was looking for Cole. She saw Connor Larkin first. He sat under the overhang of a shedlike structure at the far end of the RV camp. As Harmony got closer, she noticed the banked fire and realized it must be a portable forge.

"When you take a cover, you really get into it," she said as she came up beside him, taking a step back when the heat of the fire hit her in the face.

Conn swung around, holding out his arms.

Harmony held up her hands to ward him off. "Consider yourself hugged."

"Sorry, Harmony, I forgot," he said, urging her to sit on the stool he'd just vacated.

She did, studying the armorlike whatchamacallit on the workbench.

"It's a fish," he explained, "created out of the same kind of overlapping metal plates I'd use to make a gauntlet. The plates are smaller and shaped to look like scales, but it's the same mechanics used to make flexible plate armor."

"You could probably sell that."

"I do. Have to keep up the cover, right?"

She smiled because he expected it. "What about me and Cole? What have you told everyone?"

"Nothing. The Blisses are always taking in strays."

"No one is asking? I mean, Annie seems like the kind of person who would feed and house a complete stranger, even one who was clearly in some kind of trouble. But everyone else?"

"There are two kinds of people who participate in Renaissance fairs," Conn said. "The ones who have established businesses and use the fairs for an extra boost, and the ones who subsist on their earnings, traveling from fair to fair."

"These are the travelers, I take it."

"Some of them just prefer the lifestyle, like Annie and Nelson, her husband. But a lot of these people are on the fringe of society."

"Criminals?"

"Not the kind who'd hurt someone," Conn said quickly, "and yeah, I know I'm here for a reason, but it's nothing violent. These people look out for each other, and anyone dangerous is sent packing pretty quickly."

"What about us?" Harmony asked. "How do they know we're not dangerous?"

"I vouched for you. But while we're on the subject, what the hell are you doing?"

Harmony looked away. "Someone had to go after him, Conn."

"You know the odds, Harmony. They're going to kill him as soon as you give them what they want."

She smiled grimly. "I don't think that's going to be a problem. At least not my problem."

"What's that supposed to mean?"

"It means I think I should turn this back to Mike and let him decide what to do. I'm not capable—"

"Bullshit."

That brought her face up, her eyes meeting his.

"You started this," Conn said, "you finish it."

"But . . . You just said . . ."

"I know what I said. Now think it through. Why did you take these bastards on? And don't tell me it was all about Richard."

"He's the important part," she hedged.

"And?"

"And I wanted to prove something to Mike."

"What's it going to prove if you quit the minute it gets rough?" Conn gave her exactly two seconds to think about it before he said, "Let's try this again. They're going to kill Swendahl as soon as you give them what they want."

Harmony took a deep breath and let it out slowly. "They're not getting anything unless Richard is alive and they're turning him over to me," she said, resisting the temptation to make it into a question. Sure, her confidence had been shaken, deeply, but it hadn't been destroyed. "And then I'm going to keep the money, too."

Conn took off his glove, hunkering down in front of her and brushing a finger across the bruise on her check. "They've already tried to kill you once."

She caught his hand and held it between both of her own. "I'm still alive, aren't I? It's a miracle, and it's probably not the last one I'll need, but one day at a time, right?"

"You're trusting your life to an ex-con, and you're going up against pros," Conn said by way of agreement.

"That's the job. You make do with what you have." She smiled at him. "Unless you want to ditch the hippies and come with me."

He grinned back. "Just between you and me, these people are hippies and kooks."

"And yet I detect a note of fondness in your voice."

He shrugged. "They're endearing kooks."

"And criminals, or you wouldn't be here."

"Yep. Nice to know I can count on human nature to keep me employed."

"True," Harmony said. *Alive was a different story.*

chapter
22

IF COLE HADN'T BEEN ABLE TO PUT HIS FINGER ON why he disliked Connor Larkin, the way he was touching Harm's face was reason enough. Larkin lifted one of her feet to his thigh and tied her shoe, then did the same with the other one. He cared about her, and even though he'd said it was a brotherly kind of caring, Cole was burning.

Larkin leaned over and said something to her. She stiffened, turned to peruse the area, and her eyes landed on Cole. She was burning, too, he realized. And not in a good way.

She shot to her feet, then took a few seconds—visibly in pain—before she brushed off Larkin's hands and made a bee-line for Cole. She stopped a few feet away, her hand out. "Keys," she said shortly.

"No."

"This is my operation."

"Not anymore."

She looked over at Larkin, who was leaning against his workbench, arms crossed, watching them and not getting in the middle.

"I took your phones, too, both of them, and your laptop."

She stared at him a second, mouth open, before she stalked into Sal and Larry's RV, managing to put anger into her walk and favor her side at the same time. By the time Cole joined her, she'd dumped everything she owned out on the tiny galley table, and she was staring blankly at the empty duffel.

"You took the money, too."

"You're staying put," he said. Not to mention it was his money.

"You can't hold me prisoner."

"Doesn't feel so good when it's you, does it?"

"The circumstances are different," she said.

"Sure, the circumstances are what matters."

"We don't have time for this."

"We have plenty of time."

She fisted her hands around the duffel, and Cole could see her struggling for control. "Conn told me you called the kidnappers," she said calmly enough to impress him.

"They called your phone, actually. Last night, after you passed out . . ."

Her eyes narrowed.

"After you fell asleep in the car."

"And?"

"I told the guy on the phone I wasn't taking their offer, and if we see Boris and Natasha again, I walk for good. There were the usual threats, and I explained that if Richard isn't okay and able to move when we get there, the deal is off."

Harmony's gaze snapped to his. "When we get there?"

"He knew we were coming, Harm. He tried to claim they weren't in Los Angeles, but—"

"Damn it." She paced a few steps away, then back.

"You can call in the cavalry now," he said, on the defensive and getting pissed off about it. He'd done a good thing and she acted like he'd sold her out. "Call your boss."

"And where are you going to be?"

"I guess I didn't consider that. I was thinking of you."

"Because you don't believe we can do this—that I can do this."

"You didn't believe it either an hour ago."

"I talked to Conn—"

"You talked to *Conn*, and that changes everything."

"He reminded me why I started this, and it made me think about what would happen if I didn't finish it."

"Well, hurray for Conn." It was Cole's turn to pace away and back, work off a little of whatever was jumping around inside him. "I'm glad he's around to keep you on track."

"What's wrong with you?" Harmony wanted to know, studying his face.

"Nothing," Cole shot back, not meeting her eyes. "You've decided you want to finish this thing. You should get some rest and try to heal up."

"Well, that was patronizing. Not like that's a new attitude, considering."

"Maybe I should call Larkin over here. You listen to him."

She crossed her arms and raised an eyebrow, and he felt childish. It stung, more than taking second seat to a muscle-bound FBI agent. "At least we have a couple of days to figure out how to handle this."

"Thanks to you? You make a few threats and you think the kidnappers are going to sit there waiting for us like toddlers in a time-out?" She huffed out a breath. "This isn't kindergarten, Barney."

"Is that where you think I spent the last eight years? The FBI doesn't screw around, even when they're wrong. Why do you think I want you to bring them in?"

"They've already made their call on this."

"But now that you're in danger—"

"Because I didn't follow protocol. Mike isn't a miracle worker. He has to get approval for an operation like this, and he won't get it."

"If you ask him—"

"If I ask him, he'll send in agents, but it'll cost him his career. And don't even think about Connor. No matter how it appears, he's on a job."

Cole scrubbed a hand over his face. "I guess it's still just you and me."

"And you're having doubts."

"I was looking for a way to take some of the risk out of this. For both of us."

Harmony shook her head. "This is a chess game, Cole. You made our move when you called and threatened them, but they're not going to take it lying down. They're already planning their next move."

"They don't know where we are, so we have some time."

"You're wrong. They're not going to wait for us to surface again. If we leave now, we might be able to surprise them."

"Fine, where are we going?"

"LA."

"Where in LA?"

"What's with all the questions? No, never mind. If you won't help me, I'll find someone who will."

"Go ahead," Cole said, shrugging. "I'm sure someone will lend you a phone, but don't call Mike."

She stopped at the door, turning back. "Two minutes ago you wanted me to call him."

"To send in agents. He won't help you put yourself in danger."

"Now you're an authority on my boss?"

"I don't have to be. He told me if anything happened to you, he'd make sure I regretted it."

"You're not talking about the conversation last night, are you?"

"I'm talking about the first time we spoke. On the boat. I keep you safe or else, that's what he said."

She went still, her expression carefully blank. But there was something to the way she seemed to draw into herself, almost as if she were hurt, although Cole couldn't fathom why.

"Is that why you're still helping me?" she asked almost too calmly.

The easy answer would have been *yes*. It would be better for her to think he'd stuck with her despite everything, and that he'd turned down the deal the Russians had offered him, because he was afraid of FBI retaliation. Best not to give her any reason to romanticize their relationship.

What he said was, "No."

"Then why are you still helping me?"

"Larkin told me about your family," he said, which clearly wasn't any of the responses she'd expected.

"So it's fear *and* pity."

"I understand your motivation."

Harmony shifted sideways, and when the physical evasion wasn't enough, she said, "How could you possibly understand?"

"My parents aren't dead, but I lost them when I went to jail." He thought back, remembering how he'd burned to get away from that tiny three-bedroom tract house where he'd grown up. Now he'd give his right arm to go back there and start over. He'd make better choices this time, or at least thank his parents for the sacrifices they'd made to give him a first-class education on a blue-collar income. And he'd apologize for the heartache he'd caused them. "They live in a small town in Minnesota. Even if they could have afforded to make the trip East, I didn't want them visiting me in that place. I've only seen them once in eight years, and that was bad. For all of us."

Harmony could imagine how hard it must have been for him. She'd have given anything for a chance to see her parents again, but she couldn't change history. She could, however, stop it from repeating itself. "If you won't help me, I'll have to find a way to get there on my own."

She stepped out of the RV, shielding her eyes from the insanely bright sunshine. Sunglasses would have been nice, and she had a pair in her duffel, but Cole would probably hide those, too, if he thought they'd help her get out of there. She made a beeline for the nearest patch of shade instead, and found a family of RVers who clearly took their reenacting seriously. The dad wore a tunic and tights, the mom a wench dress that cinched her breasts up around her clavicle. Two little girls of indeterminate age, wearing tunics and the sparkly pink plastic sandals called jellies, played nearby.

The remains of their lunch covered the picnic table where the parents sat under a huge, spreading cottonwood. By the time it occurred to Harmony that she was staring at them like they were a zoo attraction, she realized they were staring right back.

"I'm sorry, it's been a strange couple of days," she said, not even realizing how true that was until she heard herself say it. Two days ago she'd been in charge of the quest to free Richard, now the reins had been taken out of her hands, and Cole was driving the wagon. Or rather Cole had parked the wagon, unhitched the horses, and stranded her in the midst of a band of traveling historical anachronisms.

"You're Connor Larkin's friend, right?" the woman said.

"Harmony."

"Cindy Brewer." She took the hand Harmony offered and shook it briskly. "This is my husband, Dan, and our daughters."

Harmony felt a tug on her pant leg and looked down into the angelic face of a towheaded ragamuffin about five years old. "My name's Corey," she said with an endearing lisp.

Harmony smiled, really smiled, for the first time in what felt like forever. She stooped down to eye level and shook the little girl's hand, saying with the proper amount of solemnity, "It's my pleasure to meet you, Miss Corey Brewer, and your sister . . ."

"Jessie," Corey said, pointing to her sister sulking next to her. "She hasta go to school today, but I done that already and I only hafta go in the morning 'cuz I'm five." She held up a hand, checking to make sure the finger count matched, then reached out and touched one of Harmony's blond curls. "You're pretty."

"Just between you and me," Harmony said, "pretty is okay, but smart gets you everything."

"Smart and hard work," Cindy chimed in.

Jessie hopped off the picnic table bench and said to her sister, "I'm gonna have everything," and raced off to join a group of kids sitting under an awning across the way, where two young women conducted a sort of group home school.

"I'm gonna get everything, too," Corey said.

Her mother caught her before she could tag along after her sister, redirecting her toward her father instead. "Right now you're getting a nap."

"They're adorable," Harmony said to their mother.

"Spoken like a woman who only spent five minutes with them," Cindy said, but she was smiling.

"You wouldn't happen to have a cell phone I could borrow, would you?"

Cindy reached into the folds of her skirt and came out with a state-of-the-art iPhone. "We're only selectively crazy."

Harmony wished she could say the same, but she'd come to the conclusion that she'd gone completely around the bend. It didn't help that Cole and Connor Larkin were standing by his forge, shoulder to shoulder, watching her like she was a lab rat. Nothing like a little rampant chauvinism to promote male bonding. Okay, that wasn't really fair. They thought they were protecting her. But the end result was the same. She had an agenda; they were standing in the way. So she was going to find someone else to help her, just like she'd said.

"It's about time you called," Mike said when she got him on the line. "Larkin caught me up already, and I agree that it's best for you to lay low for a couple days, heal up."

So the testosterone brigade was closing ranks all around, Harmony thought bitterly. "What about the kidnappers?"

"Hackett has them by the short hairs. They won't make any stupid moves with millions of dollars on the line."

"So I'm just supposed to take the weekend off?"

"Either that or I'm pulling you in."

"You can't pull me in if I don't work for you anymore."

"That supposed to be a threat? If it is, it's a damn poor one, especially if you think it will stop me."

"I can't just sit here and do nothing, Mike."

"Swendahl will be okay."

"It's not about him," Harmony said. "At least not entirely. It just feels . . . wrong to stay here."

Mike didn't say anything, and she knew he was thinking it over, just as she knew he wouldn't trust her gut feeling. She had no experience to back it up.

"Look, Treacher is out of the picture now."

"He wasn't the bigger threat," Harmony said.

"Maybe not, but it's a complication you didn't need. Give it a couple more days before you go after the kidnappers again, get back on your feet a little more."

"It's not like you've left me a choice," Harmony said, letting him hear her frustration. "I ought to sue you for gender discrimination."

"Yeah," Mike said, deadpan, "shame you're on—
There was a lot of rusty laughter after that.

Harmony disconnected and handed the phone to Dan, since Cindy had taken her youngest daughter off to nap.

"Man trouble?" he asked her.

"You could say that." Men trouble, anyway. Mike was probably still laughing, Conn was leaning against his forge, arms crossed, grinning. Cole wasn't smiling but even from there she could feel his smugness.

She closed her eyes and took a couple of deep breaths, and when she opened them again, she was able to see the snow-capped mountains, the incredible blue of the sky, and smell the fresh air.

"Don't get no better than this," Dan said.

Harmony smiled and nodded, thinking if it didn't get any better than having the closest thing to family held for ransom with an FBI-hating felon all that stood between him and death because she'd failed, utterly, the first time she'd had to really prove herself, then she might as well blow her brains out now, before Irina got the satisfaction of doing it.

"SHE'S CALLING MIKE," LARKIN SAID, AS IF COLE DIDN'T know that already. "He won't help her go off on her own and get into trouble."

Cole knew that, too. He had a threat hanging over his head to prove it. Not that it stopped him from worrying. "There's no telling what she'll do," he said. "She's kind of pissed off."

She shot them a look, and he revised the *kind of* to *extremely*, and added Mike to the names on her shit list.

"She won't do anything stupid," Larkin maintained.

"You mean like break a federal prisoner out of jail? Or take on a pack of Russian kidnappers? Not to mention the havoc she's wreaked on her fellow FBI agents." Of course, taking out a couple of feds wasn't a bad thing to his way of thinking.

"Yeah, she's gonna take hell for that." Larkin grinned

ney're going to take for
of them."

he said. "All that blond hair and
smiles at you, and you figure she's
and then *wham!* she puts two guys into
gun on you, or drives her boat over another
as it into kindling, which leaves the passengers
wi   ile-long swim."

"She pulled a gun on you?"

"She shot it, too. I'm just glad she wasn't actually trying to hit me."

Larkin chuckled, shaking his head.

"She warned me first," Cole said, trying not to smile over the memory. He'd had her by the throat, literally, but she'd kept her head, and still managed to come out on top. He ought to remember that more often.

"I blame Barbie," Larkin said. "Everything was fine when all Barbie wanted was a pink car and a dream house. Then she got a job and pretty soon it's Fighter Pilot Barbie and Corporate Raider Barbie, and little girls are getting the notion they can do anything. Not that they can't do anything, but it makes it damn hard on a guy, you know? How are you supposed to make an impression? Hell, look at Ken."

"No balls at all," Cole deadpanned.

"In more ways than one. Which makes Ken obsolete."

"I get your point, but I'm not sure you can blame Harmony on Barbie. It'd be more appropriate to name a hurricane after her. Or at least a tropical storm."

"You must bring out the worst in her."

There were some good moments, too. There were some amazing moments, and some that absolutely blew his mind. But Cole kept that to himself.

Harmony returned the phone she'd borrowed, and then she swung around and looked their way.

"It feel like the wind just picked up speed to you?" Larkin asked mildly. "Whatever Mike said to her, Hurricane Harmony isn't happy about it."

Cole could tell Larkin was grinning again, although he didn't confirm it visually. He was afraid to take his eyes off

Harmony as she crossed the open space inside the RV circle, real purpose in her step.

She stopped within shouting distance. Not that she was shouting. More like she was grinding the words out through clenched teeth. "You. Win."

"So do you. You're safe, at least long enough for your ribs to heal up some."

"I don't need you to protect me."

"See what I mean, Ken?"

They both whipped around. Connor Larkin put up his hands and backed off a step or two.

"And what about Richard?"

"Richard can take care of himself," Larkin interjected.

Harmony swung around again. "Still not talking to you."

"But I'm standing right here, and I am sort of involved."

"Don't remind me."

"You're mad at me," Cole said, "not him."

"What? You two friends now? Because Cole doesn't even like you," she said to Larkin.

"I'm not all that fond of him, either."

Harmony's eyes narrowed. "You really want to stay out of this, Conn."

"Okay." Larkin went back to work, pumping up a bellows with his foot so the fire glowed red. He picked up a pair of tongs with a bit of steel clamped between the blackened ends and plunged it into the firebox. After a few seconds he pulled it out and hammered on it, red-hot slag showering everything in proximity. It wasn't a task that allowed for anything but absolute concentration. Cole still had the impression Larkin was keeping an eye on them, even when he walked twenty yards away, forcing Harmony to follow him.

"I know you're upset," he began.

"Upset? You lined everything up the way you wanted it, my boss, that simpleton over there." She pointed to Larkin, who stiffened, proof that he was eavesdropping. "Even the kidnappers," she continued. "And then you took the car keys, both my cell phones, and my laptop."

"What did you expect me to do?"

"Talk to me."

"I tried that. You weren't being reasonable."

"Of course not. My friend, the only family I have, is in trouble."

"I get that."

"Do you? What if it were your parents?"

Cole jerked, imagining, just for a second how he'd feel if one or both of his parents were in Richard Swendahl's shoes. Panic, terror, and the kind of urgency that couldn't be put into words, and that was just the beginning because next came blind rage and the urgency took on a violent edge. He'd want to make someone pay. Hell, he'd want to kill the kidnappers with his bare hands . . .

But it wasn't his parents, he thought, unclenching his fists. If it were, if he'd been feeling half of what Harmony was, he hoped there'd be someone rational around to keep him from getting himself killed. He couldn't help anyone if he couldn't think straight.

And he didn't dare say that to Harmony, any of it.

"I thought you trusted me," she said.

"I do trust you. Damn it, Harm, I . . ."

She waited for him to finish his thought, let the silence hum for a few seconds, before she got that closed look on her face again. The one, he now realized, that masked hurt. "Nothing else to say?"

Cole had a lot to say to her, but most of it he hadn't actually said to himself yet, and it was the kind of information that needed a hell of a lot of forethought, which, since he was hoping he'd get over it, he didn't see the need for.

Harmony stared at him for a moment without comment, then she walked away. Nothing she could have said would have tortured him as much as watching her turn her back on him and leave without saying a word.

chapter
23

AROUND FIVE IN THE AFTERNOON, A HALF-DOZEN
charcoal barbecue grills were fired up in the big open space
within the circle of RVs. Three picnic tables sat behind the
guys manning the grills, and in an amazingly short time,
they were covered in plastic cloths and loaded with food. No
turkey legs or Scotch eggs, but there were bowls of pasta salad
and fresh fruit and everything else imaginable. Stacks of
hamburgers and hot dogs followed, and everyone came out
and loaded plates, sitting wherever they could find a seat.

It was a strikingly similar scene to the one at Juan's. People weren't as different as they thought they were.

Connor Larkin came over and parked himself beside Harmony on the steps of Sal and Larry's RV. Cole was MIA.

"Not eating?" Conn asked her.

"Not hungry."

"Still mad at me, huh?"

"You're a jerk," she said without any actual heat.

"That's actually a step up from what my last girlfriend
called me when we parted."

"I don't have the kind of firsthand experience it takes to

formulate a really demoralizing insult," Harmony said. "I know a couple of good generic ones: scum-sucking bastard, dickless wonder—"

Conn looked shocked.

"What?"

"I've never heard you swear before."

"Get used to it. I could come up with even better insults, but—"

"You lack firsthand experience."

She gave him a dirty look. "So, we done here?"

"Not until you get your head out of your ass. Hackett was concerned about you because that Russian woman almost killed you."

"Yeah," Harmony said on a heavy exhale. "I'm not exactly a testimonial for FBI training."

"You need to take all that rage you're aiming at Hackett and store it up for the next time you run into that bitch."

"There might not be a next time."

"There'll be a next time."

"Then I'm bringing a gun."

"That works, too."

They sat there awhile in silence, watching kids race around, thwarting the efforts of various adults to corral them into eating their dinner.

"This is like a commune," Harmony observed

"In the best sense of the word. They work together like a big family. There's conflict sometimes. Joe the roasted turkey leg guy was caught with a wench who wasn't his wife, and there was a wicked campaign to dethrone the current Queen Elizabeth. She was getting a bit snooty, if you ask me . . . What?"

Despite his scowl, she kept smiling. It felt good. "If I didn't know you better, I'd say you were getting personally involved."

"Good thing you know me better," Conn said.

"Hard to believe there's criminal activity here."

"Yeah."

Harmony let it go. Conn's case was off limits and she'd

crossed a line even alluding to it. "I don't see any kids over the age of sixteen."

Conn shrugged. "It's like living in a small town. The kids get restless and go off to college or the big city to chase their own dreams. Doesn't mean this is a bad place to raise 'em. Annie and Nelson raised their daughter this way. She was homeschooled, went to the University of Michigan and now she's some big-shot accountant."

Annie Bliss came over, a loaded plate in each hand. She gave one to Conn, the other to Harmony.

Harmony surveyed the mounds of food, her stomach pitching and rolling at the idea of putting anything into it.

"You make sure she eats some of that," Annie said to Conn.

"Nope. She calls me names when I force her to do things for her own good."

"Then don't force her, dummy. Reason with her."

"You're talking to the wrong guy," Conn said. He got up and headed off, taking his plate with him.

Harmony watched him go, thinking if he had any notion of finding Cole and sending him over, he was going to have to give it up. Cole was making himself scarce for a reason. And she didn't miss him. Really she didn't.

Annie Bliss sat down in Conn's place, nudging Harmony companionably with her shoulder. "Trouble in paradise?"

"More like hell is living up to its reputation."

FOR THE FIRST TIME SINCE HE'D LEFT JAIL, COLE WASN'T hungry. The food smelled amazing, took him back to the times when his dad had tied on his "Grillin' Man-iac" apron and turned ground beef into hockey pucks while his mom put the rest of the meal on the table, including the chicken or meatloaf because she "wasn't a hamburger person." Mom lied to Dad because she didn't want to hurt his feelings. Dad knew she was lying, but he never said as much because she loved him enough to lie to him.

Harmony didn't get that. Not that they were in love with

each other, and sure, there was more at stake than a couple of singed hamburger patties, but she still ought to get that he'd done what he'd done because he cared about her.

Cole took a swig of his sixth . . . seventh . . . his current beer, and followed it with a shot of the breath-stealing moonshine Annie's husband had been handing out earlier. He hunched his shoulders because night had fallen sometime while he'd been feeling sorry for himself, and while it wasn't chilly enough to overpower the nice buzz he had going on, being alone in the dark made him think of Lewisburg. So he concentrated on what everyone else was doing and stopped thinking about himself. It didn't change anything anyway.

Dinner was over, the grills and picnic tables were gone, and a huge bonfire had been lit. Cole stayed where he'd been the entire evening, in clear view of the action but not in danger of getting dragged into it. At Annie Bliss's urging, Harm had moved from the steps of Sal and Larry's RV to a seat around the bonfire, where she could watch the Renaissance kooks putting on their crazy.

Jugglers juggled, guys dressed like Hamlet did sword tricks, and comedians in rags told jokes that grew bawdier as the peewees were trundled off to bed. Other performers took the place of the comedians, trying out new material for the little stages peppered throughout the fairs. There were Irish dancers, Scottish dancers, and belly dancers. The reenacters really liked dancing. Some of them even joined in, carried away by booze and *joie de vivre*.

For a little while Harmony kept her seat at the edge of the firelight, but before long she was in the middle of everything, smiling, then laughing, so damn beautiful she was almost too bright to look at. And yet he couldn't take his eyes off her.

The kooks took to her like she was their long-lost queen, urging her to try her hand at juggling, clapping and laughing when she bobbled three potatoes and one of them fell into the bonfire and exploded. She was outfitted in a wench dress that did amazing things for her cleavage, and someone put a flower wreath in her hair, making her look like the Beach Boys had her in mind when they sang about California girls.

Cole took a step forward and nearly fell on his face, staring blearily down at his feet and wondering why they weren't cooperating as he blundered into the outermost group of RV-ers. Harmony looked over her shoulder, fairly sparkling with happiness, and he was lost, even after her smile faded and she turned away. He still wasn't getting with the medieval spirit, but he forgot his feet, forgot he was mad at her, so focused on getting that smile back he shoved his way through the crowd to get to her.

She met him halfway, apologizing to people he couldn't see because he was focused so completely on her.

"You're drunk," she said when she got to him.

"Not smiling," he slurred out, adding, "either one of you," because although he blinked and rubbed his eyes, there seemed to be two of her, and both of them were shaking their head and walking forward until he lost sight of them. But he felt a shoulder brace him under his armpit and pull him away from the fire.

That was all right with Cole. He couldn't tell if she was smiling, but she was touching him, which was even better, and they were alone, which was really good. And she was undressing him. He reached for the snap of his jeans but she batted his hands away, made short work of the snap and the zipper, then gave him a shove backward. He fell over, his addled brain struggling to figure out why he stopped short of the floor. Bed, he realized, belatedly noticing he'd landed on something soft.

Bed was good. Bed was just what he wanted, but not alone. He reached for Harmony but she backed away, bending to remove his shoes and strip his jeans the rest of the way off. That worked, too. The only thing better than being in bed with Harmony was being in bed naked with Harmony. When she didn't join him, he struggled upright, weaving for a second while he got used to the way the place was spinning, and then he reached for her again.

"Why is it that men think they're Casanova when they're drunk?" she said, smacking his hands away and shoving him onto his back again. She retrieved some aspirin from the bathroom and brought them out, along with a glass of water. "Take these."

"Don' wanna," he mumbled. "Want you. Love you. Come to bed." He held out a hand, but his eyes were already closed, and he couldn't stop himself from spiraling down into the peaceful darkness.

HARMONY SAT ON THE END OF THE BED THE NEXT morning, her back braced against the wall, and shoved Cole with her foot for the fourth time. He still didn't move. She'd been up for hours, and she was tired of waiting for him to wake up. She shoved him again. All she got for her effort was a half snore, so she went into the tiny bathroom, wet her hands, and came back to the bed, sprinkling water on him.

"Wha'?" he mumbled, running a hand over his face and opening his eyes to stare at his damp palm in confusion.

"Time to get up," Harmony sang out as loudly as she could, grinning when he winced and pulled a pillow over his head.

She tugged the pillow away and poked him in the ribs a couple of times, easily avoiding his attempts to stop her, especially when he gave up and cradled his head like his skull was going to explode.

Harmony laughed. "Hungover, huh?"

"My head is pounding, my mouth tastes like a cesspool, and my gut is burning. *And what is that smell?*"

"Your breath," Harmony said, waving a hand in front of her face.

"The other smell," he groaned, hands leaving his head to clutch at his stomach.

Harmony shifted out of the line of fire. "Breakfast. Eggs, toast, and some nice fresh sausage."

Cole heaved off the bed, swiping her out of the way with one arm and tearing into the bathroom. She could hear him retching, and it served him right. Then she heard him gargling, and when he came out he smelled like mouthwash, for which she was grateful.

"I was never much of a drinker, and in jail—"

"It wasn't available."

"No, it was available. Lots of guys made home brew, but getting drunk was contrary to my personal safety." He sank onto the bed, smiling weakly. "I guess I've lost my tolerance."

"How much of last night do you remember?" Harmony asked him, even though she'd sworn she wouldn't because what she really wanted to know was if he remembered saying he loved her, and what she wanted to ask him was how he'd meant it. *Was it a thanks-for-getting-me-home I love you, or a desperate-for-sex I love you? Or did he mean it, from the heart, no strings attached?*

"I remember Nelson giving me a couple swigs of some sort of homemade hooch—"

"Which you were stupid enough to drink."

"There was beer, too."

And there went her hopes for a clarification. "Go back to bed and sleep it off."

"About last night," he said, catching her arm before she could do more than stand up.

Her heart started to race, jumping into her throat. But it wasn't the explanation she'd been imagining.

"I'm sorry, Harm," he said, and although she looked pointedly at his hand still banded around her wrist, he didn't let her go, "about everything. I shouldn't have taken your phone and your computer and the car keys. And calling your boss was probably wrong, too. I just wanted to make sure you wouldn't . . ."

"Do anything stupid?"

He gave her a one-shouldered shrug, wincing when even that slight movement made his head pound.

"I suppose I did overreact a little."

"If that's an apology, it's a darn poor one."

"You want me to apologize for getting angry because you were being an overprotective jerk?"

"Well, when you put it like that . . ." He dropped her wrist and collapsed back on the bed, pulling a cool pillow under his head.

When he woke up again, Harmony was gone. His head still throbbed so hard even the suggestion of daylight made him wince. He got up, took four aspirin, drank about a gallon of water, and went back to sleep. The next time he woke up his arms were full of Harmony, and the throbbing had moved south. And he'd apologized, he reminded himself, not to mention she'd crawled into bed with him, so she probably wouldn't reject him if he woke her up.

He'd start by kissing her neck just below her ear where she liked it, and then he'd slip his hand up from where it rested at her waist. Or maybe he'd slip it down. Either way he could already predict the way her breath would sigh out, how she'd rub her soft curves against him, how he'd nudge her over onto her back, or maybe her stomach.

He had it all choreographed, and then a funny thing happened. He relaxed into the mattress again, at least most of him did. He couldn't bring himself to wake her out of a sound sleep, and not because he was afraid she'd reject him.

"Are you going to do something"—she shifted carefully onto her back—"or are you just going to think about it?"

"I don't want to hurt you. Your ribs . . ."

"My ribs don't have a starring role in the kind of performance I'm talking about."

Cole feathered his fingertips over the bruise on her cheek. "Your ribs aren't the only problem." She still wasn't a hundred percent. She probably wasn't seventy-five percent, and if he ever saw that bitch, Irina, again, he was going to rethink his policy on guns.

"Hey." She took his chin in her hand and turned his face to hers. "What's going on?"

"I don't know." Cole slumped onto his back.

Harmony lifted the blanket and looked underneath it. "There doesn't seem to be any physical problem."

She eased over so she was draped across his chest and kissed him, lightly, but when she started to pull away, Cole took her face in his hands and kissed her back. She shuddered as his tongue touched hers, feeling the whole hard length of his body against the whole needy length of hers. He slipped his hand underneath her and pulled her completely on top of him, rocking his hips against hers. It felt so good that she wrestled off Sal's shirt, which was all she'd slept in besides her panties, and rubbed her breasts against his chest. The three points of pleasure collided somewhere in her abdomen, coiling so tight she let herself drop into the pleasure.

He slid her panties down, eased his hand between her legs and slipped two fingers into her, curling up a little to take her breast into his mouth at the same time. She shattered. The coil in her belly exploded outward, wave overlapping wave until every nerve ending sang and every speck of consciousness focused on the orgasm, her center still tight, holding in the pleasure while the rest of her muscles went loose and shivery.

She dropped her forehead to Cole's shoulder and whispered his name, almost silently because she didn't have enough breath left to get out even that one syllable with any force.

"Harm," he groaned, sounding like he was in pain, which he probably was.

She shifted to one side long enough to help him remove his boxers, long enough for him to put on a condom. Then she straddled him, the flesh between her legs so sensitive she wound up doing a bump and grind routine, wanting him inside her but needing to take it slowly. Her inner muscles stretched and shuddered as she took him into her by agonizing inches.

"You're killing me," Cole said, grabbing her hips and lifting her off him.

He stacked the pillows, nudged her, chest down, on them, grabbed her hips again, and slid into her from behind, coming hard against something inside her that felt even better than before. And then he began to move, long strokes that made her blood pound and her muscles tremble. His hands were sure at her waist, his mouth hot, his teeth nipping at the place where her shoulder met her neck.

She fisted her hands in the sheets, nothing to do but lie there as he came into her, again and again. The loss of control was both frustrating and exhilarating, every stroke of his body, every touch of his mouth or hands a surprise that stole her breath and pushed her back toward climax.

His breath grew ragged and he surged into her harder, one hand moving to her breast as he curved around her so she felt him everywhere, on her and in her. She didn't know where he left off and she began, and she didn't have a choice when he feathered his thumb across her nipple as he drove into her one last time, locked himself deep, and dragged her over the edge of reality into that shattered, throbbing place she'd been before, where everything was bright and amazing and filled with pleasure almost too intense to bear.

She couldn't say how much time passed while she struggled for sanity, and breath, but it helped when Cole moved his bulk, sprawling onto his back next to her. Then she could bask in the pleasant afterglow.

"Are you all right?" he asked her.

"Oh yeah," she said. "How is your head?"

"I'm not sure I even have a head."

Harmony was sure she had ribs because they were aching, along with every bruise she'd gotten from Irina. But it was worth it because other parts of her ached, too, wonderfully.

Cole slipped out of bed, and when he came back, he dragged one of the pillows out from under her head, where she'd moved them, and curved himself around her, brushing her hair away from her neck so he could kiss her before he settled into the bed with a satisfied sigh.

Harmony rested her hand on top of his where it lay across her waist. He twined his fingers with hers, and her heart lurched. She almost told him what he'd mumbled the night before, the words trembling on her lips for just a second before she swallowed them back. The possibility that he hadn't meant it was too great a risk, so she relaxed against him and settled for what she had. And tried not to think about the fact that she was in love with Cole.

chapter 24

HARMONY WOKE UP, HER MIND SHARP BUT HER BODY still humming with afterglow, which might have had something to do with the two additional times they'd made love during the night. Being in Cole's arms, her head on his shoulder, was just the icing on the cake.

She eased back so she could see his face, tracing the lines bracketing his mouth, two days' worth of beard growth tickling her fingertips.

He started awake, instantly alert, his eyes narrowing on her face. Their gazes held, his hand came up to press her palm to his check, just for a second, before he pulled away. Harmony told herself she didn't see something . . . soft in his eyes. But his fingers curled around hers, and his voice, when he spoke, was gentle, even gruff with sleep.

"Insatiable," he said, "not that I'm complaining."

"I didn't wake you up for that. I didn't intend to wake you up at all. You've been sleeping for thirty-six hours—"

"Not exactly true."

"—and you were just ready to wake up."

"You got the ready part right."

"I don't think I can walk now, let alone if we—Ohhhhh," she said, because he'd kissed her neck while she was talking, nibbling his way down her shoulder to her breast, drawing her nipple into his mouth, lifting her knee and sliding into her at the same time.

He took it slow this time, achingly slow, his mouth gentle but insistent at her breast, his body moving surely on hers, pleasure building to a climax that broke over her as softly as a spring rain. Cole followed her over, gathering her close, barely breathing hard as he settled beside her. In seconds his breathing deepened, verging on full-fledged snore.

Harmony shoved him. "You are not going to sleep again."

Cole yawned, blinking his eyes rapidly as he sat up and swung his legs over the side of the bed. "If you want me to get up and stay up, I'm going to need a shower first."

"Make it cold," Harmony said, putting her foot on his butt and helping him on his way to the bathroom. She wanted him up, but not *up*. Any more *up* and she'd really have troubling walking. She hadn't been kidding about that.

As soon as she heard the water stop running, she eased out of the bed, favoring more than her ribs. She pulled on one of Cole's T-shirts because she was pretty sure whatever control they'd gained by separating would be destroyed if she was naked when he ran into her again.

She shouldn't have worried.

Cole came out of the tiny bathroom and met her in the narrow hallway. They both turned sideways, Cole slowing as they tried to pass one another and their bodies brushed. His eyes dropped to her mouth, and for a moment she thought he might kiss her. He didn't, just shifted away and went into the bedroom. Considering what she'd been feeling last night, it was the distance she needed, and if it stung a little, it was nothing to the pain she was facing if she didn't get her heart straightened out.

The shower helped, not only pulling her out of the intimacy of the last nine hours, but easing her sore muscles. And when she dug into her duffel to get some clothes, she noticed her phones and laptop had been returned.

"We should talk about our plans," she said when she came

out of the bathroom, fully dressed and combing her wet hair. "We've been here two days already. Today makes it three."

"And you think it's time to get on the road."

"I think it's past time."

Cole didn't say anything for a minute. "Let's talk it over with Larkin," he finally said. "We can't go off half-cocked again. I know we can't prepare for every possibility, but if we think this through before we get on the road again, we'll have a better shot at success."

Considering how hard it must have been for him to even consider consulting Conn, let alone returning her phones before they'd agreed on what to do, Harmony figured the least she could do was compromise. Besides, his suggestion was reasonable and cautious. But there were limits. "Fine, we make a plan," she said. "But the first part is that I'm leaving today. Whatever you need to do to get comfortable with that, you need to do it."

"You'd leave without me?"

"There's enough money—"

The RV door opened and Connor Larkin stepped in, easing the door shut behind him. "There's a police cruiser pulling in," he said, which not only derailed their argument, it brought them to instant accord.

Harmony went to the door, looking through the window behind Conn's bulk to where two uniformed Colorado State Police officers were talking to Annie and Nelson. They must have mentioned her name, because Corey Brewer, who was standing not far away, perked right up. So did one of the cops. He left his partner with the Blisses, walked over to the little girl, and stooped down in front of her. Cindy Brewer stepped between them. Even from a hundred yards away Harmony could see the trooper trying to badger his way through the mother to get to the child, who must've already spilled the beans about Lady Harmony.

"I'll handle it," Conn said, fending Harmony off when she tried to brush past him and go to the little girl's defense. He pulled out his cell and dialed. Annie Bliss wandered away from the cops, surreptitiously reaching into her pocket.

"She always keeps her phone on vibrate," Cole explained.

"Says the ringing is disruptive to her chakras, whatever the hell that means." He held up a finger, listened for a few seconds, then said, "Got it, thanks," and disconnected. "Annie says the state police received an anonymous tip that an escaped felon and his accomplice were hiding out here. They had your names."

"You think one of the people here made the call?" Harmony asked him.

"Nope. Cops are disruptive to their chakras, too. Besides, none of them know your last names, and even if your mug shots were still being shown on the tube, these people aren't big TV watchers. The tip had to come from somewhere else, which means you might be in bigger trouble than a couple of state cops. Get your stuff together and hightail it out the back. I'll buy you as much time as I can."

"You're going to get arrested," Cole said, coming up behind Harmony with their bags in his hands.

"Exactly. And guess to whom my one phone call will be?"

Harmony put a hand on his arm, stopping before he opened the door. "I'm sorry, Conn."

"Mike will get me out of this without blowing my cover." He looked over her shoulder and said to Cole, "Take care of her."

"That sounds like a threat, which is overkill since your friend Mike already covered that ground with me."

"The only threat that matters is the one from the kidnappers," Harmony said. "And I can take care of myself."

Conn ruffled her hair, which was very brotherly, and left her both annoyed and touched, before he stepped out of the RV, stretching and yawning like he'd just gotten out of bed.

Harmony peeked through the window long enough to see him pretend to catch sight of the cops and change direction. When the officers saw him coming, both right hands moved to rest on the butts of both guns and they put a little distance between them. For a second she thought they were going to draw their weapons, but Conn spread his hands, it was clear he wasn't armed, and the immediate threat passed.

"Here," Cole said, and when Harmony looked back at

him, he had her laptop case slung over his shoulder and he was holding out her duffel.

Harmony took it and followed him to the cab of the RV, staying out of sight of the passenger window when he slid into the driver's seat. The RV's were parked bumper to tailgate, like a parade of elephants single file, tail-in-trunk. The big side door, which was also on the passenger side of the vehicle, faced the inner part of the RV circle. That meant that the driver's side door led to the outside of the circle. Cole slid into the driver's seat, eased the door open, and stepped out.

Harmony slipped out behind him, her feet barely touching the ground before something thunked into the RV beside her head. Instinct sent her to the ground almost before her brain could shriek *bullet*, another plinking into the RV right where her chest would have been.

Cole dragged her to her feet and they ran flat out into the wooded area just behind the RV park, where Conn had moved the GT the day they'd arrived. Bullets cut through the branches and leaves around them, splintering bark and getting steadily closer until she swore she could feel the wind of their passage on the back of her neck. The shots stopped before they made it to the car, probably because the GT was hidden in a fairly thick patch of trees and the shooters had lost sight of them.

Harmony found herself at the driver's-side door before she realized she didn't have the keys. She looked up just as Cole flipped them to her. Her surprise must have shown because he said, "Just drive," and folded his long body into the passenger seat.

She got behind the wheel, taking a precious second to adjust the seat before she turned the key and jammed the car into gear. She hit the gas, shooting out of the underbrush and into the road, almost colliding with the police cruiser.

Out of the corner of her eye she saw Cole brace himself between the armrest and the console as the car fishtailed and she fought for control. The tires finally caught pavement with a screech that rocketed them forward, Cole yelling, "Holy shit!"

"Getting deeper all the time," Harmony said, her eyes on the rearview.

Cole twisted around. "There's another car behind the

cops," he said needlessly since Harmony had already seen it swing in on the cruiser's rear bumper. "It's keeping pace."

Which was saying something since they were already doing seventy-five, and on a curvy, two-lane road that was just asking for trouble.

"The Russians," Cole said.

"Yeah."

"Not the same car that picked us up in Pennsylvania."

"That one was probably stolen. They needed a car that looked nonthreatening."

"This one's built for speed and anonymity."

That pretty much summed it up, although she could all but see Irina's face despite the black-tinted windows. And even from inside the GT she could hear the engine roar.

"The good news is that they're taking out the cops," Cole said, still half-turned and watching the action.

Harmony heard a couple of muffled gunshots and looked in the mirror just in time to see the police cruiser careen off the road and nose down into the ditch, air bags going off like more gunshots.

Cole turned to face forward. "The Russians shot out their tires."

And they were next, Harmony figured. But she didn't see the guns nosing out the side windows again, which made sense when she thought about it. "They don't want to risk hurting you," she said to Cole.

"But they'll follow us and take another shot at you when they can. Unless we stop them." Cole pulled out the laptop and booted it up.

"What are you doing?"

"Just drive."

He monkeyed around for a minute, then set the laptop on the center console, the keyboard turned to face her. "Type any password, up to ten characters."

"Kind of busy here," Harmony pointed out.

"They're not going to do anything but follow us."

Harmony eased off the gas, and sure enough Irina slowed down as well. "Any password?"

"Ten characters or less," Cole said, looking out the passenger-side window. "And don't tell me what it is."

Harmony did as he asked, and when she was done, Cole got her duffel and pulled out Harmony's FBI cell. Harmony knew he was calling the kidnappers, and she knew why. She reached over and took his hand.

"It's not going to stop them for long," she said.

"It's a chess game, that's what you told me." He squeezed her hand once, then let her go.

"Remember what I told you?" he said into the phone. "I said if you attacked again it would be over." He listened for a second, then said, "It would be a mistake to kill Agent Swift. She has the password to the offshore bank account. Even I don't know it. Anything happens to her and the money is gone, and I won't get you more. And yeah, you could probably figure out the password, but it'll take time. Do you want to chance the FBI figuring out where the money went and retrieving it while you're trying to luck your way into Harmony's password?"

Cole glanced over at her, and she figured the kidnapper on the other end of the phone was digesting his threat. She caught movement in the rearview mirror, Irina pulling her car into the oncoming traffic lane and accelerating to pull abreast of the GT.

Harmony was reaching for her gun when the window of the other vehicle motored down. Leo was sitting in the passenger seat, staring out the front window. Irina looked past him, her eyes meeting Harmony's with cold intent. Harmony responded with a slight, bring-it-on nod that she hoped was convincing since her insides had turned to jelly. Irina faced forward again, Leo's window sliding closed as she punched the gas pedal and passed them, swerving back into the correct lane and disappearing around the next curve.

"That was scary," Cole said. "On both sides."

"Sure, she was quaking in her mukluks. Ask the guy on the phone how they knew where we were."

Cole repeated the question into the phone, then said, "He hung up," and snapped the phone closed.

"He's got some thinking to do," Harmony said. "So do we."

She slowed the car, pulling off the road on a scenic over-look, in the open where they could see the Russians coming, just in case.

"First things first," she said, getting her gun out of the duffel and handing it to Cole, saying, "Just take it," when he hesitated.

She got out of the car and ran her hand around the inside of all four wheel wells, felt under the front and rear bumpers, then bit the bullet and lay down on her back in the dirt, checking first one side of the undercarriage, then the other. "Pop the hood," she said to Cole.

He did, then watched her check the underside of the hood and the motor well.

"As far as I can see, there are no tracking devices," she said.

"And no one followed us after the fight." He handed her the gun back. "I made sure of that."

"Then how did they find us?" she said, more to herself than Cole. "The police got an anonymous tip and came running, which forced us out of the RV camp for the first time since we got there. And the Russians were waiting to take us—to take me out."

"Which means the kidnappers are the anonymous tippers."

"It also means they had to get their information from inside the FBI," Harmony said grimly. "It's the only answer. The last time we used the FBI phone, before today, was just after the fight in Tulsa. There's no way they could know we were in Colorado Springs, even if they'd traced it."

"Mike's the only one who knew we were there. Except for Larkin, and neither one of them would tell anyone where you are."

"Unless they didn't realize they were giving us away." Harmony met Cole's eyes and saw he was coming to the same conclusion—the only possible conclusion. "It had to be Treacher," she said. "I let Mike in on your history with him, and Mike shut him down. He had to do something, so he must have tapped into Mike's phone and computer, and since it was before Mike sent us to Conn, Treacher knew where we were, and he knew why. He let the kidnappers know, then sent the cops to flush us out, figuring you'd get arrested or killed."

"Son of a bitch," Cole ground out. "It's not bad enough that he ruined my life, now he's trying to end yours. Kovaleski shut him down once; he can do it again."

"Conn will fill Mike in," Harmony said. "And he'll figure it out, but he won't shut Treacher down. Think about it a minute, Cole. If he can get real intelligence, he can be fed bogus intelligence, and through him the kidnappers."

"We can use him," Cole said, sounding a little mollified. "If we need to."

"I hope we do, and I hope it ruins him."

"That's already a done deal. No matter how this turns out for us and for Richard, Mike will make sure Treacher burns for using him against me."

Cole grinned, but there was no humor in it. "If he doesn't, I will."

chapter
25

THEY HEADED NORTH TO DENVER, TO PICK UP THE
main highway that would take them west through the Rockies before turning southwest toward Los Angeles. The mountain views were spectacular, and all the wide-open space came close to satisfying Cole's need for, well, wide-open spaces.

Harmony had elected to drive, which left Cole to navigate, and except for a hum of acknowledgment whenever he gave her directions, she was keeping her thoughts to herself. There'd been times when Cole had really wanted Harmony to shut up, but this wasn't one of them. This silence wasn't peaceful; it was full of unspoken words and barely acknowledged feelings, all of it overshadowed by the real possibility they wouldn't survive long enough to make the rest of it necessary.

Not that he couldn't hazard a guess at what she was thinking. And feeling.

The end was coming, and he was a stew of emotion, anticipation, trepidation, fear for Harmony, and, yeah, for himself. When he charted out the possible outcomes of going after Richard Swendahl, none of them ended well for him. And if he was this jacked up, with his relatively even keel, he could only imagine what kind of fireworks were going off inside Harmony. Then again, she'd become pretty good at compartmentalizing. Sure, she had an intense emotional stake in the outcome of this operation, but at the moment all that seemed to matter to her was getting to Los Angeles. She'd set the cruise control at seventy, she barely took her eyes off the road, and she had her sights set on Los Angeles. It was all Cole could do to get her to stop around noon for food. He never even considered asking her to find a motel and get some rest. Until they hit Vegas.

THEY WERE ON I-15, HEADING FOR CALIFORNIA. THE VEgas Strip paralleled the highway, and it was lit up like an alien landing pad, probably visible from Pluto. Cole had never been in Vegas before, so he directed her off the highway and back along the Strip the way they'd come, just so he could take it all in.

"Slow down," he said. The place really got his juices flowing, and for once he wasn't thinking about food. Okay, he wasn't thinking *only* about food. He'd heard the buffets in Vegas were incredible, but what he really wanted was to try his hand at poker or blackjack. He was damn good at math, and he knew the principal behind counting cards. And he knew right where he could lay his hand on a seven-million-dollar stake. "It won't do us any good to be exhausted when we hit LA. We need to get some rest, and this is as good a place as any."

"What is it with guys and Vegas?"

"Let's see, legalized prostitution, cheap food, gambling, and violent sports. And I hear what happens here stays here. What's not to like?"

"Go for it," Harmony said.

"Really? How about if I take the seven mil and put it down on one roll of the dice," he said, only half teasing.

"Sure, that wouldn't get us any attention at all, especially if you won."

"We don't have to stop here," he said, pulling his eyes off the lights and putting them on Harmony's face, just as she turned to look at him.

"But you want to." She focused her attention out the windshield again, but this time she was checking out the food and lodging possibilities, putting his preferences above her own.

Just as he was putting her wishes above his. And the job.

"I'm hungry, too," she said, sounding slightly defensive.

Cole figured they were on the same page, both uncomfortable with the shift in their attitude toward one another and what it might say about their relationship. And neither of them was willing to open that can of worms.

Harmony pulled into valet parking at the Sahara. The Sahara had been built in the fifties, so it was smaller than the huge new metropolis hotels like the Bellagio and the MGM Grand. And since it was at the eastern end of the Strip, the throngs of people were sparser, which was a double-edge sword since they couldn't get lost in a crowd if they needed to, but they could see trouble coming more easily. Not that either of them was expecting trouble.

Then again, "Do you think the Russians really gave up after they found out you have the password?"

"I don't think the Russians know when to quit. But I think we can take the time to have a meal."

She stepped out of the GT and handed the keys to the valet, who was standing there, mouth open, eyes shifting between Harmony and the car. He eventually settled on the car. Blondes were a lot more common than GTs.

"I don't hear you saying we'll spend the night," Cole said, taking Harmony's arm and escorting her inside before she could change her mind about the food, too.

"I feel like we should push through to LA," she said.

"We're so close."

"And you want to get to Richard as soon as you can, but if we drive all night we'll be too tired to take on a bunch of Russian kidnappers."

"I'm familiar with Los Angeles and its surroundings, so I have a better idea where it's safe to stay. We can rest when we get there."

"Any idea how we're going to find out where your friend is being held?"

Harmony gave him a sidelong look as they entered the buffet line, which was pretty short at that time of night. "You're not going to try to talk me out of it again?" she asked as she paid.

"Would it do me any good?"

"You could leave. I won't try to stop you."

She'd said something like that before back at the RV park, asked him why he was still helping her. He had an answer this time, but it wasn't one he wanted to verbalize, for her sake or his own. "We have a deal. I help you; you help me."

"You might want to hear the rest before you make any rash promises," she said, following him from one food station to another.

She wasn't putting anything on her tray, so Cole used it for his overflow, trying to choose some things she might eat.

"You asked me how we were going to find out where Richard is," she continued, juggling the heavy tray. "The answer is we're not. I'm going to call the head Russian and set up a meet. It's our only option. I wish I could say I had more of a plan, but . . ."

"Have you ever had a plan? Past breaking me out of jail."

Her eyes cut to his, but she smiled. "Not really."

"So why is today any different than the last week?"

"It's different because this time we're taking on the Russians, on their turf. Our goal is get Richard out without giving away the bank. They'll do whatever it takes to get the money, even if it means killing us.

"I broke you out of jail to move the money, and once you transfer enough to satisfy the kidnappers, your part is done. There's no reason for you to be in on the exchange."

"Except I have the bank account number." Cole chose a table in a secluded corner of the seating area and dug in.

"I take it that means you're not giving it to me."

"We've come this far together. Now you just need to trust me enough to let me help."

"I do trust you."

"Good. Eat something."

"I'm not really hungry.

"You're still healing, and your body needs fuel for that. You won't be any good to either of us if you're weak from lack of food. And I don't mean green stuff," he qualified when she aimed her fork at a chunk of broccoli. He moved every dish with a side of vegetables out of her reach, shoving a plate full of red meat to her side of the table. "Try the prime rib."

"It's a bit too rare for me."

"Consider it a training tool. You could stand to have a little more carnivore in your attitude."

She gave him a look, but she actually managed to put away a respectable meal for a change. *Nothing like appealing to her pride*, Cole thought, eating everything she didn't. And, as much as he would have liked to visit the blackjack tables, he followed her to the exit, waiting while she handed the claim ticket to the valet.

The kid took the ticket and stood there, fidgeting from foot to foot, eyes wide, his face shifting between panic and fear. What struck Cole the most was that he didn't go to retrieve the GT.

"You're not going to get the car," Harmony said, clearly on the same page as Cole.

"I, uh . . ."

Harmony flipped out her badge and held it up in front of his face. "You have exactly ten seconds to produce our vehicle."

"Jeez, lady, I didn't know you were a cop. They said they were just playing a joke—"

"They who?"

He pointed a finger. Cole turned around to see a black Cadillac easing up to the curb in front of the valet station. The rear window slid open. Cole stooped to look in and got a face full of gun. Harmony came over to see what was going on, and the gun shifted to point at her.

It was no surprise to learn that the guy behind it had a Russian accent. "Get in," he said. "You in back, her in front."

Cole exchanged a look with Harmony. She had to realize what the seating arrangement meant. If they followed instructions, the guy in the backseat could shoot her without risking harm to Cole, which was exactly what Richard's kidnappers wanted.

Harmony's guns were in the duffel, which was still in the GT since the casinos wouldn't let in armed patrons and she'd preferred not to announce her profession. Even so, Cole was prepared to make a stand, then and there, but she shook her head. "Just be grateful it isn't the trunk." She opened the front door and heaved a sigh. "God, I'm sick of Russians," she said as she angled into the front seat.

"You have problem with Russians?" the driver asked her as he pulled out, heading away from the lights of the Strip.

"I didn't before they started wanting me dead."

He shrugged, one-shouldered. Very Russian. "Nothing personal. Just a favor for a friend."

"Irina," Cole stated the obvious. No one felt a need to comment further.

"How'd you find us?" Harmony asked.

"The word has gone out, how do you say, on the grapevine. In every city between Denver and Los Angeles, our friends look for you. Here in Las Vegas we have spotters along the Strip."

"So what now?"

The guy behind the wheel steered the Cadillac onto a side street that was less well lit and a lot less traveled than the Strip. "Now we take you to Irina," he said.

"So we can give her the money right before she kills us," Harmony said. She half turned in her seat, as if the comment was directed at him, Cole noticed. It definitely got the Russians' attention.

The driver's eyes cut to Cole's in the rearview mirror, then shifted back to the road. "Money?"

"Seven million," Cole said. "Irina forgot to mention that, huh?"

The driver took his attention off the road again, looking at his partner this time. Harmony struck, slamming her fist sideways into his face. She caught everyone by surprise, but not so much that Cole failed to take advantage of it, grabbing the gunman's hand so the shot he squeezed off thunked into the door.

The Russian in the backseat was older; he couldn't hope to outmuscle Cole. There was a short, silent struggle, ending with the muzzle of the gun pointed at the Russian's stomach. Cole tried to figure out what was going on in the front seat, but he couldn't take his eyes off his opponent, not in such close quarters. Cole couldn't see Harmony, but the driver was fighting more than the wheel, the car swerving crazily as he tried to keep it on the road and fend Harmony off at the same time. Cole was waiting for the crash. Instead, the driver's-side door flew open, the Russian behind the wheel yelled as he sprawled sideways out of the car, and Harmony popped up, grinning when she saw Cole holding the gun.

"There's nobody driving the car," Cole yelled, but she was already scrambling over the console.

She dropped into the driver's seat and took control of the car, pulling the door shut at the same time. They sideswiped a pickup parked along the street, but she eventually steered them straight again.

"Keep driving," Cole said, waiting until she was a few miles away before he had her pull over. They kicked the other Russian out, Cole got in the front seat, and they headed back to the Sahara.

The valet took one look at them and tried to run.

Harmony caught him by the shirtfront. If he hadn't been so scrawny, she'd never have hung onto him, but she was amped up on anger and adrenaline.

"I'm not even going to ask how much they paid you to keep us waiting," Harmony said to the valet. "But if anything happened to our car, you'd better pray your future cellmate doesn't think prison orange is flattering on you."

Cole tried to intervene before Harmony throttled the poor guy. "Okay," he said, "first you shove a guy twice your size out of a moving vehicle—"

"He was trying to kill me."

"—and now you're terrorizing a teenager."

"Because he took a bribe from the guy who wanted to kill me."

"Jeez, lady, get a grip," the valet said, "it was only forty bucks."

"Yeah, it's so much better knowing my life is only worth forty—"

Cole pulled her off the kid. "No more red meat for you."

She turned her glare on him, and he almost took an involuntary step back. Then some of the crazy started to fade away.

He still wasn't all that eager to get in a car with her behind the wheel. "I don't suppose you want to get a room for the night."

"I want this to be over," she said, looking at the valet again, not as furious as before but angry enough to have him quaking in his high-tops. "Car," she said to him.

"O-over there," he stammered, pointing in the direction of the Sahara's parking garage. "Right by the exit." And he handed Cole the keys, keeping well out of Harmony's reach.

"Didn't have time to sell it, huh?" Harmony said, her hand moving to where she normally wore her holster.

"C'mon, Dirty Harry," Cole said, dragging her off before she could realize she wasn't wearing her gun and go after the kid with her bare hands again.

The GT was parked right where the valet had said it would be. Cole deposited her in the passenger seat, then went around and climbed in the driver's side, exhaling in relief as he put the key in the ignition.

"I'm tired, too," Harmony said, "but we can rest when this is over."

"True." Cole pointed the GT toward I-15, and LA beyond. "I just hope it's not six feet under."

EVEN THOUGH COLE DROVE THE THREE HUNDRED MILES between Vegas and Los Angeles, Harmony didn't sleep. How could she when her brain refused to shut itself off and her nerves were jumping around like a drug addict needing a fix. Adrenaline, that was the problem. Damn Russians. They got her all worked up and didn't stick around long enough to help her work off the rush. Not that she wasn't relieved they were gone, and not that she didn't feel a small measure of satisfaction in shoving one of them from a moving automobile. But it wasn't the same as beating Irina.

This Russian had been trying not to crash them into a building, for one thing, so he hadn't given her his full attention. And she'd been enraged. Not just angry and sick of Russians interfering in her business, she was talking about mindless, last-straw, seeing-red fury. Berserker rage, the kind only violence could appease.

Not really what you'd call progress in her ongoing struggle to think first and emote later. Not that rage didn't get the job done, but rage didn't leave a lot of room for rationality, and an FBI field agent needed to be clear-headed at all times.

"Now what?" Cole asked her when they hit the outskirts of LA. "They won't be in one of the better parts of town."

"But we will," Harmony said, redirecting her thoughts from past shortcomings. Okay, she'd been wallowing in self-pity. But it was time to focus on the final confrontation. A confrontation she expected to win. No other possibility could be considered. She still had hope. Not to mention a towering case of exhaustion. No way could she face another gang of Russians, especially a gang that included Irina, without some downtime.

She directed Cole to the Hotel Bel-Air in Beverly Hills, a Mission-style hotel with gorgeous rooms, beautiful gardens, and the price tag to go along with it.

"We can't afford this," Cole said, but since he'd stopped the car in front of the hotel's main entrance when he said it, Harmony gathered up her duffel and laptop and climbed out. Cole had no choice but to do likewise.

"Great, another valet," he said, handing the GT's keys to a twentysomething in a hotel uniform.

"This one isn't likely to rat us out for pocket change," Harmony said.

"Unless more of Irina's comrades are lurking around somewhere."

"Irina didn't expect us to get this far," Harmony said with absolute certainty, because if there was one thing she was certain of, it was that Irina had underestimated them in at least that regard. "And this is the last place they'll expect us to stay."

"It's the last place I expected us to stay," he said, taking the laptop out of her left hand.

Harmony suppressed a smile as she dug into the duffel, looking for her purse. Cole was gawking at the lobby like a tourist from small-town Wisconsin, which, under other circumstances, he might have been.

"We don't have enough cash left," he said under his breath, eyes on the stuffed shirt staring down his nose at them from behind the registration desk.

Harmony placed her driver's license on the counter.

The desk clerk typed her name into the computer, then said, "Welcome back, Miss Swift. What can we help you with today?"

"Is the honeymoon suite available?" she asked, never taking her gaze from Cole's face. The adoration she pasted on wasn't much of a stretch.

Cole didn't seem to be having much trouble acting the part, either. He didn't take his gaze off hers when the registration clerk said they didn't have a honeymoon suite, per se, but the Bel-Air's garden suites were very romantic.

Cole said, "Fine," and when the clerk slid key cards and Harmony's license across the counter, Cole gathered them in one swipe, took her hand, and pulled her toward the depths of the hotel, all without sparing anyone or anything else a glance. Until they were safely out of sight of the front counter.

"Honeymoon suite?" he asked, steering her toward the elevator.

"The garden suites are on the first floor," Harmony said, "hence the word *garden*."

"Which you already knew, so again, honeymoon suite?"

"You're awfully freaked out about it," Harmony said. "Not the marrying kind, huh?"

"No, I, uh . . . I guess I never thought about it. Considering my living arrangements, it wasn't going to be an issue."

Harmony just smiled and took the cards from him, opening the door to a room decorated in pale yellow and warm oak. French doors led to a secluded garden patio with wicker furniture, and there was a separate bedroom with a huge bed.

"Do you think it was a good idea to use your credit card?" Cole asked her, not appreciating the accommodations at all, which made Harmony sigh.

"Look," she said, "I labeled us honeymooners so the hotel staff won't be surprised if they don't see us on a regular basis, and I chose this hotel because I have an account here. This is where I always stay when I'm in the Los Angeles area. Richard knows that, and if they . . . ask him . . ." She didn't finish the thought. She didn't have to. "I can't use my credit card, even at a bank or ATM, because Treacher will have it flagged."

"And you don't want him to find us. But what about the Russians?"

"I don't want them to find us, either, but I want them to waste time looking." And talking it through seemed to steady her again. "Order some breakfast, would you?" She pulled out her cell and dialed the kidnappers.

COLE RETRIEVED THE ROOM SERVICE MENU AND DID AS she asked, but he kept an ear on her side of the conversation. It wasn't a long one.

"They won't agree to meet today," Harmony said, not sounding particularly surprised. "And he asked for thirty million dollars."

"They never mentioned a specific number before," Cole said. "Why now?"

"The Russians are trying to stall us long enough to figure out where we are. He put a number to the ransom for the same reason. He knows we haven't transferred that much, knows we'll need time to meet his demand, so we won't balk at waiting until tomorrow to meet. Except we won't be waiting here to be found."

"And when they realize we used this place as a decoy?"

She shrugged. "If I know my criminals, this isn't the only hot water they have boiling."

"The meet tomorrow."

"Is a double cross," Harmony said by way of agreement.

"So what are we going to do about that?"

"First we're going to eat breakfast. Then we're going to hang the DO NOT DISTURB sign on the door and take off. We'll find somewhere else to stay and get some more money into that account."

"And we're going to talk about Richard, right? Try to come up with a plan."

Harmony bumped up a shoulder. "There's no way to plan for the unknown."

chapter
26

THEY SLIPPED OUT THE GARDEN ENTRANCE OF THEIR
room at the Hotel Bel-Air, careful not to be seen, then walked
a couple miles, give or take, to Sunset Boulevard. They picked
up public transportation from there. Harmony figured their
best bet was to lose themselves in an area of the city that ca-
tered largely to tourists, and Santa Monica fit the bill. She
chose a hotel on the lower end of the price scale, one that
would accept cash without insisting on identification. It wasn't
right on the beach, or even the next level of accommodations
away, but it wasn't so far off the beaten path that they'd stand
out.

"Why don't you transfer the rest of the thirty million,"
Harmony suggested when they got into their room. "They
won't set up the meeting unless the account balance is what
they want."

"I think I ought to wait until tomorrow," Cole said. "There
shouldn't be any problem getting into the FBI system. Hell,
Treacher will be waiting for me to show up again. It'll be better to move the funds just before we leave when it's too late
for anyone to track us down."

"Then I guess we rest."

Cole looked toward the bed. "How exhausted are you?"

"Exhausted." But she couldn't settle. Her nerves were jumping around under her skin, and she couldn't hang onto a thought for more than a few seconds at a time. "I have to get out of this room," she said. She'd spent too much time in cars and cheap rented rooms, racing a mile a minute and still feeling like she wasn't doing enough for Richard. And now she couldn't do anything but wait.

She took one of the key cards and made a quick trip to the gift shop, stopping at the front desk on her way back to the room. Cole was channel surfing when she got back. She dropped a bag in his lap, said, "I'll meet you at the pool," and disappeared into the bathroom.

COLE WASN'T REALLY A SUN WORSHIPPER, SO HE TOOK A detour around the hotel. Not much to see. It wasn't the kind of place that boasted a restaurant, or even a seating area in the lobby. Just a bored desk clerk who barely stirred out of his stupor when Cole walked by.

The pool, however, was a pleasant surprise. For a low-rate hotel, the pool was beautifully kept, clean and calming, surrounded by flowering, tropical plants and palm trees, with the requisite umbrella-shaded tables and plastic-strung chaise lounges.

When Cole arrived, he found Harmony sitting poolside, on the edge of a towel-covered chaise, rubbing sunblock on all her exposed skin, which was a lot, considering she was wearing a bikini composed of metal rings holding small triangles of white cloth together so they barely covered the critical parts of her anatomy. And he wasn't the only one who'd noticed.

Cole sat beside her, taking the lotion and rubbing it on her back. "I thought we were trying not to attract attention."

"Speak for yourself," Harmony said.

Cole looked around. He met an alarming number of gazes, female gazes, and they weren't interested in Harmony—at least not most of them.

Harmony took the sunblock out of his hand and squeezed some on his back. He jumped, the cool lotion a shock on his hot skin.

"Jail pallor is so over," Harmony said, rubbing the lotion in. "Relax, this is LA. We aren't anything out of the ordinary."

She had a point, Cole thought. The pool patrons looked like a casting call for porn. But so did Harmony.

"And now that it's clear we're together, there's nothing to worry about."

She was right about that, too. The other sunbathers had gone back to minding their own business. Harmony lay back on her chaise and closed her eyes, sighing blissfully. Cole tried to do the same, but he'd never been one for idleness.

"Having a hard time shutting your brain off?" Harmony asked him the third time he sat up and looked around the pool.

"Something like that," he said. "I was never very good at doing nothing."

"Jail must have been hell, then."

"I managed to keep myself occupied."

She looked over at him and smiled. "What are you going to do after this is all over?"

"If I'm still out of jail? I don't know." He hadn't actually given it much thought, he realized. Staying out of jail, sure, but what would he do with his freedom? He had no idea. And when he did put his mind to the future, it didn't take long for his thoughts to become depressing. He'd still be an ex-con, for starters. "No one in my field will hire me," he said.

"The FBI will be needing an IT security specialist."

"They won't hire me, either." Even if he'd consider working for them. "What about you?"

She shifted back and closed her eyes. "I'm not going to worry about it right now."

Because it might not be an issue, Cole reminded himself. But it did seem to be the end of their conversation. He spent another twenty minutes in the sun before he moved to a table with an umbrella. Harmony stayed out in the sun alternating between the chaise and the pool, coming out with water sluicing off her slender body, nipples peaked, looking amazing.

At one point she disappeared for a little while, and not long after she came back a guy delivered a pizza loaded with every topping under the sun and a couple of sodas that were ice-cold going down, but did nothing to cool him off.

By the time they'd wiled away the rest of the afternoon and had a takeout dinner from a nearby restaurant, his internal thermostat was set at slow simmer. And when Harmony went off to take a shower to wash the chlorine from her skin, he was pretty sure a shower would help with his problem, too.

HARMONY STEPPED UNDER THE HOT SPRAY, HOPING IT would make her relax. Nothing else had worked, basking in the sun, swimming, talking with Cole about everything but Richard. She should have known it wouldn't be so easy to distract herself with the endgame only hours away.

She squeezed shampoo onto her palm and lathered her hair, shrieking when she felt something at her waist.

"It's just me," Cole said.

She stepped forward long enough to duck her head under the water and rinse the shampoo out of her hair and face. Cole followed her, one hand curling around to her breast, the other slipping down her belly. Harmony leaned back, letting her head rest on his shoulder and trying to throw herself into it.

Cole was in such a state of need he was shaking with it. She felt like a block of stone. Where was the oblivion she needed so desperately, the spike of heat and hunger she always felt for Cole? He was offering her sex—hot, animal sex—so why was she even able to think?

"What's wrong?" he asked, and she realized he'd stopped what he was doing.

She turned into him. "I'm sorry," she said, her voice muffled against his shoulder. "I'm just so . . ."

"Tense." He lifted his hands to her shoulders, kneading and rubbing, his large hands surprisingly gentle.

Harmony looked up, Cole met her eyes, and there was a connection, nothing she could put a name to, but it hummed between them. He stooped and hooked his hand behind her knee, lifting it along his hip and slipping into her, never taking his eyes from hers, taking her heart as he took her body. And she surrendered.

She loved Cole, and with the admission something broke free inside her. Sensation swamped her, coupling with emotion, freeing her from the prison of thought and letting her simply feel. Cole's hands on her breasts, his body moving against hers and inside hers, the sweet friction sending heat rushing through her veins, settling in to throb at pulse points, pleasure making her draw together and fly apart at the same time, so that all she could do was hang onto him while her senses flew, and her muscles shuddered and jumped until she could stand no more. And still he moved, taking her mouth, drawing more from her than she'd ever imagined possible, until he pulled her tight against him while his own orgasm overtook him.

He let her leg go and gathered her against him, resting his chin on the top of her head. And she tumbled even further— nearly too far. "I—" she said, barely managing to catch back the rest of the sentiment before she put them both in an uncomfortable position.

"What?" Cole murmured, easing back far enough to look into her face.

She turned around before her verbal control deserted her completely. But she could feel him staring at her back, waiting for her to finish her thought. Which wasn't going to happen. She might be foolish enough to fall in love with Cole, but it would be complete idiocy to tell him because he didn't love her. Knowing it and seeing it on his face were two different things. There was a good chance she wouldn't live to see another sunset, so why get her heart broken tonight?

HARMONY WOKE UP THE NEXT MORNING AND DISENtangled herself from Cole, trying not to feel bereft as she did it, definitely not thinking about how it might be for the last time. Her feelings for him were the least of her worries.

Her palms were sweaty and her stomach felt squishy, a combination of nerves and achiness and, yeah, fear. She wasn't stupid; the kidnappers had no intention of releasing Richard. They'd do whatever it took to get the money, and they'd leave as few witnesses behind as possible. Cole was probably safe, since he'd be useful to them, but the odds of her and Richard coming out of this alive were pretty low. Single digits. Like zero. Which was a self-defeating thought, and she wasn't giving up until five minutes after she was dead.

Cole came into the bathroom while she was in the shower, and the need rose in her as it always did. But she couldn't put herself back there again. She couldn't afford the distraction.

"Can you put the rest of the money into the account?" she asked him, already reaching for a towel when he pulled back the shower curtain.

There was silence, and she knew she'd hurt his feelings. She stepped out of the shower, lifted onto her toes, and kissed him—more than a kiss, it was a plea for understanding. He didn't disappoint her.

"Okay if I take a shower first?" he said.

"Sure, I even left you some hot water." But she reached behind her and turned it off, laughing when he yelled because the water was ice-cold, and then shrieking herself when he splashed some on her.

It was only a small bit of horseplay between the two of them, but it made her feel better, as if this day was like any other. Of course, normal for them meant everyone from Russian kidnappers to federal officers was trying to give them grief. Which would all be over in a few hours, she told herself, for better or worse. It was a little tarnished as silver linings went, but she couldn't be too choosy.

She didn't waste a lot of time getting ready, just let her hair dry into her natural curls and swiped on some mascara. She put on a T-shirt and jeans, topping it off with the jacket that hid her shoulder holster. She was strapping on her ankle piece when Cole came out of the bathroom.

He didn't say anything as he pulled on his clothes, not until she picked up her phone.

"Can we talk about how this is going down, first?" he asked her before she dialed.

"I get the feeling you don't want to talk so much as make a point, which is?"

"Don't go into this expecting you can somehow atone for the past, Harm. I know that's why you're here, but saving Richard now isn't going to change what happened to your parents."

"I know that," she said, although if she'd learned one thing over the last ten days, it was that she couldn't keep her emotions completely in check. The trick was to accept what she was feeling instead of fighting it. Take last night, for instance, in the shower. Fighting her emotion had completely blocked her off, but when she'd let go . . . Well, the undertaking had turned out successfully, she thought with a small smile.

Taking on the Russians was no different—scarier and a lot more dangerous than sex with Cole, but the principal was the same. There was no way to plan ahead, only outwit, outlast, and outplay. It was like *Survivor*, only the stakes were her life and Richard's. And Cole's possibly, which pained her the most. If she was going to keep them all in one piece she'd need her wits sharp and her mind clear. Fighting her emotions would only split her focus and hamper her ability to adjust to whatever situation presented itself. And Step One was to mitigate the risk.

"Look," she said to Cole, "I think you should stay here. Your part in this is done."

"Nope," he replied with infuriating nonchalance.

"I dragged you into this. You should take off, get lost, stay out of jail." *And stay alive.* "You won't be any good to me, anyway. Everyone will have guns except you."

"It's not going to come to guns. They can't kill us."

"Until they get the password and account number."

"By then we'll be gone with Richard." He looked up from the laptop, his gaze intent on her face, uncomfortably intent.

She had to turn away. "It's not like you to be so negative," he said to her back. "Where's the famous optimism?"

"I'm just trying to be realistic. The chance of success is pretty low."

"You'll think of something, Harm. You always do."

"Well, now we know where the optimism went."

"It's not optimism; it's faith in you. In us."

Harmony closed her eyes, unbelievably touched, another emotion she couldn't afford at the moment. "I'll try not to disappoint you," she said, dialing her FBI cell with her back still to Cole. Her voice was even, but she knew her face would give her away.

The head kidnapper picked up the phone on the first ring, and she shifted the heartache to one side and let necessity dictate her actions.

"Is good to hear from you," the now recognizable voice intoned with the now familiar Russian imperiousness, "as you are no longer at the Hotel Bel-Air."

"We're just full of surprises," Harmony said.

"Leave the password and acc—"

"It'll be a trade. Face-to-face."

"*Nyet.*"

"Then the deal is off."

"Very well." And he hung up.

She put the phone down on the table next to Cole. "Whatever happens, don't let me touch that again for thirty minutes." Then she handed him her guns, too.

Cole set them by the phone, staring at them for a minute like they were alien artifacts. Then he looked at her the same way.

"Just in case," she said.

Twenty-two minutes of sheer torture ticked by before Harmony shot to her feet, unable to take anymore. "It's been long enough."

"You said thirty minutes."

"I've made my point," she said. "Give me the phone."

Cole slid it away from her. She dove for it, coming up with her ankle gun instead, and pointing it at him.

He rolled his eyes. "You won't shoot me."

"That's what you said last time," she reminded him.

"And I was right. You missed on purpose, remember? And you don't know the account number," he added, seeming a little concerned when the gun didn't waver. "You can't do this without the account number."

"Fine." She put the gun down and went for the phone again.

Cole lifted it out of her reach.

"Really," she insisted, "I've made my point."

She jumped in an attempt to reach the phone. He only lifted it higher, so she dropped her hand to his crotch, cupping her fingers around him, not with the intent to hurt, but he hunched instinctively anyway, so she grabbed the phone and slipped out of reach, putting a heavy armchair between them.

"Dirty pool," Cole said.

"There are no rules in life-and-death situations. And thirty minutes was just a guideline."

Cole shrugged. "You've got the phone, make the call."

Harmony took a couple of deep breaths, trying to get a grip before she could call. She couldn't have the kidnappers hearing her breath hitch and thinking they were getting to her.

"Want me to call?" Cole asked, smirking, which immediately ticked her off.

"I'll do it," she said, already dialing since irritation had steadied her nerves. Which was probably what Cole had intended. "I've got it under control, so you can stop with the reverse psychology," she said to him, although she didn't have time to give him even the abridged explanation because the kidnappers answered on the fourth ring. "Are you ready to come to an agreement?" she asked.

"If your friend is dead, no agreement is necessary."

"Then I see no point to this conversation," Harmony said. Her heart was pounding hard enough to bang against her ribs. She let it bang, regulating her breathing so it didn't affect her outwardly. "I guess that means you can kiss the . . ." She looked at Cole, he gave her the thumbs up. ". . . thirty million dollars good-bye." And she hung up.

This time she had no problem waiting. She didn't have to. The phone rang, she gave it a beat, then answered. "I'm listening."

"You wish to meet in person."

"There's no other way I'll do this."

The kidnapper named an intersection in Los Angeles.

"That's South Central."

"Correct."

It had been renamed South Los Angeles, but it hadn't altered reality. "Not a very safe area," Harmony observed blandly.

"The neighbors will not bother you if you do not bother them."

He had a point. Asking questions in a place where people would shoot you as soon as look at you was dangerous. So was taking a meet, but she'd pushed the Russians about as far as she could—with the exception of one last request, and they'd surely be expecting it. "I want to speak to Richard before I agree to anything."

"Nyet."

She huffed out a breath. "Are we going to have to play this game again?"

"What game?"

"The one where I hang up and call you back to prove I'm serious about walking away. Or maybe I won't call back this time. What point would there be if I don't have proof of life?"

There was the customary three-second silence before Richard came on the line again. Russians didn't waste time or words. "Harmony?" he said, sounding tired but pain-free.

She had to swallow, so relieved to hear his voice tears came to her eyes. "How are you?" she managed to get out in a credibly even voice.

"I've been better." Richard paused, and there were only background noises, the kind of tinny voices, bonging, and scratchy music that probably came from a television playing some old movie in the background. Richard loved old movies, so it gave her hope they were treating him well.

"It sounds like you're strong at least."

"I am," Richard said. "I don't know what you said to them, but it's been . . . tolerable."

"It's almost over," Harmony said. "Try to hold on."

"Listen, be careful, they're planning some—" There was a yelp and he went silent.

"Richard, are you all right?"

"Yeah," he said, breathing heavily, his voice strained. "I just have to watch—"

"Agent Swift," the kidnapper said, clearly having wrenched the phone away from Richard.

"Yes."

"You come now."

Her phone beeped a low battery warning, but there was nothing she could do about it now. "I'll be there, but you won't get a dime unless Richard is well and able to walk out of there on his own steam. You don't get the password until he's free."

"This is not how exchange works."

"It's how *this* exchange is going to work."

"How do we know to trust you?"

Harmony snorted. "I'm not the criminal."

There was another moment of Russian silence, then he said, "I suggest you get moving, Agent Swift."

Harmony disconnected and picked up the room phone. "I requested you arrange for a rental car yesterday," she said. "Can you have it out front in ten minutes? Thanks."

"Let's go," she said to Cole, hanging up the room phone and dropping her cell into the duffel. A minute ago she'd been shaky and nauseated. Suddenly she couldn't wait to be in the same room with the bastards who'd kidnapped Richard. Finally being able to take action was a hell of a nerve steadier.

She holstered her main gun and lifted her foot to a chair to seat her ankle piece.

"If you do that in front of the kidnappers, it'll be enough of a distraction," Cole said.

"I doubt Irina would be impressed." Unless she got a look at Cole's eyes. Cole's eyes were intense, and hot enough that they should be outlawed in California wildfire territory. It wasn't all about sex, either. He was a computer geek, but he'd spent eight years in jail, and this wasn't just about freeing Richard, it was about freeing himself, too.

chapter
27

BY THE TIME THEY ARRIVED AT THE FRONT ENTRANCE
of the hotel, a late-model Chrysler was waiting for them, a
dull brown, four-door sedan with no rust and absolutely no
curb appeal.

"This is a step down," Cole said.

"Trust me, where we're going, the GT would be a liabil-
ity."

Cole got in the driver's side. Harmony didn't argue, climbing in and plugging her phone charger into the old cigarette
lighter port. She directed him to the Rosa Parks Freeway,
which took them east from Santa Monica to South Central,
now known as South Los Angeles. She filled him in on her
brief conversation along the way.

"It's a setup" was his immediate conclusion.

"Of course, but what choice do we have?" But as she was
replaying the conversation in her head, she remembered the
sound she'd heard, the sound that had struck her as familiar
before it had been drowned out by the phone's warning beep.

"What?" Cole asked her.

"There was this sound in the background while Richard

was speaking. A kind of bonging. I felt like I'd heard it some-where before, but . . ." She frowned and shook her head. "I can't place it."

"What did it sound like? A foghorn? A streetcar? No, that's San Francisco. Church bells, maybe?"

"I don't know. It was deep, reverberating, like wind chimes only not so tinkly." She blew out a breath, frustrated. "There's no telling what it might be in LA. There's a movie filming on every other street corner. The sound could be anything."

Like maybe a death knell. She shook off that depressing thought and put the sound out of her mind, watching the signs and directing Cole to the right exit.

"Now I know why you wanted this car," Cole said, steer-ing the ten-year-old Chrysler off the highway into a neigh-borhood with gang graffiti on everything stationary, including a couple of street sleepers. "We're not going to just walk into this meeting with absolutely no plan at all, are we?"

"What do you propose we plan for? I know where we're going, I know the general makeup of the neighborhood, but I can't tell you any specifics."

"Irina and Leo are probably waiting to ambush us; we know that much."

"They won't be waiting out in plain sight with their guns drawn, taking potshots at us. All we can do is take it slow and wait for them to make their move."

"No matter what we do we're going to be surprised."

"That pretty much sums it up," Harmony agreed. "The good news is they don't want us dead, not until they get the new account number and password. And it should only be Irina and Leo. Based on history they think they can han-dle us."

"We handled them."

"You handled them, and they've adjusted for that, but so have we, and at least the numbers will be even. The really sketchy part will be getting to the meet. We're going into gangland USA, the home turf of some of the nastiest, mean-est criminals . . . Home turf. Home . . ."

Cole glanced over at Harmony, just as she grabbed his arm, her frown turning slowly to a smile of dawning realization.

"Turn the car around, Cole."

"What? Why?"

"I know where Richard is, and it's not South Central."

"LET ME GET THIS STRAIGHT," COLE SAID, HIS EYES ON the road as they headed back to the freeway. "You have a house?"

"In Hollywood, to be exact. Why are you surprised? You know I'm from California."

"But you live in Washington. Kind of extravagant to have a house you never use."

"It was my parents'." Which said it all, judging by Cole's expression, and made her add defensively, "I do use it. It's a pretty good bribe. A bunch of stars live in the neighborhood, including this guy just down the hill from me who likes to meditate in his backyard. Naked. He's been doing it for years, which should tell you how old he is and what a treat it would be to see him sitting cross-legged on a bamboo mat. Not that I ever saw him meditating, because my mother would never let me look out the west-facing windows from two to four in the afternoon, which is a shame because there are some really great views of the Pacific Ocean. And after the kidnapping I didn't want the house sold. It was the last place I lived with my parents, you know, but I couldn't live there again, so I only ever heard him meditating—"

"Okay, I get it," he said, looking bemused.

"I'm sorry," Harmony said, "too much information. I'm a little nervous."

He got that, too. "You think they're holding Richard at your house?"

"Yes."

"Because your neighbor is into meditation."

"And he rings a gong while he meditates."

"In his backyard. Naked." Cole took a few seconds to get that mental picture out of his head. "Why would they use your house?"

"It's the last place I'd expect them to be."

Cole pulled the car over just before the entrance ramp to the freeway. "How sure are you?"

"Nowhere near a hundred percent."

"If we don't go to the meet and the kidnappers are there with Richard, they may kill him when we don't show. If we go to your house and the kidnappers are there, they may kill him when we show up unexpectedly. There's no way to be a hundred percent certain, but you need to think about this, make sure you're going with your best bet."

Harmony exhaled carefully, running everything through her mind again, then running it by Cole. "I'm sure South Central is an ambush and Richard won't be there."

"I'll agree with that."

"And Richard uses my house whenever he's out here and not on a case. They didn't grab him there, but they would have been watching him, so they must have known about it."

"And even if we don't show up in South Central, I don't think they'll kill him with thirty million dollars on the line. They've waited this long, my bet is they'll wait to hear from us again before they do anything that final."

"Then we have to go now," she said. "Get on the highway, follow it north to Mulholland Drive, then head east, and don't worry about speed limits. The Russians are expecting us to show up for the meet in less than fifteen minutes. When we don't, they'll head for the house, too. If we want the odds to be even, we need to get there before Leo and Irina."

She pulled out her phone, speed-dialed Mike by touch and put it to her ear. Nothing happened. She pulled it back and stared at the display, puzzled for a second before the "no service" message on the screen made sense, and then she went cold, her blood beginning to pound in her temples.

"Treacher had my phone shut off." She dumped it in her bag and grabbed the prepaid phone instead. She flipped it open and went through the same motions. Again, the phone was dead. "This one doesn't work, either, but there's no way Treacher could know about it."

"Shit," Cole said.

She looked over at him. The muscles in his jaw were knotting and unknotting, his knuckles white on the steering wheel.

Nausea joined her other bodily reactions. "What's going on?"

"It got wet the night we were apart."

"Wet?"

"It was raining cats and dogs. A mudslide put me in the ditch."

"Under any other circumstances, that would be hilarious."

"Yeah, it was a real laugh riot."

"Get off the highway," Harmony said, ignoring Cole's wounded dignity. "Take the next exit. Find a pay phone."

He did, but they were back in Beverly Hills, among the expensive shops, restaurants, and gated homes.

"Damn it," Harmony said, "there aren't going to be any pay phones here. Everyone has a cell phone, and we don't have time to buy another disposable."

"Now what?"

Try not to panic, she thought, racking her brain and coming up empty.

"This is no time to draw a blank."

"You're not helping." Harmony closed her eyes, shutting out everything—the fact that time was growing short and Cole was expecting her to come up with a miracle solution, one that probably didn't involve the cops. The FBI wasn't going to ride to their rescue, either, which pretty much left them on their own. Her biggest impulse was to throw up and so what if it was on the doorstep of one of the snooty fusion restaurants that were popping up . . .

"Pull over here," she said, dragging her tiny purse and her useless phone out of her duffel, practically out the door before he stopped the car because her brain had finally kicked back in. She leaned back inside to meet Cole's eyes. "I'm going to call the cops, but we'll sort it out later. I promise."

"We don't have much choice," he said, looking miserable.

Harmony kneeled in the passenger seat and kissed him, intending it to be a short, sweet reminder that she had his best interests at heart.

He slipped a hand around the nape of her neck and took it deeper. "In case we don't have time later," he said when he finally let her go.

Harmony wrapped her hand around his wrist. "We will."

He returned her smile. "Nice to see the optimism is back."

She squeezed his wrist once, then backed out of the car, taking a precious moment to straighten her jacket and pull "privileged California blonde" around her like an invisible cloak.

She couldn't go to the police station. They'd probably recognize her. If she told them about the kidnapping, they'd call in the FBI, and while they were hashing it all out, Leo and Irina would get back to the house and who knew what would happen?

She needed to buy some time to go in and get Richard out, which meant alerting the LAPD and hoping like hell they'd show up in time.

She opened the door and stepped inside, took one look at the restaurant's hostess, and pasted a vapid smile on her face, walking in like she owned the world and concocting a lie on the spot. "I'm, like, meeting my boyfriend for brunch, and I'm, like, unforgivably late," she said to the hostess. "Again."

The hostess, whose name badge proclaimed her as Christine, never batted an eye. Harmony had to give her credit; she was obviously sick and tired of the entitled rich, but she never showed it. "I'm sorry, Miss, no one is waiting."

Harmony let loose a little giggle. "He probably left and now he's all, like, mad and stuff." She huffed out a breath, letting her shoulders get into the action, then took out her cell phone, rolling her eyes dramatically as she held it up. "And I forgot to charge my phone, see? So I'll have to use yours."

"I'm not supposed to," Christine said, but she didn't stop Harmony from leaning over the reception desk and picking up the cordless phone.

"It'll just take a sec," Harmony said, waving her hand in dismissal, and walking toward the front door to keep the hostess from hearing her lie to the police.

She dialed information and let the operator connect her,

working her way through the phone tree and smiling over her shoulder at Christine, who was getting antsy. "He's back at work," she lied, "so he put me on hold, and, like, I just have to, like, *hold*. You know how it is. Men can be so, like, touchy about stuff like this."

Finally a real person came on the line and she turned away, pitching her voice low enough, she hoped, so the hostess couldn't hear what she was saying but the police could. "I need to report a vagrant wandering around my house in the Hills," she said. "Yes, I'm inside with the doors locked, but there's a lot of glass on the canyon side of the house, and he looks crazy. I live all alone at the end of the road— Viewmont Drive," she said to the obvious question, adding her address. "No, he hasn't done anything yet, except dig through my trash. No, I didn't see him do it, so it might have been coyotes . . . Okay, I pay a lot of taxes, and I know the police chief . . . Good, come as soon as— Oh, darn, I think I see him again." And she disconnected abruptly in the hope it would lend her story more immediacy.

The police still weren't going to take her very seriously, but they'd eventually send an officer, hopefully after she and Cole had had enough time to do what they needed to do. As backup plans went, it left a lot to be desired, but it was the best she could do with two dead phones and a looming deadline.

She turned back to the reception desk only to bump into Christine, who'd been standing about three inches behind her, eavesdropping. She snatched the phone out of Harmony's hand and marched behind the desk, glaring at her.

"Sorry," Harmony said, "it's a, uh . . . a punk! You know, like Ashton Kutcher," and when the hostess looked out the windows, she said, "he's not here, he's at the address."

"You're making it up."

"I wouldn't use Ashton like that," Harmony said, walking out the door in a huff, which she lost before she got to the car.

"Well?" Cole said as he floored it away from the curb, hanging a U-turn in the middle of late-morning traffic and leaving car horns blaring in their wake.

"There's hope."

Cole snorted. "That might make me feel better if it wasn't your own personal motto."

THE HOLLYWOOD HILLS WERE JUST THAT, A SERIES OF graduated hills that were actually part of the Santa Monica Mountains. On a smog-free day you could see the mountain peaks, the city sprawl, and the Hollywood sign. It wasn't a smog-free day.

Homes were set on the crests of the hills, most of them built into the hillsides, with the garage and entrances on the street side and what would normally be the back of the house overlooking undeveloped valleys full of wildlife, both plant and animal.

Harmony's home was no different. It sat at the end of the street, a little higher and a little apart from its lone neighbor. Cole parked down the street, out of sight of the house, which wasn't difficult since the area between her and her neighbor had been allowed to remain natural with scrubby underbrush and trees growing wild.

The yard around the house was a different story. The lawn was well-kept, studded with flower beds, flowering shrubs, and trellises sat at one side of the house covered in flowering vines. The house itself was a castlelike fantasy in natural stone and weathered cedar, with turrets and alternating roof levels.

"Jeez," Cole said, keeping his voice down, "where do you keep the dwarves and the house-cleaning forest creatures."

"I don't live here, remember? And I'm not exactly Snow White."

No, but it was the kind of fairy-tale-looking place he could see her living in.

"I don't recognize the car in the driveway," she said quietly.

"At least we know they're here."

"Someone is."

"Who else could it be?"

"Who else," Harmony repeated grimly.

Cole wrapped a hand around her arm and pulled her back, out of sight of the house. "You don't have to do this," he said to her. "Now that you know where he is, you can call the FBI and let them deal with the Russians."

"If the FBI shows up, it won't be to negotiate. They'll come in with guns blazing and Richard will be the first one killed."

"Then come with me and we'll disappear."

She leaned into him, but not before he swore he saw tears in her eyes. He didn't hear them in her voice. "You don't mean that, Cole. If you wanted to spend the rest of your life looking over your shoulder, you'd be gone already."

"I'll go if you will."

She didn't say anything, but he felt her take a breath, then another. She was probably chanting mantras, too, but he couldn't tease her about it. "C'mon then," he said. "I'm going to make sure you get through this in one piece, and you're going to make sure I don't go back to jail."

She nodded, and when she stepped back her eyes were absolutely dry. "The front entrance leads to the main level of the house, with the bedrooms above," she said. "There are two more levels below the main floor, built into the hillside overlooking the valley, and there's no telling where they're holding Richard."

"You know the layout. What do you suggest?"

She got to her feet and walked across the front yard like she owned the place, which she did. "If it was me, I'd stay in the lower two levels. Everything they need is there—kitchenette, maid's quarters—and there's nothing behind the house so they could even use the pool without being seen."

"Maid's quarters? Pool?"

"It's California."

And she was rich, which was something he'd been trying not to think about. Kind of hard to ignore it when she retrieved a key from a false stone near the front entry and led him through the door to a world he'd only dreamt of building for himself. It took a real effort to remember he might meet a different destiny altogether there.

Harmony stepped inside and shut the door behind them,

easing back so she was leaning against it, her hands behind her. They ought to get moving, but Cole didn't try to hurry her. It had to be hell to walk into that house again and remember the last time she was there, the moment she'd learned her parents were never coming home. It had to be hell knowing the last person she considered family was facing the same danger, and she was the one who stood between him and death.

She faced it, though. She pushed away from the door, slipped out of her shoes, and moved silently across the foyer and up the stairs directly across from the front door. This time Cole was rooted to the spot, dealing with a flood of . . . pride and respect—and optimism—that caught him off guard. They might actually get through this, he thought to himself, as long as they stuck together. She motioned him to stay there, but he followed her while she made a quick check of the four palatial bedroom suites on the topmost level of the house, then went back downstairs and made a similar check of the living areas, kitchen, dining room, media room, entertainment area and home office.

And then she headed for the stairs leading down. Before they'd descended halfway she stopped and looked over her shoulder at him. He didn't hear anything but the pounding of his own heart, but it felt . . . different. Not deserted. She pulled her gun and took the rest of the stairs two at a time, Cole right on her heels, ending up in a huge room that ran the length of the house and held a pool table, jukebox, pinball machines, and Leo and Irina. Her left eye was still puffy and just turning from purple to green.

A figure sat in the shadows at the end of the room. Harmony stared in that direction, her shoulders relaxing just for a second before she squared them again. By her reaction Cole assumed it was Richard, but they had only a split-second to assess the situation and react.

Irina was on the same page, pulling a gun and stepping up to Richard. "You move, he dies. Put down gun."

"You won't shoot me," Harmony said, "and you won't shoot Richard as long as you need him to gain our cooperation."

"And where's the third Russian?" Cole asked.

Harmony paid him no attention, completely focused on Irina.

Irina held her gaze, smiling coldly. "You wish a rematch."

"It was always going to come down to this," Harmony said. "Cole's right, you can't shoot us. Your only hope is to capture us and make us give you the account number and password."

Irina shrugged with one shoulder, a thoroughly Russian movement. She pulled the gun from Richard's head, popped the clip, and tossed it aside, and set the gun in his lap. It didn't do them any good since Richard's hands were tied behind his back, but the balance of power swung to their favor. Until Harmony took the clip out of her gun, and set them both on the pinball machine next to her.

"What the hell are you doing?" Cole asked her. "I thought you wanted to get Richard free."

"I will," she said, never taking her eyes from Irina's face.

Cole shot a glance at the pinball machine, but Leo shifted to within a few feet of him. He could go for Harmony's weapon, but he had no experience with guns. Leo would be on him before he could get the clip in correctly, let alone get a shot off.

He could only stand there and watch the two women circle before Harmony attacked. She caught Irina by surprise and got in a blow that rocked the other woman's head back. Irina responded with a flurry of punches aimed at Harmony's ribs. At least one of them landed. Harmony hunched over, eyes closed, breath wheezing out, absorbing what had to be excruciating pain.

Irina moved in for the kill—or at least the take-out, and for a minute Cole thought it was over. He should have had more faith, but then he'd never seen Harmony so . . . scary.

The California girl was gone, anger taking over, cold anger comprised of everything the Russians had put her through, days of helpless worry, of hearing a man she loved like a father tortured, of losing that first fight and questioning everything she was and wanted to be. She went after Irina relentlessly, using every fighting trick in the book, clean and dirty.

Cole stayed out of it, but he was staking everything on Harmony. If she lost, there was no way he could take on both Russians. Leo clearly felt the same. When it was apparent that Irina wasn't going to come out the winner he moved, but not toward Cole, and not toward Harmony's gun. He dove into the corner where Irina had tossed her clip.

Cole went after him, but Leo got there first, the whole thing going into slow motion. Cole's feet moved but didn't seem to get him anywhere. Leo scrabbled in the corner for the clip. Harmony still struggled with Irina, and Richard was still tied up in the shadows.

Then everything happened at once. Leo came up with the clip, but instead of going for Irina's gun, he flipped the clip into Richard's lap then turned and lumbered at Cole. Cole couldn't stop his forward momentum. He crashed into Leo and they went down in a tangle. Leo's head hit the floor with a sickening thud, and when Cole climbed off him he didn't get up. He was, however, snoring.

Cole turned to see Harmony standing over Irina's inert body. She was savoring the moment, Cole thought, but only briefly before she ran over to Richard, intending to set him free.

Richard pulled his hands out from behind his back and slapped the clip into Irina's gun as he stood up. The light fell on his face for the first time, and Harmony's steps faltered. He had no bruises, no cuts, and they already knew he hadn't been tied up.

"You're the third kidnapper," Harmony said. "You set up the whole thing."

"Dos vedanya," Richard said in the Russian-accented voice that Cole recognized from his one phone call to the kidnappers. He opened his arms wide and smiled at Harmony. "How about a hug for your uncle Richard?"

chapter
28

"SHOOT HIM," COLE SAID TO HARMONY UNDER HIS breath.

"He's got the gun."

"But—"

"She has an ankle holster," Richard said, his accent completely gone now, "but she wants answers. She has always been too curious for her own good, and too impulsive, as your presence here is ample proof. Not that I'm complaining. Your involvement has provided . . . opportunities."

"Victor Treacher. That's how you knew we were at the RV park," Cole said. They'd always assumed as much, now they had confirmation.

Richard smiled proudly. "That was a good bit of adaptation on my part," he said, his eyes shifting back to Harmony. "The ability to adjust to changing circumstances is something every successful agent must develop," he said to her. "It's a shame you won't be around to learn such a useful lesson."

Harmony wasn't up to talking yet, but she was doing a whole lot of nonverbal communicating. Behind the clenched fists and the scowl of absolute fury on her pretty face, behind the brilliant blue of her narrowed eyes, though, was pain. Soul-deep, heart-wrenching agony. The person she'd trusted most had betrayed her in the worst possible way, by using the heartache of her own past against her. And now he had the stupidity to gloat about it.

Cole stood back and let him talk. Whatever Harmony did—and she was going to do something, of that he was sure—he wasn't getting in the line of fire.

"After Irina tried to capture Hackett and failed," Richard was saying, "we lost track of you. Irina alerted her friends in the Russian mafia to keep an eye out for you, but I feared they would be unsuccessful in finding you. All I could do was wait for you to reach Los Angeles—until Victor contacted me, or rather contacted Richard Swendahl's Russian kidnappers.

"I didn't even have to tell him why I was looking for you," he continued. "As soon as he discovered who'd had his agents called back to D.C., he began to monitor Kovaleski's phone activity. When Mike reached out to Larkin, Treacher learned exactly what you were doing and where you were going."

"And he told you where we were so you could kill me," Harmony said with an eerie calm in her voice. "He thought he was getting a kidnapped FBI agent killed, too. But of course you were never in any danger."

"Thanks to my friends at the Bureau. I knew they would refuse to negotiate, and I knew they would keep it quiet. Can't let the other agents know just how disposable they are."

"Isn't that supposed to be part of the job description?"

"Perhaps in theory. Even while they take every possible step to prevent it, every agent knows they may give their life for their country," he sneered. "In your case, you would be correct."

"You're talking about the *meet* in South Central. But your lapdogs weren't there."

"And you weren't supposed to die there. We made arrangements with some of the local residents—"

"Gang members," Harmony said.

Richard shrugged. "You were not to be hurt, simply taken

hostage so we could get the password and the bank account number."

"Which you couldn't have gotten without hurting us."

"Again, this is your choice," Richard said, just a little puzzlement and a tinge of concern leaking into his expression. Harmony was being far too calm, and Cole could see that was rattling him. "How did you know to come here?"

"Background noise."

He closed his eyes, shaking his head slightly. "That idiot next door and his gong."

Harmony just shrugged.

"None of this has gone as it was supposed to," Richard said with a slightly accusatory tone, as if it were all Harmony's fault. "You were to transfer the money from Washington. You were not intended to rescue me."

This time Harmony smiled a little. It wasn't pleasant. "Apparently you don't know me as well as you think you do."

"I know you're going to die one way or another," Richard said, lifting the gun a little to show he meant business. "It's your choice how you go. You can give me the account information and get a nice, quick bullet to the brain, or I'll let Irina and Leo have you. They're pretty good at getting what they want even when there's no personal stake for them. After this," he gestured to the inert forms on the floor, "Irina in particular will want some retribution for the humiliation she's suffered."

"What's with all the talking?" Cole burst out. It was time to end the game before Richard got his henchmen back. In her current state, Harmony probably would have loved for Irina to wake up so she had someplace to take out her aggression. Cole wasn't so eager to have another dance with Leo. "Haven't you ever heard of *shoot first and ask questions later*?" he snapped at Harmony. "It's a saying for a reason."

Harmony only glared at him. "So is out of sight, out of mind. If you're so worried about your safety, feel free to leave."

"He's holding a gun on us."

"That didn't stop you before."

"Before it was you holding the gun, and you needed me."

"So does he. He's not going to shoot you."

"He can't kill me," Cole reminded her, "but he can still hoot me."

Richard laughed. "You two really are very entertaining."

"Glad to be of service," Cole grumbled, meeting Harmony glare for glare until she turned her back to him again.

"You were talking about your master plan," she prompted Richard.

"Ah, yes. But of course you can deduce the rest for yourself."

"You are Russian, then." And her last hope to salvage anything from this situation died. "You were a double agent in the beginning, with your allegiance to Russia."

"During the Cold War, yes. When the Iron Curtain fell, I stayed in the United States rather than go back to the hellhole Russia became in the chaos that followed the advent of so-called democracy. But I had never prepared . . . Had things remained as they were I would have gone back to my country a hero. A very well-compensated hero."

"But you had no retirement savings here, so you set me up."

"No, but I did use you." And he almost looked sorry for it. "If you'd done as asked and transferred the money from the safety of Washington D.C.—"

"I'd be on the hook for the money, which means I'd be going to jail."

"But you'd be alive."

"Somehow I don't think I'd have been grateful."

"You weren't supposed to discover the truth," Richard reminded her. "I was to be taken for dead, and the kidnappers would have gotten away with millions of dollars."

Harmony might have been able to see the genius of his plan, under other circumstances and after the passage of time. At the moment it felt like she'd had her heart ripped out. But there was still one more question. The answer was sure to hurt her more deeply, but she needed to know just how big a fool

she'd been. "Have you been planning this since I was eight
years old?"

"Let's say the seeds were planted then, but they would not
have taken root had my circumstances not been irrevocably
changed."

She shook her head, some of her anger giving way to sad-
ness. "I would have given you the money."

"I don't want charity," Richard spat, "and you don't have
the kind of money I deserve."

"Deserve?"

"I put my life on the line every day. For two countries.
I was being pulled from the field, did you know that? The
next step would have been retirement. On a government pen-
sion, and I wasn't about to live in quiet poverty, or take some
desk job in the private sector. Not while the criminals are living like kings—in both countries. So I called some contacts
from the old days. Most of the KGB officers I knew have
found other uses for their talents. Before long, Irina and Lev
showed up."

"The Russian mafia sent them," Harmony said, not feeling
quite so naïve anymore, compared to Richard's willful igno-
rance. "They're not the kind of people who would let you
walk off into the sunset with millions of dollars. You'd have
gotten your cut, but you'd have proven yourself useful, and
there's no retiring from that kind of employment."

"My affiliation is now to myself."

"Oh, I think the FBI would want to talk to you about
that."

"The FBI will never find out."

When his gaze shifted, ever so slightly, Harmony took his
words as more than just arrogance. She glanced around in
time to see Irina stirring. She walked over and kicked the
other woman in the ribs, then smashed her fist into Irina's
temple. It hurt like hell, and Irina got to her feet anyway, but
Harmony was spoiling for more violence.

Richard put a hand out before Irina could try to retaliate.

"I'm impressed," Harmony said to Irina. "Do you know
'sit' and 'roll over,' too? You did a pretty good job on 'play
dead.' "

"Are you done?" Richard asked her.

"Not even close. I won't be done until you're in jail."

"Big talk from someone on the wrong end of the gun." Richard held out his free hand. "And you can hand over your clutch piece."

"No."

"Don't think I won't shoot you. I'm prepared to do what it takes to get the information I want."

"Then shoot me."

Richard cocked the gun and brought it to bear on Cole.

Before Harmony could even begin to decide how to handle the threat, the doorbell rang, and then she knew just what to do. She smiled. "That'll be the police."

"Get rid of them," Richard said to Irina.

Irina sent Harmony one last look filled with hatred and promise, and took herself upstairs.

That level of the basement was built into the hillside and fronted by windows that overlooked the valley beyond. There were French doors at Richard's end, with a small brick patio, terracing down to the pool. Harmony looked past Richard, out the glass doorway, and smiled.

Irina came back, bumping Harmony on the way by. "It was some stupid American looking for a movie star."

"Ashton Kutcher?" Harmony asked, grinning.

Irina nodded, meeting Richard's eyes.

"What don't I know?"

"On the way here I stopped and called the police."

That just made Richard chuckle. "This is Hollywood. The police spend most of their time doing traffic control for some movie or premiere or award show. They'll never arrive in time to help you."

"No, but the paparazzi will."

And right on cue the photographers she'd seen peeking through the glass doors began to snap pictures, one after another, flashbulbs going off like lightning. The half-dozen or so paparazzi on her terrace couldn't possibly know who they were photographing, but film was cheap, and you never knew when you'd get that big-money shot.

"Smile for the cameras, Uncle Richard."

He automatically lowered the gun and brought it in tight so his body hid it from the cameras. Harmony dropped to one knee, pulled her clutch piece and pointed it at Richard, all in that split-second before he turned back to face her.

"You won't shoot me," he said.

"That's what I thought," Cole told him.

"And she didn't shoot you."

"Because I needed him." Harmony adjusted her aim and pulled the trigger.

Richard dropped his gun to clutch at his thigh.

Harmony had already turned her gun on Irina, who had crouched to retrieve the pistol that had fallen near her feet. She froze, but she was clearly thinking over her choices.

"Go for it," Harmony said to her. "Please."

chapter 29

"SAVED BY THE PAPARAZZI," MIKE SAID.

Harmony could see his smirk all the way from Washington. "It worked, didn't it?"

"Only in California."

He had a point. After she left the restaurant in Beverly Hills, it seemed the hostess had called the police back and told them Harmony's fugitive sighting had been a prank. Then she'd called the paparazzi—who'd called the police when Harmony shot Richard.

The police were followed closely by a foursome of FBI agents in black suits and black sunglasses. They'd been sent by Mike, of course, who'd been keeping tabs on police activity in the Los Angeles area. The FBI agents took over the crime scene, much to the disgust of the LAPD, and Harmony's relief since it meant she wouldn't be arrested. Cole's fate wasn't as clear.

Richard had been rolled out on a gurney, moaning like he was at death's door, which nobody bought, including his FBI escort. Irina and Leo had been cuffed and taken directly to jail to await transfer to federal custody. And all of it had taken place before the voracious cameras of the paparazzi.

"So tell me the rest of the story," Mike said.

"I only injured Richard slightly," she said, because Mike already knew everything that had led up to the actual shooting. "The paramedics said the bullet went through the muscle on the side of his leg, and it was a small caliber, so he'll be up and around in no time. I had no choice. There were innocent bystanders all over the place, and he had a gun, too. And he didn't believe I'd do it," she added grudgingly, since that was at least half the reason she'd pulled the trigger. She was getting tired of everyone taking her for a creampuff.

"He underestimated you," Mike said.

"He's not the only one."

"You gonna shoot me, too?"

"If you don't stop laughing."

"I think I can manage that by the time you get your butt back to Washington."

"You mean our butts."

"I mean your butt, and if there's any chance of saving that butt, you need to get as much mileage as you can out of bringing down a double a—"

"What about Cole?"

Mike sighed heavily. "You know what has to happen."

"No, I don't. Why can't we take him into federal custody and hold him someplace in D.C.? Some nice, comfortable hotel, maybe."

"It'll be hard enough to convince the warden, not to mention all the suits around here, that we had to break him out like we did," Mike said. "We can't go around procedure again if we hope to come out of this without having *our* asses handed to us."

"He was just as instrumental in catching Swendahl as I was," Harmony reminded Mike, "along with a couple of Russian mafia members, all of whom can provide invaluable information about the rest of their little conspiracy. I couldn't have done this without him, Mike. You know that."

"Yeah, but it's nice to hear you say it."

"So I learned a few lessons. You don't screw over your friends, that's one thing I knew going into this."

"You made promises you knew you wouldn't be able to keep."

"But Treacher—"

"Is going down. Soon. In the meanwhile Hackett has to go back to jail."

"I'll post bond."

"You know it doesn't work like that. He's already been convicted. We have to reopen his case, investigate, and get all the facts in front of a judge. And if the conviction is overturned, then he'll get out."

Harmony searched desperately for an argument that would change Mike's mind. She came up empty. Because Mike was right.

"Look, I'll go to bat for him, and I know an ace lawyer who'll take the case as a favor to me."

"Daniel Pierce," Harmony said, her eyes on the door.

"He's already in Los Angeles, working on a case, so I called him."

"He just walked in." Tall, handsome, and commanding, Pierce's slight limp was just another facet of what made people immediately trust and respect him.

The two FBI agents bracketing Cole came instantly to attention, and not just because of the way Daniel Pierce's presence filled a room. He had the reputation to back it up. Daniel was a former FBI agent, wounded in the line of duty, who'd become a federal prosecutor. He'd prevented the Irish mob in Boston from consolidating, which would have resulted in a turf war between the Irish and Italian crime factions.

Along the way he'd been marked for death, and he'd survived several murder attempts with the help of Vivienne Foster. Vivi considered herself a psychic. So did Daniel. Now. As far as the Bureau was concerned, her vocation was just a rumor.

Harmony had never met the woman, but she'd spent one long night trying to help Daniel locate Vivi after she'd been kidnapped by the bad guys. Harmony could still remember the way Daniel had channeled his anger and frustration, the intensity of his focus. Of course, it turned out he was in love with Vivi.

Daniel had since left the U.S. Attorney's office to start his own investigation firm, but if she had to go in front of a jury, Harmony couldn't think of anyone she'd sooner trust her fate to. Daniel Pierce was serious legal muscle. It said something about the gravity of Cole's situation.

Daniel raised a hand in greeting to Vivi, but he headed directly for Cole.

"Put Hackett on the phone," Mike said, mistaking the reason for her silence. "He's a smart guy; he'll understand."

"He already knows," she said, seeing Cole's eyes shift to her about three seconds after Daniel introduced himself as a lawyer.

She disconnected and crossed to the group of four men. The two FBI agents nodded politely. Daniel stepped forward and gave her a hug. Cole wasn't looking at her anymore.

"I'd like a moment with my client," Daniel said to the agents.

They exchanged a glance, but they moved to the other end of the room, out of earshot. Harmony stayed where she was.

"I'm going back to jail," Cole said, his gaze skipping over Daniel to land on Harmony.

She nodded, all the words disappearing from her brain when she saw the bleakness in his eyes.

"I'm not blaming you, Harm. We both knew it would probably come down to this."

"It won't be permanent," Daniel put in. "Just until we can get your case reopened and prove Treacher is the real villain here."

"There isn't any more proof than there was the last time," Cole said.

"There's his wimp of a son. I looked over the trial record after Mike called me," he added by way of explanation.

"My lawyer tried to get Scott Treacher to admit he stole my system and all the documentation, and wiped my computer, but he lied through his teeth."

"He's never been questioned by me."

"No offense, Mr. Pierce—"

"Daniel."

"Daniel. Scotty isn't going to admit he committed a crime."

Daniel didn't reply, unless Harmony counted the slight smirk on his face. Her money was on Daniel. Ten minutes alone in a room with him, and Treacher's son would probably confess to being Jack the Ripper.

"I can probably make a case for holding you in Washington," Daniel said. "Under the circumstances, considering what you know about all this"—he gestured around him—"I imagine they'd agree."

"I'd rather go back to Lewisburg," Cole said. "I know what to expect there."

"No," Harmony said to Daniel. "I'm not letting you put him back in that place."

Daniel stepped forward, but Cole blocked him. "Let me," he said, taking Harmony by the shoulders while Daniel slipped away to give them some privacy, keeping the two agents with him. "This is how it had to happen, Harm."

"No, I can—"

"Listen to me," he said, giving her a little shake when she tried to brush his hands off. "The only reason I'm letting them put me back in there is because I know you'll get me out. Which you won't be able to do if you're in trouble yourself."

"But I lied to you—"

"To save someone you loved. I'd have done the same."

She fought for another second, trying to pull away so she could do . . . She had no idea what she could do. She could barely think around the idea of Cole being back in that tiny cell he'd hated so much.

"I'm trusting you to keep your head and do what you have to do."

She relaxed, all the fight going out of her at the word *trust*.

"Harm?"

"I'd promise you, but I don't know how you can possibly believe any promise I'd make."

"Like I said, I trust you."

"Touching scene," one of the agents grumbled loud enough for them to hear, and when they turned, he was reaching for a leather holder on his belt.

"No cuffs," Daniel said when his intention became clear. "Harmony."

She ignored Daniel, holding the arresting agent's eyes until he followed Daniel's instructions.

"Wrap up here," Daniel said when she finally turned her attention back to him.

"Okay," she said, steadying as she focused on what she could control. She needed to close the house up, get the rental car back, and check out of both hotels so she could make the next plane to D.C., whatever time that was.

"Mike mentioned something about a car."

"A GT," she said, adding it to her mental list.

Daniel whistled slightly under his breath. "No wonder he wants it back. He said he'd let you know where to take it. Call me as soon as you arrive in Washington. If I'm going to get Hackett out of jail permanently, I'll need your statement." And he was gone, following the two agents and Cole up the stairs.

Harmony just stood there watching them disappear, and then her brain kicked back in.

Cole might be resigned to this outcome, but she sure as hell wasn't. She'd had to accept a lot of things in her life—the death of her parents before she'd ever really known them, working a job she loved for people who had no faith in her abilities, and now being betrayed by the only family she had left. She'd be damned if she stood by passively while Cole went back to jail.

Besides, he was right about the FBI. The powers at the Bureau handed down orders and expected everyone to fall in line so things worked out the way they wanted. And what they'd want here was to keep quiet what Richard Swendahl and Victor Treacher, two of their own, had done. They'd probably get Cole back in Lewisburg and decide that was the best place for him and his inside information about the double agent and the thief who'd held prominent, long-term positions at the FBI.

And that was exactly why she'd get what she wanted this time. Unless she didn't get her backside moving.

She raced up the stairs to the main level and found the four men still standing in the foyer, Daniel and the two agents talking quietly. It made no sense until she caught movement beyond the stained glass sidelights. The paparazzi would have left when they realized no celebrities were involved, but they'd have been replaced by newspaper and television reporters, along with their camera crews. Judging by the number of shadows on the other side of the glass, there seemed to be enough media people to make it impossible to leave the house without becoming a part of the story. Which worked to her advantage.

She put herself between the agents and the door, her hand resting on the butt of her gun. Not that she would have pulled her weapon on two FBI agents, a former U.S. Attorney, and a civilian. She just wanted to make sure they knew she meant business.

Daniel stepped in front of the agents and Cole, and said, "I'll handle this," just as the front door eased open.

Harmony automatically looked over her shoulder, expecting to see a reporter or photographer. Instead she came face-to-face with a slim, beautiful woman with long, dark hair.

"Vivienne Foster," she said, "but you can call me Vivi."

"Harmony Swift." She shook the hand offered without thinking, even though she had to let go of her gun to do it. She felt a little jolt when their hands touched, which was probably just her own imagination, and Vivi's reputation. She looked like she might be a gypsy, so it wasn't that difficult to imagine her with a crystal ball and tarot cards.

"I didn't get to meet you in Boston," Vivi said, "or to thank you."

"I had to get back to Washington. I, ah, wasn't exactly on the clock, if you know what I mean."

"You're an Aries," she said with a slight smile. "Willful, enthusiastic, adventurous, honest."

"I could add an adjective or two to that list," Cole put in.

Vivi smiled. "People who are Aries are warriors, and warriors have no patience for obstacles."

Harmony ignored Cole. "I'm glad everything worked out," she said to Vivi.

"As it will with you. With both of you," Vivi amended, tipping her head to one side. "In all matters."

Harmony felt better just hearing her say it. Maybe it was her own optimistic tendency, but there was something . . . calming and reassuring in Vivi Foster's manner. She wasn't placating. She *believed* what she said, and that gave it weight.

"I thought you were going to wait in the car," Daniel said to Vivi.

"I prefer to avoid the media," she explained for everyone else's sake, "but I was concerned that something . . . unfortunate might happen."

"Like me doing something idiotic so I could rescue Cole?" Harmony said.

"I don't need to be rescued," Cole put in crankily. "I can handle my own problems."

"This isn't your problem. I promised you wouldn't go back to jail." The ragged edge of tears in her voice embarrassed her, but it softened Cole's anger.

"There's no reason for you to ruin your career, Harm. And I won't be in Lewisburg long, right?"

The question had been directed to Daniel, but Harmony answered first. "I know what I'm doing. I've thought it all through."

"In the last two minutes?"

"Are you going to make me shoot at you again?"

"No." Cole stepped away from the agents.

"You won't get away with this," one of them said.

"I wouldn't be too sure," Harmony shot back. "There's all the explaining the FBI will have to do about the hundreds of photos of Richard and his Cossacks being taken off in handcuffs. The Cold War is over, but I think national television news might still be interested to know what really went down today. If they find out Cole was instrumental in outing a double agent, they'll wonder why he's still in jail, and they'll ask a lot of questions about subjects the FBI doesn't want to become public knowledge. And let's not forget the thirty million hostages."

"Thirty-five million," Daniel said.

It took a minute for that to sink in, and even then she didn't want to believe it. "Where's the other five?" she asked, although she already knew because suddenly Cole wouldn't meet her eyes.

"We'll sort it out in Washington," Daniel said.

"All the money will go back where it belongs," Cole added, his gaze lifting to Harmony's. "But it's not about the money, is it?"

Harmony saw the apology in his eyes, but it wasn't enough. He'd stood right in front of her, ten short minutes ago, talking about trust and not meaning a word of it. And it wasn't just ten minutes ago. They'd spent days together, days when she'd agonized over telling him one ridiculous little white lie. And the moment she'd felt like they had a real partnership she'd told him the truth, knowing he'd be angry. Even then, when the fireworks were over and they'd promised each other there'd be no more secrets, he'd been lying.

"No," she said, "it's not about the money."

chapter
30

BY THE TIME A WEEK PASSED, MOST OF THE MESS HAD been mopped up. Richard Swendahl and his partners in crime were still in federal custody, and Harmony had given her report. As far as the FBI was concerned, the trial was just a formality. Richard's completely uncoerced confession to Harmony while he'd been holding her at gunpoint meant he'd spend the rest of his life in jail. Known Russian *mafiya* members had denied any connection to Irina and Leo, but their collaboration in perpetrating a fraud on the U.S. government, not to mention the attempted murder of an FBI agent, meant lifelong incarceration for them as well. Harmony felt sorry for the other inmates of whatever prison Irina landed in.

Scotty Treacher had been brought in for questioning. Fear of his father wasn't nearly enough to withstand the combined efforts of Mike Kovaleski and Daniel Pierce, not to mention a strategic twenty-four hours in jail. He'd sung like a stool pigeon. He'd still go to prison—minimum security—but the testimony he gave in exchange led to Victor's arrest, and the house of cards Victor had built on top of a stolen security system and a framed software specialist began to collapse.

The fallout included two geeks masquerading as FBI agents, which explained why it had been so easy to get the better of them—time after time after time. It also answered the question of how Mike Kovaleski had been kept in the dark. Treacher being the head of Systems Security, no one questioned how he ran his department. It had been easy for him to talk two desk-ridden geeks into fulfilling their secret agent fantasies. They were singing, too, now. No one had been hurt, so all they could be charged with was impersonating federal officers. They'd get a slap on the wrist, and a ticket to the unemployment office. Treacher would face two more criminal counts: hindering a federal officer and attempted murder.

Cole provided the coup de grâce, and he didn't even have to give a statement to do it. A first-year law student could have tied the current testimony to the transcripts from Cole's criminal prosecution eight years before, and come up with more than enough rope to hang Victor Treacher. Daniel Pierce did that, and forged it all into a key that unlocked Cole's jail cell permanently. Despite Cole's attempts to lock himself into a new one.

Harmony had promised him he'd take no heat for her actions. She made sure he didn't. Her gamble had paid off in a big way, sure, but the suits weren't happy about the way she'd pulled it off—the U.S. penal system and the FBI made to look incompetent, not to mention the potential for serious trouble she'd risked in her balls-to-the-wall race across the country. The fact that no one had been hurt wasn't nearly enough mitigation.

It wasn't even the truth.

Another week had passed since Treacher's arrest, but Harmony still felt sick to her stomach. Because she hadn't faced Cole yet, and there'd be no hope of moving on with her life until she did.

She took a couple of deep breaths and pushed through the revolving door of the Washington hotel where Cole was staying. She nearly ran into him.

Harmony froze, her eyes dropping to the small black duffel he carried. "Going somewhere?" she asked him, amazed at her ability to speak, let alone breathe.

"To find you," he said, and the hope she'd thought dead began to warm her heart.

"Then I saved you a trip."

He looked down for a minute, smiled a little, sadly, before he met her eyes again. "All business, Harm?"

"I wanted to thank you for helping me—"

"You didn't come here because you're grateful. You came here because you're in love with me."

It was Harmony's turn to smile, and her smile was just as sad as his had been.

"You're not denying it."

"Love isn't blind, and it isn't magic. I love you, but—"

"You can't forgive me for diverting the money. I gave it back, every cent."

"Maybe you'd like to have this conversation by yourself."

He blew out a breath. "I've done that about a dozen times in my head over the last two weeks."

"Then you know how it turns out?"

"It turns out bad," he said. "That's why I was coming to find you."

"So I could let you off the hook? Fine, you're off the hook. You can stop trying to convince everyone the whole thing was your idea. They don't believe you anyway, and you've done nothing to be punished for."

"I lied to you."

"You had a lot on the line."

"So did you, but you told me the truth."

Harmony wasn't sure how to respond to that, so she didn't.

"Look," Cole said, "I went into this hoping to find that new evidence you told me about. Failing that I intended to set myself up, disappear, do whatever it took to stay out of jail. But I should have told you what I was doing. I should have made it clear that it wasn't you I didn't trust. It was the Bureau."

"But you weren't sure I'd choose you over my job."

He scrubbed his fingers through his hair, the prison buzz cut grown out an inch or so now. It made him look younger, and even more endearing. "In the beginning, yeah. You're

FBI. Going after a bunch of Russian kidnappers is one thing. Taking on one of your own—not just a couple of half-baked agents but someone with real power—is totally different. I figured when you found out about Treacher, you'd bolt."

"And you had no intention of going back to jail. I get it."

"No, you don't." He took her by the elbow and pulled her out of the doorway so the other guests could go in and out. The warmth of his hand, even through her light sweater, nearly brought her to her knees.

"You proved me wrong, Harm," he said, letting her go and putting some distance between them, as if he, too, had a hard time concentrating when they were close. "I meant it when I said I trusted you, but when it came to proving it—"

She kissed him, just a peck on the lips, actually, but it did the trick. "I know you rehearsed and everything, but you need to let me talk."

Cole rubbed his fingers across his heart, his smile dawning slow and wide. "As long as you start all your sentences that way."

"If I did that in a building full of rooms with beds, we'd never settle anything."

"Verbal communication is highly overrated."

A typical male viewpoint, Harmony thought, and she needed to get the past cleared up if they were going to have a chance at a future. "I was hurt that you didn't trust me enough to tell me about the five million dollars," she began. "I was still stinging from Richard's betrayal, and it took me a little while to work through that, but once I had time to think it over it occurred to me that I'd be a fool to let the money matter.

"You followed me into that basement, Cole, and you stood there while I blew the only advantage we had by putting my gun down and facing Irina one on one. You kept Leo out of my hair long enough for me to prove myself, and not to you." She shook her head, realizing just how big a fool she'd been. "I was the one doubting my abilities. You gave me a chance to regain my confidence, and it could have cost you your life."

"You came here to thank me for that?"

She bumped up a shoulder. She'd come there for so much more, but she couldn't tell Cole that. She'd already told him she loved him, and he'd felt no urge to make any declarations of his own. When, or if, he did, she didn't want it to be coerced.

So she changed the subject. "Mike told me your system is going to be returned to you. Well, not returned, but at least attributed." According to Mike, Scott Treacher had been paid five million for the software originally. Daniel Pierce felt that was too low a figure for a system of such magnitude—not to mention eight years of Cole's life—and Daniel made sure the price tag included the cost of the frame Cole had worn for so long. "I'm glad everything worked out for you."

"That sounds like good-bye."

Harmony crossed her arms, rubbing one hand over the ache just below her breastbone. "It seems like we've said everything there is to say."

"Have we?"

"Why don't you tell me? You're the one who rehearsed."

He slipped his hands into his jeans' pockets and hunched his shoulders. "I never got this far before," he said, just his eyes shifting from the floor to her face. "But I've been doing some thinking. A lot of thinking, actually."

"And?" she said, barely getting the word out because she was holding her breath.

"I've always wanted to start my own security company—computer security." He straightened, excitement lighting his face. "I have some ideas that will make my old system look like Swiss cheese. It'll blow the computer security community's collective minds." He sobered. "But it's not likely anybody will put their trust in me."

"You've been exonerated."

"It doesn't matter. I was convicted. Once people hear that, they won't want to know anything else about me." He took a step toward her, just one step. Hoping, but not too much. "Which is why I need someone to front for me. Like a former FBI agent with an extremely trustworthy face."

"You told me I look like Barbie."

"Not a bad first impression. Especially if the client is male. Or Ellen DeGeneres."

"She and Portia need a lot of computer security?"

"You never know."

Her heart soared. After everything she'd put Cole through, he was still willing to take a risk on her. "So . . ." She started walking toward him, very slowly. "You're offering me a job?"

"I know how much the FBI means to you, but—"

"Meant," she said. "Past tense."

"You were fired?"

"I quit. Sort of. I'm sure they would have fired me anyway, or at least encouraged me to find other employment. Somebody's head had to roll."

"And you sacrificed yours."

"Believe me, it was no sacrifice. And you were willing to go back to jail for me."

Their eyes met, held, and then Cole reached out and pulled her against him, hugging her so hard she could barely breathe. She didn't care.

They stood there like that for a minute or two, just holding one another, oblivious to the staff and guests of the hotel. Harmony lifted onto her toes and kissed him. Cole took it deep, shifted his arms, and dragged her up until her feet were off the ground and he was her entire world. The taste and heat and scent of him enveloped her, and he became the one pillar of strength in a maelstrom of emotion and sensation.

When he put her down, she stumbled. And then she heard catcalls and applause, and realized they both needed to get some control before they gave the tourists a real show. She stepped back a little but she slipped her hand into Cole's and held onto him while her head stopped spinning.

Cole swiped his other hand over his face, and when he met her eyes, she saw the intensity that always made her body tremble and her heart stutter. But he was grinning.

"God, I love you," she said.

He squeezed her hand. "I must be crazy because I love you, too."

She reared back to glare at him. "Crazy! I waited in agony for you to tell me you love me, and you qualify it?"

"You're an FBI agent."

"*Ex*-FBI agent, as in *ex*-con. I quit, remember?"

He gathered her into his arms and kissed her again, a long, deep kiss she felt everywhere, but mostly her heart.

"I'm glad you quit," he said when they came up for air. "Getting fired would have a negative impact on your credibility. You won't be much good to me without it."

"You know, you could hire someone. You can afford the best." He'd been paid enough to hire all the legitimacy he could ever want.

"I could hire someone," he agreed. "Even if the FBI doesn't give me a dime, there are kids coming out of college who'd jump at a chance to get in on the ground floor of the kind of enterprise I intend to start. But they'd be employees. I was thinking you and I would be more like partners."

"And I'd be the front man."

"Front woman," he said with a smile. "Believe me, you'll be working hard, going to companies and selling the system. And someone has to make recommendations about the physical security: motion detectors, video surveillance, that sort of thing. You're better qualified for that, just like I'm better at the computer end."

"I'd get to tell very powerful men what to do?"

He laughed. "It's not as exciting as being a field agent for the FBI—"

"True, no car chases or flying bullets—"

"—but at night we get to come home to each other, and god knows we'll fight often enough."

"And then we'll get to make up." Harmony turned into him, snugging her arms around his waist and lifting onto her toes. "Making up sounds really good."

He held her off. "So it's just the sex you're interested in."

"It's the sex and the job."

"I don't know . . ."

"Maybe we should do a trial run."

Cole pretended to think about it for a minute, then said, "Okay, how about the next fifty years or so?"

She smiled, her heart beating wildly as he wrapped his arms around her. "Some men would call that a prison sentence."

"Well, I know the difference, don't I?"

Penny McCall lives in Michigan with her husband, three children, and two dogs, whose lives of leisure she envies, but would never be able to pull off. Her children and husband have come to accept her strange preoccupation with imaginary people. The dogs don't worry about it, as long as they're fed occasionally and allowed to nap on whatever piece of furniture strikes their fancy. Come to think of it, that pretty much goes for the husband, too. Visit her website at www.pennymccall.com.